... IS A
VERY HARD THING
TO BE

THE
BOY
ON THE
BRIDGE

M. R. CAREY

www.orbitbooks.net

ORBIT

First published in Great Britain in 2017 by Orbit
This paperback edition published in 2018 by Orbit

1 3 5 7 9 10 8 6 4 2

Copyright © 2017 by M. R. Carey

Excerpt from *The End of the Day* by Claire North
Copyright © 2017 by Claire North

The moral right of the author has been asserted.

*All characters and events in this publication, other than those
clearly in the public domain, are fictitious and any resemblance
to real persons, living or dead, is purely coincidental.*

A CIP catalogue record for this book
is available from the British Library.

ISBN 978-0-356-50356-1

Typeset in Bembo 11.75/14 pt by Palimpsest Book Production Limited,
Falkirk, Stirlingshire

Printed and bound in Great Britain by CPI Group (UK) Ltd,
Croydon CR0 4YY

Papers used by Orbit are from well-managed forests
and other responsible sources.

Orbit
An imprint of
Little, Brown Book Group
Carmelite House
50 Victoria Embankment
London EC4Y 0DZ

An Hachette UK Company
www.hachette.co.uk

www.orbitbooks.net

To Camille Gatin and Colm McCarthy,
with thanks and love

PART ONE

IN COUNTRY

1

The bucks have all been passed and the arguments thrashed out until they don't even bleed any more. Finally, after a hundred false starts, the Rosalind Franklin begins her north-ward journey – from Beacon on the south coast of England all the way to the wilds of the Scottish Highlands. There aren't many who think she'll make it that far, but they wave her off with bands and garlands all the same. They cheer the bare possibility.

Rosie is an awesome thing to behold, a land leviathan, but she's not by any means the biggest thing that ever rolled. In the years before the Breakdown, the most luxurious motor homes, the class A diesel-pushers, were a good sixteen or seventeen metres long. Rosie is smaller than that: she has to be because her armour plating is extremely thick and there's a limit to the weight her treads will carry. In order to accommodate a crew of twelve, certain luxuries have had

3

to be sacrificed. There's a single shower and a single latrine, with a rota that's rigorously maintained. The only private space is in the bunks, which are tiered three-high like a Tokyo coffin hotel.

The going is slow, a pilgrimage through a world that turned its back on humankind the best part of a decade ago. Dr Fournier, in an inspirational speech, likens the crew to the wise men in the Bible who followed a star. Nobody else in the crew finds the analogy plausible or appealing. There are twelve of them, for one thing – more like the apostles than the wise men, if they were in the Jesus business in the first place, and they are not in any sense following a star. They're following the trail blazed a year before by another team in an armoured vehicle exactly like their own – a trail planned out by a panel of fractious experts, through every terrain that mainland Britain has to offer. Fields and meadows, woodland and hills, the peat bogs of Norfolk and the Yorkshire moors.

All these things look, at least to Dr Samrina Khan, very much as she remembers them looking in former times. Recent events – the collapse of global civilisation and the near-extinction of the human species – have left no mark on them that she can see. Khan is not surprised. The time of human dominion on Earth is barely a drop in the ocean of geological time, and it takes a lot to make a ripple in that ocean.

But the cities and the towns are changed beyond measure. They were built for people, and without people they have no identity or purpose. They have lost their memory. Vegetation is everywhere, softening the man-made megaliths into new and unrecognisable shapes. Office blocks have absent-mindedly become mesas, public squares morphed into copses or lakes. Emptied of the past that defined them, they have surrendered

4

without protest, no longer even haunted by human meanings.

There are still plenty of ghosts around, though, if that's what you're looking for. The members of the science team avoid the hungries where possible, engage when strictly necessary (which mostly means when the schedule calls for tissue samples). The military escort, by virtue of their weapons, have a third option which they pursue with vigour.

Nobody enjoys these forays, but the schedule is specific. It takes them into every place where pertinent data could lurk.

Seven weeks out from Beacon, it takes them into Luton. Private Sixsmith parks and locks down in the middle of a roundabout on the A505, which combines a highly defensible position with excellent lines of sight. The sampling team walks into the town centre from there, a journey of about half a mile.

This is one of the places where the crew of the Charles Darwin, their dead predecessors, left a cache of specimen cultures to grow in organic material drawn from the immediate area. The team's brief is to retrieve these legacy specimens, which calls for only a single scientist with an escort of two soldiers. Dr Khan is the scientist (she made damn sure she would be by swapping duties with Lucien Akimwe for three days running). The escort consists of Lieutenant McQueen and Private Phillips.

Khan has her own private reasons for wanting to visit Luton, and they have become steadily more pressing with each day's forward progress. She is afraid, and she is uncertain. She needs an answer to a question, and she hopes that Luton might give it to her.

They move slowly for all the usual reasons – thick undergrowth, ad hoc barricades of tumbledown masonry, alarms

5

and diversions whenever anything moves or makes a sound. The soldiers have no call to use their weapons, but they see several groups of hungries at a distance and they change their route each time to minimise the chance of a close encounter. They keep their gait to a halting dead march, because even with blocker gel slathered on every inch of exposed skin to deaden their scent, it's possible that the hungries will lock onto rapid movement and see potential prey.

Khan considers how strange they must look, although there's almost certainly no one around to see them. The two men each comfortably topping six feet in height, and the small, slight woman in between. She doesn't even come up to their shoulders, and her thighs are thinner than their forearms. They could carry her, with all her gear, and not slacken stride. It's past noon before they reach Park Square, where the Darwin's logs have directed them. And then it takes a long while to locate the specimen cache. The Darwin's scientists cleared a ten-foot area before setting it down, as per standing orders, but a whole year's growth has happened since then. The cache's bright orange casing is invisible in snarls of brambles so dense and thick they look like tank traps. When they finally locate it, they have to use machetes to get to it.

Khan kneels down in pulped bramble and oozing bramble-sap to verify the seals on the specimen containers. There are ten of them, all battleship grey rather than transparent because the fungus inside them has grown to fill the interior space to bursting. That probably means the specimens are useless, offering no information beyond the obvious – that the enemy is robust and versatile and not picky at all about pH, temperature, moisture or any damn thing else.

But hope springs as high as it can, and the mission statement is not negotiable. Khan transfers the containers to her belt pouches. McQueen and Phillips stand close on either side of her, sweeping the silent square with a wary 360-degree gaze.

Khan climbs to her feet, but she stands her ground when McQueen brusquely gestures for her and Phillips to move out.

'I need to do a quick sortie,' she says, hoping her voice does not betray her nerves.

The lieutenant regards her with a vast indifference, his broad, flat face showing no emotion. 'That's not on the log,' he tells her curtly. He has little time for Khan and doesn't try to hide the fact. Khan believes that this is because she is (a) not a soldier and (b) not even a man, but she doesn't rule out other possibilities. There may even be some racism in there, however quaint and old-fashioned that seems in these latter days.

So she has anticipated his answer and prepared her own. She takes a list out of the pocket of her fatigues and hands it to him. 'Medicines,' she says as he unfolds and scans it, his lips pursed thin and tight. 'We're doing okay for the most part, but the area north of Bedford saw a lot of bombing. If we can stock up on some of this stuff before we get into the burn shadow, it might save us a lot of heartache later.'

Khan is prepared to lie if she has to, but McQueen doesn't ask her whether this is an authorised detour. He takes it for granted – and it's a very fair assumption – that she wouldn't prolong this little day trip without direct orders from either Dr Fournier or the colonel.

So they stroll on a little way to the Mall, which is a mausoleum fit for an ancient pharaoh. Behind shattered shopfronts, flat-screen televisions and computers offer digital apotheosis.

Mannequins in peacock finery bear witness, or else await their long-delayed resurrection.

Ignoring them all, Lieutenant McQueen leads the way inside and up to the mezzanine level. Once there, he stays out on the concourse, his rifle on full automatic with the safety off, while Khan and Phillips gather up the precious bounty of Boots the Chemist.

Khan takes the prescription drugs, leaving the private with the much easier task of scoring bandages, dressings and painkillers. Even so, she presses the list on him, assuring him that he will need it more than she does. That's true enough, as far as it goes. She's well aware of what's in short supply and what they can reasonably expect to find.

But it's only half the truth. She also wants Private Phillips to have his head down, puzzling over her shitty handwriting as he makes his way along the aisles. If he's reading the list, he won't be watching her. She'll be free to pursue her secret mission – the one that has brought her here without authorisation and without the mission commanders' knowledge.

The prescription meds are hived away behind a counter. Khan tucks herself away in there and fills her pack, quickly and efficiently. She mostly goes for antibiotics, which are so precious in Beacon that any prescription has to be countersigned by two doctors and an army officer. There's a whole pack of insulin too, which goes straight in the bag. Paracetamol. Codeine. A few antihistamines.

With the official shopping list covered, it's time to switch agendas. She was hoping she might find what she was looking for right here in the pharmacy area, but there's no sign of it. She raises her head up over the counter to check the lie of the land. Private Phillips is fifty yards away, scowling over the list as he pads from rack to rack.

Khan crosses the aisle in shuffling baby steps, bent almost double and trying not to make a sound. Fetching up in front of a display themed around dental hygiene, she scans the shelves to either side of her urgently. Phillips could finish his task and come looking for her at any moment.

The part of her body she's concerned about is a long way south of her teeth, but for some esoteric reason the relevant products are shelved right there on the next unit along. There is a choice of three brands. Ten long years ago, on the last day when anything was bought or sold in this place, they were on special offer. Khan can't imagine how that can ever have made sense, given the very limited circumstances in which these items are useful. You either need them or you don't, and if you do then price doesn't really factor in. With a surge of relief, Khan grabs one and shoves it into her pack.

On second thoughts, she takes two more, giving her one of each brand. Ten years is a long time, and even behind airtight seals most things eventually degrade: three throws of the dice are better than one.

Popping her head up over the parapet again, she sees that Private Phillips has his back to her. Perfect timing. She steps out into the aisle and rests one hand nonchalantly on the pharmacy counter. Here I am, her stance says. Where I've been all along. Where I have every reason to be.

'Done,' she tells him.

Phillips doesn't answer. He's looking at something down on the ground.

Khan goes and joins him.

He's found a nest, of sorts. There's a sleeping bag, rumpled and dirty; an open rucksack in which Khan can see the tops

9

of several plastic water bottles and the handle of what might be a hammer or large screwdriver; two neat stacks of clothes (jeans, socks, T-shirts and a few sweaters, nothing indisputably female except for a single pair of knickers and a black blouse with ruffles on the sleeves); a few dozen empty cans laid out in rows, most of which once held baked beans or soup, and a paperback copy of Enid Blyton's *The Wishing-Chair*. There's no dust here to speak of, but it's clear that none of these things have been touched in a while. Dead leaves from a broken window somewhere have silted up against them, and tendrils of black mould are groping their way up the lower half of the sleeping bag.

Someone lived here, Khan thinks. The Mall must have looked like a pretty good place to hide, offering food and shelter and an enticing array of consumer goods. But it was a death trap of course, with a dozen entrances and few defensible spaces. This hopeful hermit probably died not too far away from where they're standing. Private Phillips is looking down at the pathetic display with a thoughtful, distant expression on his face. He scratches his lightly stubbled chin with the tip of one finger.

Then he squats, sets down his rifle and picks up the book, riffling the pages with his thumb. He has to do this very gently because the decades-old glue has dried and cracked and the pages have come loose from the spine. Khan is amazed. She can only assume that *The Wishing-Chair* must have featured somehow in the private's childhood; that he's communing with some buried part of himself.

Something falls out onto the floor. A narrow rectangle of thin card, pale gold in colour. It bears the single word *Rizla*.

'Knew it,' Phillips exults. He tosses the book aside. Pages

10

spill out of it when it lands, splayed like a hand of cards. He delves into the rucksack with serious purpose, throwing aside the half-empty water bottles and the tool (a claw hammer) to come up with his prize: a half-empty packet of Marlboro Gold cigarettes and a second pack that's still sealed. Hard currency in Beacon, but there's no way these cancer-sticks are going to travel that far.

Khan dips her gaze and looks at the scattered pages of the book. One of them has a picture, of two children sitting in a flying chair, holding on tight to the arms as they soar over the rounded turret of a castle tower. There is a caption below the picture. *'Why, our magic chair might take us anywhere!'* *Peter cried.*

'Got what you need, Dr Khan?' Phillips asks her. He's cheerful, expansive, riding on an emotional high from the mere thought of those smokes.

'Yes, Gary,' Khan tells him, studiously deadpan. 'Everything I need.'

The journey back to Rosie is blessedly uneventful but, like the trip out, it's protracted and exhausting. By the time they're through the airlock, Khan is pretty much done and just wants to lie down in her bunk until the day goes away. But John Sealey needs to greet her and – under the guise of a casual conversation – to ascertain that she's okay. The boy Stephen Greaves is less demonstrative but she knows his body language: he needs even more reassurance than John, and on top of that he needs, as always, to restore their normal status quo through the rituals they've established over the years they have known each other – greetings and exchanges whose importance lies entirely in their being said rather than in any meaning they carry.

'Good day's work, Stephen?'

'Not too bad, Dr Khan. Thank you.'

'You're very welcome.'

'Did you enjoy your walk?'

'Very much. It's a lovely day out there. You should take a stroll yourself before the sun goes in.'

She disentangles herself delicately, first from John and then from Stephen, and now she's free and clear. The colonel is up in the cockpit. The rest of the crew have their own shit to deal with and no wish to get mixed up in hers.

Khan goes into the shower, since Phillips has already grabbed the latrine. She locks herself in and undresses quickly. Her body is slick with sweat but there is no smell apart from the slightly bitter tang of e-blocker. If there had been, of course, she would have found out about it before now.

One by one she unwraps the three packages, stowing the wrappers in her pockets. The boxes, folded down tight and small, follow. In each package is a flimsy plastic wand. The designs are slightly different, but each wand has a window halfway along its length and a thickening at one end to show where you're supposed to grip it.

Squatting on the floor of the shower, legs slightly parted, she does what needs to be done.

The chemistry is straightforward, and close to infallible. Anti-hCG globulin is extremely reactive to certain human hormones, including the hormone gonadotrophin. Properly prepared, it will change colour in the hormone's presence.

And the hormone is present in a woman's urine. Sometimes.

Having peed on the business end of the three wands, she waits in silence, watching the three little windows. A negative result will tell her very little. The protein layer on the prepared strip inside the wands may have degraded too far to catalyse. A positive, on the other hand, will mean what it always meant.

Khan gets the hat-trick.

Mixed emotions rise in her as she stares at these messages from her own uncharted interior, a high tide of wonder and dismay and disbelief and misery in which hope bobs like a lifeboat cut adrift.

Seven weeks into a fifteen-month mission, ten years after the world ended and a hundred miles from home, Dr Samrina Khan is pregnant.

But this is not Bethlehem, and there will be no manger.

2

There are twelve of them, but they break neatly into two groups of six.

The science team is headed by Dr Alan Fournier, the civilian commander with overall responsibility for the success of the mission. He is a thin, overly precise man with a habit of stopping in the middle of a sentence to get his thoughts in order. It's an unfortunate habit to find in a leader, but to be fair nobody thinks of him as one.

The escort, comprising soldiers and officers of the Beacon Muster, is under the command of Colonel Isaac Carlisle, sometimes known as the Fireman because of his association with the offensive use of chemical incendiaries. He hates that name. He hated that mission. His feelings about this one are not on record.

In the science team, there are three men and two women:

Samrina Khan	epidemiologist
Lucien Akimwe	chemist
John Sealey	biologist
Elaine Penny	biologist
Stephen Greaves	nobody is entirely certain

In the escort, likewise, two women and three men:

Lt Daniel McQueen	sniper and second in command
Lance-Bombardier Kat Foss	sniper
Private Brendan Lutes	engineer
Private Paula Sixsmith	driver
Private Gary Phillips	quartermaster

The ruling bodies in Beacon, the civilian council called the Main Table and the Military Muster, did not choose their best or their brightest, though they made a great show of doing exactly that. What they actually did, or tried to do, was to strike a balance that gave them the most plausible shot at survival. A larger escort would have been possible simply by allocating more vehicles to the expedition, but every soldier sent out would have weakened Beacon's own defences. McQueen and Foss, trained in the sniper corps, are elite soldiers and the hardest to spare. Their skill set is needed every day to thin out the hungries gathering at Beacon's gates. The scientists are a different matter, but in their case too there are issues of day-to-day urgency to which their expertise could be applied. By sending them out, Beacon is making a commitment to the future. But it is a commitment filtered through a bed of pragmatism.

Twelve men and women in a great big armoured truck are not such a huge risk, when all is said and done. They carry a great many hopes and dreams with them, but if they should chance to be lost, their loss can be borne.

They know very well that they are expendable.

3

Seven weeks brought them to Luton. Seven months carry them on to Scotland.

The year is closing in on them, and so is everything else. The last of the good omens evaporated long ago. They have made no progress, no discoveries. Thousands of samples have been taken and tested, thousands more are still to come, but nobody on the science team believes any longer that there is any point. Each hides his or her resignation, cynicism or despair for the sake of the others, reduced to hoping now at second hand.

They have stayed close to the Charles Darwin's course throughout, and they have succeeded in retrieving all but one of the specimen caches. The one they missed was on the Cairngorm plateau, close to the summit of the mountain Ben Macdhui, and it was Dr Fournier who made the decision to leave it where it was. He claimed he was unwilling to risk Rosie on the steep slopes, but everyone translated *Rosie* in that sentence into *my own arse*. It's a sign, either way, of imminent surrender.

The civilian and military commanders are simply not fit for purpose. They hate each other and they avoid the crew – the alternative being to force them to take sides. It falls to Lieutenant McQueen, most days, to organise the escort roster, and to Dr Khan or Dr Sealey to assign tasks for the sampling runs.

Khan is showing. There was a time when her pregnancy was ambiguous and deniable, should anyone have pressed her. That time is over now, and she will be pressed very soon.

And then there's Greaves, though people wonder why. Who thought bringing a kid along on a mission like this was a good idea? When will Dr Fournier formally remove him from the roster instead of working around his inadequacies?

When will they give up, and turn around?

When will this ever end?

That rhetorical question is still hanging in the air when their comms fail. The radio still seems to be operational but Beacon, their home and source, rationale and reference point, stops answering.

They're on their own.

PART TWO

GESTATION

4

They deploy in three waves.

The grunts go first. That's Lieutenant McQueen's term, nobody else's, a heavy-handed joke. The three privates pretend to think it's funny but Dr Khan is offended on their behalf. Lutes is the best engineer in Beacon. Sixsmith was a commercial pilot before the Breakdown and is as comfortable with wings as she is with wheels. Phillips has the perfect physique of a classical statue and can perform card tricks that still dazzle you after he explains how they're done. There is nothing grunt-like about any of them.

They trot over the brow of the hill in a quick, broken stride. Fifty metres down, they dig in behind some gorse, which offers no protection at all but might diffuse their outlines a little from a distance. Something as small as that could make the difference between life and death.

'Clear,' Private Phillips says quietly. Sound carries a long way out here. There's no need to shout and a lot of good reasons not to.

In the absence of Colonel Carlisle, McQueen is in command. He gestures – a circular wave of his arm, which is bent at the elbow, the hand pointing upwards. To Khan, maybe because Dr Fournier's three-wise-men analogy lodged deeper in her brain than she would have liked, it looks as though he's bearing witness to heaven.

But in fact the gesture is for the science team, and they go over next. Or rather two thirds of them do, comprising Dr Khan, Elaine Penny, Lucien Akimwe and John Sealey. The remaining two members of the team are absent, recused from this day's work: Alan Fournier, as the leader of the science team and the mission's civilian commander, is above it. And he has left Stephen Greaves out of the day's roster, not trusting him to play his part in a coordinated group action and knowing that the rest of the team (apart from Khan) don't trust him either.

Khan feels that insult to Stephen more deeply than he feels it himself, but for the most part she is grateful for his absence. He's still her boy, if not by blood then by something just as thick and just as binding. A part of her has never been able to relinquish the self-imposed responsibility of looking out for him. Also, although she wouldn't admit it even to John Sealey, she's keen to keep Stephen away from these culls because they're such degrading and brutalising spectacles. The hungries may not be human any more but they still look like real people. To see them being mown like wheat turns her stomach, no matter what her brain asserts.

She tops the hill and scuffles down it on feet, hands and bum (leaving her dignity way behind her, but she's not going to risk a fall at this point). Her passenger kicks a couple of times anyway, maybe to register a protest. Just before she gets in among the bushes she catches sight – out of the corner of her eye – of a cluster of hungries standing further down the slope. Sidelong is how you're supposed to see them. The safest way. If you meet their gaze, they attack. If you move too fast, they attack. If you sweat through your e-blocker or God forbid break a fart while you're out in the field, they follow the chemical gradient and attack.

But she's safe at home plate now, with Phillips to one side of her and Sixsmith on the other, their rifles promising a refuge. Akimwe slides down right behind her, barely in control of his speed. His leg bumps her side and he is instantly appalled. 'I'm sorry, Rina,' he mutters. 'Please forgive me.'

Khan shakes her head to show it's fine, she's not bone china after all. But she wishes he would remember to take it more slowly. That descent might easily have been fast enough to register on the hungries' perceptions, and if they start moving they won't stop. They could be heading up here right now, heads down and arms dangling in the ugly swallow-dive run that puts their gaping jaws front and centre. But she tells herself that's just her hind-brain talking. If there were any sign of a massed charge, Phillips and Sixsmith and Lutes would be firing and the whole team would be retreating back up the slope and all hell would be breaking loose.

It's fine. It has to be fine.

Because here come the snipers, walking with no particular haste, their muscular grace making Khan feel ashamed to be so dusty and dishevelled and afraid. They come over the hill side by side as though they're on a country ramble, just the two of them, their over-long M407s slung casually across their shoulders. The three privates always carry their rifles at the ready, but Lieutenant McQueen and Lance-Bombardier Foss flaunt their unreadiness, make a show of empty hands. And Kat Foss is almost as tall as the lieutenant, an elegant, long-limbed predator with cropped white hair like exhaled smoke – the only woman who has ever made Khan feel that her five feet and two inches might be less than adequate.

Once he's level with them, McQueen whips them on to the task with a single word. 'Targets.' The members of the science team, well conditioned, stick up their heads above the gorse flowers' yellow exuberance. They must look like so many rabbits.

Triage. This is where they get to weigh souls against feathers, assuming there are any souls left in this valley besides their own. That's a burning question, not a philosophical exercise: it keeps Khan awake at night.

She lets her eye travel the length of the valley. It's breathtaking. A salt-and-pepper day where the sun breaks from cover and runs a little way before being swallowed up again in curdling banks of cumulus. A day where the threat of rain makes you revel in the dazzle when it comes. Cloud shadow drifts across the forested upper slopes, making it seem as though the whole vista is under water. Further down, light green meadows shelve towards the loch, which is as smooth as a mirror despite the bustle in the upper air.

Here and there in the broad valley, at every elevation and regardless of the terrain, human figures stand; their arms hanging at their sides, their heads mostly bowed at an angle on their necks. They stand up to their calves or knees in thistles, mud, bracken, water. They wear faded and ragged clothes made piebald by the rust of old bloodstains. They look for all the world like sleepwalkers about to wake up.

And that's what they are, Khan thinks. Except that they won't wake, ever. The human minds that once inhabited these carcasses will slumber on for always. If they open their eyes, something else entirely will be looking out.

'Two over there,' Elaine says. 'At the foot of the big rock. Lots of grey on both of them.'

'And another.' Sealey raises his hand – slowly, carefully – to point. 'Same vector. Downslope. Good field of fire.'

Khan almost smiles. Vectors. Fields of fire. That's how McQueen and Foss talk. John wants so much to play with the cool kids, but whatever he does or says he'll always be a nerd rather than a lethal weapon. Her heart stirs a little, asserts itself inside her for his gentleness and for his trying too hard.

'I'm good with all three of those,' she says, and Akimwe nods. 'Lots to work with,' he concurs.

The snipers kneel and set up their weapons. They don't say a word, or waste a movement. Nobody else speaks either. This is their mystery and everybody knows not to step across its rituals and observances. For all she knows, Khan might be the only one in the whole team to feel any ambivalence about their free and easy attitude to killing. Possibly she's an outlier when it comes to the practice of shedding blood.

Certainly she's a hypocrite. When Foss and McQueen are done, she'll go in and cut a slice or two from the chosen sacrifices. Different instruments, same agenda. She's got no business mistaking this verdant hillside for the moral high ground. Particularly when she thinks about what's waiting for her back at base once this expedition is over.

Nobody expects the Spanish Inquisition. Which is faulty learning because it always comes.

'Why are there so many of them way out here?' Penny

25

murmurs. 'It's so remote.' Her freckled face scrunches up, perplexity changing its topology as all emotions instantly do. She wears her heart most visibly of anyone in the crew except for Stephen, who of course has no disguises or defences at all.

'Look at their overalls,' Akimwe tells her. 'Most of them were working at the water-testing station, up at the head of the loch. They were probably infected in a single incident.'

Khan tries not to think about how that might have gone down. One hungry finding its way into the big cement bunker. Biting the first man or woman it saw, passing on the infection. The two of them, all at once on the same team, wandering on through the corridors following the rich scents that led to fresh prey. Biting, infecting, recruiting. A lethal chain reaction that didn't end until there was no one left in the building. No one without the pathogen in their system. No one still human and self-aware.

'From the water's edge,' McQueen says. 'Lead off.'

Foss is lying full length on the grass now, her neck pressed against the 407's padded stock, her eye up against its sight. If she were standing up, it would look like the opening position of a hot tango.

She pulls back on the trigger. It's a beckoning motion, not quick or sudden. The gun – wearing a phase-cancellation sound suppressor that would give a yearling stallion penis envy – makes a noise like a man spitting out a pip.

Down in the valley, half a second later, one of the standing figures – one of the chosen three – leans sideways, thrown off balance by having its right leg shattered at the knee. Then it topples headlong into the waters of the loch. Red-brown spray hangs in the air where it fell.

The sound of the splash reaches them a heartbeat later, a

discreet whisper in the air. The hungries closest to the one that fell turn towards the sound and the movement, but neither of these stimuli is quite enough to push them from passive to active state.

McQueen goes next. His shooting stance is up on one knee, spurning the extra stability of the rifle's bipod support. He fires, and the second target is punched backwards off its feet. The bullet has gone through the centre of its pelvis, effectively immobilising it. It lies where it fell, not even twitching. Only its head moves, its eyes roving as if to seek the source of the shot that dropped it.

Foss takes out the third and last of the chosen ones, then the two snipers switch out their magazines to clear the area around the fallen.

The aim, first and foremost, is to avoid a stampede. If the hungries run – and when one runs, they all will – they will trample the ones already down, who have been chosen for sampling. There would be no use in trying to take tissue samples from the resulting slurry of flesh and bone. So radically invasive hollow-point – RIH for short – is the order of the day. These are flechette bullets, breaking up inside the body to pulp everything in their path. Every shot is a kill. As though he's forgotten this, McQueen goes for the head shot every time. And every time he makes it.

The man and the woman work to a rapid rhythm, each of them pulling back the bolt to eject the spent cartridge and slamming it home again while the other aims and fires. When in due course they empty their magazines (limited to five bullets so as not to throw off the rifles' exquisite balance), the reloading barely creates a pause in the syncopated carnage.

Within two minutes, a space has been cleared around the

three chosen hungries. This is what the team has come to call fine clearance. What comes next is mass clearance: it's done by the grunts using SCAR-H heavy assault rifles on full automatic. The three privates heft their weapons and take aim, insofar as aim is needed.

'Safeties off,' McQueen says to the grunts. 'On my mark.' He holds up his hand. *Wait for it.* Why does he do that? Khan wonders. Is he testing the air or something? But that makes no sense. They're wearing e-blocker gel to mask their bodies' natural smorgasbord of scents, and in spite of that they're standing downwind of the hungries, taking no chances. Either the drawn-out pause is some aspect of kill-craft that the laity can't be expected to understand or else it's pure melodrama.

The moment stretches. 'Okay,' the lieutenant says at last. 'Let's—' But another voice, loud and clear, cuts him off.

'Hold your fire.'

It's Carlisle. The colonel. He's standing right on the shoulder of the slope, in full view from all directions. He has come up behind them while they were focused on what was going on down below and he has been watching all this.

To McQueen's strong disapproval, evidently. The sniper pushes out his cheek as though there's some half-chewed mass in there that he wants to eject.

'Permission to speak, sir,' he says.

The colonel doesn't give it. He doesn't not give it either: he just doesn't acknowledge the request. 'Guns down,' he says to the three soldiers on their knees in the gorse. 'Watch and wait.'

McQueen tries again. 'Sir, operational guidelines call for a complete clearance of—'

He stops because he's just seen what everyone else has

28

seen. Topping the rise a quarter of a mile away, standing for a moment on the summit in full, heraldic glory, is a stag the size of the wrath of God. It's the most beautiful thing Khan has ever seen, or she thinks it is at that moment. They all gawp at it, reduced to tourists by the monarch of the glen as he makes time in his busy schedule to stop by and remind them of how small they are.

Then he starts down the slope. Khan registers what's about to happen. But she can't look away.

The stag is unaware of any danger. Nothing is moving. There are no loud noises. A few tattered clothes are drifting in a skittish wind, and the waves are lapping around a few recently deposited corpses. Nothing to see here, nothing to get alarmed about.

The animal is in among the hungries before the ones closest to it start to stir. Their heads come upright on their necks, swivel around to take in range and distance. And then they're on the move.

The stag finds itself, with no warning, at the centre of a vast convergence.

It breaks into a gallop, but that's not going to help because there's nowhere to run to that isn't already crowded. The hungries may have looked sparse spread out across the valley, but Jesus, do they rally to the sound of the dinner bell! They come sprinting in from every quarter, backs bent and heads thrust forward. Now there are sounds: the working of their jaws, the pounding of their feet, the occasional brute, blunt impact as one runs up against another in its haste and they both go sprawling down the hill.

The first hungry to reach the stag sinks its teeth into its flank. The second into its throat. Then it's impossible to count, impossible to see. The stag disappears under a living wave of human bodies (or post-human, Khan corrects herself reflexively). The sound of its fall is a dull thud, muffled by distance.

The hungries feed. Dipping their heads, locking their jaws, tearing away whatever they can get in quick, convulsive jerks. The movement is like a collective peristalsis, a wave that goes through them all in sequence.

Khan understands now why the colonel said not to fire. The hungries – all but the ones already felled – are gone from the nearer slope. There's nothing to stop the science team from strolling right on down and reaping what the snipers sowed.

5

The snipers stay high up on the slope, providing cover as the scientists go in. The grunts go in with them, rifles slung, catch-cans in hand. Time is still of the essence, and everyone has their job to do.

Which is why Khan carries a sampling kit even though her role on the mission roster is as an epidemiologist. The only line that matters here is between the people with rifles and the people with doctorates.

Three hungries. Three subjects, each with a brain, a spinal column, a skin surface and numerous organs. Four scientists, each with a field kit that accommodates a maximum of twenty-four separate samples. Fun for all.

The soldiers wield their catch-cans with practised skill. It's a tool that was designed for animal handling, an extensible metal pole that locks at any length and has a running loop at the business end. The loop is made out of parachute silk,

31

with braided steel ribbon woven through it. You slip it around the neck – or any available limb – of a hungry and use it as a pinion point. Usually the drill is to loop and lock down the head and both arms of the chosen target, completely immobilising the upper body. The hungry still flails and squirms, but unless you actually put your hand in its mouth you're not going to get bitten.

It's not always easy to remember that. These hungries were infected years before. The *Cordyceps* pathogen has been growing through their bodies for all that time, and by now there is a rich carpet of fungal threads on the surface of their skin. It's not dangerous: the only vector of infection is via bodily fluids, through blood and saliva. But some deep-seated instinct always makes Khan want to avoid the touch of that bleached, blotchy flesh with its coat of grey fur.

She can't. Every second matters here. With a specimen secured, each of the scientists becomes a different kind of butcher. John Sealey wields the bone saw, with absolute and unblinking concentration. Akimwe is Mister Spinal Fluid, punching in with a hypo at the L5 vertebra without knocking. Penny goes for epidermal growth, a brief that has her ducking in and out between the two men with her little plastic scraper like the shuttle on a loom.

And Khan?

Khan cuts out the brains.

In this context, the brain is the prime cut, although it certainly doesn't look like it. It looks like mouldering cheese, dried out and shrunk to about a third of its normal volume, swathed in fungal matter like clotted cobwebs. She doesn't take it all. What she wants is a snapshot of penetration and mycelial density, which she can get from a biopsy.

So as soon as John levers off the top of each skull, Khan dips in with the eight-centimetre punch, driving it diagonally through the *corpus callosum* into the desiccated, unhealthy tissue beneath.

There's a series of steel canisters hooked onto her belt. The filled punches slot into them so perfectly it's practically a vacuum seal even before she screws on the lids.

'All good here,' she says.

'I'm done,' Akimwe answers.

'Give me a second,' Penny mutters. She's running her scraper repeatedly around the curve of a shoulder as though the still-twitching hungry is a pat of butter straight out of the fridge. 'Okay,' she says at last, spooning the grey froth carefully into her last empty sample jar. 'Ready.'

John Sealey gives McQueen the okay sign, forefinger and thumb joined at the tips. Once again he's trying to speak the lieutenant's language, which is touching in a way but also futile. McQueen barely looks at him.

And in any case, now that Carlisle is here it's him rather than McQueen who's the ranking officer. 'All finished, colonel,' Khan says, not wanting to correct John's solecism but also quite keen not to let it stand. She feels respect for the colonel – respect deepened by her personal debt to him into something a lot harder to define. For McQueen, although he keeps her alive on a daily basis, she mainly feels a sort of uneasy mixture of awe and mild distaste. He's very, very good at what he does. But what he does is not something to which she can entirely reconcile herself.

'Withdraw,' Carlisle orders. 'Single file, on your name.'

He calls them home, and they come. All this time, he hasn't troubled to duck his head or take cover: he just keeps a weather eye on the hungries down at the bottom of the slope, who are still feeding on the remains of the stag. But whatever risks the colonel takes with his own person, he's chary of the rest of them. He brings them out in good order, the scientists and their hard-won prizes at the centre of a protective cordon of outward-pointing ordnance, like a delicate flower in a nest of thistles.

At the head of the rise, Elaine Penny looks back down into the valley with a puzzled expression.

'What?' Khan asks.

'That was weird,' Penny says. 'I thought I saw . . .' she points. 'There were some kids down there.'

'Hungries?'

'No. I don't know.'

'Well, who else is going to be down there? Junkers would have more sense.'

Penny frowns, then shrugs. 'I suppose.'

Khan finds herself walking beside the colonel as they return to Rosie. That puts her at the back of the column, because even when he's using his cane the colonel's lopsided, rolling walk is not fast. His tall, gaunt body, carved into a stick by the winds of a dozen or so assorted battlefields, towers head and shoulders over hers. His face with its right-angled jaw and boat-prow nose, bald dome framed between two sparse brackets of grey hair, is no less heraldic than the stag's. It's so retro it's actually funny. He turns to look down at her, shifting his grip on his (equally timeless) spiral Derby walking stick.

And they've known each other a long time – much longer than the two hundred and some days of the current expedition – so he can see that Khan is not happy. But he mistakes the reason. 'You've no need to be afraid of Dr

Fournier, Rina,' he says. And then when she doesn't answer: 'You've committed an infraction, and he feels as though it will send the wrong signal if he ignores it. But he can hardly stand you down from the mission, and since it's impossible right now to refer the matter back to Beacon, he doesn't have any other sanctions to call on.'

Khan knows these things. She's not looking forward to that particular interview, but she's not afraid either. She just wants it to be over. But the colonel has just broached the Forbidden Subject. Now she's thinking about the radio silence and what it might mean, and those thoughts are a spiral you have to pull out of before you hit the ground and explode in a stinky cloud of existential angst.

They're in among the trees now and the soldiers have closed in, tense and alert. Visibility is bad here. A hungry could come running from any direction. They can't even rely on sound because the wind has picked up: the trees are making a noise like the crowd in a distant football stadium cheering from hoarse lungs. The smell of wild flowers comes to Khan, and underneath it the smell of rot. The world has dabbed a little perfume on its spoiling wounds.

Colonel Carlisle can see he's missed the mark. He guesses again.

'You think that was cruel,' he says. 'What I did just now. Letting the stag draw off the hungries.'

'No,' Khan protests. But she's hiding behind semantics. She thought it was ugly, and she doesn't associate the colonel with ugliness. 'I was geared up for something else, that's all,' she half-lies. 'It took me by surprise.'

'I was thinking of waste, Rina.'

'So was I,' Khan says.

'But you mean the stag. I mean the bullets.'

'The bullets?'

'Back in Beacon there's a whole warehouse full, scavenged from here and there. Enough to last for years. Ten years, I'd say, if you pushed me to offer an estimate. Possibly a little longer. But nobody is making any more. Not to these tolerances. Every single cartridge in these magazines, every round these soldiers fire, is an exquisite piece of engineering from a finite and diminishing stock.'

The colonel tilts his hand, miming a shifting balance. 'And if you follow the logic, every shot fired changes the odds on our survival as a species. Will our children fight with pikestaffs? Bows and arrows? Sharpened sticks? It's hard enough to bring a hungry down with a ballistic round. Half the time they don't seem to realise that they're dead. Pending your expert opinion, of course.'

He offers her a quick smile to let her know that this last is a joke rather than an attack on her. The Caldwell doctrine, that ego-death occurs at the moment of infection, is widely accepted in Beacon but has never been satisfactorily proved. The alternative hypothesis – terrible but not implausible – is that the hungries have some kind of locked-in syndrome. That they're conscious but unable to command their own limbs, sidelined by the pathogen that's set up house in their nervous system. How would that feel? A soul peeping out through stained grey curtains while the body it used to wear celebrates its freedom with acts of random carnage?

Khan maintains a stubborn belief in the future – in the fact that there is going to be one – but sometimes the present daunts and defeats her. There used to be a world in which things made some kind of sense, had some kind of permanence. But the human race put that world down somewhere, left it carelessly behind, and now nobody can find it again or reconstitute it. Entropy is increasing. In her own affairs, too.

The colonel has assured her that she's got nothing to worry about, but as a member of the science team she reports to the civilian commander, not the military one. In any given situation it's impossible to say which way Dr Fournier will jump. Most of the time he doesn't even know that himself.

They've reached the camp perimeter. Carlisle tells McQueen to deactivate the motion sensors. The lieutenant does so using the command channel on his walkie-talkie (which is still functional, proving that Beacon's silence can't be explained away by mechanical failure). There are three sets of sensors, carefully hidden among the gorse and towering thistles. The leg-breaker traps and barbed wire entanglements, by contrast, are left out in the open with no attempt at concealment. When hungries run, they run in a straight line towards their prey so there's really no point in subterfuge.

The team can now see the road ahead of them and below them. It's just a ragged strip of asphalt that's being torn apart in slow motion by weeds clawing their way through it from underneath. There's a section about thirty yards long that they cleared by hand, soldiers and scientists together, hacking at the brambles and spear-thistles with machetes. The Rosalind Franklin sits in the middle of the clear space, an armoured mother hen waiting for her chicks to come home.

Her? Khan always falls into the trap of using the female pronoun, and always resents it. It's only the name of the armoured olive-drab monster that enforces the logic. It also recalls none-too-subtly the quiet dedication of scientists who change the world and earn no glittering prizes. But by any name, Rosie is the bastard child of an articulated lorry and a Chieftain tank. Her front end is adorned with a V-shaped steel battering ram designed to function like a cow-catcher on an ancient steam train. On her roof, a field pounder and a flamethrower share a single broad turret. Inch-thick plate sheathes her sides, and broad black treads her underbelly. There is nothing in this post-lapsarian world that she can't roll over, burn through or blow the hell apart.

But right now Rosie is base camp, her warrior self disguised as home sweet home. Her airlock is fully extruded from the mid-section, her extension blisters out to their furthest extent almost doubling the interior space. She has outriggers to hold her stable in spite of external pressure coming on any vector, at any speed. She would hold fast against a hurricane; and more to the point, against a massed charge. Thousands of hungries, flinging themselves against Rosie's flanks in a flood tide of reckless bio-mass, would break and ebb harmlessly.

Have broken. Have ebbed.

McQueen cycles the airlock. He stabs irritably at the keypad, entering the day's code correctly only on the second try. Mostly, these days, the airlock features in their lives as a pain in the arse. It's like an over-large shower cubicle rigged up against the mid-section door, flimsy-looking but made of a rigid, robust plastic polymer. Protocol dictates that it stays in place whenever there's a team out in the field, but it's pointless. Nobody is afraid at this point that they might bring unsuspected toxins or biological agents into Rosie's interior. They know what the hungry pathogen is and how it travels, how it infects. The airlock defends against a risk that isn't present. It's a gesture, more than anything, a finger impotently raised against the apocalypse.

And it only holds six people, so two cycles are needed to get them all inside. The scientists go in first, with their tissue samples. That's what the mission is all about, after all. The soldiers wait, facing outwards with rifles at the ready, until the outer door slides open again and they can enter in their turn.

Inside Rosie the same demarcation lines stay in place. The scientists retreat to the lab space, which is at the stern end. The soldiers go to crew quarters up at the front. It's like some awkward high-school bop where the boys and the girls scuttle off to opposite ends of the school hall and nobody dares to go out on the dance floor. Except that the dance floor in this analogy is the mid-section, which houses nothing except the airlock and the access ladder for the turret.

Khan transfers her tissue samples into cryo. They won't stay there long, but she's going to miss out on the coming orgy of fixing, sectioning, staining and slide-mounting. She's got other places to be.

She's got to face the inquisition.

Carlisle has gone through into the engine room, even further astern than the lab. According to the book, which for the colonel is a real and vital thing, he has to check in with the civilian commander as soon as he returns from the field – and Dr Fournier has seized on the engine room, a pathetic, claustrophobic little space, as his office.

Khan asked Carlisle once how he could bear it. A man who has led brigades, having to report and sometimes defer to a neurotic little pencil-pusher. Where is the sense in it? Especially now, in the deafening silence of the cockpit radio, wondering (as every one of them is wondering, all the time) whether Beacon has gone down and their remit has disappeared along with their whole world. Carlisle evaded the question with a joke. Khan can't remember the punchline now, something about the chain of command not being an actual chain. But yeah, it is. At least if you let the powers-that-be add a padlock to it.

John Sealey is giving her anxious looks but he can't do any more than that with everyone watching. And they *are* watching. There just aren't that many topics of conversation left after more than half a year in the field. Khan is a thrilling enigma to the scientists, probably a source of filthy jokes to the soldiers. She can live with that. She has lived with worse things.

Something else is nagging at her, though, and she's just about to figure out what it is when the colonel reappears.

'Rina,' he says. 'Dr Fournier would like to see you.'

Of course he would.

'We're actually pretty busy with this stuff,' Khan says. 'Working up the new samples. It's time-sensitive. Is it possible I could come along in a little while?'

Carlisle shakes his head. 'Now, please,' he says. 'This won't take long, but you need to come with me, Dr Khan.'

Dr Khan. Such formality. But he's not freezing her out: he's giving her a warning. Stay on your toes, don't relax into this. You've still got a lot to lose.

And she doesn't dispute that.

6

The first time she met Colonel Carlisle, Samrina Khan cordially hated him. She is embarrassed about that now, not least because she is aware of the trope in romantic movies where hate at first sight prefigures an eventual romance. She could no more see the colonel as a potential lover than she could see her own father as one — and when she thinks about it, he resembles her dad in many other ways besides. Strict. Insulated from his own emotions. Fiercely honourable.

But on that first meeting, he reminded her more of Taz, the character from the old Warner cartoons who is a perpetual whirl of objectless fury.

She was in London. The Centre for Synthetic Biology at Imperial College. She was working on an epidemiological model for the hungry disease that would allow the government to predict its spread with greater than 90 per cent accuracy. And the world was way ahead of her, already falling apart.

Fortress America was still standing, just about, or at least still broadcasting. Most of the broadcast content consisted of bullish proclamations about the robustness of the newly relocated federal government, operating out of the Sangre de Cristo range in Southern Colorado. Eleven thousand feet up and enjoying the bracing mountain air! But the southern hemisphere had fallen silent and Europe was rolling up from the east to the west like a cheap carpet. The Channel Tunnel had been filled in with seventy thousand tons of cement, which sounded like a lot but turned out to be too little too late.

The hungries were just there. Everywhere at once. Wherever you tried to draw the line they were already inside it.

But Khan had always imagined that London would be the last redoubt. When you retreated, you retreated from the bailey to the motte, into the innermost sanctum. So the order to evacuate the city took her by surprise. Apparently the innermost sanctum was Codename Beacon, a fortified camp on the south coast between Dover and Brighton. All remaining government offices were relocating there, effective immediately. Presumably a fortified camp was easier to defend than a city that covered six hundred square miles and had nine major motorways by way of a front door.

By this time, all the surviving doctors and biologists were government employees, their private contracts annulled or bought up, so 'all remaining government offices' included Khan. She was given an assembly point and a time to arrive there with one suitcase and one piece of hand luggage.

She went right on working. Her model was almost done and there was no guarantee whatsoever that she would be able to get computer time at Codename Middle of Fucking Nowhere. As the desks around her emptied, she just threw herself with more determination into her work. The peace and quiet were even welcome in a way. No distractions. She had already been sleeping on the couch in her office for three weeks, so she didn't have to venture out into the hazardous and eerily silent streets. She lived on tins of Heinz lentil soup and family-sized packets of crisps.

Until the colonel came and forced her out at gunpoint.

Well, 'gunpoint' was something of an exaggeration, but he had a gun. He had soldiers. He was in a state of barely contained rage and he told her that if she didn't come of her own free will she would be handcuffed and taken away under arrest.

Khan told him to drop dead and kept on entering data.

Carlisle wasn't kidding. The cuffs were forthcoming. Two burly soldiers took Khan away from her desk, from her data, and despite her screams of protest they didn't give her time to record a back-up. The internet had long since gone from being patchy to not being a thing, so her months of work stayed where they were and she was taken south.

She was honest enough to admit to herself – eventually – that nothing much was lost by this. The research was worthless. The worst-case scenarios had already become realities. She had been clinging to her spreadsheets and models the way a child clings to a security blanket. But being kidnapped for her own good still pissed her off.

She didn't register the colonel's name right away, but she had heard of the Fireman. Everybody had. The man who burned half of Hertfordshire, who rained more napalm down on the home counties than America rained on Vietnam without causing the hungries even to miss a meal. He looked the part. And she had reason enough to hate him, even if he hadn't just erased a year of her life with a wave of his hand.

The hate was tempered, though, as they tacked across London. Picking up Khan and two other Imperial College staff had taken the colonel two miles out of his way. He had missed his transport. The four of them had to trek along the Westway to Hammersmith to join another refugee column. They met hungries three times, the third time en masse. The colonel stood his ground alongside his men, aiming low in kneecapping sweeps so the attackers in the forefront of the charge fell and became a barricade against those coming on behind.

They never found the column they were meant to meet. It had disappeared, hundreds of men and dozens of vehicles just swallowed up and gone. Lost in a city, a world, that had burned up all its history and gone back to being pure jungle. Colonel Carlisle assembled his own column of scavenged and repurposed cars and trucks, and led them south. 'Five weeks on the march,' one of the privates said, with a mixture of awe and exasperation. 'He doesn't stop. He just keeps saying we'll sleep when we're dead.'

Which was probably a little over-optimistic, these days.

They were the last ones to make it out of London. On the evidence of their own nightmare journey to the coast, there was nobody left in there to save.

Later, Khan learned that Carlisle had made the burn runs in Hertfordshire under protest – a protest that he had taken all the way to the chiefs of staff. They told him to carry out his orders and he did. Then he resigned his commission, although the top brass twisted his arm until he took it up again – and then punished him for his presumption by putting him in charge of the evacuation while they sat in the war room in Codename Beacon moving counters around on situation charts.

That was where the colonel's anger came from: the disconnect between the orders he was being given and the situation on the ground. The endless missed opportunities and avoidable screw-ups. The burn runs did nothing but kill innocents and destroy essential roads. London should have been evacuated by air, but the army wouldn't release the helicopters because they were technically assigned to combat units. Most of the decisions were coming days or weeks too late.

But Carlisle still followed the orders he was given, the bad ones included. Khan wondered even then what it would take for him to break that habit, given that the end of the world hadn't been enough to do it.

She's wondering the same thing now as she follows him into the engine room. As he punctiliously salutes the worthless man sitting in the room's only chair. Alan Fournier. A wandering arse cut loose from Beacon's large intestine. A man whose shortcomings as a scientist and as a human being are balanced by a limitless capacity for . . .

The word she is heading towards is *obedience*, but she doesn't want to concede any point of comparison between Fournier and the colonel. She settles for *time-serving*, amends it to *licking boots*. Yes, it's true that both men do what they're told. But the colonel has a moral compass. Dr Fournier just has an eagerness to please.

The engine room isn't really a room, any more than the turret is a room. It's an inspection space, just wide enough for an engineer to work in. It's so small that the cowling that covers Rosie's engine is divided into panels, allowing it to be removed in stages. If you took it off in one piece, there would be nowhere to put it and no way of getting it out of the room into the lab beyond.

But there is space, just about, for Dr Fournier to have

45

squeezed in a folding table, which he makes believe is a desk. He is sitting behind it now. Khan has to stand. The colonel doesn't, because Fournier dismisses him with a curt nod of thanks.

Despite his strict adherence to military discipline, Carlisle rests his hand on Khan's shoulder for a moment before he leaves: a reminder, in case she needs one, that she has friends outside this room.

Fournier gives no sign of having noticed. 'Close the door, please,' he tells Khan. His thin, ascetic face is solemn, almost architectural with self-conscious dignity. Sweat sticks his hair to his forehead, undercutting the effect. The engine room is uncomfortably hot, but Khan is sure some of the sweat is because he's been fretting about this conversation ever since he decided to ask her the million-dollar question (*Is that a baby in your belly, Dr Khan, or did you blow your diet?*) straight out, yes or no, and she gave the wrong answer.

For a moment, the strong aversion she feels for the civilian commander gives way to pity. Fournier has so many fears, and what he's doing now combines most of them. Fear of losing the respect and/or the affection of the crew. Fear of meeting a challenge that will be too strong for him, and will break him. Fear of seeming weak, or cruel, or indecisive. Fear, always, of being judged unfit for the job he has been given. The sad thing is that if he is unfit, it's the fear that makes him that way. It makes him second-guess himself. He could follow his instincts in almost any direction and be a better leader than he is now.

Fournier gestures at the hand-held recorder on the table in front of him. 'You should know that I'm taping this,' he tells Khan unnecessarily. 'Obviously we can't report in to Beacon just now, but the sound file will go on your record.' It's quite a grandiose claim when they're all the way out here in the wilds of Scotland, four hundred miles from the last human enclave in the United Kingdom. There are computers on board, but there are no satellites left in the sky to bounce digital signals from one end of the world to the other. The file will stay on the little hand-held until they get back home, if home is even still there, and then if anyone gives a damn it will be uploaded onto a server somewhere.

And promptly forgotten, more than likely. Beacon, if it's still in business, has bigger problems on its plate right now. And they might even solve one or two of them if Fournier would just leave them to get on with their work. Khan tries to shut that line of thought down. She doesn't want to get angry: anger will make her careless, and she might say something stupid.

'Dr Khan,' Fournier says. He seems not to like the sound of it because he tries again. 'Rina. Over the past few weeks it's become impossible to ignore the fact that you've been gaining weight. Around your—' he gestures. 'Your middle. I didn't want to pry, but the well-being of this crew is in my hands. So yesterday I asked you if you were pregnant. I'm going to ask you again now, for the record.'

Khan waits. She's not going to make this easy for him.

'Are you pregnant?' Fournier demands at last, when he realises that she is waiting for the actual question to be repeated.

'Yes.'

'Which puts you in breach of the mission statement you accepted and signed to when you came aboard.'

'No,' Khan says. 'It doesn't.'

'You received the same orders as the rest of us. You accepted, as we all did, that there would be absolutely no fraternisation, absolutely no emotional or physical bonding, between any

47

of the members of this crew. You knew that we were going to be in the field for more than a year. You knew that a pregnancy, if it forced us to return to Beacon early, would be disastrous. Yet you still decided to indulge in unprotected sex.'

Indulge, Khan thinks. Right. That's what we did. That frantic fumble was a wild indulgence. And by the way how can you miss the fact that Dr Akimwe is banging Private Phillips right under your nose every night and most days? No risk of pregnancy there, though, so looking the other way is the better part of valour.

'And when you realised you were pregnant, as you must have done several months ago, you didn't tell me.'

'No,' Khan agrees. 'I'm sincerely sorry about that.'

She sincerely isn't. She's sorry that she let her guard down. Sorry that she didn't think about consequences. But she's not sorry she kept the secret. Six months ago they would still have been close enough to Beacon to turn around and take her home. She has to be here, however difficult here is. She wants and needs to be a part of this mission. And her presence secured Stephen's, which she still believes will turn out – at some point, in some way – to be crucial.

Dr Fournier doesn't acknowledge the apology in any case. Khan wonders if he's working to a script he's prepared in advance. 'This is a disciplinary offence, Rina,' he says, 'and I'm going to have to write it up as one. I'm also obliged to ask you to give me the name of the father.'

Khan says nothing.

'Dr Khan, I said you have to tell me who the child's father is.'

'No, I don't.' She takes a deep breath. She is about to lie, and it doesn't sit well with her. She would prefer to throw the truth in the civilian commander's teeth and see how he

48

copes with it. But she can't just consult her own preferences here. Other people are involved. 'I was already pregnant when we left Beacon,' she says. 'I realised the truth a month later, and you're right that I should have told you then. I was afraid to. I didn't want to be responsible for aborting the mission.'

Fournier stares at her, affronted. 'That's ridiculous,' he protests. 'That would mean you're seven months . . .' A strained pause completes the sentence.

'Seven months gone? Yes, Dr Fournier. Thank you. I'm perfectly capable of counting backwards.' And the calculation isn't wrong by more than a week. She and John fell into each other's arms only a few days out from Beacon. It was the relief of getting away from that place. The explosive derepression. They might as well have been drunk.

Fournier frowns. 'It's hardly conceivable . . .' he protests, and – conception being precisely the issue – stumbles head-long into another silence.

'I'm happy to submit to any tests or inquiries you want to order when we get back,' Khan declares. She's happy enough to say it, anyway. There are no tests that will settle the issue, and she'll take her chances on an inquiry. The way things are going, Fournier's lease is unlikely to last any longer than the mission. Beacon doesn't reward failure.

The commander knows that too. But what can he do? Order her shot, theoretically, since the Beacon Muster and the civilian government have joint control of the mission. But short of the nuclear option, he's got nothing. The colonel was right about that. And shooting her would be such an outrageously stupid move that she doesn't even feel scared. They're short-handed already, running out of time and options and ideas. Not a good time to lose one member of the team and traumatise the rest.

49

But she has underestimated Dr Fournier. He has one last shot left in his locker. Four shots, actually, and the locker in question is the medicine locker. The four packages must have been sitting on his knee all this time. He lays them out on the flimsy folding table now as though the two of them have been playing poker all this time and he's putting down a pat hand.

Laminaria in a big, bulky box.

Oxytocin pills.

Misoprostol suppositories.

And Digoxin, in a tiny plastic bottle like a nasal spray – with an eight-inch hypodermic syringe taped to it for ease of use.

Khan stares at the pharmacopoeia, at first in polite surprise and then in queasy wonder.

'You're kidding me,' she says without inflection.

'No,' Fournier says. 'I'm not. A late-term abortion in this instance is the only course of action that—'

'Late term? That's what you call this?'

'—the only course of action that will guarantee your safety and allow the mission to proceed in—'

Khan's incredulous laugh cuts through the mealy words. She shakes her head. 'Shut up,' she says. 'My God! Shut up right now.'

'Rina.' Fournier chides her, seriously affronted. 'I'm thinking of you here.'

That makes her laugh again. 'Then think of someone else!' She picks up the ampoule of Digoxin strapped to its little rocket-ship hypodermic, holds it up for him to see. 'You think I didn't consider an abortion?' she asks him. 'Seriously? You think that never occurred to me? Seven weeks out, in Luton . . . right after I found out, I got the methotrexate out of the cabinet and I sat there in my bunk with two little white pills

50

in one hand and a glass of water in the other. I thought it through, Dr Fournier, and I decided not to go for it. So it's not likely I'd wait until my baby is almost ready to be born and then stick a needle in its chest to induce a fucking heart attack.'

It's a heartfelt speech and she holds to every word of it, but Fournier tries one last blustering end-run. He puts on a consultative face and leans forward across the table, like a hanging judge who wants to discuss drop heights and thicknesses of rope. 'Until we can re-establish contact with Beacon, Rina, I'm the sole authority on board Rosie. I'm suggesting that you do this for your own good and for the good of the rest of the crew. A baby will divert resources and distract us from the job we've undertaken to do. On my authority as mission commander—'

'Your authority ends at my skin,' she reminds him.

'But the risks, Rina. The risks associated with the birth itself, and then the difficulty of keeping a baby alive out here. Having to take you out of the roster . . .'

She waits him out. But he started that sentence without knowing how to finish it, and now he's all out of ideas. If he tells her it's just a little prick with a needle, she'll probably have to brain him with the table.

Fournier shoots a haunted look at the recorder, capturing every word for posterity. It seems to have a chilling effect on his eloquence. About time!

Finally he gives in and dismisses her. 'I'll refer this to Beacon as soon as comms are up again,' he warns. 'Obviously I'll protect you as far as I can, but the ultimate decision is in their hands. There will be consequences for this.'

'Yeah, I'm sure,' Khan says. 'Thanks for your support.'

'You'll get no exemption from your duties. And when the

51

baby is born, you will continue to receive a single ration. I can't make exceptions for you because of these unwarranted circumstances.'

She makes her exit without another word, because she really can't think of any. Her sense of relief at getting out of the sweat box is tempered by a very strong urge to go take a shower so she can wash this whole conversation off her skin. But the roster puts her next turn in the shower at 4.00 p.m.

In the lab, Akimwe and Penny and John Sealey are prepping the tissue samples and keeping up a determined pretence that they weren't trying to eavesdrop through the closed door. Khan closes the engine-room door, but then runs out of steam. Out of volition. She rests her body, which is feeling heavy and awkward and bloated, against the cold steel of Rosie's bulkhead.

John finds a way to get in close to her, pretending to stack some petri dishes in the steriliser. 'Hey,' he murmurs, letting his forearm rub up against hers. 'You okay?'

'Leave it,' she tells him tersely. 'I'm fine.' And she is. Fournier can go screw himself. If they get Beacon up on the radio again . . . well, then that will be a different situation and she'll deal with it when it comes.

They're all of them waiting for that moment. The lab and the crew space and the cockpit all one big pent-up breath waiting to be breathed out. All of them separately asking themselves whether no news is—

Wait. All of them?

With a sudden sense of vertigo Khan realises what's wrong with this scene. What's missing.

'Where's Stephen?' she demands. 'John, where the hell is Stephen?'

7

Stephen Greaves stands stock still, frozen in a posture he has held without a break for most of the afternoon. He is simply and perfectly happy: a happiness made of observations and inferences. His brain is a computer. Nothing perturbs its dispassionate calculations.

He is in the water-testing station at the eastern end of the loch, in the main pump room. He is not alone there. Hungries surround him, and will attack and devour him if they notice he is there – that is, if he moves too suddenly or makes any loud noise. They will not detect him by scent: the chemical gel smeared over his body protects him, makes him smell like nothing much at all instead of like a meal.

The discomfort of standing so still for so long doesn't trouble Greaves over-much. He has refined the skill over a long time. He started practising the day after his thirteenth birthday, two years ago, when Dr Khan first told him that his name was on the longlist for the Rosalind Franklin's crew. Close observation of the hungries was clearly something that would be highly desirable, so he trained himself in the necessary skills. He feels the strain, of course, but he lets it lie at the outer limits of his perceptions, all but ignored. This is not so bad. He has chosen a position that puts minimal strain on his arms and legs, braced in an angle of a wall so that he can even lean back and relax a little if he gets tired.

Also on those perceptual outskirts, consulted from time to time without undue urgency, is an estimate of passing time. He is counting off the seconds in a kind of mental sub-routine, a discipline he taught himself when he was ten.

He knows he will have to leave soon, that he is close to his limit. He has set an alarm. When his internal counter reaches 108,000, corresponding to an elapsed duration of approximately three hours, it will signal to him that it is time to leave. There are two reasons why he has to do this. The first is temperature. As the air around Greaves cools, the hungries will become aware of him as an anomalous hot spot in the early evening chill. They will be able to track him by his body heat.

The other reason is that the longer he stays here, the more likely it is that his absence will be noticed. That would be unpleasant. Greaves does not enjoy talking to other people, except for Dr Khan and (sometimes) Colonel Carlisle. He likes it even less when the other people are angry or upset.

He wishes he could just be allowed to assume the risk without argument, without having to justify himself. He has come here to observe the hungries in their quiet, dormant state, and there is so much to observe. Their stillness, their silence is full of meaning.

Greaves visited the water-testing station for the first time the day before and was pleased with what he found there. The station offered a large concentration of hungries in a single enclosed space: very dangerous, but (from the point of view of information-gathering) fabulously rich pickings. He was able to stand and watch for an hour, stealing the time from a soil-acidity sweep that he had officially logged in the day-book. As far as the other crew members knew, Greaves was safely within Rosie's defensive perimeter.

He is taking a bigger risk today. He has gone AWOL from a major sampling expedition, slipping away from Rosie as soon as the science team and its military escort were out of sight. Dr Fournier was still on board and might have spotted him, but Greaves judged that contingency unlikely. For the most part, Dr Fournier (like the colonel) prefers to keep to his own company and has found ways to do so even within the mobile lab's very tight confines.

It took Greaves twenty minutes to reach the station. He could have got there more quickly by running, but running would have entailed two unwelcome risks. One: any hungry that saw him would almost certainly transition into the active pursuit state. Two: the e-blocker gel that disguises his scent – the gel that he invented and gave to the Beacon authorities to copy and mass produce – would be weakened and eventually deactivated by excessive sweating.

So he walked to the station, eased his way into the huge, central pump room at a speed slower than a snail ambling across a cabbage leaf, and this is where he is standing now. The pump room is a natural amphitheatre, shelving steeply down to a central reservoir where in former times water drawn off from the loch would have been held while it was tested for alkalinity and contaminants. The roof has fallen in at some point, so the room is open to the sky.

It's also crowded: full of still and silent people with their heads bowed or tilted to the side and their arms dangling. They look as though their internal clockwork has run down for ever, but that's a dangerous illusion. Greaves knows the hungries are tightly wound, hair-triggered. He was careful not to touch them as he slid like treacle into his place. He is careful, now, not to meet their cloudy gaze.

The hungries seem as motionless as statues. But if you spend long enough in their company you come to realise that their stillness is not absolute. Their responses to sound and movement and smells are well known, but Greaves has discovered other stimuli to which they will sometimes react. A strong wind makes them turn, angling their faces to take advantage of the flood of olfactory information. Excessive heat causes them to open their mouths, possibly as a means of temperature regulation. And – a recent discovery which Greaves has spent the afternoon confirming – they have heliotropism. They follow the movement of the sun across the sky, the same way plants do.

This is what he is pondering as he watches them now. Is the pathogen that has saturated the nervous system of these unfortunates trying to photosynthesise? No, that's very close to impossible. *Cordyceps* is not a plant but a fungus. Its cells, in all the specimens he has examined, contain no chloroplasts. Moreover, it feeds through its host and doesn't need to exert itself on its own account.

So it must be the warmth that the hungries are responding to, rather than the light. Greaves thinks what he is seeing is a side effect of the mechanism that lets them hunt down living prey at night by body heat alone. They are tracking the sun as though it might be something good to eat.

It's a fascinating prospect, but there is no time to interrogate it further. His mental alarm goes off. He has reached his pre-arranged limit and he has to leave.

Has to *begin* to leave. The manoeuvre will take time. He needs to make his movements so gradual that the hungries won't notice him. He turns around, very slowly, to face the door he entered by. He takes a step towards it, and then another. Tiny steps, barely lifting his feet off the ground. He is an untethered balloon, drifting in a non-existent breeze.

But just before he reaches the door, just before he drifts through it onto the stairwell beyond, he sees something that stops him in his tracks.

Movement.

It's off to his left, at the periphery of his vision and down below his natural eye level. He almost turns. He almost looks.

Nothing should be moving here – or at least, not quickly or suddenly enough to draw his gaze. Greaves barely checks himself in time, keeps his eyes determinedly on the ground. A shudder goes through the hungries anyway as the movement impinges on their sensoria too.

His heart pounding, Greaves begins a slow turn. It takes most of a minute.

He sees immediately what has changed in the room. There is one more person present. A child. Female, and aged (he estimates) somewhere between nine and ten years.

She is not moving now, or looking at him. She is as still as any of the adult hungries, and she wears the same vacant expression. Pale grey eyes cast down, mouth half-open. Her red hair hangs lank over her face, half-hiding a puckered

57

scar that runs from her hairline across one eye and cheek, terminating in the fold of her neck.

Her immobility is perfectly convincing, but she wasn't there before and therefore it must have been her that moved. It seems most likely that she has emerged from the pump room's central well, which is now dry, but she could simply have stepped out from behind one of the other hungries. She is small enough to have been completely hidden by an adult body.

Is it possible that she has been here all along, and that Greaves has simply overlooked her? He thinks it unlikely. She is the only child present, which makes her an anomaly. The other hungries in the room, all wearing the same overalls with the same logo over the breast pocket, were employees of this facility until they became infected. She would have stood out from the start.

The girl is dressed oddly too, given that hungries always wear the increasingly ragged and filthy remnants of what they were wearing at the moment when they were bitten and took the infection. If she is a hungry, then at the moment of infection she must have been in some kind of fancy dress. Twin lines of blue and yellow paint have been daubed roughly and unevenly across her brows, two more down the mid-line of her nose. A man's shirt in a narrow pinstripe hangs loosely on her skinny frame all the way down to her knees, cinched at her waist with a brown belt made of plaited leather strings. Dozens of what look to be ornamental key rings are attached to the belt, all of them different. Greaves sees a skull, a smiley face, a rabbit's foot, a tiny shoe. Underneath the shirt, the girl is wearing what looks like the vest from a wetsuit. Her feet are bare.

Is she a hungry? If she is, then her stepping into view and then halting again defies explanation. The hungries toggle between two states: they are either stock still or running headlong after food. They don't make concerted movements and then stop. Only humans do that.

Conversely, if the girl is human why don't the hungries smell her humanity and respond to her? Turn on her and eat their fill? She can't be wearing e-blocker. Beacon is the only place in the whole of mainland Britain where the protective gel is manufactured, and she is not from Beacon.

Uncertainty frightens Greaves. Even a small amount of unresolvable ambiguity makes him unhappy at a very deep level, makes his brain itch and tears start in his eyes.

His hand begins a super-slow glide across his chest, into the pocket of his flak jacket. He keeps a relic there, whose touch comforts him. He finds it now and turns it in his fingers. A small, angular shape. A flat rectangle, but slightly convex on one side. With the tip of his index finger, Greaves traces the vertical bars of a tiny speaker grille.

Activate jump gate, captain, he mouths silently.

Neutron star at your six o'clock.

We come in peace from Planet Earth.

The plastic lozenge is the voice box from a child's toy. There are twenty-four phrases in its inventory. Five of them never play any more but Greaves knows them all. Every quirk of intonation and every hiss or crackle that the little speaker adds on its own account. In moments of personal crisis, he recites them like a catechism and it calms him.

It calms him now, but still he has to know. He needs to resolve the ambiguity before it topples his reason and makes him panic. Panicking here would be very bad.

He applies the only test he can think of. 'I see you,' he says. He keeps his voice to a murmur, doesn't move his lips even a fraction. In this pregnant silence, the sound should be loud enough to reach her without standing out in the hungries' perceptions as purposive and worth investigating.

But the girl doesn't move. Her eyes don't flick in his direction. Is their grey tone natural or is it the grey that comes with infection? He's too far away from her to tell for sure.

'My name is Stephen,' he says, trying again. Again she makes no response.

Greaves takes a slow, sidling step towards her, but then immediately stops. He is stymied. If he advances on her and she runs away, he will have killed her by drawing down the hungries' attentions on her. While if she is a hungry herself, she will almost certainly register his movement any second now and attack him. He is taking a risk even in looking at her for so long.

The only safe thing to do is to withdraw. But if he withdraws he may never have an answer. Not having an answer is unacceptable. Impossible.

He does it without even thinking. His hand, inside his pocket, is already folded around the voice box. He brings it out, very slowly.

His intention is only half-formed but on some level he is already committed. His hands move of their own accord: he parses the decision after it has already happened. He displays the little plastic box, which is bright red and no more than an inch in diameter. He holds it up so the girl can see it, turns it this way and that in his hand.

He is essaying a magic trick that Private Phillips taught him. Normally he is proficient, but normally his movements

60

are much quicker than this. Misdirection is harder at glacial speeds.

In fact, it's impossible. Greaves performs the pass, and the re-pass, but nobody watching would be in any doubt that the voice box is now in the palm of his left hand.

He tries again, elaborately (and very gradually) waving the fingers of his left hand in sequence to disguise the moment when he slides the box across to the right. The hungries stir a little. In spite of the care Greaves is taking with his gestures, he is close to triggering them into wakefulness. The girl is still not looking in his direction but something about her stance, too, suggests a heightened alertness. She is interested, but whether in the trick or in the imminent possibility of a meal Greaves can't tell.

And he can't go any further. He has to abandon the trick before it kills him.

Again, his body is quicker than his mind. His finger and thumb find the string that is the voice box's only control, and draw it out to a six-inch length.

As the string ravels back, a voice speaks into the utter stillness of the room. The voice of Captain Power, the galactic engineer. It is muted by Greaves' enclosing hand, and it seems to come from nowhere.

'We need to go to light speed.'

The girl's face flickers, just for a moment, lit up from the inside by a spark of surprise she can't suppress in time.

Greaves has his answer. Sheer amazement punches him in the heart and compresses his diaphragm tight enough so that his next breath hurts.

What now? What should he do? He has to get himself and the girl out of this room. He has to talk to her (he hates talking to anyone, but children are not as scary as adults) and find out who she is. How she came to be here. What she is using to keep the hungries from scenting her out.

He has to take her back to the safety of Rosie.

Even as he thinks these thoughts, the still life moves.

A pigeon flies down through the gaping hole in the roof. All the hungries raise their heads in a simultaneous jerking shudder, like cars cold-starting on a frosty winter morning. Their heads turn and their eyes range.

The pigeon settles on a rusted steel railing (stainless steel, it used to be called, but you can't keep out oxygen for ever) and looks around the room with its black-bead eyes. Its blue-grey head ducks and darts. Looking for food, most likely, and completely unaware that it's the best thing on the menu.

By this time, the hungries have found the bird and locked their gaze onto it. They surge forward as one. Greaves has to do the same. If you don't keep to the moves in this dance, you will pretty soon wish you had.

They're very fast, the walking dead, the ontologically departed. But the pigeon is fast too. As the room erupts all around it, it takes wing again, heading back the way it came.

Fastest of all is the girl. She runs right under the bird, gathers herself and jumps. She hits Greaves full in the chest and scales him in an instant. One foot goes into the crook of his arm, the other onto his shoulder.

He clamps down a yell. It's not that she has hurt him. She is so light it seems she must be hollow-boned, like the bird. But he has a strong aversion to being touched, especially with no warning. He feels, for a second, as though some bubble that enclosed him has burst. As though he is naked to hostile space.

The girl pushes off, vaulting and turning in the air.

Catches the bird in flight with one outstretched hand.

She lands, somehow, at the top of a wall with nothing but open sky above her. Her feet are braced against smooth concrete. Her free hand snags a steel stanchion that was left exposed when the roof fell in.

She pivots on that hand and she's over.

She's gone.

The wild, vain clapping of the pigeon's wings reaches Greaves a second later, is stilled again a second after that. For a moment or two, his mind performs a weird synthesis. It's as though he just saw her fly, and the wings he heard were hers.

The hungries' reaction is more dramatic than Greaves'. It's also quicker, since it's not mediated by any conscious thought. They throw themselves against the base of the wall the girl leapt over. The first ones to reach it claw at the damp cement as though they could rip their way through, until the ones coming up behind press them against it, crushing and breaking them.

Greaves takes the opportunity, with all eyes turned away from him, to extract himself from the room a little more quickly than he would otherwise have dared. A flight of steel steps takes him up onto what used to be a car park. Now it's a jungle of head-high weeds with a single path trampled through it.

All this while he is thinking: what is she? How did she move among the hungries without eliciting any response from them? And how did she move so fast, faster even than those flesh-and-blood machines? In the filing cabinet of his mind he puts her – unwillingly, but with quickening excitement – into a category of one. She is an anomaly.

Anomalies explode old theories and engender new ones. They are dangerous and glorious.

Greaves can't help himself. Despite the risk, he runs to the end of the path, onto a wide apron of asphalt that seems to have been more resistant to the encroaching wilderness. An old security post stands here, with all its windows broken. A traffic barrier that wasn't up to the job it was made for lies in pieces on the ground.

There is no sign of the girl. But if she ran in this direction there is only one place she could have been heading for. At the bottom of the valley, a mile and a half away and two hundred feet below him, is the town of Invercrae. It's the next place on Dr Fournier's itinerary, and the science team will be heading there tomorrow.

Greaves can't wait that long. Not with a question as big as this pressing on his mind.

He will go tonight.

8

Greaves returns to the Rosalind Franklin by the exact same path he took when he left, apart from a careful detour around a pack of wild dogs feeding on the carcase of a squirrel. The expedition has seen packs like this everywhere they have visited, and though they almost never attack humans Greaves doesn't like them or trust them at all.

Once he gets close to Rosie, he is careful to follow his outward route step for step. He carries a map of the traps and movement sensors in his head and has chosen his angle of approach accordingly.

He comes in from the front. He sees Colonel Carlisle sitting in the cockpit, reading a book (Greaves has seen the book before: it is R. T. Mulholland's biography of Napoleon Bonaparte in a thoroughly used Wordsworth Classics edition). Carlisle glances up as Greaves passes and they exchange a nod of greeting. Though he is punctilious about regulations on his own account, the colonel has no desire to be anyone else's conscience. It might be different if he were in overall command, Greaves surmises. But this expedition has two commanders. They embody the current uneasy status quo in Beacon, where the civilian government pretends to be in absolute control but depends for its continuing existence on the actions and interventions of the Military Muster. Carlisle is the military commander; Fournier the civilian one – deliberate obfuscation, twisting the loose ends of their mission statement to make a Möbius strip.

Greaves walks on around the side of the massive vehicle to the central airlock. There is no way of getting in here without being seen: the airlock is almost always guarded, and even when it isn't the act of cycling it from outside will activate telltales and alarms all over the lab and crew spaces.

The airlock is open. Dr Khan stands just inside, her restless gaze scanning the trees to left and right. When she sees Greaves, she steps aside and lets him enter. There is a rigidity in her posture that he sees at once: she is tense, afraid. She puts out her hand to touch the back of his wrist, but only with her index finger. She is allowed to touch him; he has made a special and complex accommodation in his mind for her and her alone, but she knows him and the tip of one finger is as far as she ever takes that liberty. Small though the point of contact is, a tremor in her arm communicates itself to him. Dr Khan is perturbed.

'I'm fine, Rina,' Greaves assures her. He is so contrite about having worried her that he almost reaches up and touches her fingertip with his own. But his hand hovers, unable to complete the gesture.

'I can see that,' she says. 'Thank God. But where were you,

Stephen? Were you making observations again? Close up?'

She has him. Knowing that a *yes* will make her unhappy Greaves tries to say *no*. He starts to stammer, locks his jaws on the word he is physically unable to speak.

His discomfort with deliberate falsehood is like his discomfort with uncertainty raised to its own power. If he says something that isn't true, he is bringing uncertainty into the world. He is blinding the people around him to a small part of the truth – and every part of the truth is important. You can't complete a jigsaw if one of its pieces has been swapped out for a piece of a different jigsaw.

'I knew it,' Dr Khan exclaims. 'Stephen, you can't keep doing this!' He darts a glance at her face. Her eyes, which are looking directly at him, are full and glistening. She told him a while ago (five weeks, two days, seven hours and some minutes and seconds that he could calculate but chooses not to) that the baby she is carrying will make her less in control of her emotions than she usually is. There will be a soup of hormones sloshing around inside her, and it will show itself in her reactions. Perhaps this is why she forgets that he finds sustained gaze uncomfortable. 'Whatever you're trying to find, it's not worth dying for.'

Which is true, of course – but trivially true. If he dies, he won't be able to finish his work, and it's only his work and its outcomes that will vindicate the risks he takes. Or fail to.

But they all take risks. And they have all accepted the implied logic. Without a cure for the hungry plague, or a work-around, they will *all* die, one by one. The great spreading tree of humanity will be hewn away at its base until it falls. Until the number of survivors is so small that congenital abnormalities multiply and intensify and viable births fall off to nothing. This is why the risks they take are worth taking. This is why Rosie was sent.

Rosie and Charlie. But their sister vessel, the Charles Darwin, never came home. The prevailing theory is that Charlie fell into an ambush set by junkers – roving, outlaw bands of survivalists – who then dismantled the vehicle, pillaged its tech and slaughtered its crew. But nobody knows, and most likely nobody will ever know. The most they will be able to tell – when they get to a spot where there should be a specimen cache and find nothing there – is how far the Charles Darwin got before misfortune overtook it.

So now it's the turn of Dr Fournier's team. And they will either find what they came here to find or else they will fail and the extinction event will continue at its present pace (which for extinctions is very rapid indeed). There is no contingency plan, no back-up. It's hard to quantify risk when they're already way up on the high wire without a safety net. But that seems to be what Dr Khan is asking Stephen to do.

'Promise me,' she says now. 'Promise me you won't do this again.'

He meets her gaze. This is hard for him. Like pulling something heavy up out of a well and holding it, at arm's length, in front of his face. A part of himself that he offers up to her, effortlessly.

'No,' he says. 'No, Rina.'

And he walks on past her into the lab.

9

In Rosie's cramped interior, there is no such thing as privacy. Over the months that they have lived here, the various members of her crew have adapted to this, each in their own way.

Most have not been able, as Dr Fournier and the colonel have done, to stake out a specific territory for themselves. With all other spaces owned in common, the bunks have become inviolate. Dr Khan and Dr Sealey, most evenings, eat their meal with everyone else in the kitchen area and then retire to their beds with the curtains drawn across. They are not disturbed: that tiny space is sacrosanct.

The soldiers – grunts and sniper elite alike – devote the lion's share of their down-time to a single unending game of poker. No actual money changes hands, but Private Phillips keeps score in a kids' notebook decorated with Pokémon stickers to a depth of half an inch. It is not clear to anyone where this notebook came from.

On most evenings, after the game winds up, Lieutenant McQueen goes up into the turret and cleans his rifle, whether he has used it that day or not.

Dr Akimwe and Dr Penny work late, unless there is no work at all to be done. They sing show tunes, very softly, working their way amicably through the oeuvres of Stephen Sondheim and Jerry Herman. They have agreed to draw the line at Andrew Lloyd Webber.

This uses up all of Rosie's available space, but Stephen Greaves has found another space that no one wants. He sits in the airlock and is completely undisturbed. There is no light there, apart from the dim glow from the keypad that controls the airlock's cycling mechanism. More to the point, it feels to the rest of the crew like a negotiated space, a halfway house between the safe (if claustrophobic) interior and the hostile outside. To try to relax there would be futile.

But Greaves isn't relaxing. Like Penny and Akimwe, he is still working – by natural light until there is none left, and after that by the narrow, focused beam of a portable reading lamp clamped to the top of the repurposed page-a-day diary in which he writes. He would prefer to be in the lab, of course, but Dr Fournier has placed tight restrictions on Greaves' use of lab time. He has to file requests, which will be considered only after everyone else's needs have been met. 'He's just a child,' Fournier has said on many occasions. 'A bright child, but a child nonetheless. And we have a tight remit. He can't be allowed to impede that.'

In practice, Greaves is usually able to get around these strictures, but it's by a precarious route that makes him deeply uncomfortable. He works when Dr Khan is in the lab, and if Dr Fournier asks what he is doing there Dr Khan answers for him. 'He's assisting me.' Greaves himself says nothing, and keeps his eyes on the bench, but the lie (even though it's someone else's, not his) twists in his stomach and in his throat, makes him feel as though he is going to have to vomit to get it out of him. Officially, therefore, he has no research of his own. Don't-ask-don't-tell, with all its attendant difficulties, is the best compromise he has been able to find.

When Dr Khan isn't in the lab, Greaves mostly uses the airlock – a lab for thought experiments only. On such occasions, he has a set routine that makes the most productive use of his time. He compartmentalises his brain in order to maintain a through-line for clear, undistracted thoughts. The distractions are simply sent away into sub-routines where they can be indulged without any harm to his reasoning.

He is doing this now. Cross-legged, head down, as motionless as a hungry: but vaulting on mental swing-bars.

On the top level – the most important – he is tabulating his observations from the day. Below that, he is considering the problem of the anomalous girl. And below that, on a more emotionally compromised level Greaves thinks of as the tumble-drier, he is thinking about his altercation with Dr Khan.

Greaves sees nothing remarkable in this split-level reasoning. He is not really thinking simultaneously on all three levels; he is simply swapping between them and letting each one claim his attention when he reaches an impasse on one of the others. While his conscious mind is focused on level one, say, his unconscious hovers over levels two and three – so usually, the next time one of those levels comes to the top of the stack he will have had some new insight.

Actually there is a fourth level, but he has ceased to

71

annotate it. *What has happened to Beacon, to stop them from talking to us?* is an urgent question with very wide-ranging implications but it can't be addressed until he has some data, and currently he has none at all.

All three active levels are represented in the notes he writes in the diary, in a code of his own making that reduces words and phrases to single strokes of the pencil. He uses superscript and subscript to carry the chatter alongside the capitalised font that represents the main topic. He is aware that other people don't do this; that when they take notes they try to filter out the things they think of as extraneous to the subject. Greaves finds that digressions and distractions are usually there for a reason, and can yield unexpected insights. So he writes down everything that crosses his mind, as it comes. To save time, he is cavalier with punctuation and sometimes with syntax.

Top level:
Hungries' heliotropism appears side effect of heat-seeking behaviour used for hunting at night. Could be hijacked? Used against them? But how determine level of radiant heat that will activate tropic behaviour? Contrast with background ambient temperature probably crucial. Hence no heat-seeking by day. Higher overall temperatures degrade contrast.

Middle level:
Fact: she cannot be human.
Fact: she cannot be hungry.
Define anomalies. Strength and speed clearly outside human range, but within observed parameters for

72

hungries. Also, hungries did not respond to her. Did not
identify her as prey.
But she showed volition. Reacted to non-food stimulus.
Made conscious, creative use of environment (me).
Is she new?
Determine ontological status. Priority: urgent.

Lowest level:
Dr Khan Dr Khan Dr Khan Dr Khan Dr Khan Dr Khan
Rina Rina Rina Rina Rina Rina Rina Rina Rina Rina Rina
Dr Khan Dr Khan Dr Khan Dr Khan Dr Khan Dr Khan

This is shorthand for a great many things: thoughts he
does not wish at the moment to examine too closely. It
hurts him to make Rina unhappy. She is important, in a way
that other people are not important. She is an exception to
every rule. She can look at him, and even touch him. He
is able to listen to her voice without counting the syllables
of her words or breaking them down by grammatical and
instrumental function.

He supposes he loves her. Love is a word that people use
about other people all the time, and Greaves has assembled
a reasonably clear idea of its many contradictory referents.
For more than half of these referents, he can place a positive
mark against Dr Khan's name in a polydimensional matrix
that he has imagined.

He knows, though, that the matrix does not accurately
model what he feels for her. It only defines a logical space
that she partially inhabits.

After he came to Beacon, after he went to dormitory
twelve, Rina came and found him. 'We refugees have got

73

to stick together,' she said. And she held something out for him to take. Two somethings.

Captain Power. And Captain Power's voice box.

The captain had fallen from Greaves' hand when he was carried from the transport into the orphanage. Greaves had heard the crack when he hit the concrete. Dr Khan must have found the toy, broken, and she evidently remembered how determinedly Greaves had held onto it as they marched out of London. Remembering, she took the trouble to come and bring the two pieces to him when she found them.

And as he took the captain back, with an interior lurch of relief and wonder, she sang to him. In a soft murmur that none of the other children or adults in the crowded room could hear. *He's the hero of the spaceways, the galactic engineer . . .* She stopped at that. Most likely she didn't remember the rest of the words, about the Terran Code and the Planetary League and how the captain fights for truth.

Greaves thinks of that day as the start of their relationship. On the journey from London he had been aware of her, but only in the same way that he was aware of all the other people in the refugee column.

At that moment, she became Dr Khan – and later still, Rina. Like the girl at the water-testing plant, she sits in a category of one. An anomaly.

For Greaves, growing up in Beacon was like a years-long walk across a minefield, very lonely and very arduous. Except that the errors were marked not by explosions but by humiliations, so there wasn't even the hope that a final, fatal misstep would make it all go away. The teachers at the school and the wardens at the orphanage tried to protect him when they noticed him at all, but Beacon was a refugee camp with a million people trying to find a place to stand, in a space too small for half that number. People fought to the death in the streets for frost-gnawed carrots and wire-trapped rats. The laws were just the same brawl being fought in a wider theatre.

And Greaves found that every act of kindness brought, reliably, its own reprisal. If a teacher gave him a book to read, an older child would take it from him – to trade it away for food, or just to enjoy the experience of power – and beat him for the sin of having it in the first place. The key to survival was not being noticed at all.

Until suddenly the key was Rina. She took him out of school for weeks at a time to teach him herself, in her canvas-walled lab – to teach him science mostly, but other things too. She reasoned that if he loved the captain, he would have a taste for science fiction and fantasy in general, so she introduced him to Asimov and Clarke, then Miéville and Gaiman and Le Guin. He had already learned to read, but now he learned the pleasure of stories which is like no other pleasure – the experience of slipping sideways into another world and living there for as long as you want to.

In the streets, now, he walked with slightly more assurance. Beacon was growing older along with him. Curfews had been introduced, and a hard-labour farm for people guilty of breaches of public order. Greaves carried Alice and Ged and Coraline and Grimnebulin in his head, along with the captain, and talked with them when the external world became problematic. But that happened less and less. He had found out what happiness was, and therefore was able to realise that he hadn't been happy up to now.

He stopped going to school, gave up his bed at the

orphanage. He laid out a bedroll on the floor of Dr Khan's lab each night, and stowed it in a corner each morning. Rina's presence became his peace. Her voice told him ceaselessly – whatever else she might be saying – that he was home.

Greaves' memory is eidetic and perfect, a complete record of his past to which new information is added at a steady rate of one second per second. It isn't possible for him to forget. But sometimes when he remembers his mother (her hands washing his face, her face smiling down into his crib, her body cooling beside his on blood-soaked gravel) she has Dr Khan's face. His brain has performed a semantic substitution between two nearly identical signs.

So if there were a feasible way to give her what she wants – a promise that he will not expose himself to unnecessary danger – he would do it. He would very much like to offer her that reassurance. But he can't.

Because unless he can find some new insight in the remaining months of the mission, the mission will fail. Unless

Middle level:
Unless the girl is what she seems. Different from the human baseline and from the hungries. New. Fitting into a space whose shape I can't define yet or even hypothesise. And that's good. That's very good. If known factors permit of no solutions, any solution must come from a space beyond what is known.
Focus.
The priorities haven't changed. It's only that the list of variables has lengthened. Lengthened in a way that shows promise.

Top level (but is it the top level any more, or is she?):
Summary of environmental factors found to inhibit or
retard the spread of the hungry pathogen.
NONE.

Greaves pauses, staring at the word with the top of the
pencil pressed hard against his lower lip. There are thousands
of pages of mission logs and experimental notes in the double-
reinforced filing cabinet underneath the lab's main centrifuge, but their substantive findings can be factored down to
that single word. Dr Fournier's team has studied, tabulated
and graphed the effects on the hungries of temperature,
sound, atmospheric pressure, wind speed, relative and absolute
humidity, light (duration and intensity), presence or absence
of fifty-three trace elements in air and soil, thermoperiod,
acidity and alkalinity, macro- and micro-nutrients and the
strength of the Earth's magnetic field. They have done this
both through their own sampling and through extensive
study of the specimen caches left for them by the crew of
the Charles Darwin.

The hope was to find an inhibitor. A weakness they could
seize on and weaponise. If the pathogen was adversely affected
by any of these things, Beacon and its inhabitants could adjust
accordingly. They could make themselves as inhospitable an
environment as possible for the disease to take root in.

But *Cordyceps* is robust and hardy. Its onset and progress
are the same in every case. Human tissue suits it well, and
anchors it against all trials and tribulations. Human blood
nourishes and waters it.

Which, as far as Greaves can see, leaves only two options.
One is to synthesise a vaccine or a cure, and the team are

nowhere on that. He has seen Dr Akimwe's reports, knows that they're years away from a means of countering the infection or guarding against it.

The other option is what he has been working on all this time: behavioural observation of hungries in the field. He is trying to build up a map of how the fungus shapes and repurposes the mammalian brain. A human body is not the environment *Cordyceps* was originally designed for, however much it has made itself at home there. It started out as a parasite on insects. So perhaps the fit isn't perfect. Perhaps it's loose enough that he can find an exploit – a behavioural trigger that will make the hungries damage themselves or swerve away and find some other prey.

Middle level:
Was she real?

He hates to think that thought, let alone write it, but he doesn't flinch because you can't rule any hypothesis out until you've disproved it.

It has occurred to Greaves before now to wonder about his own sanity (defined as the accuracy of the assessments he makes of the world around him and its processes, of the men and women around him and their behaviours, and of course of himself as separate from all of the above, a unique system that he observes from the inside). He knows his brain isn't like everyone else's. He is painfully aware that people in general take pleasure from things that terrify him, are afflicted by things that fascinate him. On the whole, he has learned to live with those differences. But suppose they are indications of some deeper difference that amounts to damage? Dysfunction?

78

To go mad, to lose your mind, which is the only thing that's really yours because it's really you . . . That would be an inexpressibly terrible thing. And at the same time it would be nothing, because you yourself would be unable, from within that damaged state, to recognise or reflect on it. Greaves considers this paradox. He is afraid of something that may already have happened.

No, he is afraid of its consequences. Of the queasy, unsettling possibility that he has lost touch with reality and can never re-join it.

He is sure that the anomalous girl was real. Almost. Almost sure. She had the fearsome clarity of a hallucination, but still . . .

A thought occurs to him. He undoes the buttons on his jacket, pulls up his T-shirt and examines the flesh beneath. In one small area, roughly ellipsoidal, with a long radius of three centimetres and a short radius of two, his skin is yellow deepening to blue. He is bruised in the place where she touched him. Where her heel kicked off from him.

Greaves nods, satisfied.

Top level:
The hungries have night behaviours and day behaviours. But all my observations have taken place during daylight. The use of thermal sensory organs or organelles for hunting by night was confirmed by Caldwell et al in the third and last of their WHO reports. The absence of a normal sleep cycle has been argued by Selkirk and Bales. But the evidential base is slender. A few hours of observation in each case, from a camouflaged hide whose armour and defences restricted vision and kept the hungries at a distance.
To see them at night, up close, might yield valuable insights.

But Greaves can't lie, even to himself.

If I go into Invercrae, and if she's there, I might find her.
Study her in situ, in her habitat. Further observation of
behaviours, esp feeding. Possibly find some clue to where
she lives. If successful in this, tissue sample from shed
skin or hair cells might be obtained.

Of course, leaving Rosie at night exposes him to a new
set of potential dangers. Moving in a nocturnal environment
will be slow and difficult, while at the same time it will be
easier for the hungries to locate and hunt him.

It's time to test the suit.

10

The day's work being over, the doors closed and the perimeter defences up, the soldiers and the scientists are free for an hour or two to do as they please.

Dr Fournier is in the engine room. He has let it be known that he uses the twilight hours to write up reports that he has no time to address during the day. As mission commander, he has a great many reports to write, and some of them are of a sensitive nature, so he has given orders that he should not be disturbed at these times. He plays classical music — mostly Wagner — on a portable CD player so old that Dr Sealey says its continued functioning can only be explained using a new branch of physics. The CD player belongs to Dr Penny and it used to sit in the lab until Dr Fournier requisitioned it — hence Drs Akimwe and Penny having to make their own entertainment *a cappella*.

The sound of the music, though soft, is enough to cover

the sound of Dr Fournier's voice. He is speaking into a radio set given to him by Brigadier Fry before the Rosalind Franklin set out from Beacon. He was given the set so that he could report on the actions and the conversations of his crew, with a specific focus on Colonel Carlisle. But there was seldom anything new to say. Only that the colonel was doing his job and trying not to speak to Dr Fournier any more than he had to.

And now there is nobody to listen. Since the cockpit radio went out nine days ago, the doctor's hand-held receiver has been silent too. The airwaves are empty. Rosie is a bubble of meaning in a void of . . . of the absence of meaning. A void devoid of . . .

He tries again. 'Dr Alan Fournier calling Beacon. Dr Alan Fournier calling Brigadier Fry. If you can hear me, please answer. Dr Fournier calling Beacon.'

Colonel Carlisle reads a biography of Napoleon, one of the three books he brought with him when he came on board the Rosalind Franklin. Mulholland's account of the emperor's life is often partial and poorly researched, but Carlisle appreciates his declamatory style. *Truly*, he reads, *the years that witnessed Napoleon's fall were fruitful in paradox. The greatest political genius of the age, for lack of the saving grace of moderation, had banded Europe against him: and the most calculating of commanders had nonetheless given his enemies time to frame an effective military collaboration.*

Without hubris (he knows he is no genius) the colonel looks in all the volumes he reads for echoes and precursors of his own mistakes. He has seen Beacon go from an armed camp to a proto-republic, and then he has seen that precarious democracy dismantle itself again. Now it is standing on the brink of something truly horrible and Carlisle is four hundred miles away on nursemaiding duty – having resigned his commission as an act of principle and then taken it up again on direct orders from a superior who promised – in exchange – to leave him be and raise him no higher.

Now the colonel is wondering whose trap he fell into: Brigadier Fry's or his own. Possibly the answer is both. In any event, he has traded power for a clean conscience and ended up with neither.

Mulholland again: *An overweening belief in his own powers and in the pliability of his enemies was the cause alike of his grandest triumphs and of his unexampled overthrow.*

Overthrow is a nicely judged word. It suggests a wrestler being flung to the mat. That only happens when you move outside your centre of gravity. Your enemy can't throw you if you have your feet firmly planted.

Which Carlisle himself never did have, of course. He is not a politician. He's not even somebody who weighs his words. But he is, in the end, a conformist. A man whose centre of gravity can't easily be found because he has never taken the time to work out where it is he wants to stand. He only knows his limits when he actually meets them, in the world.

As, for example, in his last face-to-face conversation with Brigadier Fry seven months ago, just before the gates opened and Rosie passed through them on her outward journey. He was trying to make the brigadier understand why the machinery of democracy is important, even if in some ways it makes Beacon run less efficiently rather than more.

The brigadier listened sober-faced to his argument – which

was about checks and balances, safeguards and redundant systems. Her own position was that these things were luxuries that came with security. You could afford to think about redecorating your house only when you could be absolutely certain that the roof wasn't about to fall in. Her politicking illustrated this perfectly. She had demanded that the Muster – Beacon's military – be granted a fixed proportion of the seats on councils and committees, including the so-called Main Table where overall policy was decided. Then she had expanded that wedge until the Muster was the single biggest voting bloc. Now she was questioning the legitimacy of having any civilian presence at all on boards that decided on military matters.

Fry listened politely as Carlisle made his case and then she corrected him, punctilious to a fault. 'You think I see democracy as irrelevant, Isaac? I don't. Please don't think that. When humankind was in the ascendant, when we ruled the world and the whole of creation bowed down to us, democratic institutions worked and nothing else did. The dictatorships were the sleazy corners where people were poor and miserable and governments were parasitic. Back then I bowed to civil authorities and I followed orders and I never once asked myself if there was something I was missing. Democracy made sense.

'But when the plague struck, that all changed. It changed for ever. You know what I see when I'm sitting at the Main Table? I see frightened sheep trying to decide which way to run. And if we put the sheep in charge of the farm, then we'll all of us die and the grass will grow over us. I don't intend to let that happen.'

'Where is the Muster in this metaphor, Geraldine?' Carlisle

had asked her. 'Assuming you're not sheep, what are you? Shepherds, perhaps?'

'If you like.'

'But shepherds only keep sheep safe until it's time to slaughter them.'

Fry's lip twitched, a movement of anger that she suppressed. 'We fight and we die for these people,' she said. 'Every day. And then they turn around and tell us to do the same thing on a smaller budget. With fewer soldiers. It's grotesque. Have we made mistakes? Yes, we have. But everybody in Beacon owes their lives to us and they put us on a par with waste disposal and street clearance.'

There was a pause. A silence that Carlisle failed to fill. He could have said: Your mistakes − our mistakes − killed thousands of men, women and children. They thought those planes were coming to save them and we dropped white phosphorus on their heads. We burned them alive.

So why didn't he? What kept him sitting there in dead silence when he could see her hiding those hideous deeds away in a box labelled COLLATERAL DAMAGE?

The same thing that had made him resign his commission instead of denouncing Fry and standing against her. He had too much respect for the frameworks of authority, was too afraid of the harm that comes when they're shaken. Sometimes they needed to be shaken. Sometimes they needed to be dismantled and rebuilt from the ground up. He had never seen himself as the one best qualified to do that; never quite found enough sand to draw a line in.

Still, he felt himself reaching a limit. He wasn't sure how much longer he could convince himself that doing nothing was the lesser evil.

And Fry knew him well enough to see that change coming. Probably she was aware of it even before he was. Certainly she timed her intervention perfectly.

'I have a new mission for you,' she said, handing him the papers. 'Top priority. It will take you away from Beacon for a while, which might be the best thing for all of us.'

Carlisle reached out his hand.

He took the papers. Abdicated yet again.

There is a knock on the cockpit's open door. With no regret, the colonel abandons the contentious past for the unfathomable present.

It's Lieutenant McQueen. 'Poker game, sir,' he says. 'The men were wondering whether you'd join us for once.'

Carlisle hesitates. In all his previous postings, he spent as much time with the soldiers in his command as he could. He is fully cognisant of the importance of knowing his troops and being known by them. *The emperor held it as a maxim*, Mulholland asserts, *not to trust his weight to any bridge he had not personally tested and assayed.*

But the look on McQueen's face irks him. The lieutenant barely troubles to hide his contempt, which he will bring with him into the game. Every hand will become an index of the greater, unspoken antagonism between them. Their mutual dislike will curdle the atmosphere and sap the morale of the other soldiers, which is already ebbing steadily.

They stare at each other for a cold second, each acknowledging the unspoken agenda. And why is it still unspoken after all these months of enforced proximity? Carlisle has no idea. He was sure when they left Beacon that there would be a flare-up, a rebellious act or word that would discharge the lightning. But here they are, seven months later, with the storm still building.

'I think not, lieutenant,' Carlisle says evenly. 'Thank you for the invitation, but I believe you'll be better able to relax without a senior officer present.'

'Yes, sir,' McQueen says blandly. 'Of course, sir. Enjoy your book.'

Which he wasn't managing to do even before the lieutenant's intrusion. He tries again, but still can't find the right mood of scholarly detachment. It melts in the universal solvent of recent memories. With a sigh, he sets Mulholland aside.

The rear-view mirror gives him a view along the flank of the vehicle. He can see the mid-section airlock and the Greaves boy sitting in it, writing furiously with a stub of pencil so short it doesn't show between his pursed fingers.

Is he still a boy, at age fifteen? Dr Khan argues that he is some kind of savant, but Carlisle can only ever see Greaves as the wide-eyed, silent child who made the arduous journey from London to Beacon wearing a single unchanging expression of shell-shocked wonder and dismay. Clutching a toy or doll of some kind. Not hugging it to his chest or trailing it along behind him the way Christopher Robin dragged Pooh Bear, but holding it clenched in both hands like a talisman that he could raise, at need, against the world.

Probably as efficacious as anything else, the colonel thinks.

11

Lieutenant McQueen returns to the game.

'Just the five of us,' he says. 'His majesty is wanking off over his war porn again.'

'The four of us,' Sixsmith amends. 'Phillips is on sentry.' Sixsmith doesn't like it when McQueen criticises the colonel, and tends to try to shut him down. She's one of those – and there are a fair number – who think Carlisle is a hero because he got eleven thousand people out of a city that used to have a population of eight and a half million. Apparently 99.9 per cent attrition counts as success.

And apparently it absolves that abject bastard of everything he did *before* the evacuation. It's like the burn runs never happened. It's like he didn't preside over the biggest peace-time massacre in British military history and lead decent, serving soldiers into a bloodletting that would stain their souls for ever.

This is what McQueen thinks, about himself, his job and the colonel:

Britain had an army once that prized and rewarded blind obedience. Sometimes that led to monumental screw-ups like the Charge of the Light Brigade, but more often than not it worked. It worked because of the context: a world where people fought against other people, century after century, in the same theatres and with the same rules of engagement.

That was what it was like when McQueen himself enlisted – and he went along with it without much thought. Did well out of it, all things considered. Tours of duty in Syria and then in Lebanon got him commended four times and fast-tracked for promotion.

Then the context changed, overnight. But some people didn't manage to change with it. Most of the people at the Main Table in Beacon are just the same old arseholes playing by the same old rules. Throwing down the ace of clubs as though it still means something when the game has switched to Russian roulette.

Why does McQueen hate the colonel? Because the colonel had the chance to turn it around. He was one of the highest-ranking officers to survive the global clusterfuck that happened when the hungry plague first broke out, and one of the most respected. He could have taken charge, and people would have rallied behind him. McQueen would have, just for one.

And instead he kept on obeying orders, even when the orders plainly made no sense. Fire-bomb the south of England! When there were people down there barricaded in their houses waiting for help to come. When there were civilian aircraft on the ground that could have been reclaimed and put into use. When your own damn troops were going to need that infrastructure if they were ever going to take one step outside the fences and the ditches and the minefields you had them hiding behind.

Yeah, McQueen thinks, actually his metaphor doesn't hold. Russian roulette is exactly what the authorities in Beacon were playing. Only they cheated by putting a bullet in every chamber. And then they gave the gun to Colonel Isaac Carlisle to fire.

No, he and Sixsmith will have to disagree on the matter of the Fireman. But she makes a good point about the game. Four of them is below critical mass. You don't get proper poker without five or six around the table.

He considers. Sentry duty is some more of the Old Man's play-it-by-the-book bullshit. They don't need a sentry. The movement sensors will trip if the hungries come, and in any case the hungries don't. Not while Rosie is on silent running. And how is it that only the grunts draw night duties? As if divisions of rank matter a flying toss when they're sitting out in nowhere's armpit with nothing coming in on the radio and no way of knowing if Beacon's even there any more. It's time to strike a blow for the common man, and maybe goad the colonel into finally facing him head on.

He goes through to the mid-section platform, where Phillips is standing by the airlock. Rifle at parade rest. Face at *back in five minutes*.

'Anything?' McQueen asks sympathetically.

Phillips nods towards the airlock. There's a light on in there, at about knee height. It takes McQueen a moment to realise that it's Stephen Greaves, writing by the light of a clip-on reading lamp with a 50-watt LED.

'Just the Robot,' Phillips says.

Privately McQueen has a few nicknames of his own for Greaves that are less family-friendly. He shakes his head as he stares, then taps his brow with the tip of his trigger finger. 'Wonder what goes on in there,' he says, although he really doesn't. He actually prefers to see Greaves as a kind of black box – like the hungries. There may or may not be a person in there, but either way it's not his problem. He only has to deal with the output.

'Listen,' he says to Phillips, 'I don't see any point in you staying out here. The perimeter is up. Nothing can get close to us without tripping an alarm. And the kid will raise a squawk if it comes to that. You might as well join the game.'

Phillips considers. McQueen watches him doing it, knows more or less what's going through his mind and politely gives the other man as long as he needs. McQueen isn't his commanding officer; Colonel Carlisle is. And Carlisle's authority has to punch it out with Dr Fournier's. But in Rosie's narrow spaces, rank and influence aren't the same thing. There is no question who looms largest in the private's mental landscape, false modesty aside.

'Aye,' Phillips says at last. 'All right, then.'

McQueen slaps him on the shoulder. 'Good man. If the colonel comes your way, tell him you were obeying a direct order.'

They go back into the crew quarters.

Greaves watches them go, and gives them a minute or two to change their minds. When they don't return, he stands and strips.

The top layer only. Underneath he is wearing something

else entirely. A matt-black suit set with small glassy studs very much like the cats' eyes you find on road surfaces. In fact the retro-reflectors in cats' eyes were one of Greaves' starting points when he designed the suit, but more because of their simplicity and durability than because of what happens at the business end of them. It's not light he's hoping to diffract, but his own body heat.

He has been working on the suit, off and on, for four months. The idea of it came to him even earlier than that, but it wasn't until they left Beacon that he had time to implement his design. He brought most of the raw materials with him, trusted to serendipity to provide the rest. The journey north offered uninterrupted stretches of whole weeks with no official lab work to be done. Sometimes he worked through the night, appreciating the opportunity to progress on the suit without stopping every half-hour or so to answer questions.

Now it's done, as far as possible given the constraints under which he has been working. He has confidence in the principle, and in the overall design. Some of the components are work-arounds and make-dos, and the tolerances are not what he would have liked, but now it's way past time for a field test. And he believes, all things considered, that it will work. In an ideal world, of course, he wouldn't risk his life on it.

But the world is the way it is and that's just what he's going to do.

12

Samrina Khan has retired to bed early. The curtains are drawn across her bunk, which signals that – awake or asleep – she is not to be disturbed. There are very few social niceties that have survived their seven-month voyage, but this one is accorded universal respect. Only a full-on emergency would cause any of the crew to pull those curtains aside. So it's unlikely that anyone will find out she's not alone in there.

Getting three tiers of bunks into a seven-foot space meant cutting everything back to basics. Each set of bunks is really just a single recess separated into three by two rows of wooden slats lying across steel supports. John Sealey, whose bunk is above Dr Khan's, has rolled back his mattress (which is easy enough as it's barely an inch thick) and removed five of the slats, opening his own bunk space up to hers. He is leaning down through this gap at an oblique angle so their upper bodies can meet up in a tight embrace. Any other kind of embrace would be impossible, all things considered.

This is a risky enterprise and they don't do it often. Tonight, Sealey has come to visit Rina in order to lift her mood after her official interrogation by Dr Fournier. As the father of the child she's carrying, he feels this is the least he can do.

But he finds Rina's mood surprisingly resistant to lifting. Surprisingly, that is, until she tells him what it is that's weighing on her mind. It's not the mission commander and his flaccid third degree. It's Greaves, her surrogate son.

'He's going to get himself killed,' she whispers, sounding choked. 'He's out there, with no camouflage and no back-up. Watching them. Not with binoculars. Watching them from a few feet away. John, all it would take would be for him to trip, or sneeze, and . . . They'll eat him alive!'

'We're all taking that chance, every day we're out here,' Sealey offers. 'Greaves isn't stupid. Or reckless.'

Rina seems not to have heard him. 'I think Fournier knows,' she says, raising her voice a little more than is safe. Only the infield chatter of the poker players a few feet astern gives them any cover at all. 'He's just decided it doesn't matter. Stephen was forced on him at the last moment, and he's never treated him as a full member of the crew.' Her churning mind hits on another explanation. 'Or perhaps he sees it as an acceptable risk. He knows by now we're not going to find any environmental inhibitors. If Stephen comes up with a new idea, we might have something to show for all this.'

'Maybe it is, at that,' Sealey murmurs. An acceptable risk, he means. If Greaves can bottle the same lightning twice – grab another genius insight out of the ether the way he allegedly did with the e-blocker gel – then humankind might not die collectively in a ditch after all. As a fully paid-up member of said club, Sealey would see that as a win.

But the odds are pretty long. Greaves might be the genius Rina says he is, or then again it might be that he just got lucky that one time. And Rina isn't even thinking about that right now. She knew Greaves when he was just a mostly broken little kid. She was there when his parents died, and through the queasy aftermath when he was an elective mute. When everyone thought he was mentally handicapped rather than a weird little alien *wunderkind* with no human emotions.

Is it possible to slide through those judgements without them sticking to you? Sealey seriously wonders. The general feeling now is that Greaves is on the autistic spectrum, but how much of his weirdness is down to his brain's basic wiring and how much of it is a trauma artefact?

It's an academic question, but it's got real-world consequences. Rina more or less twisted the arm of everyone back in Beacon to get Greaves onto the mission roster. She knew how much he depended on her, feared how quickly he might fall apart without her.

The supervisory group took a contrary point of view. They saw Greaves as a child first and foremost, and as a gifted hobbyist rather than a serious practitioner. Then they looked at his psych assessments and saw something worse: a maladapted obsessive, damaged goods, and (e-blocker notwithstanding) a potential liability out in the field. Rina won her point in the end by making it a two-for-one deal: *you want me, you take him too.*

To be fair, she didn't do that just to protect him. She genuinely thinks that Greaves can pull off a miracle here – a cure, a vaccine, a weapon, a better mousetrap. But all of that is predicated on the idea of his being different. As though his intellect cuts across the world at an angle nobody else is even aware of.

Rina wouldn't admit to any of this – to thinking of Greaves as a Hail Mary play – but Sealey knows full well she's watching the boy. Waiting for the clouds to part and a dove to descend from heaven.

It could be a long wait, in Sealey's humble opinion. He's no psychologist, but he doesn't see Greaves as being on the spectrum. He sees him as a luckless kid who started out normal – pretty bright, no doubt about it, but normal – only to get bent all out of shape by horrendous tragedy. Then found himself trapped in Rina's hopes for him. At the orphanage in Beacon, where the teachers had given up on him because they were just volunteers making it up as they went along, she took Greaves in hand. Fed him books the way you'd feed a baby bird worms and broken up bits of bread. Turned him into what he is now.

Which is what? An eccentric genius, or just an ill-equipped explorer swaying on the rickety rope bridge between sanity and madness? The way Greaves acts, the things he does . . . it *is* extraordinary. But that's just another way of saying he's got his own coping mechanisms. It's not proof of anything. And yes, there's that one astonishing breakthrough, but Sealey doesn't know anyone who accepts Khan's version of that story. A child genius finds an enzyme that leaches the sharp-smelling acids out of apocrine sweat and breaks them down into water and carbon dioxide, cooks it up in a saucepan and brings it to his best friend, biologist and epidemiological expert Dr Samrina Khan, to help him test it out. Occam's razor suggests a different sequence of events.

No matter. Rina has her perspective and she won't be shifted from it. Possibly she's the only person on Rosie's roster who actually worries about Greaves. Sealey has tried many times to have this conversation with her, but it never takes.

Gamely, but without much hope, he tries again. 'He's a member of the crew, Rina. Your co-worker, not your son. You've got to let him make his own choices.'

She looks at him as though he's just stuck out his hand to catch a ball that's already on the ground. 'Thank you, John,' she says. 'That's an admirable summary of the blindingly obvious.'

But she doesn't say it with biting sarcasm. She says it with a catch in her voice. Her lips are twisting as she tries to hold in a flood of tears. So instead of bristling or snapping back he wraps his arms around her. She gives way to her misery in absolute silence, her head buried in the angle of his neck and his shoulder. She's pulling him forward through the gap in the slats so he feels like he's going to lose his purchase and fall headlong on top of her, then probably roll out sideways and give the whole game away. His T-shirt (which doubles as pyjamas) is slowly but surely getting saturated with her tears.

Rina slips straight from crying into exhausted sleep. Sealey realises then how hard this day has been on her. Her concern for Stephen is wholly real, of course, but it comes on top of a whole set of other concerns. She might catch a reprimand for her unauthorised pregnancy that will stop her career in its tracks. Or the baby might do that all by itself, reprimand or not. She might have to give birth out here in the middle of nowhere. She might lose the baby.

He wishes he was better at this stuff. He's in his thirties but he can still count the relationships he's been in on one hand without running out of fingers. And none of them lasted. Maybe this one wouldn't have either if it hadn't been for a lack of condoms and self-control.

It was leaving Beacon that caused that one fateful lapse. After being cooped up behind the fences and minefields for so long, getting out on the road – even inside an armour-plated sardine tin – felt like freedom. He and Rina found the only way to celebrate that didn't need to be applied for, signed off on, rubber-stamped, rationed or reported.

Now they're stuck with the consequences. And with each other.

Sealey backs away from that thought in alarm. Rina is amazing and he loves her more than he's ever loved anyone. He is in awe of her courage – the way she decides on a course of action and sticks to it, no matter what the world throws in her way. He admires her honesty, which turns white lies into red roadkill. Most of all, he loves her optimism, which is something he himself is really bad at. Rina never considers the possibility that the world might already have ended. She talks about the future without irony, and even plans for it. As part of that, she has decided to keep their baby. She told him this in a way that left no room for argument.

Sealey thinks about what Beacon has become and is inclined, sometimes, to question the wisdom of that decision. But he has kept his doubts locked down. The last thing he wants to do is to leave her in any uncertainty, ever, that he's on her side. Has got her back. Will be there for her, when the time comes. Will stand up and be . . .

Where are all these clichés coming from?

He disentangles himself from Rina's sprawled body – rests his hand, for a second or two, against the indiscreet bump that is their burgeoning son or daughter – and levers himself back up through the gap in the bed frame. He does this with reluctance. Every time he removes the slats and visits her, he feels like one of the soldiers in *The Great Escape*, digging a tunnel to freedom.

Which prompts a further reflection. Maybe it wasn't leaving Beacon, after all, that got him so drunkenly and irresponsibly joyous.

Maybe it was her. Maybe it was Rina all the time.

13

Dr Khan is not actually asleep. There is a state midway between sleep and waking in which she falls back into the past and relives it. Relives it in full HD with surround-sound, all of her senses chipping in. She thinks of this state as replay, but as a scientist she knows it has another name. It's a PTS, a post-trauma symptom. It comes over her two or three nights a week, and there's no point in struggling against it. If she tries to block the images, they impinge on her waking life, which is exponentially worse.

Replay isn't like dreaming. Dreams have a logic and a structure that prevents you, while you're dreaming, from reflecting on the events you're wrapped up in. You take it all for granted because consciously questioning any one element would wake you up.

But in her replays, Khan is aware of herself now as well as herself back then. She is her current self, sitting like a passenger in her former body. (It troubles her to think that this might be how the hungries experience the world. If there is any trace of their consciousness, their identity, behind the ramparts that the fungus has erected in their brains, then all they can do is watch. Their bodies now answer to a new master.)

She's walking. Through Guildford and Godalming and places with even more innocuous names. Milford. Haslemere. Hawkley. Heading south to Beacon in a column of about eight hundred desperate people shepherded – harassed, it sometimes seems – by soldiers in urban camouflage colours.

Their journey makes as much sense to her as the crazy careering of clown cars at the start of a circus act. Sometimes they're in trucks, buses, white vans and ambulances. Sometimes they're on foot. *Then*-Rina, sleep-deprived and starving, has no sense of why they keep getting out of the safe, warm cars and walking along the man-made valley of the A3. *Now*-Rina understands that when the road is blocked – by the crashed, burned-out remains of cars and trucks that ferried earlier waves of fleeing people – they don't have the time or the resources to clear it. The colonel gives the order, each time, to abandon the vehicles and trek to the next stretch of clear road. He sends his soldiers on ahead to find and requisition a new set of viable wheels.

So their pace varies, and her mileage likewise. Sometimes she sits. Sometimes she lies on a truck-bed staring at the sky, someone's limp arm draped across her legs, harsh breathing and sobbing all around her mingling with her waking dreams. Mostly she walks, staggers, limps, shambles, hobbles along the endless road that has become their Calvary.

There are two constants: the first is the hungries. This is

101

several years before the advent of e-blocker gel. They have no way of disguising their scent, their sounds, their body heat, so they are an endless, ever-moving invitation to dinner. The hungries chase them down from behind, charge them from in front, assail them from both sides.

The colonel is their rampart. The other constant, always in between. *Don't look back* is his mantra. What's done is done and here we are, still moving forward. He wields his rifle like a scythe, cutting their persecutors off at the knees with precise, horizontal sweeps of the weapon. He hands out guns to the refugees, teaches them the principles of covering fire. He rigs up flamethrowers from oxygen cylinders and insecticide sprayers. Once, he fills a Bedford van with petrol and C4 and rolls it down an incline they have just climbed so that a dip in the road becomes a lake of fire in which hundreds of hungries drown and sink.

They are in hell, but the devil is on their side.

He is changing, in their minds. Most of them thought of him as the Fireman before this, because of the burn runs that turned most of south-east England into a carbonised desert. Now he is the Old Man. Spoken as though you know him, whether he's ever said a single word to you or not.

From time to time, people join their column. They are never turned away. The gap between exposure to the infection and ego-death is so short for most people that the risk of accepting newcomers is non-existent. The few who – defying the mass of statistics – turn more slowly and gradually are killed with a single bullet to the head. Dr Khan steps over their bodies and walks on.

She is hallucinating from sheer fatigue. The colonel is Moses and they are his children. *Don't look back*. The hungries part before him like a sea. Half-congealed blood is the ebb-tide, making the pavement suck at her feet as she walks. The air smells of sweat and blood and shit and cordite, petrol and plasticine and overcooked meat. He holds them to him. He walks them home.

The A3 becomes impassable – one vast thousand-car pile-up strewn with the half-eaten dead. They abandon it and walk through deserted villages. In one of them, on an overpass above the road they left not long before, they find a small cadre of survivors fighting for their lives. They've closed off the ends of the bridge with junk and repurposed white goods and retreated to the centre, but hungries have swarmed over their barricades to assail them from both sides.

The colonel is bringing salvation, but he brings it too late. Courageous last stands like this deconstruct from the edges into the centre. Bitten once, the brave defenders fight on – for a few seconds. Then they stiffen momentarily as the fuse of their consciousness burns to its end. A heartbeat later, they've turned around and joined the scrum, bearing down on their nearest neighbours and dragging them to the ground. Khan watches it happen to a woman who is swinging an aluminium baseball bat; a man with a dustbin-lid shield and a carving knife; a blonde cherub who has been entrusted with the family's lop-eared spaniel (the dog is her first meal).

By the time the colonel's fighting wedge breaks through to the centre of the group, there's no group left. The people they hoped to rescue became enemies, became targets, are all gone.

Almost all. As the soldiers move around handing out full-metal *coups de grâce*, Khan's gaze finds a small boy – maybe five or six years old – lying in between two adults. Their

103

bodies are bowed outwards, shielding him from attack on either side. They are like a pair of brackets around him, cordoning him off from the world. The couple bear so many wounds – bite marks, incisions and lacerations, in the man's case a gunshot wound to the head – that it is impossible to piece together how they died. Certainly they were trying to protect the child.

Who has no visible wounds or injuries at all.

A soldier touches the stock of his rifle to the boy's temple. 'Wait!' Khan shouts.

Just in time. The boy lets out a breath. Someone says, 'This one's alive,' and someone else swears. The soldier steps back, a look of shock and fear replacing the stolid frown on his face. When Khan steps in and claims the boy, scoops him up in her arms, nobody says a word.

Until Carlisle nods and tells them to move.

Replay ends here. The ordeal wasn't over – they didn't reach Beacon for another three days – but it had entered another phase, for Khan at least. She had acquired a role, a function. Keeping the silent, wide-eyed little boy alive. It kept her alive too, she was and is convinced.

Stillness was Stephen's natural modality even then. Perhaps it was the last thing his mother or father said to him: lie still and they might not notice you. Don't make a sound. But over the hours and days that followed, as they slogged on towards Codename Beacon, that stillness never left him. Khan believes he had it long before his parents were killed and partially eaten while he watched. It's a wonderful and scary thing. When there's nothing to run or reach for, Stephen doesn't run or reach. He can fold himself down, his volition, his emotions, until – seen from any angle except straight

104

on, through any eyes except hers – they're invisible. For a scientist, that's an amazing asset.

But it's more than that. The stillness took a different tincture on the day she met him, the day his parents died.

Khan knows better than anyone how far Stephen has come, how much he has achieved. He was only twelve when he synthesised the e-blocker gel that saves their lives on a daily basis, though everybody credits her with that discovery. He was one of the first to suggest *Ophiocordyceps unilateralis* as the fungus that was responsible for the hungry plague (and then his name was mysteriously omitted from the paper Caroline Caldwell ultimately submitted). He has proved that the pathogen grows directly into the nervous system of its hosts and controls them by means of myco-transmitters – long-chain fungal proteins that mimic and hijack the signalling apparatus of the mammalian brain. In the whole of Beacon, there is nobody who has a fuller understanding of what the human race is up against.

But it seems to Khan that a part of Stephen is still lying on the damp asphalt of a Surrey street. In parenthesis. Waiting for an all-clear that will never come.

14

Ten years after the Breakdown, the night is a foreign country, and not a friendly one. Its borders begin at your door. Unless you want to mount a major expedition, an armed incursion, you do not trespass.

Nonetheless, Stephen Greaves is walking through the dark.

There are field glasses that turn dark into light, but he doesn't have those. A single pair of them sits in the gun locker on board the Rosalind Franklin, squirrelled away for the exclusive use of the snipers. Greaves could have retrieved them from the locker by breaking the access code, but he could not have erased all the traces that he had done so. There would have been unpleasant conversations.

So he relies on starlight and a quarter moon, on a pocket torch that he uses very sparingly, and on his very clear recollection of walking this route by day. The last of these three is the most reliable. Greaves carries a map in his mind and charts his progress on the map by means of an imagined red dot moving along a fractally plotted course. Where the stars and that slender rind of moon cease to be a help, as when he is walking between high trees which shut out their light completely, he expands the detail of his map so that it warns him of ditches, potholes, boulders and barbed wire. He can do this almost indefinitely, the limit being his eyes' ability to resolve detail. Whatever he has seen, even once, he can remember.

He has come well equipped for this short but perilous journey. A bulky kit bag slung across his shoulder carries spare batteries for the torch, his notebook, a bottle of water and an emergency signal flare. Also a knife, although he can't justify its presence. If he is attacked, he will not use it. He has a deft hand with a scalpel and has dissected dozens of cadavers with no qualms at all, but the thought of cutting into a living body, human or animal or hungry, is nauseating. Impossible. Like telling a lie or initiating touch, it is simply not in his behavioural repertoire.

But so far he has not been attacked. He is pleased and re-assured by this fact. He would not, however, wish to extra-polate from it. It might be an accident of geography and distance that has saved him up to this point. The nearest hungries may be so far away from his current position that even though they have caught his trail, they have yet to reach him. But he believes it is more likely to be because of his camouflage suit.

At a turn in the road he is given the chance to test this theory. Rounding the bend, stepping from darkness into light, he is suddenly in the presence of a hungry. It is, or used to be, a woman. In the livid moonlight she is an unnerving spectre, a bleached-out effigy like a ghost unexpectedly showing up on a photographic negative. She sways like a tree, arms hanging at her sides. A dark stain down the front of her blouse is probably blood, whether her own or that of someone or something she has fed on. One of her arms has been eaten almost to the bone, from elbow to wrist. The moon shines down on her like a spotlight, and Stephen thinks the satellite and the woman carry their history in much the same way, both scarred by ancient impacts.

As he comes into view, the woman lurches towards him – then stops. He takes another step and the same thing happens again. She twists and shuffles as he approaches her, but she can't seem to find her mark. Her feet march in place, her upper body writhes and rocks.

Greaves walks on by, skirting widely around the hungry and taking care to keep his movements slow and steady. She keeps making sallies in his direction, or almost in his direction, keeps fetching up short and turning again, to the left and then the right. Her jaw works with a dry-leather creak. Her one functional hand clenches and unclenches, claws the air with futile yearning.

She staggers after him a little way, but stops again. She is losing the signal. When he is thirty yards away, she slides once more into her dormant state.

All of this is good news. It is consistent with how the camouflage suit is meant to work.

As soon as the hungries' heat-seeking ability became verified fact, Greaves began to study it. He tried in dissections to identify the organs or structures involved, but there is no single front-runner. He has established that the visual cortex of a human brain undergoes extensive changes shortly after the onset of infection, which suggests that the pathogen may heighten visual acuity in the infra-red range. It's equally plausible, though, that the passive thermoreceptor cells at the base of the tongue have been co-opted for this purpose (which would explain why hungries gape their mouths when they hunt).

At a certain point, he put this question on the back burner and switched his attention to counter-measures. Whatever the precise mechanism of heat detection may be, in order to confuse it all you need to do is to smear or block your heat emissions in some way. Blocking is problematic. It leaves you the problem of what to do with stored heat, which if it can't be vented will kill you as surely as the hungries will. So he decided to go with camouflage.

Before the Breakdown, the Israeli army were trialling a heat-signature camouflage system which they christened *Adaptiv*. Even in its prototype form it was able to make a tank look like a car or a flat-bed truck to thermal scanning systems, or to make it invisible against background ambient temperature. The secret was a layer of flat tiles on the vehicle's surface which could be separately heated and cooled, effectively providing a coat of many colours in the infra-red.

Inspired by *Adaptiv*, Greaves has produced an actual coat of no colours at all. He used whatever was available – scraps he had scavenged up from Rina's lab and brought with him, materials laid in for Rosie's repair and maintenance, serendipitous finds from stops along their journey – and stored the work-in-progress in one of the freezer compartments intended for whole cadavers. There are ten of these compartments and only seven of them have been filled.

The heat-suit covers his body like a second skin. Its exterior surface is dotted here and there with modified cats' eye studs – like the *Adaptiv* tiles but three-dimensional – which focus and channel heat rather than light. The visual effect is grotesque in the extreme, like a diving suit designed by a sexual fetishist, but in theory the suit will broaden and flatten his heat signature and even create hotspots in the air around him. It's like throwing your voice, but what you're throwing is your energy, the exhaust from your ever-working metabolism. Instead of a single source of heat from which the hungries can take a range and a direction, he's the centre of an ever-changing thermal disturbance. The effect he is hoping for is confusion: if the hungries can't track him consistently from one moment to the next, perhaps their tropism – their heat-seeking mechanism – will fail to engage. Based on the available evidence so far, the theory is holding.

There's a downside, though. The suit does, after all, store heat. The radiant vents work reasonably well when he is still, but now that he is walking he can feel his core temperature climbing up. It's a serious problem. He wishes he had installed a temperature read-out of some kind, an LED thermometer in one of the suit's sleeves. It would be useful to know whether he is actually in danger of heat prostration, or close to it. Subjectively, he feels uncomfortable but not weak or dizzy or sick. He judges that he will reach Invercrae before any critical thresholds are passed.

He crosses the Telford bridge over the River Moriston, a tourist attraction in former times. The roar of the falls above the town makes him pause for a second, afraid for no definable reason. He steels himself, annoyed at the irrational response, and walks on into the town.

Although to call it that seems like comical exaggeration. It's a main avenue and a square, with a few short, blunt side streets, most of which end at the river. Even before the

Breakdown, it could never have had more than five hundred inhabitants. Now a few hungries stand at street corners as though they're waiting for someone to come and lead them back into the lives they lost.

They will stand like this until their body's systems fail, barring occasional headlong sprints in pursuit of local fauna. It's an afterlife that not even the grimmest and least user-friendly of the old world's religions ever imagined.

Greaves walks along the main street, his pace a controlled and inconspicuous amble. He is careful to keep his distance from the hungries. The scatter effect of his heat-suit will be aided and abetted at wider distances by the inverse square rule, and ought to be enough to protect him. At close quarters, he may still become a focus. Again and again, the nearest hungries react like the woman on the road did. They jerk into life as Greaves goes by, dance on the spot for a few moments but fail to translate their agitation into forward motion.

But the heat and discomfort are becoming more acute. He has to stop exerting himself and allow his body to cool down naturally as his metabolism slows. This will take more time than it would if any part of his skin were open to the air. But he has sweated heavily inside the suit, almost certainly undoing the masking effect of the e-blocker gel. Taking any part of the suit off now is impossible.

He finds a café whose windows have been folded back, years before, to open its frontage entirely to the street. It stands at the top of a steep rise, a vantage point from which most of the town is visible. Back before the world ended, this must have been an attractive spot to sit and watch some tiny fraction of it go by. Greaves steps in off the street and finds a place to stand, in shadow and – he hopes – safe from detection. He doesn't try to sit: the suit is too rigid to allow him to do that in comfort, and once down he would not be able to get up again quickly.

His immediate problems aside, the primary goal of this sortie remains unchanged. From here he can see nine hungries, four males and five females. He will observe them for as long as he can, and take mental notes on their nocturnal behaviours.

And the girl? He has no idea, no clue as to where she might be. Unless she walks across his field of vision he will be forced to seek her out. Slowly. Very slowly. If the suit fails, his situation will become untenable.

He stands still for a few minutes, letting his breathing return to normal and hoping that his body temperature will follow.

In the meantime, there is a great deal for him to observe and think about. The hungries do behave differently at night, as he had surmised. The visual and aural environment is richer, of course, since a great many small mammals are nocturnal. The scents must be richer, too. As a result, the hungries stir from their dormant state much more frequently. Almost immediately, Greaves sees a badger brought down. A few minutes later, more impressively, a male hungry standing out in the middle of the road snaps into sudden, staccato life and snatches a bat out of the air. Greaves hears the crunch of bones as the animal – most likely a noctule, *Nyctalus noctula* – is devoured. It troubles him momentarily to think that the bat is screaming its pain in a supersonic register that his ears (especially hampered by the suit) cannot access. The world is information. An endless torrent. Whatever escapes you becomes something you will never completely understand.

Other things trouble him, too. He is still much too hot.

The suit is not working. If his temperature doesn't stabilise, he will die from heatstroke. He may be able to find a safe place in which he can barricade himself and remove the suit, but he will still be trapped. The science team may find him when they arrive for their sampling run tomorrow. Alternatively the hungries may find him a lot sooner than that: he will be filling the air with the scent that they follow most fervently and urgently of all, the scent of human flesh and pheromones.

Greaves finds the prospect of his own non-existence fascinating and dizzying. While he thinks about it, he becomes abnormally preoccupied. The stream of sensory data that he is used to receiving and parsing continually goes unanalysed for whole seconds at a time.

Movement in the middle distance pulls him out of this self-absorbed spiral with an uncomfortable jolt. He has allowed himself to be surprised, a thing that he hates even when nothing is at stake.

They come loping up the street from the river, heading his way: the wild dogs he saw earlier, or another similar pack. In that first glimpse, Greaves thinks they must be hunting him, but he quickly sees that he's wrong. Their heads are down, and their flanks heave with panting breaths. Some of them are limping.

Behind them come the children. A dozen of them, then twenty, then more than he can easily count in the bad light. The youngest look to Greaves to be around three or four, the oldest no more than ten. Like the girl from this morning, they are fantastically dressed. Some are wearing adult clothes: T-shirts that hang as low as skirts, hoodies and knitted sweaters with the sleeves rolled back or ripped away.

113

Others are naked, or else they're dressed in things that aren't technically clothes at all, random scraps of cloth and leather scavenged and repurposed. Their feet are bare. Their faces are painted, as the girl's was: a horizontal line across the forehead, a vertical one down the centre of the face. Some of them carry weapons: knives, walking sticks, hammers, trowels, in one case what looks like the metal shaft from the centre of an umbrella.

The dogs are not the hunters here: they are the prey. They are being driven. And the children don't hunt as the hungries do, which is by running full at the thing they want to eat. They work in a coordinated way, fanning out into a broad semi-circle to keep the dogs penned in as they run, to control and corral them. Some, though, mostly the youngest, seem to have no part to play in the hunt: they run alongside the others but further out and make no movement to close the distance.

The dogs are used to being on the other side of this equation. They're cowed and terrified. Their gait is faltering. They stumble, cringe, duck their heads in expectation of an imminent attack. Greaves guesses that this chase has gone on for some time and is nearing its end.

It is nearing Greaves, too, not to mention the hungries he has been watching up to now. The hungries respond to the oncoming flurry of movement, all at once waking from their torpor and running forward. And now Greaves sees that the younger children at the periphery do have a reason for being there. Most of them are carrying long sticks, branches and knobkerries and the handles of brooms, which they use to trip the hungries so that they can't interfere with the work in progress. In some cases, when a hungry

114

refuses to stay down, two or three of the children jump on it together, pinning it to the ground. One or other of them then draws a knife and expertly hamstrings the hungry. The children run on without a sound, leaving the hungry flailing spasmodically in the dirt.

The children seem to be all but invisible to the hungries. Their movements can trigger a response, a running charge, but up close the hungries seem to lose track of them altogether. They're not acknowledged either as threat or as food!

Greaves looks for the red-haired girl from the water-testing plant, and finds her – easily identifiable by the livid scar across her face. She is in the vanguard, leading the hunt. She brings one of the dogs down herself, almost at his feet. Greaves knows from earlier experience what she is capable of but even so he is awed at the flying leap that lands her on the dog's back. She bears it down, strong arms locking on its neck to twist its head around, and she is the first to feed on it once it falls. The dog gives a single high-pitched yip, which ends abruptly as her teeth close in its throat.

But she's not greedy. Some smaller children run to share the feast and she steps back at once, leaving them to it. Her chin is awash with blood. She wipes it with the back of her hand, then licks at her knuckles absently as she stares around her.

By this time, two more dogs are down. Everyone is eating. The girl seems satisfied with this, like a hostess who has done her best and is glad to see her efforts appreciated.

A small detail catches her attention. She pulls an older boy away from one of the three kills to allow a skeletally thin girl half his age a space at the dinner table. The boy glares at her, utters a long and inflected growl, but doesn't press the point. He is an outlandish figure, even in this company.

His blond hair has been hacked away from the sides of his head leaving a soft, unruly mohawk stripe down the centre. Splashes of black paint around his eyes make their whites stand out with the vividness of shattered porcelain, and he has drawn vertical white lines like the teeth of a skull around his real mouth, turning it into a perpetual grimace even when it's closed.

Greaves is enthralled by all this, so excited it's all he can do to make himself breathe. The children shift in his mind, semiotically adrift. They are hungries, but not hungries. They have the feeding urge that defines the condition, the preternatural strength and speed, but they are social beings with some degree of intelligence. *Cordyceps* wipes the mind like a slate and then writes on it the single word: FEED. As a hungry, your mental landscape is blindingly simple. In the presence of food, you eat. When it's absent, you shut down and wait.

So the children, as he thought when he first saw the girl, as he has been hoping ever since, are something new. Something unprecedented. They have found a middle ground that was never there before. He needs (oh, he needs so very badly) to find out what that middle ground is.

The meal is short. The metabolism of a hungry is highly efficient, needing only a small and occasional intake of live protein to survive. One by one, the children eat their fill and then relinquish their place. The scarred girl kneels and eats a second time, from a different carcase, perhaps to reinforce her status. Around her the children gesture and murmur. Greaves has no doubt whatsoever that this is language: after-dinner conversation is flowing, and the mood is mellow.

He is so rapt in his observations he has forgotten that he wasn't invited to this feast. But he is reminded of the fact, forcibly, when he sees that one of the children – the blond boy who was displaced when the girl thought he had had his fair share – is staring at him. Has been staring for some time, but his hooded eyes have become lost in the broad black smear of his war paint so that Greaves isn't conscious of the gaze until the boy turns his head to face him directly.

Greaves feels an urge to freeze on the spot, but he has already been frozen all this time. He has honed his stillness, with long practice, to perfection. The suit holds in his heat and his smell. He can't think of any signal he has let slip that might have given him away.

But then again, he realises as the boy takes a step towards him, that logic only applies to hungries. It wouldn't hold with a human child of any age. In the heat-control suit, he is an outlandish sight, and part of the basic equipment of human beings is curiosity – the desire to test out the immediate environment and come to an understanding of it.

He has assumed that the children will react like hungries rather than like people. He has underestimated them, and he is about to die for it.

The boy advances, pauses, advances again. He is about ten feet away now. He tilts his head on one side as he studies Greaves in his strange get-up, his face hidden by a featureless mask, his kit bag dangling from his shoulder like an ornament on a Christmas tree.

(A stray memory intrudes: brightly wrapped parcels under the tree at home in Witley, before home became a complex abstraction best represented by the face of Dr Khan. It was the best Christmas ever, because one of those parcels held Captain Power. Greaves suppresses the chain of ideas. He wants to live, and that will take full concentration.)

117

The boy takes another step. Other children are following him, but cautiously and at a distance. They have no idea what Greaves might be. He doesn't smell like food, clearly. He might be taken for a hungry but then he didn't come running when the dogs passed by. The odd paraphernalia hung about him invite exploration.

He wonders how far he would get if he ran. Not far at all, he thinks. Even without the encumbrance of the suit he would be slower than the children. If running served any purpose at all, it would probably be to end any ambiguity about what he is. The dogs ran, and the dogs were food. It's a short chain of reasoning with a warm meal at the end of it.

The boy raises his hand and reaches out.

The scarred girl is suddenly in his way, crossing in front of him to examine Greaves from right up close. Then from closer still. She takes two steps and thrusts her face up against his, standing on tiptoe.

Through the micro-pore mesh she stares into Greaves' eyes.

Greaves experiences a curious dislocation. If anyone from Rosie's crew, anyone from Beacon were doing this he would flinch away violently from the imposed intimacy. He would hate it. A child's gaze would be less unsettling than an adult's, but only fractionally.

The only thing that makes this bearable is that the girl is still uncategorised in his mind. There is no defined place in his highly organised mental landscape where he can set her down and feel that she fits. She might be nobody, devoid of meaning or value. But it doesn't feel like that. If anything, it feels like the opposite. She is supercharged with potential meanings, none of which can be subtracted until he knows her better.

The skull-faced boy is carrying a carpenter's claw hammer

with a black rubber grip and a head that still shines in places through a thick crusting of old blood. He tilts it to the vertical, pressing the spread fingers of his left hand lightly against the upper end of the shaft as though he is bringing some finely tuned piece of equipment into perfect alignment.

Greaves improvises. He raises his hands (bringing a grunt of astonishment from all the children) and performs the pass and re-pass from his magic trick. The girl's eyes widen, then narrow.

There is nothing in his hands. Nothing up his sleeve. Nothing between him and death except the hope that she might remember.

'We need to go to light speed,' he says, imitating the captain's inflection exactly. But his voice is muffled by the material of the suit and he is not, at the end of the day, the hero of the spaceways, the galactic engineer.

The boy raises the hammer. He grimaces, not with effort but with the anticipation of effort. He steps up level with the girl.

She thrusts him aside, without ceremony. Over his squeal of reproach and outrage, she speaks a single syllable. There are no consonants in the sound she makes, but there is plenty of authority. She is still staring at Greaves, barely acknowledging the skull-faced boy. The boy accepts the command or the rebuke, whatever it was. He steps back, ducking his head in abasement. There is a grimace on his face, as though his submission is something sour that he can taste.

The girl speaks again. She turns from Greaves, but gives him one final, sidelong glance. Her hands move, imitating the pass and re-pass. Then she steps away from him, very deliberately, and signals to the other children to follow her.

Nothing to see here. Let's go.

They move away quickly, walking between or over the still-twitching bodies of the hungries they felled in the hunt.

The street is like a battlefield. And Greaves is a casualty, though he hasn't been touched. The girl's gaze bored a hole in him, through armour much older and much, much thicker than the heat dispersal suit. Her mercy twisted the knife. He stands in some relation to her, and he doesn't know what it is.

Also he is going to die, even without the children's intervention. His body is burning up in the suit. He won't get back to Rosie or even out of the town before he collapses. He has a few minutes at best.

The solution comes to him – as solutions often do – in the form of a memory. Bath night. His mother testing the water in his yellow plastic baby bath with her elbow, to make sure he won't be scalded. She wears her own face this time, not Dr Khan's. She murmurs something to him that he can no longer reconstruct. His verbal memory is only accurate for memories after he reached the age of seven months, when he first began to extract actual meanings from the soundscape around him.

But the words don't matter here. The water does.

Greaves staggers across the street and into one of the side alleys that lead down to the river's edge.

A minute later, he is on his hands and knees in the shallows of the swift-flowing Moriston, his upper body bowed so that the flood breaks over his shoulders. The ice-cold water cools him and then chills him. Saves him from his own bad design.

But the girl saved him first.

15

By the time Greaves gets back to Rosie, it is almost morning. Private Sixsmith, standing guard inside the airlock, is astonished and more than a little alarmed to see him looming out of the pre-dawn shadows to stand on the threshold like bad news.

But at least she recognises him. Greaves has removed the suit for his final approach, presenting himself in his regulation olive-drab uniform. He's hoping that will be enough to shield him from comment, but he is saturated with sweat, shivering, exhausted. Sixsmith gives him a hard, quizzical stare as she opens the airlock doors and lets him in.

'What the fuck have you been up to?' she demands.

Checking the motion sensors, Greaves thinks. It might be a serviceable lie if he could say it aloud, but he can't because it isn't true. He only shrugs.

Sixsmith shakes her head, as though his idiocy and

waywardness make her sad, but she doesn't press the point. 'Well, nobody else is up,' she mutters. 'You've bloody well got away with it again, you mad bastard.' Greaves nods and says thank you. He wonders if Sixsmith knows that he waited in the dark for an hour to emerge as soon as her turn on watch began, preferring her over the much more uncertain quantity of Private Phillips.

Maybe she's figured that out, because she doesn't take the thanks kindly. 'Just get inside,' she says. 'And take a shower. You stink.'

And he takes her advice, recognising that she is right. Greaves is fastidious about his own body odour, thinking of smell as a kind of long-distance touch, unsolicited but unavoidable. He rubs the carbolic acid soap over his body until he is covered from neck to toe in stinging, prickling lather. When he washes it off, his skin is furious red, but that's a guarantee that he is clean.

By the time he is finished in the shower, the rest of the science team are awake and queuing for their own turn, along with Privates Lutes and Phillips and Lance-Bombardier Foss. The rainfall has been high since they came north into Scotland so showers aren't rationed quite as strictly as they used to be. The crew are making hay while the sun fails to shine.

Greaves goes about the rest of his waking-up ritual, in spite of the fact that he hasn't been asleep. It's not just to forestall questions. He needs to do it because each day has a shape and the waking-up ritual is one of its load-bearing components.

He brushes his teeth and shaves at the fold-out sink in the crew quarters, then goes back to his bunk to dress behind closed curtains. Though they are all routinely naked in each other's presence, dressing is for Greaves a very private thing. The most private part of it is when he puts on the watch that Rina gave him when he won his place on Rosie's roster. It belonged to Rina's younger brother, Simon, who was in America when the Breakdown happened and never made it home. Greaves wears the watch every day, the strap's loose grip augmented with an elastic band because Simon had a considerably thicker wrist than his own.

The captain's voice box is a part of the ritual, too. Greaves pulls the string and listens to what Captain Power has to say to him. Nobody knows that he does this, not even Rina. He would feel foolish explaining it, because it is far from being a rational act. The captain's words have no bearing on the events that will take place as the day goes on. Greaves doesn't take them as advice, or prophecy. It's just part of dressing. When he was younger, he would sometimes ask the captain what to do in a difficult situation, playing both sides of the conversation, giving the advice as the captain and listening to it as himself. He hasn't done that since he was thirteen, hasn't needed to. But hearing the captain's voice is like putting on a little of the captain's strength, the captain's courage.

Today the scratchy, rumbling voice declares, *'We've broken through into another universe!'*

You're right, Captain. We have.

Greaves goes to Dr Fournier and tells him that he wants to be included in today's work party. The science team is going into Invercrae and he wants to be with them. He hopes that Dr Fournier will not ask him why. There are so many reasons, and none of them have anything to do with the day's scheduled work.

Dr Fournier is reluctant. 'I thought you were happier

pursuing your own research, Stephen,' he says. 'With the rest of the team in the field, you'll have access to the lab for once. Besides, today's cull will be in a built-up area, which makes it a great deal more dangerous.'

'And I'll just be one more thing to worry about,' Greaves supplies. 'Yes, I know. I'm sorry, Dr Fournier. I am very happy doing my own thing, and I know the rest of the team will be more comfortable if I'm not there.' That's even true of Rina, he thinks: when he's there she worries about him. He steels himself for the next sentence. He's going to tell the truth, of course, but because of what he is omitting he will be skirting the black hole of a lie. 'But today I need to take some observations of my own.'

'Observations of what?' Dr Fournier demands.

Greaves swallows. Braces himself. Gets it out with some difficulty. 'Of outlying activity. I'm looking for . . . hungries who don't entirely fit the behaviour profiles we've seen so far. Anomalous patterns.'

The civilian commander shakes his head. 'Stephen, there are no outliers. No anomalies. If there were we would have found them by now.'

'I think . . .' Greaves tries. 'I'm not sure. Some of my recent findings . . .'

Left to himself, he would blunder into a full confession. Fortunately Dr Fournier breaks in before that happens. 'We're only going to have two or three more sampling runs at most,' he says. 'Invercrae. Then Lairg. Then Thurso. By all means come along today if you want to help. But if you come, I'll require you to stick to the agenda we've already worked out. No wandering off on your own. Understood?'

Greaves is frowning in concentration. He has been sieving

the doctor's speech, breaking it up into grammatical and semantic and intentional units, hoping to find some room for manoeuvre. He is close to despair until the last word – which is functionally a question – saves him.

'Yes!' he blurts, fists clenched to hold back whatever other words might rise in his throat. 'I understand, Dr Fournier.'

Fournier gives him a pained and worried stare. 'All right then,' he says. 'I'm going to deliver a final mission briefing in thirty minutes. Dr Sealey will give you your sample kit and tell you what to collect. Please do exactly as you're told, even if you can't always see the reason for it. There's no time for debate out in the field. You just have to accept that the soldiers and the rest of the team know what they're doing and that there's a reason for everything that happens.'

Greaves can find no answer to this. He can see that determinism might be very comforting as a philosophical position, but he doesn't feel that it maps very well onto individual human actions. If everyone always knows what they're doing and acts in a perfectly rational way, how did most of world history happen? As an alternative to saying anything at all, he nods – which is really just saying 'I understand' again – and retreats quickly.

The other members of the science team are assembling equipment and conducting a big, rowdy conversation with lots of interruptions – the kind of unfocused discussion that Greaves hates, because it's hard to know which thread to follow through the babble of competing voices. At the best of times, that's hard for him to deal with. Now, having come so close to telling an outright lie to Dr Fournier, he is in far too delicate a state to bear the slings and arrows of light conversation.

125

He goes out onto the mid-section platform instead and, finding the turret free, climbs up there to be out of sight and alone. He feels safe now to tell the empty air what he should have said to Dr Fournier. 'I want to go into the town because there are children there who I need to study,' he whispers. 'Infected children, almost certainly, because they hunt and eat like hungries. But in other ways their actions are closer to the normal human repertoire. They seem to still be able to think. If it's possible to be infected and retain some degree of consciousness and self-awareness . . .'

He doesn't finish the sentence. The possibilities proliferate and make him mute. The prospect of a cure for the hungry pathogen has become remote. *Cordyceps* grows into and through nerve tissue so quickly that there is no way of eradicating it without destroying the host's nervous system. A 'cure' like that might get you a clean bill of health but you'd be a quadriplegic vegetable. But if Greaves is right about the children – and if he gets some samples to work with – he might be able to produce a vaccine that mediates or even negates the pathogen's effects.

There's more, though. And as with his notebook, Greaves is aware of the currents of thought riding above and below the main signal.

Above:
The girl. She saved his life, stopped the skull-faced boy from splitting him with the hammer. Now the science team is doing a cull, right where she lives. Where the children live. What happens if they meet? What good are hammers and sharpened sticks against hollow-point ammunition?

126

Below:

Everyone? Everyone always knows what they're doing, except for him? No. That's simply not true. He sees more than anyone thinks. More than anyone else does, because he knows how to interpolate and extrapolate and he never stops looking or listening even if they think he does.

He knows that Dr Fournier has a radio that's all his own and that nobody else has been told about. He has heard Fournier talking late in the night when the rest of the crew are asleep, and afterwards he searched for and found the fake panel in the engine room where the radio is kept.

He knows that Dr Fournier and Colonel Carlisle are not friends or allies. On both sides there's wariness and mistrust, a split that has prevented the mission team from ever really becoming a team in more than name.

He knows that Lieutenant McQueen dislikes the colonel. A lot.

He knows that Beacon, when they left, was changing – shifting from one state to another, like milk when the bacteria suspended in it processes its molecules into lactic acid. Beacon was souring into something new and frightening.

He knows that John Sealey is the father of Rina's baby, and that he is scared of it being born.

They think he doesn't understand. That he can't see.

They can't see him.

127

16

The civilian commander's briefing is a waste of time, but that's fine. Everybody knows what to expect and nobody is listening. Fournier has taken over the lab, though, so actual preparation for the sampling run has had to stop. Bureaucracy must have its way.

Dr Khan is performing a mental sum involving times and distances and dates. She feels the taut fullness of her lower body very acutely, where even a month ago she could pretend there was nothing there. Her back just twinged as she sat down. In many different ways, the baby is announcing itself. Starting the drumroll that will end when Khan screams and sends it out to meet the world.

'Urban environments present unique threat profiles,' Dr Fournier is saying, as though this is the first town they've encountered rather than the twentieth. He's right, of course, but they don't need to be told. Or if they do, it ought to be one of the soldiers who does the telling. They're the ones who take the weight of those extra risks. Especially the snipers, who in a stampede situation will have to rely on the grunts with their automatic rifles to pull their irons out of the fire. Dropping one hungry at a time doesn't count for much when there are two or three hundred running at you.

'Lines of sight become problematic in a heavily built-up area,' Fournier is saying now, 'and exit strategies even more so. Lieutenant McQueen is responsible for your safety in the field, but he can only keep you safe if you do what he tells you to do in all circumstances. You should already have memorised the street maps he has provided, but keep them with you nonetheless. Anything else, Lieutenant?'

McQueen has been leaning against one of the work surfaces, his elbow resting on the main centrifuge. He comes erect now, with something of languor in his movements. You can lead him to water, he seems to say, but he'll drink in his own good time.

'Only the obvious,' he says. 'If you're separated from the main party, you go to ground. Find some height if you can. There's always more hungry activity at street level. Radio in and we'll come and get you. Don't strike out on your own because that's the best way to get killed.

'Everyone should refresh their e-blocker before stepping out of the airlock, and again at one-hour intervals. If you break into a sweat, give yourself a top-up right there and then. Don't wait until the hungries start to compliment you on your rich bouquet.

'As far as the firing goes, usual drill pertains: you choose; we shoot. Once we start to shoot, you stay absolutely still.

I don't want anyone ambling into our sights and messing up the clearance. You don't want that either. Any questions?'

There are no questions.

'Very well,' Fournier says. 'Dr Sealey has assigned each of you a specific sampling brief. He'll go over those with you now. I'll be in the engine room if I'm needed. The lieutenant will lead out from the mid-section airlock in ten minutes.'

The scientists scatter. Everyone has already assembled their kit, but now they check everything again in case they've left some crucial piece of equipment on their bunks or out in the workspace. John does not repeat their individual shopping lists: he knows he doesn't have to.

Khan glances across at Stephen, who is prepping an additional specimen box. She watches as he slips this second box into his rucksack. In spite of the briefing, he seems very much inclined to further some project of his own.

She was surprised when she learned that Stephen had asked to come with the team today. Normally he works with the samples they bring back but will do anything to avoid going out in their company. She understands, or thinks she does. Company, for Stephen, is equivalent to unresolved tension. His interactions with other people are awkward, and their interactions with each other are a distraction he finds hard to cope with.

So what's different about today? Khan could ask him, of course, but hitting Stephen with a direct question feels like rolling him for his spare change. He has no defence against questions.

So she says nothing, and returns to checking her own sample kit for the third or fourth time.

★

130

John Sealey is watching Khan as she watches Greaves. He feels, not for the first time, a twinge of jealousy at her solicitude for the boy. It seems sometimes as though the two of them have an intimacy he can't break into.

That's crazy talk, of course. You can't get intimate with Greaves; with the Robot, as the soldiers call him. When it comes to the muddled give-and-take of human relationships, Stephen doesn't have a functional interface. Which means Sealey is jealous of a mirage.

Do we always fret about our partners' exes? he wonders. And do we extend that to everyone they knew before they met us? Is it their whole past we're jealous of, as though we want them to be born again when we walk into their lives? It's a depressing thought. He has believed himself to be bigger than that, and a whole lot more rational.

All the same, it hurts him just a little when Rina is so worried about Stephen Greaves that she forgets that anyone else – including himself – is even in the room.

He touches her shoulder, bringing her back. 'All tooled up?' he asks her unnecessarily. She shows him her sample kit, like a schoolkid brandishing her lunchbox. 'Ready to rock,' she says, with about a half of a smile.

'Then let's go,' John suggests. 'Last one in the airlock is a smelly cheese.'

Lieutenant McQueen doesn't greatly appreciate babysitting duties, but he does like getting out of the big tin can. He likes being in charge, which he always is on these expeditions (the colonel remains in the vehicle on account of his bad leg; Dr Fournier stays behind too, just because). And he likes using his expertise.

Dr Khan accused him once, on some occasion when a bottle or two of hard spirits had eroded the usual demarcation between the scientists and the soldiers, of having a relaxed attitude to killing. He didn't take any offence at that. In fact, he laughed. She was so far off the mark that he couldn't even feel insulted.

He is no more casual about killing than she is about science. It's a discipline, that's the truth of it, and some men (some women too, with Lance-Bombardier Foss pre-eminent among them) are better fitted for it than others. It doesn't mean they don't care about life. Quite the opposite. You shouldn't kill a man without being aware of the possibilities, the futures, you're snuffing out. The younger the target, the more of those possible futures there are. Killing a child is like killing a vast multitude.

And conversely, killing a hungry is like swatting a fly. There's nothing there, no future possibility left. It's only a shell, a cast skin that a man or a woman or a child shucked off. What Dr Khan thinks of as his indifference to death is really a by-product of how well he understands it.

He thinks, briefly, as he cycles the airlock and lets her out, about the possibility of killing her. Not because he wants to. He dislikes her but not nearly enough for that. It's just that the complexity of the equation in her case makes the thought-experiment interesting: killing a pregnant woman carries a greater freight of consequences than any other killing. However contemptible the doctor is (and she is contemptible, sneering at things she doesn't understand, endangering the mission in order to get laid, talking down to decent men while she treats the Robot like an overgrown baby), the life inside her has its own potentiality that isn't related to hers in any way. He would pause before shooting her, if it came to it. Pause for the kind of reflection that she thinks him incapable of.

Then he would do the job because it needed to be done and he doesn't flinch from something just because it's hard or dangerous or ugly. Not that Khan does either, he has to admit. This is why he can't bring himself to despise her all the way down to the ground, the way he despises Fournier and Sealey. Whatever else you can say about her, she does the job that's in front of her.

The airlock cycles again and the team assembles around McQueen. It would be possible to drive the lab closer to the town and reduce the risks that come with moving a large cohort overland. But the noise of the engines, even shielded, will bring any hungries in the area at a dead run. They'll end up churning their axles in crushed and pulped corpse-meat, and any chance of an orderly sampling will disappear. This way is better, even given the amount of shepherding the scientists will require en route, like a crocodile of skipping schoolkids on a trip.

McQueen gives some orders, gets them started. They move off in good shape with Foss and Lutes up front, Sixsmith and Phillips at the rear, leaving him free to move around as needed. The scientists stay in a tight huddle, which is fine. He tried to teach them broken field movement once, and once was enough.

They're all geared up for anything that might come along, but the road into town is as quiet as the grave. The absence of hungries is surprising, given how many they saw running loose up and down the valley. Maybe something has happened at some point to disperse them from the town. Migrating animals would have been enough to do it; hungries will run a long way in pursuit of food on the hoof. But then McQueen would expect to see some gnawed bones, maybe the odd half-eaten carcase.

No news isn't always good news, in the lieutenant's book. He has been in too many bad situations that blew up out of nowhere: he tends to view any invitation to let his guard down with open suspicion.

And he's right, of course.

It's all fine until they cross the bridge and enter the town. This was a beautiful place once. The water pouring over the falls, the old stone bridge right under it, so close the spray flecks your face like a wet kiss. You could have come here any time in the last two centuries and nothing about this scene would have looked any different, except maybe the weeds wouldn't have been so high. McQueen likes that a lot.

What they find in the town's main street, a hundred yards further on, enthuses him somewhat less. There are bodies on the ground. Nothing much in themselves but the blood, still sticky underfoot, makes him wary. He signals a halt and goes on alone to examine the kills up close. Without needing to be asked, Foss circles into the centre of the street to give him cover.

One good look at the fresh remains makes the lieutenant swear out loud. Just over half of them are animal carcases. Dogs. The rest are hungries, and they're not dead. They've just had their tendons slashed so they can't stand. As he approaches, they raise their heads, their hunting reflex triggered by his movement, and start to haul themselves towards him on their hands and elbows.

Has a raiding party of junkers passed through here? That's

134

a definite possible. The mad survivalists are more than happy to eat dog when dog is on the menu, and if they ran up against hungries who were hunting too they would have taken them down fast and kept right on moving.

But when he examines the dead dogs, the lieutenant is inclined to modify this initial diagnosis. The animals haven't been dropped with small arms fire or arrows: they've been overrun and eaten on the spot. The absence of any other wounds apart from the bite marks suggests that they were eaten alive.

If junkers were here, they lost this one. The hungries – apart from the ones now feebly clawing their way across the cobbles towards him – ate their fill.

The members of the science team are drifting up behind him, as if the order to halt is a volatile spirit that gradually evaporates in air. McQueen has to resist the urge to bawl them out, which until he has figured out this little conundrum would be self-indulgent and stupid.

'What's the score?' Foss asks, from off on his right shoulder. She looks tense but her tone is level.

'Not sure,' McQueen says. 'Looks like we've had company. Someone sliced up these hungries with edged weapons.'

Murmurs of dismay from the scientists, who have set their little hearts on some more tissue samples, bless them. The soldiers look around, weighing up the pros and cons of this open street from a defensive point of view. They're all thinking it. Nobody actually says it.

'Whoever it was, there's nothing to say that they're still here.' This from Dr Sealey, who out of all of them is usually the most skittish when there's a whiff of any actual risk. McQueen has always held that the least impressive kind of

135

courage is officer courage – the courage to give filthy orders other people have to obey. On this mission he's met tourist courage, and he has had to revise his league table.

He gives Sealey a hard stare. Sealey returns it, not knowing how close he is to getting his head smacked. 'No,' McQueen agrees. 'Nothing to say they left, either. That's why we're currently considering our options.'

He's still thinking it over as he says this, and he's finding a lot of things now that don't fit in at all with the junker hypothesis. No vehicle tracks on the road into town. Weeds taller than a man, on both sides of the bridge, that were almost completely unbroken. At the edges of the street where the cobbles give way to dirt, there are a few scuff marks from (arguably) recent feet, but if you marched a whole junker cadre through a town this size you'd leave a much bigger footprint than a few dead dogs. They're like locusts. They would have gone through the houses and thrown everything out onto the street for a game of trash-or-treasure. Plus they would have fucked and fought and had a pig roast and generally raised hell. The street would be full of their detritus. McQueen has walked through a town after junkers went through it and he knows exactly what the aftermath of their hideous diversions looks like. It's not something he's ever likely to forget.

So most likely this little piece of work was done by local boys, who have either moved on or else are keeping their heads down until the scary men with the big guns go away again.

It's still an unquantifiable risk. McQueen is fairly sure it's minimal, but his first priority has to be the safety of the team.

Everyone is looking to him for a decision. Well, everyone except for Greaves: the Robot is preoccupied, his eyes darting from side to side as though he's expecting company. He doesn't seem to be taking this as seriously as it deserves.

McQueen turns back to Sealey. 'Do you think you can work with what you've got here?' he asks. 'I mean, the hungries who are already down?'

Sealey looks up and down the street. At the felled and broken hungries still intent on the chase, arms scraping on the cobbles, closing with their prey one painful inch at a time. He's doubtful at first, but as his gaze flicks around and he sees the full extent of what's on offer he gets a little perkier.

'Well, there's plenty to choose from,' he admits. 'And a lot of these have got visible epidermal growth. We might have to mix and match a little because of the tissue damage, but yeah. I'd say we're probably good.'

'All right,' McQueen says. 'This is the plan. There's no mileage in a full-scale cull when we don't know if there's anyone else in the neighbourhood. Best to keep the noise down to a minimum and make sure everyone stays together. So you take what you can get from these guys and then you call it a day.'

They all nod their understanding. 'We might even get to go home early,' Dr Penny says.

But McQueen has to rain on her picnic. 'No,' he says, 'you won't. In fact, it's going to take you a fair bit longer than usual because I'm putting all my men on perimeter. You'll have to do your own pinning and skinning. Phillips, Lutes, hand over the kit.'

The two privates set down the bags that contain the catch-can poles. Dr Akimwe and Dr Sealey take delivery, maybe a little too quickly: it seems they have a definite preference as to which end of this messy procedure they want to be on.

McQueen leaves them to it, addressing his own people. 'Let's flatten the risk profile as far as we can. Phillips, Sixsmith, take the two ends of the street and lock them off. Lutes, you stay right here with the whitecoats. Make sure they can pick their flowers in peace. Foss, follow me.'

Everyone jumps to it, absolutely happy that someone else has taken responsibility and told them what to do. Sometimes McQueen despairs of the human race.

He and Foss need to get some elevation to be of maximal use, and ideally they need to do it without going into any of the buildings that line the street. Letting sleeping dogs lie is his default option. He stations Foss on top of a high-sided van about fifty yards away from the scientists, who are already beavering away. What does that leave? A flat roof on top of that café over there, with a drainpipe alongside. Good enough. He scales it in seconds, finds a good nest and settles himself in.

He can't see everything from here but he can see far enough. It's virtually impossible for anyone with bad intentions to get close to the science team without tipping their hand to the soldiers first.

The lieutenant is confident that he has this situation in hand. He relaxes a little, and draws some innocent amusement from watching the geeks trying to corral their first specimen. They're all over the place, scared of their own shadows, almost catching their feet in the running loops as they dance around looking for a good angle.

Something is wrong with this picture, though, and it takes him a moment to realise what it is. There are only four geeks in the parade. One of the science team is missing.

McQueen experiences a momentary twinge of alarm. He

138

does a head count and sees that it's Greaves who is AWOL, which in most circumstances he would just live with. But if person or persons unknown are wandering around Invercrae with more machetes than inhibitions, this is not a good time for Greaves to be out there doing whatever the unfathomable fuck he does.

The lieutenant unships his walkie-talkie and thumbs it to channel three. Down on the street, Private Lutes picks up and speaks his name.

'You've lost one; Bo Peep,' McQueen says. He tries to keep the irritation out of his voice: he gave Lutes the easiest job because Lutes came onto Rosie's roster from the royal corps of transport, primarily as an engineer. He is the under-achiever of the group. And now he has screwed up his very simple, very explicit brief.

'It's just the Robot,' Lutes says.

'I know who it is. Go and get him. Out.'

Lutes puts the walkie-talkie back on his belt with a truc-ulence that McQueen can read from fifty metres away. He detaches himself from the group down in the street, takes a forlorn look inside the nearest of the shop frontages, then chooses one at random and wades in.

The scientists don't even see him leave. They're doing their own dirty work for once and making heavy weather of it.

It rains on the just and the unjust, McQueen reflects. Nothing you can do but turn your collar up.

139

17

Greaves was forced to wait for his moment, and it was a long time in coming. But when the soldiers went to their stations and the science team started to look around for the first specimen to work on, the opportunity was suddenly there. He stepped backwards off the street into the window display of a shop whose glass frontage had long ago been shattered.

Faceless mannequins dressed in sun-bleached rags jostled him, but he steadied them with both hands and passed on through. In the space of a second, he had become invisible.

He pauses now to savour that feeling. Privacy and anonymity appeal to him strongly.

The interior of the shop has a rich smell of damp and rot. Sodden cloth, mulched down two or three inches thick, sucks at his feet as he walks. He gropes his way through interior doors, passageways, storerooms, back out onto an alley so narrow that he has to keep his body flat to the wall as he walks. The sound of the river is loud in his ears. It must be close at hand, probably on the other side of the rough-cast wall that faces him.

He comes out onto a side street, finds it deserted. Picking another shop, he dives in through the gaping, dislocated doorway and keeps on going.

Greaves moves quickly, even though he has no idea where he is going. He is painfully aware of how little time he has. On previous excursions when he has struck out from Rosie on his own, he has chosen a time when nobody had any expectations of him or any reason to look for him. This time is different. This time he is on the mission roster and his absence is bound to raise alarms as soon as it gets noticed.

And normally Greaves has a plan, but this time no. He was lured astray by the urgency of his desire. His strongest passion, sometimes his only passion, is for explanations. When he encounters something that runs so contrary to his understanding of the world, he needs to interrogate it until it yields to his intellect.

This time, though, it's more than just a quirk of his nature. Understanding the children may lead him to a cure for *Cordyceps*, a medicine for all the world's ills.

Somewhere in this town, the children are hiding. And the town is so small it seems that he must inevitably run into them, but that feeling is an illusion mostly attributable to his having grown up in Beacon. Beacon began life as a camp. Its structures are mostly single-storey. Thousands of people live in tents, or in temporary shelters that have insidiously become permanent.

By contrast, a town from before the Breakdown, even a town as small as this one, is an upside-down rabbit warren in which spaces proliferate vertically upwards. Every building is made of many rooms, with more rooms piled on top of them and more above those, and so on. Not quite *ad infinitum*, but in London Greaves sometimes met his own limits halfway up a glass and stone tower that reared itself so high above the ground his stomach seized and cramped with nausea whenever he looked out of a window.

Greaves knows his way here, is confident that he will not get lost. He has memorised the ordnance survey map of Invercrae, and he has perfect recall of his journey of the previous night. Even so, it's hard to align these vivid, fractal spaces with the idealised abstract presented by the map. Uncertainties proliferate. A room he passes through is full of shoes piled as high as the ceiling – wellington boots and high heels, slippers and sandals and baby shoes. Across walls and windows in the next street is a mural painted in a rust-brown colour that reminds Greaves of dried blood: a man, a woman and a child, arm in arm, smiling. Memorial? Magic charm? Mere insanity?

The river is his guide of last resort, but it betrays him. Following its sound, he traps himself in a dead end bounded on three sides by high, windowless walls. This does not correspond to anything on the ordnance survey map, and almost certainly postdates it. Greaves is starting to panic a little. He steps through a doorway into a fetid corridor whose carpet has become an indoor garden of weeds and lichen. He has neither claustrophobia nor agoraphobia, but any unfamiliar place has the potential to become an enemy. It would be a comfort right now to lie down and cover his face with his hands. He has to force himself to keep moving.

He tries to retrace his steps, but rising adrenalin assails

and confuses him. His memory, normally indelible, begins to blur at the edges. He is in a dark room, walking into walls, tripping over indeterminate objects. Another room. A third.

Filtered daylight beckons to him.

He blunders out into a large, enclosed yard: a vehicle bay, for cars that died long ago. One is up on blocks, another missing its doors and windscreen. He can see the sky at last, and a gate through which he can exit to the street.

He bolts.

Gets to the gate. Through the gate.

Then stops dead in his tracks.

The sound of weapons firing bounces off his skin and off the walls around him. What makes Greaves freeze and look around, bewildered, is not the volume. The soldiers always use suppressors, because where all animals bolt away from loud, sudden noises, hungries run straight towards them. So this is not a boom of thunder; it's just the hawk-and-spit sound he has become used to.

But it's full auto, and it's close. So who is firing?

And what have they hit?

18

Private Lutes is an engineer first and a soldier second. Although actually the gap between the two roles is bigger than that suggests. He never wanted to join the army, but after three years on the dole he did very much want a proper apprenticeship that he could turn into a proper job. A four-year army contract, he reasoned, would see him at age twenty-five walking into a sweet deal at Swain's or Eddie Stobart's with a good chance of having his own garage somewhere down the line.

Then the Breakdown happened. The hungry plague. And here he is, more than a decade later, still stuck in his fatigues in a world where even engineers who never enlisted belong to the army by default. To be fair, he loves his job – or at least, the part of his job that consists of taking broken machines and making them sing and dance by the application of his skilled hands. That gig is magic. It's Zen. It's the perfect peace of the unclouded mind, so completely engaged that it's somehow completely free.

But he hates all the rest of this shit. Hates being taken away from his real work to do things that don't mean anything, for people who aren't grateful. Particularly hates being outside the Beacon perimeter fence (at the moment, four hundred miles outside) and at risk. If he's happiest with a spanner in his hand, a rifle fills him with a kind of disgust. Spanners take things apart, yes, but they put them together again too. With a rifle all you can do is dismantle.

Feeling hard done by, he trudges through the streets of Invercrae looking for Stephen Greaves. And wouldn't he like to open that one up with a spanner! Lots of fascinating things to be discovered inside Greaves' cranium, no doubt, although the Robot is the very definition of NSK – non-standard kit. If you wanted to fix him you'd need to make your spare parts from scratch, by hand.

The sun comes out for a minute or so, and Lutes' spirits lift. He walks on the sunny side of the street for as long as it lasts. Then the cloud closes in again and the sky is all watery porridge. That seems to be the normal state of affairs in this miserable bit of the world.

The private is so lost in his thoughts that he loses a second in responding when he hears the sound. Just the clink of metal or stone on glass, but an intentional sound is different from what the wind or the rain does. It has its own profile that is hard to mistake.

Something is moving in the building on his right-hand side. Moving quietly, but the deserted town provides no cover, no distractions. After the clink, a shuffle. Perhaps the hiss of a barely voiced command.

These things add up to ambush. Lutes saw the hungries hacked and felled like trees, and has no wish to end up the same way. He has been moving with his safety on, as per regs, but now he flicks it free and — he doesn't even have to think about it — fires.

The rifle is on semi-auto, stepped down, but Lutes has the trigger in a death grip. He empties his magazine in three seconds, remembering to fan diagonally downwards and to the left for maximum coverage.

The shop front explodes as the bullets rip through glass and brickwork. Hollow-point, yes, but maximally configured for shallow penetration. These mixed-alloy, mosquito-nosed rounds will bite three inches deep into anything, then repent and weep molten metal when they get there. The sound is deceptively soft, like papers being incautiously toppled from a desk and scattering across the floor.

Immediately followed by shrill yips of pain or shock and the sudden, concerted movement of many bodies.

It was a trap and he triggered it. Too bad for the trappers.

In the exhilaration of that moment — of ducking the blow and turning the tables — Lutes loses all perspective. He does the last thing in the world he should do.

He charges into the shop, where drifts of brick and plaster dust make the air into a cocktail whose main ingredient is wall, and on through an open doorway into the depths of the building in pursuit of his fleeing enemies.

He reloads as he runs, and fires again. Full auto this time. There's nothing to fire at, but fuck it. These guys thought they could wait in the dark for him and trip him as he passed by. Cut his tendons and leave him crawling in the dust the

146

way they did the hungries. Well, let them try a taste of that and see how it goes down.

Out the back door, into a closed courtyard where eviscerated black bags bleed ancient, unidentifiable rubbish. Then into the street. Now he can see the fleeing shapes ahead of him, heads down and bodies low to the ground as they run flat-out. They look too small. Perspective, probably. He gets off another burst, and one of them falls. One of them is down. He's actually made a kill.

He jumps right over the prone body and keeps on going, processing what he saw slowly and piecemeal in the seconds that follow. He's got his mind on the chase, lunging into another building, an office of some kind, through cubicle farms now empty of all livestock, inspirational posters exhorting him from the walls. *Just hang in there!*

But then the penny drops, and echoes round his skull. A kid? It was a kid?

They're all kids. And they've stopped running now. Lutes stops too, stares at them in utter wonderment. He can't imagine what they're doing here, where their parents are, where they got their ridiculous trick-or-treat costumes from. No, they're not dressed for Halloween, although one of them has turned his face into a stylised skull. The rest seem to be playing dress-like-mummy-and-daddy-do, with about the same hit rate that kids normally average.

Dear Christ, he just killed a kid!

He opens his mouth to apologise, to explain, to reassure, but right at that moment one of the children – the skull-faced boy – whips his arm around like a jockey urging his horse towards the last fence.

There's a sensation in Lutes' left eye like a door slamming shut. A big steel door with a lot of weight and heft to it.

A second, bigger impact turns out to be the ground, standing on its end to smack him hard. Now he is lying on fouled carpet tiles and his thoughts have slowed to a syrupy crawl. The children's feet appear in his monocular field of vision (his left eye is welded shut), stepping softly and cautiously around and over him as though he might still have some fight left in him.

'Don't be . . . don't be scared,' he slurs. 'It's okay. It's okay.'

But they're not. And it isn't.

19

Greaves sees the body as soon as he rounds the corner.

He looks to left and right, quickly. His first reaction is simple confusion. Why would the children leave one of their number to lie where he has fallen like one more bag of spilled rubbish in a street that seems to offer nothing else? Bodies are not rubbish. Bodies in the field – bodies of hungries – are specimens. Bodies in Beacon are important for other reasons. Ceremonies. Memories. Regrets. One way or another, it seems, this body should be tended to.

Noises reach Greaves' ears, muffled by a wall or two but very close. Running feet, the crash of something falling. Something is in the middle of happening, which (it's not an unreasonable inference) might have forced the children to defer the decision of what to do with this corpse.

In the space between two breaths, Greaves feels a decision swell to ripeness inside him. He scans the street again, quick and tremulous, to make sure he is not observed. He is keenly aware of the danger here. The children are much faster and stronger than he is. There is no way he could either fight them or outrun them.

But the enigma, the impossibility, is drawing him on like a hook tugging at his brain. The children are hungries, but they don't respond like hungries. They can still think and feel. Higher brain functions have not been completely erased. He needs to understand them. Needs it on a level so fundamental that his nerves are screaming at him to move. To forget the risk and just do it. What does his physical safety matter? What terrors does death hold compared to having to live without answers?

He is moving forward. Out into the open where the body lies.

He is kneeling beside it. He tries to postpone investigation, analysis, but it is obvious to a cursory inspection that the boy has received two bullet wounds, either of which would most likely have been fatal. One bullet has passed directly through the throat, the other (Greaves moans aloud in dismay) has punched through the boy's left temple and more or less obliterated that side of the brain.

Greaves is shaking, less from the perception of danger than from the sheer mental pressure of what this find might mean – the piled up weight of possibilities. He can't think about it. If he thinks about it, that weight will fall on him and he will freeze in place.

He slides his hands underneath the boy's shoulders and knees. There is no weight there. It's as though he is holding a ventriloquist's doll, a hollow replica of a boy. The ruined head falls against him. Greaves remembers lying like this in his mother's arms, when he was so young that he couldn't speak in full sentences. Remembers lisping the word *bedtime*, and his mother laughing out loud at his precociousness. 'Listen to that! He knows the drill, don't you, my love?' Under the sour tang of blood, the boy's body smells like a forest floor, warm and damp and old.

Greaves scoops the little broken thing up in his arms and runs.

Not to the main street, but to the river. The map has activated in his mind. There is a way back to Rosie that doesn't go past the science team and the soldiers.

It goes instead through reeds and bracken, through ribbons of sand and shallows back to the bridge. A voice shouts behind him – Lieutenant McQueen's – but the words are impossible to make out and Greaves doesn't think the lieutenant is calling out to him.

The boy's head slides down into the crook of his elbow. The blood that stains Greaves' overalls is more brown than red, although there's certainly some red in there too. He can see the parapets of the bridge up ahead now and he slows involuntarily, starting to see how hard a task he has set himself.

How is he going to do this? Getting back on board Rosie by himself is complicated but not impossible. Carrying the dead body of a child through the airlock is a very different proposition. He will need to vary his route so that he doesn't go by the cockpit. But that won't be enough. With a team in the field, it's more than likely that either the colonel or Dr Fournier will have taken manual control of the airlock and will be waiting there to check the crew back in when they come. If he evades them at the airlock, they will still hear him enter and come to greet or debrief him, thinking that his arrival heralds the return of the team.

151

Perhaps he should hide the body and come back to retrieve it later? But that opens up the possibility that the children will search for it and claim it back. In fact, if their sense of smell is as strong as that of regular hungries they won't even need to search: they'll just go straight to it.

Greaves has reached the bridge, and now he starts to climb the steep bank that leads up to the parapet. He picks his way one-handed, the cooling weight of the corpse pressed hard against his chest.

He has to find a way back into Rosie, before the rest of the field team arrive there. He has to stow the body where it can't be found. And he has to make sure that no questions are asked about his own absence, because if they are asked he will have to answer them.

Right then is when the stone wall of the bridge starts to vibrate under his hand. He takes a step back and looks across the river.

He won't need to go to Rosie. Rosie is coming to him, with her airlock and extensor wings drawn in and her guns elevated.

She roars down the narrow, overgrown road and out onto the bridge, which is barely wide enough to take her. The weeds are trampled and torn up by her treads, rise again behind her in a column of green confetti. An angle of the parapet wall, struck by the edge of her front-end ram, explodes. Chunks of stone as big as clenched fists fly over Greaves' head as he ducks and covers.

Rosie is level with him, then she's past him, then she's gone. She didn't even slow.

It seems his problem has just become part of a wider problem.

152

20

After Lutes has been gone for twenty minutes, McQueen tries to raise him on the walkie-talkie. When that fails, he calls a halt to the sampling and orders a search.

There is no question of splitting the team up. If there is an enemy out here who is picking them off one by one, the lieutenant is damned if he's going to make their job easier for them. They search the main streets first, then the side streets. They stay clear of the buildings, where anyone so inclined could mount an ambush in the time it takes to blink. Searching the interiors will be a last resort.

The scientists have put their sampling gear away and have rifles at the ready. McQueen only hopes they remember which end of the bastard things to point with.

They don't find either Lutes or Greaves at first, but on one of the side streets they pick up a trail. Dr Khan sees it first. She has the sense not to shout. She touches McQueen's shoulder and points in silence. Her face is pale. Most likely she is thinking about Greaves, who is her protégé, pampered pet and just possibly (he's only a kid but you have to wonder) the one who knocked her up.

What Khan has seen is blood, which as far as bad news goes is the first but not the worst. There's a broad pool of the stuff out in the middle of the street, fresh enough that it's still tacky to the touch. A set of booted footprints leads from it into the nearest building. It looks as though Lutes hit something here, and brought it down. But maybe he didn't hit it hard enough, because whatever it was it's not here any more. It looks to the lieutenant as though it took off towards the river. There's a second, fainter trail of dark red smears and spatter patterns that leads off in that direction.

'Oh my God!' Sealey mutters. And Penny, who is no shrinking violet, shakes her head violently as if she's refusing to admit that any of this is happening.

Whatever went down and didn't die is still a potential threat. They would be stupid to turn their backs on that. But Lutes is the priority, and he should be easier to find now they've got a vector. Most of all, McQueen thinks, he's got to get this done before the civilians start to fall apart.

'Foss, on my six,' he raps out. 'Phillips, Sixsmith, stay out here. Cover both ends of the street, and the river. Anything happens, even if it's a cloud in the sky, you squawk me.'

'Yes, sir,' Phillips says.

'Can I come with you?' Khan asks. 'If Stephen is in there—'

'I'll call out if I need you,' the lieutenant says. It doesn't mean anything but it shuts her up.

He walks into the building, with Foss stalking silent at his back. She has left her M407 in its canvas sheath-holster across her shoulders: it's a liability in a narrow space. In its place she holds a Glock 22 (whose magazine, McQueen knows, is filled with bespoke rounds that Kat makes herself using the .40 Smith & Wesson case as a starting point) and a .357 powerhead contact shooter. Good choices. He's bringing Sixsmith's SCAR-H to the party, so they've got both ends covered – the surgical and the indiscriminate.

But they don't need either, because the party is over. Lutes lies on his back staring one-eyed at the ceiling. The eye that looks as though it's winking has in fact been permanently closed by a smooth grey stone that has embedded itself in the socket. The blood welling up around it has already begun to scab. The private's throat has been slit so deeply that the top of his spine has been severed. Nubs of bone glisten in the blackness of the wound. There are a number of other wounds distributed widely across his limbs and torso, incised and abraded and any damn flavour you can think of.

Whoever killed him brought a lot of energy to the task, and a lot of implements. One of the implements lies on the ground beside him. A knife, but not a knife that was designed to be a weapon. It has a short blade and a sculpted plastic handle. The Kitchen Devil logo adorns it.

'Where are you, you bastards?' Foss whispers. She turns a quick circle, looking for a target. She already has a round in the chamber and her finger is tight on the Glock's finely balanced trigger, where half a foot-pound of extra energy will push the bullet down the slipway.

'Stand down,' McQueen orders her. In case that's not enough, he grips her wrist and points it at the ground.

His own instincts are the same as hers. He was playing poker with Lutes less than twelve hours ago. He has spent a

155

lot of the last seven months listening to the man's bad jokes and untenable claims about how good he is at the nearly extinct game of table football. So yeah, he wants to find who did this and teach them the going rate for eyes and teeth.

But it's a luxury he can't afford. He doesn't know the ground, and he is heading up a force that balances three actual soldiers against four armed liabilities. You can't churn butter with a toothpick, no matter how much you might want to.

Go to ground, then, and get their licks in later. But as a fortress, this place doesn't thrill him. Too wide. Too open. Too many doors. Walls too thin to stop a sneeze. Lines of sight fuck-awful in every direction.

He throws Foss the signal to retreat in good order, and she knows better than to argue. They back out the way they came, leaving Lutes' thoroughly tenderised remains where they lie. It hurts like hell but it's the only thing to do.

Out on the street McQueen rounds up the geeks, who predictably are full of questions he doesn't have time to answer.

'Lutes is dead?' Sealey keeps repeating, as if he can scrape the unpalatable fact away by abrasive repetition.

Dr Khan grabs McQueen's arm, which he doesn't like over-much. 'What about Stephen?' she demands. 'Did you find him?'

'There's no sign of him,' he tells her. 'Probably means he's lying low somewhere. We'll get to him when we can.'

'When we can?' Khan spits the words out as though they're poison. 'We've got to find him now, before we do anything else.'

McQueen wants to grab her by the throat and shout in her face that Greaves *caused* this by wandering off in the first place. Greaves brought Lutes this hideous, unseemly death. But he doesn't say that, because it's the part of the truth that matters least. The senior officer takes the decisions, and the rap. Everything that's happened here is down to him, first and last.

So he just pulls his arm sharply away from her grasp and gives the order again. 'Follow the leader. Single file, ten yards apart. Start and stop on my mark. If any of you steps out of line, I'm going to handcuff them and frog-march them, which will be bad news for everybody.'

Khan looks like she's inclined to argue again, but then she thinks better of it. The fact of Lutes' death is sinking in. Her face twists in surprise and pain as though something sharp just dug into somewhere soft. Well, it's tough all over. Every one of them can see that they're playing a bad hand in a bad place.

'Single file,' he repeats. 'Don't close up.'

McQueen leads them away from the killing ground, sticking to the shadows and the angles of walls, spacing them out along a skirmish line, making them as difficult a target as he can.

They're being followed. Something is fucking pacing them. The enemy don't let themselves be seen, not clearly, but there are flicks of movement from the buildings on either side, skitters of sound. Again McQueen is tempted to cut loose, but the middle of the street is no place to make a stand. Dig in first, then see what comes, unless the bastards force the issue.

They don't. The lieutenant gets the science team into cover in what used to be the Corn Exchange. He manages to find a place he can actually fortify, a first-floor room with a wide view of the street and a flat roof at the back that will make a good line of retreat. He establishes a perimeter, about twenty feet across.

He calls Rosie. Tells the colonel they're in a hole they can't climb out of and if he can find time in his busy schedule to stop by, the field team will be delighted to see him. Informal dress, guns prepped and armour up.

Carlisle doesn't bother asking questions he doesn't need the answers to. 'Wait there,' he orders McQueen. And McQueen does. Meanwhile, he finds a nice place to sit by the window with his rifle resting in his hands. *Come on, you bastards. Let's see you.* But there's nothing to see now. Nothing moving. The only sound is a pigeon cooing from up on the roof.

The radio is silent for three minutes, which is the time it takes to retract the airlock and the extension blisters. When the colonel pings them back McQueen can hear the sound of Rosie's engines in the background, already warming up. Evidently he succeeded in conveying a suitable sense of urgency.

Foss and Sixsmith have got the windows; Phillips is at the door, which he's cracked open seven eighths of an inch with the barrel of his rifle right up against the gap. The whitecoats are sitting in a tight circle on the floor, facing outwards. They've got their guns at the ready but McQueen has told them to keep the safeties on. He is not going to put his own or his people's skins in between a terrified amateur and a moving target.

Khan is as pale as a sheet and her hands are shaking. Funny, he would have thought she would be one of the last to lose her nerve. But she's sweating it for the Robot, of course.

The radio squawks again. Carlisle, asking for a GPS. McQueen gives him both that and his take on the situation. 'It's quiet right now but they're close and I think they'll make a move before you get here.'

'I'll bring Rosie right to you,' Carlisle says. 'ETA two

minutes. Use the time to locate enemy positions if you can. Anything you spot, I'll light up from the street before I retrieve you.'

'Copy,' McQueen says tersely. And he doesn't bother with 'Out'.

Khan is practically gnawing her fist off. Her eyes show darker than ever in her bleached-out face. 'Can we try to send Stephen some kind of message?' she asks McQueen. 'So he can find us?'

'Like what?' Foss snaps, reaching the end of her tether. 'A fucking smoke signal?'

'We don't want him to find us,' Private Sixsmith says, with less of an edge. 'It wouldn't be a good idea for him to come into the open right now. He's better off keeping his head down until we come.'

She glances across at McQueen as though McQueen might have an opinion on this. The lieutenant doesn't say a word, and prominent among the words he doesn't say are, 'Small loss.' He is much more concerned with the silence and stillness out in the street. The enemy were practically treading on their heels and now they've disappeared. It doesn't make any sense.

'How long will we have to wait here?' Akimwe demands.

There is no answer to that question that will do justice to the lieutenant's feelings, but he's about to give it a shot when something he has been noticing subconsciously makes it into the forefront of his mind.

That sound he just heard was wings. Birds taking off from the roof.

He looks up. Listens. When Akimwe starts to speak again, he grunts a terse 'Shut up.'

A loosed pebble chatters and chuckles its way down the roof ridge.

McQueen aims at the ceiling. The next thing that moves is going to get a bullet, just to make a point.

But the next thing that moves is Penny. She screams as the window shatters, showering her with broken glass. She goes down into a crouch, clutching her face.

That was no gunshot. It came in on a curved trajectory and it lost height too fast. McQueen guesses what it was even before he sees the pebble lying on the naked floorboards at his feet. A stone out of a slingshot. He snaps his fingers to get the whitecoats' attention. 'Take off your coats,' he says quickly. 'Now. Wad them up and cover your faces. A headshot is the only thing that can actually kill you.' They scramble to do it, all except for Penny who is still praying to Mecca. Akimwe asks if she's hit but she's not answering.

A slingshot is a low-tech weapon even by junker standards, but it's effective. Much more worrying are the scraping and wrenching sounds from right over their heads. The bogeys are ripping the slates off. They're going to come in through the roof.

Needs must. McQueen strafes the ceiling with a short, wide burst, doing more damage than their unseen assailants but at least he's breaking up their party. As he does this the rest of the windows blow out. Small chunks of stone punch the plaster on the far wall with impacts as crisp and clean as bullets. One of them hits him in the back but his pack absorbs most of the force.

'Lie down,' he orders the science team, and they do. The soldiers are down too, on their knees and peering at an oblique angle around the edges of the broken windows, trying to get a glimpse of the enemy without swallowing a piece of ballistic geology.

'Foss,' McQueen snaps. 'Phillips.' He points at the ceiling, where the sounds of digging and scrambling are suddenly louder. The enemy made short work of the slates and now they're going through whatever else is up there. With luck that will be wooden beams. Otherwise it's just lath and plaster. They've probably got a couple of seconds before they have to deal with vertical incoming.

But Rosie comes first and she comes like thunder, the sweetest sound McQueen has ever heard. The bogeys up on the roof are hearing her too, and no doubt seeing her as she rolls up the steep incline of the main street towards them. Good. Rosie with her guns up is a terrifying sight. They must be shitting breezeblocks right now.

The colonel can't take the corner cleanly. There just isn't room to turn something of Rosie's generous dimensions without hitting something. So he doesn't even try. He comes round wide, smashing through the frontages of shops, folding benches and litter bins down to two dimensions, then he swerves at the last moment to scythe into the street they're on. Even so, he doesn't have enough room to manoeuvre. A lamp post is torn out of the ground and falls full length across the road, from pavement to pavement. It lies there like a toppled tree for half a heartbeat before Rosie's treads crush it flat.

McQueen grabs the radio. 'Extend the airlock,' he yells. 'We need an umbrella!'

The massive vehicle comes to a stop at last, with the mid-section door right opposite the door they entered through. The scientists scramble up and start to head for

161

the exit, but McQueen brings them back with a terse bark. 'Wait for it.'

The colonel extends the airlock, all the way to the door of the building. That glass is everything-proof. If someone up on the roof has a gun pointed down at them, or even just a pebble and a leather strap, the crew will only be exposed for a fraction of a second as they sprint across from the protection of the doorway to the sanctuary of the airlock. Even McQueen would have trouble setting up a decent shot in that kind of timeframe.

'Okay,' he tells his people, 'lead off. One at a time, like before. Cover the civilians, then go over yourselves. Foss, you and me run tail.'

The geek squad is quick and efficient for once. With their lives on the line they remember every combat drill they were ever put through, every skip and jump. They descend the stairs quickly and quietly. McQueen notices as Dr Penny runs by that she is uninjured. Her duck-and-cover was a reflex, not a response to a wound.

He lingers in the doorway, and Foss stays behind too without a word being spoken. They wait, rifles in hand, to see if anything comes down through the ceiling, but nothing does. Finally they retreat backwards out of the room and slam the door.

When they get to the bottom of the stairs, the whitecoats are already scooting through the airlock doors with Phillips and Sixsmith to either side, watchful and ready.

They get the hell out of there, by the numbers. Only Khan seems a little breathless as they duck and run, a little clumsy, but then she's used to manoeuvring without a seven-month baby bump.

162

Dr Fournier is waiting for them right inside the mid-section door, trying to look like he's actually got something to do here, yelping out orders as though anyone is listening.

'Keep the platform clear! Leave room for the people who are coming in behind you! Cycle the doors as soon as the last man is in!'

The last man is McQueen. Foss, who was second to last, has shuffled in backwards so she can cover him as he comes. He gives her a curt nod of thanks and walks on by, trusting her to lock up behind him.

'What if Stephen—?' Dr Khan protests, but McQueen isn't really listening so he misses the rest of the sentence. He dumps his gun and climbs into the turret.

The doors slide shut and the airlock retracts. Rosie backs out the way she came, smashing a lot more infrastructure with her arse end.

They reverse onto the main street where they swing around in a wide, destructive arc. But not as destructive as it's about to get.

The field pounder, in these close quarters, is useless. The shells would punch through the walls of Invercrae and sail right on. The flamethrower, though, is a different proposition entirely.

The lieutenant slams down the priming lever and rotates the turret through most of a circle. He aims at the building they've just come from and cuts loose, sweeping the house from the roof on down.

In seconds, it's one big bonfire. After that, he sprays the buildings on either side, with a view to catching anyone who saw the turret turn and jumped clear. Finally, he picks targets at random. Invercrae goes up like dry tinder around them and behind them.

McQueen hears a yelling from the bottom of the turret steps, in more than one voice. He shuts off the primer, rests the gun and descends to find Dr Khan and Foss wrestling while the men look on in various states of bemusement or horror. Khan was trying to get up into the turret and stop him, presumably, and Foss blocked her way.

The lieutenant gestures to Phillips and Sixsmith, who restrain the doctor as gently as they can, pulling her off Foss like a limpet off a rock. 'Motherfucker!' she yells, with the accent on the third syllable. She immediately tries to throw herself at McQueen, but the soldiers hold her tight. He sees Dr Sealey contemplate a rescue, then very sensibly take a step back as his sense of self-preservation kicks in.

'You bastard!' Khan shouts. 'Stephen is out there! Stephen is out there and you burned it down!'

He doesn't have any answer to that. He hadn't forgotten Greaves; he just didn't believe there was any chance at all that the kid was still alive. Or if he entertained a doubt, a small one, it didn't weigh very much against the urgency of paying out Invercrae and her invisible residents for what they just did to Lutes. He is groping for a way to put this into words that Dr Khan will understand, but she's still screaming at him so he can't get any headway.

It's right then that Rosie slows.

Stops.

The intracom hisses and crackles.

'Friendlies,' the colonel says. 'Mid-section door. It's Greaves. Bring him aboard.'

Khan is the first to move. She hits the lock. Sealey and Akimwe join her, quickly throwing the manual safeties that Foss has only just engaged.

Only Foss out of all of them has the presence of mind to provide any cover as they pull the door wide.

They've stopped by the river, just before the bridge. Stephen Greaves steps in. Nothing to say for himself, he just jumps right up onto the platform as the doors open, like a hitchhiker who can't believe his luck is in. His kit bag bulges at his side, even fuller than usual.

'Thank you,' he says. 'I'm very sorry to have slowed you down. We probably should go now. The town is on fire.'

21

'You violated standing orders,' Colonel Carlisle says. 'I need to know why.' He is aware that he has said it before, and he is aware of how inadequate it sounds, but it is the least of a whole box of evils. He needs to adhere to the bloodlessness, the formality of regulations and procedures in the same way that Odysseus needed to tie himself to the mast when he passed by the island of the sirens. The seductive voices in this case will lure him into anger, and Lieutenant McQueen will meet him more than halfway.

'You didn't see what Lutes looked like when they were through with him,' McQueen says, as though that's an answer. After a half-second pause he adds a 'Sir,' like throwing a scrap to a dog.

The two men face each other across the long diagonal of the crew quarters, as though this is a duel. The rest of the crew stand around the edges, all except for Greaves who has hidden in the lab, away from the dangerous emotions. The boy's instincts are sound, the colonel reflects grimly. His own men and the science team are all still stunned by what just happened, but as they thaw out, their reactions are tending to extremes. The soldiers are angry and hurting because one of their own is dead. Samrina Khan is furious for a different reason, the lieutenant's unilateral barbecue party far from forgotten, and her voice carries a lot of weight with the whitecoats. However this plays out, it has the potential to polarise them, to set them all at odds.

So the colonel treads lightly. He stands by the book. The book isn't angry with anyone, and the demands it makes are ones the soldiers accepted the first time they put on their uniforms.

'Explain to me,' he says to McQueen, 'why you fired the flamethrower in the absence of a direct order.'

McQueen shakes his head as though that's the sorriest excuse for a question he has ever heard. He doesn't answer. So Carlisle tries again. 'Lieutenant, you used the mid-section guns without permission, and without verifying that all personnel were aboard. If there was a clear and present danger that justified this course of action, I need to know about it. Because if there wasn't, you endangered the entire crew for no good—'

'They're still alive,' McQueen says, between his teeth. 'All but one of them. All the ones who stuck with me. Did you miss that? I did what had to be done to bring us out of there. I secured a position and then I requested an extraction exactly as per standing bastard orders. The flamethrower was just to let them know that if they hurt one of ours we hurt them back.'

'Damn right,' mutters Lance-Bombardier Foss.

Samrina gives Foss a look of incredulous contempt. She

167

hasn't bounced back yet from the whole ordeal. Her face is haggard with stress and exhaustion. 'Damn right?' she echoes. 'What, did they teach you that at sniper school? Somebody hurts you, you hit back with the biggest weapon you've got, no matter who might be in the way?'

Foss shrugs. 'Nobody was in the way. We got out. We got out in one piece.'

'And the ends justify the means. Right.' She indicates McQueen with a jerk of the head. 'You're a bigger idiot than he is.'

Foss arches an eyebrow. 'Well now,' she says mildly. 'That's a conversation we can take up another time.'

Samrina talks over her, eyes on the colonel. 'Stephen was MIA,' she says. 'He could have been in any one of the buildings this fucking moron torched. I don't know how this works, but I want some assurance that he can never touch those turret guns again. I'd rather take my chances with the hungries.'

McQueen lets the insult pass. 'In this instance,' he points out levelly, 'you would have been taking your chances with junkers. And let's not forget that Greaves going off-mission was the catalyst for all of this. Lutes was killed trying to find him and escort him back.'

'If I might be permitted to voice an opinion,' Dr Fournier breaks in. 'Speaking as civilian commander.'

'With due respect, Doctor,' Carlisle says heavily, 'I'm attempting to settle a matter of military discipline.'

'Which impacts on the mission.'

True enough, but so does everything. Which is why having two mission commanders never made any sense.

'Lieutenant,' Carlisle presses, 'what prompted you to fire the mid-section guns? Please explain.'

McQueen makes a gesture, palms up and open. *This is all I have to give you.* 'I suppose, sir,' he says, 'I fired them because I felt that Brendan Lutes' death mattered. If you disagree, feel free to discipline me in any way you see fit.'

The challenge rests there. Carlisle gathers himself to pick it up.

'If I may be allowed to speak,' Fournier tries again. 'The presence of junkers in the town more than justifies the lieutenant's action. I would be inclined to overlook the breach of regulations.'

'The presence of junkers wasn't verified,' the colonel tells him bluntly, and turns right back to McQueen. 'You used the flamethrower contrary to regulations. In an enclosed and compromised space, and without regard to the safety of the crew. You were firing in a broad arc, ignoring the headwind and our own acceleration. Not only could you have killed Mr Greaves, you could also have set fire to Rosie if the propane stream had blown back on us. I respect your feelings, but I can't condone your actions.'

'I can live with that,' McQueen says.

'I'm therefore taking away your commission.'

McQueen takes that blow full in the face. He blinks a few times, as though to clear his sight. There is a silence that spreads out from him to take in the rest of the room. Even Dr Khan can't find anything to say right now, although she nods just once. *Good.* The slamming of drawers and the clatter of instruments – Greaves, at work in the lab – seem to come from a great distance.

'Whether or not the demotion becomes permanent,' the colonel goes on, 'is a matter for the Muster's senior officers as soon as we're able to re-establish radio contact.' He tries to temper his tone. The punishment is what it is, and it needed to be public, but there is no need to take the man's humiliation any further than that. 'Until then, your acting rank is private. The official reprimand will stay on your docket regardless, of course. Lance-Bombardier Foss, you are now ranking officer in field parties and on any occasions when I'm not present. You will carry the acting rank of lieutenant.'

'Sir,' Foss says mechanically. She's just acknowledging the order. She clearly needs some time to figure out what it means.

'Permission to speak, sir,' McQueen manages. His voice is tight. His face is starting to look a little taut too, as though suppressed emotion is pressing on it from the inside.

'I don't agree with this decision,' Dr Fournier says.

'You're not required to,' Carlisle reassures him. 'It's mine to make.'

'Sir, permission to—'

'We'll speak later.' The colonel hauls himself to his feet, wincing at the pain in his damaged leg. 'Take a while to think about it, then come and find me in the cockpit.'

'If you don't mind, Colonel,' Dr Fournier says, his voice rising now. 'I think there's a wider decision to be made. About the mission as a whole.' He stands up too, rigidly tense, his head moving as his gaze flicks between Carlisle and the rest of the crew. The colonel knows hurt pride when he sees it: Fournier doesn't like to be brought up against the limits of his authority. But there is fear in his face, too. He's not just throwing his weight around: he's serious about this. About whatever it is he's about to say.

And what he has to say is serious stuff. It brings the house down.

170

22

The argument is ugly. But it is taking place in the crew quarters, so Greaves is able to retreat from it into the lab. He hates raised voices, raised emotions, words turned into cutting tools, but the upside is that it provides some cover for what he needs to do. He gets to work, doing his best to tune out the noise.

The voices still get through, though. The loudest ones belong to Colonel Carlisle and Lieutenant McQueen, with each man repeating the same statement in a lot of different ways.

Colonel Carlisle is angry with Lieutenant McQueen because he used the flamethrower when he hadn't been told to. He violated standing orders. He was in breach of regulations.

The lieutenant is angry because the colonel isn't angry enough about the death of Private Lutes, which made using the flamethrower the right thing to do. He also says that it was all Greaves' fault and not his own.

Greaves tries not to think about this last argument. Lieutenant McQueen must be wrong. It must be a lie, somehow, even if it doesn't feel like one.

The rest of the team are angry too (he didn't kill Private Lutes) because they almost died and Dr Fournier is angry (but what if Private Lutes died because of him?) because nobody is listening to him even though he's meant to be in charge (he didn't he didn't he didn't he didn't he didn't).

So everybody is angry and Greaves has to work and not think about any of these things, but especially not that one thing. Private Lutes killed the boy and the rest of the children killed Private Lutes. That was how it happened and Lieutenant McQueen doesn't know because he wasn't there.

Greaves feels the stinging in his eyes, the wetness welling and tumbling down his cheek. He can't wipe it away because he has put surgical gloves on. And he can't sob or snuffle in case the crew members hear him and decide to look in on him. He is doing something very dangerous and delicate out in plain sight. He bites down on his lower lip and glares through the filming tears.

The lab has ten freezer compartments for whole cadavers. Seven of them are full, the remaining three empty. Greaves unlocks and opens cabinet number ten, the one that in the normal run of things is least likely to be used. The one where he has been hiding his stealth suit all this time.

He takes the boy's body from his kit bag. It is incredibly light, incredibly small; folded in on itself like a hedgehog or a woodlouse. Greaves puts it directly into the cabinet, which now hides it from any crew member glancing casually into the lab.

Greaves is at war with himself. He is lying by his actions,

172

without saying a word. But what else can he do? Before Invercrae, he could have told them what he had seen, what he suspected. He can't – he really doesn't think he can – say to them, now, *I swapped Private Lutes for this. I'm sorry I didn't warn you, I'm sorry I didn't tell anyone what I was doing, but I got all I needed so on balance it worked out well.*

They already hate him. Despise him, at any rate. Dr Fournier will never allow him into the lab again, and nobody will ever speak to him, and the mission will fail and Beacon will fall and it will all be his fault.

The bag has to be hidden, too. Its bottom is caked with blood and brain tissue. The seams are holding the liquescent mass, just about, but dark stains are showing on the bag's surface. Greaves stows it at the bottom end of the cabinet, below the feet of the small cadaver and alongside the stealth suit. There is plenty of room there, since the space was designed with the body of an adult hungry in mind.

He has to work. He has to find something. And then, when he has found it he can tell them. It has to be that way round.

Contamination of the specimen is going to be extreme and complex, but Greaves can't think of any way to prevent it. The exposed tissue in the head wound is crusted with dust and grit from the road surface and unidentifiable particulate matter from his bag. To remove it all would take hours of work with the autopsy table fully extended, taking up half the total lab space, and the body laid out in full view.

It can't be done, so there is no sense in worrying about it.

The volume of the voices behind him has reached a new peak. Dr Sealey and Dr Akimwe are shouting at Dr Fournier, which is troubling but also opportune. For the moment, he is unlikely to be observed.

173

He exposes the skull on the side that has not already been laid open by the bullet. This will provide the cleanest sample he can get. He selects a three-millimetre bit and screws it into the high-speed drill. Setting the extractor fan on maximum to mask the noise of the drill, he quickly and crudely punches his way through the skull into the cranial vault. The smell of burned bone almost chokes him. The fan can't take it all away in time, so he will just have to be quick.

Be done before they realise. Before they ask.

He retracts the drill, unscrews the bloody, clogged drill bit and drops it into the freezer cabinet. There is no time to clean and disinfect it, and he doesn't want to explain what he has used it for. Selecting the widest of the biopsy needles, he slides it into the excavated space and takes his sample.

Just as Dr Khan – Rina – steps into the lab and comes up behind him.

He can tell her by her tread, although right now it is heavier than usual (because of the baby) and more uneven (no hypothesis as yet). Greaves doesn't turn to face her. Reaching up to switch off the fan, he slides the freezer cabinet shut with his knee. He hopes that Rina won't track the movement with her gaze.

Now he turns. 'Wow,' Khan says, wincing. She waves her hand in front of her face with exaggerated disgust. 'Who burned the toast?'

It's a joke, not a real question, so he is not meant to answer it. But still, the pressure builds. Greaves casts around for something he can use to fend it off. Rina does not look well. Her eyes are shiny with unshed tears and her posture is rigid. These are signs he has learned to interpret, at least up to a point. 'Why are you upset?' he asks her. 'What's happened?'

Rina shakes her head. She touches his forearm for a moment – one fingertip, their agreed and minimalistic hug – then takes a step back to compensate for the dangerous intimacy. 'I'm fine,' she says. 'It's fine. Dr Fournier has decided to cut the mission short. We're going home, a little earlier than expected.'

'Home?' Greaves is confused, and then alarmed. 'But we haven't made all the stops on the schedule. There are still two more samplings before we—'

Rina is nodding. 'I know, I know. But if there are junkers up here, it changes everything. It's just not safe to keep going when we don't know what's in front of us. And it's not as though we're finding anything different. Anything we can actually use.'

Greaves swallows hard. 'What if we were?' he asks. There is a tremor in his voice.

But Rina doesn't seem to notice it. She shrugs, almost dismissively. 'Well even then, I think I'd vote for going home.'

'But the mission . . .' Greaves protests again.

Rina laughs, but the laugh has a catch in it. 'The mission needs some fresh thinking,' she says. 'And I need to get back home and have this baby. I wish it hadn't happened like this, but I'm still glad to be going back. It just feels terrible to be relieved about something that's so . . .' A vague motion of her restless hands picks up where the words leave off.

Greaves interprets: she is happy on her own account, but unhappy because Private Lutes is dead. The disparity between these two emotions makes her uneasy. He is amazed to find his own experience – the mingled guilt and excitement he feels – reflected in hers. It doesn't happen to him often.

He wants to explore the similarities, but he is afraid to.

He is still holding the biopsy needle close against his side. The longer the conversation goes on, the more chance there is that Rina will see it and ask him about it. Or else that she will want to know what he was doing off by himself in Invercrae.

As though his thought has triggered hers, Rina looks over her shoulder into the crew quarters. 'They're not very happy with you,' she tells him. It's not entirely clear who she means. The crew quarters have emptied out. The soldiers have gone outside, most probably to replace the motion sensors and perimeter traps now that Rosie is stationary again. The colonel has gone up front and Dr Fournier has contrived to disappear too, leaving only Akimwe, Sealey and Penny. Despite this, Greaves decides that Rina's words must apply to all the crew, irrespective of uniform.

He wants to say he's sorry, but that will invite further discussion. He says, instead, 'I won't do it again.' It's a reckless promise, but the future tense pulls them both away from the dangerous waters of the recent past.

Almost.

'You can't, Stephen,' Rina tells him gently. 'Not any more. You're not responsible for what happened back there, but if there's a junker cadre somewhere close by then we're in real danger. You know it was probably junkers who got Charlie.'

'We don't know that,' Greaves points out. But he's being pedantic. The commander of the Charles Darwin talked in her last transmission to Beacon of being pursued by a large group of junkers riding battle-trucks to which hungries had been harnessed like oxen. She said she would avoid engaging as long as she could, but would fight back if attacked. Her last words were, 'They're flanking us.'

'They're really dangerous,' Rina insists. 'People think of them as savages because they choose to live out in the wild rather than in Beacon. But they live by scavenging and they're really good at it. They have to be, or they wouldn't have lasted this long. They look at Rosie and they see guns, ammunition, equipment, food. All kinds of things they need. We're worth a lot of effort, in their eyes.'

Greaves nods cautiously. He is agreeing with the explicit meaning of her words (the junkers are a serious threat) rather than with their secondary implication (there are junkers here). It's not a lie, because he hasn't opened his mouth, but once again he is allowing someone to believe a thing that isn't true. His mind itches and an iron bar of tension presses against his shoulders.

But Rina seems satisfied with his reaction. Possibly she mistakes his tension for a salutary fear. 'So when Dr Fournier decided to turn us around,' she continues, 'he was doing the only thing he could do. We'd have to be crazy to carry on all the way to the coast, with the junkers behind us.'

She is looking at Greaves expectantly. He nods again. 'Yes,' he says. But this time he is compelled to add, 'If there were junkers here, that would be bad.'

'So we're doing the right thing. Everybody thinks so. Everybody agreed with the decision.'

Greaves glances into the crew quarters again. He finds it very hard to parse emotion, but the cues he has learned to associate with celebration are notably absent. Dr Akimwe is sitting in silence at the table, his chin resting on his fist, his eyes wide but unfocused. Dr Penny rubs her pursed lips with the knuckle of her thumb. Dr Sealey talks to them both in low tones, striking matches from the box above the kitchen unit and letting them burn down in his hand before dropping them, one by one, into the sink.

These are not the behaviours Greaves would expect to see if everyone is really comfortable with Dr Fournier's decision. But then, agreeing with something is a cognitive rather than an emotional response. Rina has already told him what the dominant mood is.

They're not very happy with you.

Greaves can't make this right. Private Lutes is dead. The mission is over. There is nothing that he could put on the opposite scale that would be big enough to balance these huge, remorseless facts.

Nothing except a new and radically important discovery. A cure.

A cure for the hungry plague.

Rina tries to temper what she has already said, to spare him further pain. 'Stephen,' she tells him, 'they're mostly unhappy because the mission is a washout. Today was bad, but even without today . . . We weren't getting anywhere. You know that. The whole point of the sampling runs was to find an inhibiting agent. Something that makes *Cordyceps* grow more slowly, or stops it from growing altogether. But we haven't managed to do that because there isn't one. We're going home empty-handed. That's what hurts.'

She leaves him to it. She has done what touch can do, and what words can do. The only other variable is time.

Greaves watches her rejoin Dr Sealey and the others. The weight and import of the moment make her forget herself enough to reach out and take Dr Sealey's hand. They look into each other's eyes, enjoying some wordless communion. Greaves would find that combined touch and gaze unbearable, but he knows that for lovers, meaning people who share physical intimacy, such things are an important means of overcoming the isolation of monadic consciousness. Or seeming to.

We're going home empty-handed. He replays the words in his mind, three times over. It was true yesterday, but it's not true now.

The contents of freezer cabinet ten.

The slender cylinder of cortical tissue in the biopsy needle.

He can still make this right.

23

Dr Fournier is afraid that he may have overreached his authority.

In the engine room, with the door closed and locked, he tries once again to raise Brigadier Fry on his secret radio, which despite its tiny size has always out-performed the main cockpit radio in terms of reach and signal strength. But yet again the brigadier fails to pick up.

Fournier wishes very fervently that he had been able to ask her *before* he gave the order to turn around.

It wasn't fear. He didn't do it because he was afraid, although he is. Afraid of dying, and even more afraid of not dying – of being bitten and left abandoned up here in the north while Rosie rolls home; a living but *Cordyceps*-ridden scarecrow standing out in a field for ever while the seasons wheel and turn.

But it was anger, in the end, that pushed him over the

precipice of decision. He is going to be judged on what the expedition has achieved, and he will be judged harshly because they have achieved nothing. They left Beacon to cheers and fanfares, bottles of bootleg liquor smashed across their bows. The twelve of them in their tin can, carrying the blessings of the million and a half they were meant to save. Now they will sneak home through the back door and be forgotten. Suddenly, seeing that shame and blame vividly in his head, he found in himself an unexpected eagerness to face it full on and answer it. *You could have done no better. Nobody could have done better. We didn't find an answer because there isn't one!*

And perhaps there was a part of him that was thinking: Lutes is probably only the first. He's proved that it's eminently possible for us to die out here. And after the proof, you can expect to find more and more instances that support it.

Perhaps, yes. But it doesn't really matter now.

He found his voice. He found his authority. He made his decision and he carried it. This – squatting over the radio, teasing its tiny frequency controls with cold and clumsy fingers, waiting once again to be put in his place – is the price he has to pay for that.

After three failed attempts to raise the brigadier, he decides to wait a while. Rosie is stationary, of course, so there is no chance of moving into an area with better reception, but the fall of night sometimes sharpens the signal all by itself.

This digging in was at Carlisle's insistence, and Fournier didn't argue. For Rosie to move at night is a hazardous proceeding. Most of the roads are blocked with rusting cars, the poignant remains of a ten-year-old exodus. The going is hard, even with full visibility. The colonel has decreed that

181

they will bivouac for the night and move out in the morning.

It seems to be so easy for the colonel to constitute himself as an authority when other authorities fail. For Fournier it's very hard. His natural mode is submission.

His relationship with Brigadier Fry fits very well into this pattern, and always has since the first time he ever met her. It was before his status as civilian commander was officially confirmed. He had been interviewed by three representatives of the Main Table and he felt he had done well, portraying himself as a safe pair of hands, a man who would stick to his orders no matter what. But then the brigadier, as senior officer in the Military Muster, asserted a right to interview him too. After some toing and froing, she won her point.

In her command tent between the second and third of Beacon's seven perimeter fences, she welcomed him without using his name and poured him a whiskey without asking him whether he drank. She had some questions about his relevant experience, both as a scientist and as a team leader, but they were generic enough that they didn't even prove she had read his file. She seemed a lot more interested in talking about Colonel Carlisle. 'The colonel is an important man, and he's going to be away from Beacon and the Main Table for a long time. He'll be missed here.'

Fournier had no opinion about this, but he nodded emphatically. 'Oh yes. I'm sure of it. The mission will be lucky to have him.'

That seemed to him to be the answer that was required, but the brigadier didn't appear overly enthused by it. 'I would like to think,' she went on with cold and careful emphasis, 'that the civilian and military commanders will form a mutually supportive team. Watching each other's backs, as it were.

Assessing each other's competence, even, and stepping in as necessary to provide whatever assistance or corrective might be needed.'

This time Fournier said nothing, but only nodded. A safer bet all round.

'We here in Beacon – in the Muster, I mean – are quite keen to keep track of the colonel while he's outside the fence. Not just where he is, but what he's thinking and feeling. We're concerned for his well-being.'

Dr Fournier chewed this over for a few tense seconds. Would another nod be enough of a response? He was pretty sure that it wouldn't.

'May I be frank?' he asked, too late to keep the pause from becoming noticeable.

'By all means.'

'Are you asking me to spy on the colonel?'

Fry breathed in and out, audibly. Not quite a sigh, but most of the way along. 'Morale here in Beacon is volatile at the moment,' she said, which seemed to Fournier to be no answer at all. 'The Muster works at the behest of civilian authorities who often don't entirely understand our workings, or share our priorities. Hence the double command for this mission, and hence our being allowed to vet you, even though your role – if you were accepted – would be civilian commander.'

'I understand that,' Fournier said.

'I'm glad. The candidate we interviewed before you – and if I may return your frankness, the preferred candidate for the position – didn't. She seemed determined to misunderstand us, and to define her role entirely in terms of the mission's scientific objectives. We felt that this was too narrow a point of view. That to ignore the political dimensions of what's happening here was obtuse.'

Fournier tried to hold back, but couldn't. The feminine pronoun was a deliberate tease, dangled in front of him to see whether he had enough self-control to keep from guessing. He didn't.

'Caroline Caldwell? Caroline Caldwell was your first choice for this?'

Fry affected to be surprised at the question. 'I said she was the preferred candidate overall, Doctor. I didn't say she was *my* choice. In fact, I would much rather have someone in post whom I could rely on to see, and serve, the bigger picture. Science and politics are not two worlds; they're two hemispheres.'

Fournier, who had never seen himself as a politician but now at least had an inkling of the job description, agreed. Two hemispheres, yes. Very aptly put. Very insightful.

Caroline Caldwell in the Rosalind Franklin, and him left behind in Beacon polishing other people's test tubes, other people's reputations? No no no. This was the future, if there was to be one. The forge on which the future would be made. He knew very well that he was a competent researcher rather than a great one, but still. He couldn't choose irrelevance when greatness was on the table. Surely nobody could.

With the stakes clearly established, he continued to agree with every proposition the brigadier put to him.

Fry suggested that he might need to form a judgement on the robustness of his staff. Their morale. The clarity of their motives. He said he was good for that.

She demonstrated the operation of the radio, emphasising

184

that its existence must remain a secret. He promised her that he would be the soul of discretion.

She indicated that the Muster might wish to give him additional orders in the course of the mission, depending on how certain events in Beacon itself fell out, or failed to fall out. He said that he would not object to that.

When he left her office, he was brimming with self-disgust, his stomach sloshing and griping with it. He wanted to be sick.

But by the time he got back to the lab, he was already feeling much calmer. Compromise wasn't a swearword and expediency wasn't a sin, especially not when it came to the big turning points in your life. The world was going to be saved. Rosie was the surgical instrument and humanity was the patient. Who in their right mind would choose to lie down on the slab when they could be the one holding the scalpel?

Now, seven months on, he feels that the scalpel is at his throat. The mission was already a shambles, even before the death of Private Lutes. In despair of finding anything of value, wearied to death with this confinement and cowed by two strained, awful weeks of inexplicable radio silence, he jumped at the chance to turn the car around and head for home.

Brigadier Fry's last words to him: 'You may be tempted at some point to renege on our agreement, Dr Fournier. With everyone calling you commander, it would be easy to fall into the trap of actually trying to command. But that's really not what you're there for. As far as your scientific expertise goes, I won't presume to advise or direct you.

'But everything else is mine.'

24

McQueen sits up in the turret while the sun sets and the stars come out.

In his mind, he identifies and names the constellations he can see. The Dragon. The Little Bear. Cepheus. Mostly he learned them for their use in orienteering, but he is struck too by the beauty and profligacy of their display. The daytime burns with a single fire, and a lot of the time it burns fitfully. The night is a million suns exploding all at once, igniting the whole sky. With no man-made lights to dim them, they have reclaimed the glory, the pre-eminence they had back in the dawn age when humans lived in caves. Even through the distorting curve of the turret glass, they make McQueen feel as though he is about to fall off the tilted world into the immensity beyond.

No hungries in that infinite light-show. No junkers. No lies or bullshit. The world ended more than a decade ago, but the news hasn't made it out there yet and it won't make any difference when it does. Perfect truth is black and white and it doesn't know our names.

McQueen is wrestling with his pride and with his definition of himself. He isn't enjoying it, but he doesn't shrink from it either. It's absolutely necessary to know who you are, as the basis for knowing anything else.

Cutting loose with the flamethrower felt necessary and obvious at the time, as though it was just the part of the equation that comes after the equals sign. He didn't think about wind speed or their own displacement as they moved. He just thought about the response that needed to be made to that dead man on the ground, hacked to the bone like meat on a slab.

In other words, he lost control. Carlisle called the play, and he called it right. You don't do a broad sweep with a flamethrower from a moving vehicle unless you want to fry yourself and everyone who's riding with you.

There are only two ways you can go from that realisation. You can make up stupid stories about how you were actually right all along because X and Y and Z and all the rest of it. Or you can admit you screwed up and try to be better.

McQueen climbs down from the turret. His limbs are heavy and he feels tired to death. It seems appropriate that emotions should have recoil in the same way guns do, because after all they're just as dangerous. But that doesn't make it any more pleasant to endure.

To get to the cockpit, he has to walk through the crew quarters. There is a mixed bag of soldiers and whitecoats in there and they all look up when he comes.

Foss is the first to react. She stands up quickly and rips off

187

a salute. As a signal it's pretty unambiguous. Phillips is right behind her, Sixsmith a little slower but inside of a couple of seconds the three of them are standing there, defying regulations and telling him he's still ranking officer here.

'You have got to be fucking kidding me!' Dr Khan exclaims, appalled.

McQueen enjoys that part, at least. But he needs to nip this little revolution in the bud.

He returns Foss's salute, crisply and punctiliously. 'A little confused, aren't we, Lieutenant?' he says. 'Never mind. It will sink in eventually.'

He walks on, leaving silence in his wake.

The cockpit door is open. He goes in and closes it behind him. Carlisle sets his book aside and nods towards the shotgun seat. McQueen stays on his feet, even though he has to stoop a little because of the low ceiling.

'Permission to speak, sir,' he says.

The colonel shrugs mildly. 'Of course,' he says.

McQueen doesn't beat about the bush. There is no point. 'You were right about the flamethrower,' he says. 'I used it without authorisation and without due care, as you pointed out. In doing so, I risked the safety of the crew and the vehicle. I deserve a reprimand for that, and I accept it. But I'd like you to restore my access to the turret guns. We're in a bad place and with junkers in the mix it could easily get worse. You may need me, and I can't do much if I'm not allowed to touch the silverware.'

Carlisle is silent for a moment or two. McQueen waits for the verdict, wanting this to be over.

'Will you sit down, Private McQueen?' the colonel asks him.

'No offence, sir,' McQueen says, 'but I didn't come here to kick back and talk about old times. I just need a yes or a no.'

'Then it's no.'

The colonel's tone is flat, emotionless. McQueen feels that recoil again, this time in the form of a cold fizz of static through his nerves. He thinks he must have misheard. Considering the magnitude of the climb-down he has just made, the Fireman's answer makes no sense.

'Sir, I don't think one error of judgement—'

'Mr McQueen.' The colonel drops the words like a baulk of timber, cuts him off dead. 'If the flamethrower were the only issue, I would agree with you. But it's not.'

The colonel stands, wincing as he momentarily shifts some of his weight onto his injured leg. Clearly it's important to him that they be on the same level for this, one way or the other. 'Your whole attitude,' he says heavily, carefully, like a doctor delivering a terminal diagnosis, 'is at odds with military discipline and the outlook required of a soldier. To serve in an army, in a militia of any kind, is to subordinate your own wishes and instincts to the orders of your commander. A soldier may have his doubts, but he does what he is ordered to do. Whereas you, Mr McQueen, seem to regard orders of any kind as an insult to your professionalism.'

McQueen can't believe he's hearing this, or who he's hearing it from. And maybe he should keep his mouth shut until the sermon is over, but there are serious arguments to be made and he already has permission to speak. 'I know all about following orders, sir,' he says. 'I also know where it can lead to.'

'Thank you,' Carlisle says gravely. 'That is exactly the point I'm trying to make. It seems to me that you obey where it's absolutely required, but that you do so in a spirit of reluctant compromise. Knowing that your own instincts are more reliable and that you could achieve more if you were left to your own devices.'

'That's not true,' McQueen says.

'Really? Standing orders dictate—'

'Shit, I already admitted I got it wrong! Once! I got it wrong once!'

They're matching point-blank stares, practically stepping on each other's toes. The cockpit's narrow confines are pushing them towards confrontation whether they want it or not. 'Standing orders,' Carlisle repeats heavily, 'dictate that if the situation on the ground materially changes, you notify your commanding officer.'

'I did that.'

'When you found Lutes' body, yes. You should have done it the moment you saw the dead dogs.'

'I made a judgement call.'

'Of course.' The colonel nods. 'You always do, Mr McQueen. One judgement call after another. Most of them have been good, I have to admit. But it was only a matter of time.'

'Why?' McQueen demands, contempt thickening his voice. 'Because your judgement is so much better than mine?'

'No,' the colonel says, with the same infuriating calm. 'Because armies work by simple algorithms. Procedure, however point-less it seems, is there to lessen the chance of error. It filters all the decisions you make through a bed of cross-checks and failsafes. But only if you use it. You could be a fine soldier, Mr McQueen, if only you weren't in an army of one.'

McQueen shakes his head, bitter but also – now that the

190

first rush of anger and surprise has passed – coldly amused. This has a symmetry to it. Carlisle is describing him exactly as he sees himself, but upside down so that all his virtues are vices, and presumably all the colonel's own failings are strengths.

'I have to ask,' he says. 'Were you following the algorithms when you bombed Cambridge and Stansted? When you did the burn runs, and fried all those people in their beds? Did that decision filter through okay?'

Carlisle's mouth tugs down as though he's got a hook in his lower lip. That one hurt. 'Yes,' he says, 'and no, respectively. I did what I could within the system to stop the burn runs from happening. But it didn't work. The wrong decision was made. I offer no excuses for that.'

'No,' McQueen agrees, his face inches from the other man's. 'And you got no reprimands for it, either, did you? I put a dozen men and women in danger but they all lived. You killed thousands and walked away with a medal.'

'You're mistaken. Nobody gave me a medal.'

'I'm sure they'll get around to it, sir. Just a matter of time, if you don't mind me saying.'

The colonel is silent for a moment or two. 'Is there anything else?' he asks at last.

'Only what I already said. I've got more experience with the field pounder than anyone. The flamethrower too. Let me do my job.'

'If I thought you could do your job, we wouldn't be having this conversation.'

Words are bubbling up in McQueen's throat. Saying them won't do any good. He leaves the way he came, runs the same gauntlet of resentment and solidarity. He has no use for either, but in Rosie there's only ever one route from A to B.

25

Sunrise finds the crew up and at it. Kat Foss, as ranking officer (and how crazy is that?), leads the charge.

Not that there's much need for leadership, as far as she can see. Everyone does what has to be done without being told. The motion sensors and immobiliser traps were a sacred mystery once, but seven months have made their operation tediously familiar. So the whitecoats dismantle the perimeter while Foss leads a detail down to the loch with the ten-gallon water drums. Rosie has integral tanks that fill with rainwater run-off, but Colonel Carlisle is a belt-and-braces man.

When they get back from the loch, the roles rotate. The whitecoats add purification tablets to the water drums and stow them in the galley; Foss puts the soldiers on to the maintenance allocation checks. The MAC routine is prescribed by Rosie's operational manual, which Foss keeps in her hand the whole time and cribs from about ten times a minute. There's a long and exhaustive list of checks covering the treads, the engine and the environmental controls. Some of them are just diagnostic; others involve getting down and dirty with oilcans, spanners and wrenches. Lutes knew the book by heart, and gave everyone else the reassurance of a safety net – a better pair of eyes verifying everything they did. Lutes being unavoidably dead, Foss does the best she can. She stands over Phillips and Sixsmith the whole time, watching them with a nervous, critical eye. Then when they're done, she makes them go through the entire list again, out of a general sense that cock-ups are hovering over them and waiting to descend.

They're going home. Not a one of them quite believes that yet, and not a one of them wants to jinx it.

But in spite of Foss's slightly obsessive thoroughness, it's still early when they leave. Colonel Carlisle surrenders the driving seat to Sixsmith, its rightful occupant, but remains in the cab so he can use its comms rig to talk to everyone in the main crew space. Foss takes the mid-section look-out and gives Phillips the turret. She is still hesitant about giving orders to McQueen.

Everyone apart from the look-outs straps in and waits for take-off. They won't stay strapped in, of course. Rosie's top speed is twenty miles per hour on a good road, but there are no good roads left. She picks her way slowly along Britain's rutted, sclerotic arteries, and drops to an 8 mph average when she leaves the tarmac for the scenic route. Most day-to-day activities, whether work or leisure, aren't inhibited by her easy trundling. But this is turn-around, a day they have been anticipating for a long time. Soldiers and whitecoats alike are showing a due respect.

In fact, the scientists seem downright sombre. Foss can see where they're coming from, too. More than half a year on the road and nothing to show for it. For all the good they got out of those endless shoot-em-ups and cut-em-ups, they might just as well have been picking blackberries. Better off, in fact. Fresh fruit is hard currency in Beacon.

If Beacon is still there. But it must be. Nothing would have torn the whole camp down so completely that they couldn't even squeeze a word out. So the lack of comms must be a technical hitch. That's all it can be.

So personally she's in a pretty buoyant mood. The image of Lutes' body almost cut up into pieces is still vivid in her mind – much more vivid than any particular memories of him alive – but the fact that they're heading home early is the best news she has had since they set out.

And going back with a field commission would be the icing on the cake if she didn't feel so bad for (it's just force of habit, but she can't break it) the lieutenant. McQueen only did what the rest of them were thinking of doing, so where's the sense in pretending he's the one to blame? When he put his hands on the guns and the turret turned and the fire spewed out, Foss felt almost like it was happening because she was willing it to. If anything, she wishes she'd got there first. Now, vicariously, she feels herself slapped down by McQueen's punishment. She doesn't believe she's alone in that.

Damn if she isn't sliding into the same grim mood as the whitecoats. She drags herself out of it again by thinking about what she'll do when she gets home. First, go to the Twenty-Seven Pavilion and get wasted. Then take a tumble or two with some guy blessed with a respectably sized dick and a sense of direction (there are exactly two men on board Rosie who she was ever sexually interested in, Phillips and Akimwe, and – story of her life – they only have eyes for each other).

194

Finally, go home and wave her lieutenant pips in her father's face – *How do you like that sleeve-candy, quartermaster sergeant?* That's a recipe for a good day right there, and now that they're heading south again it can't be more than a few days away.

Rosie's frame shudders as the engine comes awake. The throbbing climbs and peaks. Sixsmith is dropping down through the gears for a start that will lift them up out of the footprint made by their own massive weight: she knows Rosie better than anyone, now Lutes is dead. They rock back and forth a little as she makes herself some room to manoeuvre, then with a huge lurch and a basso fart of hydraulics they're underway.

That counts as a smooth take-off, and it gets a fair bit smoother as soon as they're moving. There's a scatter of applause from the crew quarters.

'Too kind,' says Sixsmith on the intracom. 'Your steward-esses will be passing down the aisles shortly serving drinks and recreational drugs.'

There's a click and the colonel's voice takes over. 'Mid-section,' he says tersely, 'report in.'

'We're good here,' Foss answers.

Phillips begs to differ. 'Sir,' he says, from up in the turret, 'I'm seeing movement.'

Shit! What has she missed? Foss puts her fantasies of home sweet home aside for later and takes a look through the tell-tale in the mid-section door, which she should have done before she opened her mouth. She sees nothing but tall trees and weed-choked fields, blurred into green soup by their motion.

'Port or starboard?' she demands.

'Your side. Five o'clock.'

195

'I'm not getting anything, Colonel.'

'Ten o'clock, too,' Phillips says, tense as hell. 'We've definitely got company.'

Foss looks again. Still just landscape in her field of vision. Nothing moving that shouldn't be.

'Phillips, tell me what you're seeing,' the colonel orders.

'I can't, sir. Sorry. It's just glimpses here and there, among the trees. I'm not getting a clear line on it.'

'Rabbits?' Foss guesses. 'Foxes?' Not great suggestions, either of them. There just isn't a whole lot of wildlife about these days. Anything with a pulse is fair game for the hungries. They prefer warm blood but they'll take what they can get.

There's a long, strained silence, then Phillips swears.

'Gone?' the colonel asks.

'I don't know, sir. I keep thinking I'm seeing something, but they're way low down.'

Which implies animal rather than human. Junkers might crawl to stay under the cover of the weeds, but they couldn't do that and keep pace with a moving tank.

'Still nothing here,' Foss says. She's looking a lot harder now. She trusts her own eyes, but from upstairs Phillips has two metres of height on her position and he doesn't panic easily.

Neither does the colonel, but as previously noted he likes to go belt and braces. 'Sixsmith, give us some legs. Phillips, see if there are any blips in the infra-red.'

'Nothing, sir,' Phillips reports in due course. Foss can hear the relief in his voice, and she shares it. Junkers would show as hot spots in the infra-red, as would live animals of any kind. So it's just hungries, most likely, drawn by the sound of the engines as they started off. There are only so many layers of baffle you can add to an engine cowling and still move.

196

Hungries *can* outrun Rosie, but only in the short term. It shouldn't be long before they've got the road to themselves again.

'All good?' the colonel demands.

This time Foss and Phillips agree that it is. The phantom blips are forgiven and forgotten.

Rosie's going home.

26

As soon as they're underway, Greaves springs his seat strap and retreats from the crew quarters into the lab. He hopes he might get a little time to himself there, since working when they're on the move isn't a popular option. It's too hard to compensate for the rocking of Rosie's chassis. A few shattered test tubes and ruined samples were enough to wean most of the science team off the habit.

But not today. He is followed almost immediately by Rina. He's afraid for a moment that she will offer to help him, but it seems she's got a project of her own to pursue. She flashes him a smile as she moves past him towards the further workbench. It's a weak smile. Greaves assigns it meaning *c* (*you are my friend*) on a list that goes all the way to *n* (*I'm thinking of something that you wouldn't understand*).

'Getting harder and harder to work around me, isn't it?'

Rina asks, patting her protuberant belly. 'Don't let me get in your way, Stephen.'

He considers telling her that there is still more than a foot of clearance on either side of the central walkway if she stands in its centre. But he is almost certain (from her smile, which has now transitioned into a *d*) that she intends the comment as a joke. He offers a smile in return, usually the safest option, and goes back to his work.

From the crew quarters come the voices of Sealey and Akimwe. They are discussing *Cordyceps*, the great adversary – its cultural and historical significance, with special reference to Chinese folk legends about its life cycle. Greaves is well aware that the Chinese, almost three thousand years ago, saw the fungus sprouting from the exploded bodies of caterpillars and thought they had chanced upon a magical metamorphosis. A creature that was an animal in summer and a mushroom in winter! They prized *Cordyceps* as a treatment for heart disease and impotence, the distilled essence of life itself. Later generations found that the fungus could grow through damaged nerve tissue and partially repair it. There's a prevailing theory that these medicinal uses of the fungus were the precursors to the hungry plague – the doorway through which *Cordyceps* infected human populations.

Tuning out the voices, Greaves prepares the tissue collected by the biopsy needle for examination. He uses the ATLUM, a machine perfected at Harvard's Centre for Brain Science in the years immediately preceding the Breakdown. It's a microtome, a lathe for slicing neural tissue into ultra-fine sections of a single cell's thickness. The ATLUM mounts the sections onto a continuous ribbon of tape rather than onto conventional slides. It therefore allows the user – at least, the user with a scanning electron microscope ready to hand – to build up a three-dimensional view of brain structures and to follow them down through successive strata of tissue. Greaves finds the operation of the ATLUM utterly enthralling. It peels tissue samples the way you might peel an apple with your pocket knife, then rebuilds them into an apple again.

When he mounts and examines his sample, though, he is confused.

The children have already demonstrated that they are not at all like other hungries. Their behavioural repertoire is vast, perhaps as large as that of regular humans, so he expects to see little or no fungal penetration of the brain tissue. Instead he finds himself staring at a dense mat of fungal mycelia. The brain is one vast spider web of threads, woven about and through the regular neurons all the way from the outer cortex to the thalamus and transverse fissure. By volume, this brain is half human and half fungus.

But where is the damage? The human cerebral matter ought to have been hollowed out, devoured by the fungal invader. There ought to be a 55–80 per cent reduction in actual brain mass and a visible degeneration of whatever tissue still remains. A crust of microglial cells overlaying the damaged cortical areas. Myelin sheaths stripped away leaving bare neurons firing fitfully and futilely into synaptic gaps that have become mud wallows of necrotic juices. None of that is present. If this brain has been invaded, it is mounting a robust defence.

Or is this a moment rather than a state? Just a brief equilibrium before the cerebral tissue surrenders and the fungus carries the day? But in that case, how has the brain held out for so long, surrounded and besieged? There is some factor at work that he has never seen before, and the implications are immense. Almost dizzying.

Greaves raises his head from the eyepiece and looks around furtively. He feels for a moment as though the beating of his heart, the tremor in his breathing must have been noticed, but Rina isn't looking at him at all. She is focused on her own work, her preoccupied calm contrasting with his own sudden burst of excitement and near-panic.

He goes back in. This time he abandons the microscope for a while, draws off another tissue sample and begins a series of tests for the presence of the major neurotransmitters – the chemicals that turn the brain from a lump of inert flesh into the world's biggest communications hub. There are well over a hundred of these chemical couriers, but Greaves limits himself for the moment to a sample of about thirty: the ones that show up quickly in the presence of off-the-shelf reagents.

Half of the chemical transmitters are present in the same strengths and proportions as a normal human brain. The rest aren't there at all.

Which is impossible.

He knows how *Cordyceps* is meant to work – how it works in every hungry studied so far. Seconds after primary infection, it floods the human host's bloodstream where it proliferates with breathtaking speed. Carried through the blood-brain barrier, it lodges in the brain stem and launches a pre-emptive strike, deactivating normal neural functioning by destructive super-stimulation of the nerve cells. It burns the brain out.

Then it grows downwards again, into and through the spine, extending its mycelial system along the host body's major afferent nerve trunks. With the brain out of the conversation, apart from a few powerful, instinctive behaviours controlled through the pons and medulla, the fungus is free to hijack the peripheral nervous system and use it to take direct control of the host's motor functions.

So in a heavily infected brain, native neurotransmitter activity should be minimal to non-existent. There may still be a consciousness in there – the experts at Beacon have argued it back and forth without reaching a conclusion – but either way it doesn't matter. The strings have been cut.

This brain is different. Structurally it's intact and chemically it's halfway functional: but what good is half a brain? You can't drive a car if it has a carburettor but no spark plug, cylinders but no pistons. It's not as though half a brain could run half the body's systems. Your limbs can't be made to move without dopamine or acetylcholine. You can't have a proper sleep cycle without adenosine, or hunger and satiety reflexes without noradrenaline. So the fungus must still be running the show, surely, however healthy the brain tissue looks in cross-section.

But Greaves has seen how these children behave. Aside from the hunger, they remind him of real people.

Turn the question on its head. If this child, when he was alive, had a partial immunity to some of the hungry pathogen's effects, then what was the mechanism? There is nothing unusual in the cellular structures Greaves is seeing, except that they are still pristine, still viable, when they should be bombed-out shells.

He ponders. Form follows function, but it also dictates function. There is a reason why the hungries are called that, after all. Obviously the hunger reflex is the first thing that

Cordyceps hijacks. More than anything else it needs its hosts to eat, carrying the infection with every bite. He saw the little girl go after that pigeon, and he saw her tribe feeding on dog-flesh in the streets of Invercrae. The children have that instinct, that drive, just as strongly as the regular hungries have it, however different they may be in other ways.

So what is happening here? Is this just a refinement of the pathogen's normal onset and progression, or is it something completely new?

He needs to look at spinal tissue to see what *Cordyceps* is doing down there. But he can't take a fresh biopsy with Rina in the lab, working right beside him.

Reluctantly, he dismounts his slides and samples and stows them in his personal area where they won't be touched. Rina hasn't looked up once in all this time. What she is doing shouldn't be that absorbing, though. It's a fairly basic mechanical procedure. She is neutralising sulphuric acid with magnesium carbonate, which is a quick and easy way to produce . . .

Oh.

Dr Khan looks up at last and meets his stare. The guarded blankness of it confirms his guess.

Greaves has had to learn people the hard way, but chemistry is easy. He knows magnesium sulphate very well indeed: its molecular profile, its chemical properties and its bio-regulatory effect. Dr Khan almost certainly intends to take it as a toco-lytic, to suppress contractions in her birth canal. The baby is coming, or at least announcing its intentions.

'What?' she asks, not realising that her cover is blown.

Greaves has no idea what an adequate response might be from the point of view of emotion and its abstruse architecture. But again, he is confident about the chemistry.

'Nifedipine, Rina,' he tells her. 'Nifedipine would be better, if you want to delay the birth. We've got some in the med cabinet, for hypertensive trauma.'

Rina looks stunned. She puts down the retort she's been holding all this time, leans away from it a little as though she wants to disavow all knowledge. After a moment she laughs, and shakes her head. 'Amazing, Holmes,' she says.

'What? Who is Holmes? Why is he amazing?'

'Never mind. Don't say a word to anyone, Stephen. I don't want to slow us down or make this stupid situation any worse than it is. Don't say anything. Please?'

Greaves nods. He may not be able to lie, but he is a hundred per cent sure that nobody is going to ask him this particular question. And if anyone asks the more general question 'Is something wrong with Dr Khan?' he can probably keep from giving away the secret by saying she is taking medicine commonly prescribed for stress. So he is confident that he can keep his word.

He wishes he could defuse his discovery of her intentions by confiding in her about his own immense project. But this is not the time.

Soon. When he has findings rather than suppositions. When he has more to show her than a dead child.

A dead child, he strongly suspects, will only add to her troubles right now.

27

Dr Fournier is still trying to coax a response out of the radio but he has long since resigned himself to failure. He's only doing it now because he can think of nothing else to do that's of any value. So when the voice of Brigadier Fry's adjutant, Mullings, oozes weakly out of the radio in a viscous froth of static, he starts so violently that he cracks his right elbow on the engine cowling.

'Beacon. Please identify.'

'Get the brigadier,' the doctor snarls, doubled up around his injured arm. 'It's Fournier. Field report. Urgency one.'

'She's conferring with her chiefs of staff, Dr Fournier. You'll have to—'

Another voice murmurs in the background. Fournier can't hear the words, but Mullings' robust 'Yes, Brigadier!' is loud enough to make him clap his hand over the radio's speaker and whisper a curse.

'Go ahead then,' Fry says. 'Report, Dr Fournier.'

He tries to:

'You—we— There hasn't been a transmission through the main cockpit radio in two weeks, Brigadier. We didn't know what was happening—'

'I'm well aware of that, Doctor. I asked you to report on your own status, if you please.'

'We had an incident. We lost a man – Private Lutes.' He tells her about Invercrae, in somewhat unnecessary detail, steering away from the substantive point for as long as he can. But finally he says it. 'We're heading home.'

'Are you now?' the brigadier asks mildly, after a momentary pause. 'And whose decision was that?'

'All of us. It was . . . it was the group decision. We had hard evidence of junker activity, after all. It— it seemed—'

'You had a man down. That in itself isn't evidence of anything. Frankly, I'd say the fact that Rosie herself was not attacked argues against any junker presence.'

So here they are. And of course Fournier is being required to bow his head and bear the blame. How very convenient a scapegoat is, especially in a situation where success is almost impossible. This time he fights back. 'I made a judgement call based on the facts available to me. I also took into account the morale of the team, and the frictions – very considerable frictions! – between Colonel Carlisle and Lieutenant McQueen.'

Fry sweeps these arguments away. 'What matters now,' she says, 'is to manage the situation. The timing is very unwelcome. We're in the middle of significant structural upheaval here, which is why there has been a hiatus in our communications to you. The colonel's return at this point could be highly disruptive.'

Fournier is ready to dig in his heels and argue his case, but now he feels a stirring of unease. Structural upheaval! He imagines the bleak landscape lying under those anodyne words and he is unable to keep from lifting the blanket.

'When you say upheaval,' he ventures, 'do you mean . . . ?' He tries to think of a neutral way to phrase the question, discovers that there isn't one. 'Has the Muster taken charge of the Main Table?'

Fry's tone is surgically precise. 'The Main Table has voluntarily ceded executive authority to the Muster. A peaceful handover of power. We are not talking about a regime change, Doctor, but a logical reallocation of existing roles and priorities. Unfortunately, some extremist elements have refused to see it that way. They're taking this opportunity to press their own private resentments, and we're having to come down very hard on that.'

'Is there an emergency?' Fournier asks anxiously. He means besides what she has just described, of course. Was there some reason to do this apart from the end-in-itself of taking power?

'There was a need,' the brigadier says, 'for firm and focused management of a volatile situation.'

Fournier has no further questions. He has just heard a military coup being defined in words that make it sound like a school detention. He doesn't want to hear any more, in case it's worse than what he is already imagining.

All his fight and all his grievances are gone out of him, suddenly. He thinks of asking 'What do you want me to do?' but even in his head that sounds feeble and vacillating. He can't let those words out into the world. He edits them into slightly better shape. 'So what are your orders?'

'First of all, and most urgently, disable the main cockpit

radio at your earliest opportunity. We've been maintaining radio silence, obviously, but we want to guard against anyone else managing to contact Rosie.'

'Anyone else?' Fournier hazards.

The brigadier doesn't seem to hear. 'You can render the cockpit radio inoperable,' she tells him, 'by opening the fascia up with an Allen key and removing the smaller of the two circuit boards inset at the rear of the main motherboard. It will unclip very easily. Do this quickly, Doctor. The longer you delay, the greater the risk. If the colonel is apprised of events here at Beacon, he may wish to intervene. That's unacceptable.'

'Very well. I— I think I can do that. Is there anything else?'

'Yes, of course there is. I need you to stay out in the field until further notice. We don't want Carlisle here and we don't want Rosie. Not yet. When the situation stabilises, we'll bring you in. Until then, find a way to stop or slow down.'

Dr Fournier feels that this is a very easy thing to say and a difficult thing to deliver. He is about to ask, with a carefully modulated amount of sarcasm, how the brigadier thinks he's going to stop a tank. But at that moment there is a lurch so abrupt that it slams his chair and his shoulder right up against the bulkhead.

Rosie has stopped.

28

'I— I'm really sorry, sir!' Private Sixsmith stammers. 'I didn't see it until we were right on top of it. The leaves—'

She shrugs helplessly, then puts her hands back on the wheel – gripping it as if to draw some strength from it. 'The leaves hid it,' she says again. 'I didn't think there was anything there. I'm sorry.' She isn't finished with apologising but Carlisle shuts her down as gently as he can. They have to respond to what has just happened: everything else can wait. 'It's fine, Private,' he says quietly. 'You reacted quickly and appropriately.'

He opens the ALL channel on the comms rig, speaking to the crew quarters, lab, mid-section and turret. From the crew quarters comes a chorus of raised voices. Sealey keeps asking what just happened and Penny is crying, 'Did we hit something? What did we hit?'

'There's nothing to worry about,' the colonel broadcasts.

'Everybody stay where you are, and please don't block the channel. Phillips, go to infra-red again. Scan for hostiles.'

'Sir,' Phillips says, and then there is silence for most of a minute. A provisional silence, anyway, with only breathless whispers from the crew quarters – and from the lab, very distinct, Stephen Greaves' voice saying with rising panic, 'Rina's hurt! Somebody. Everybody. Rina's hurt!'

'Dr Akimwe,' Carlisle says, 'please go to Dr Khan. Mr Greaves, help is coming. Please stay off the channel.' That done, he waits in silence. He approves of the fact that Private Phillips is taking his time. This is not a situation where an off-the-cuff answer will do.

'Nothing out there, sir,' Phillips says at last. 'Nothing warm, anyway.'

Which doesn't rule out hungries. But hungries didn't make the thing they've just rolled over. It was a barricade stretched across the full width of the road. Mainly branches and twigs, but the grinding squeals from Rosie's underbelly suggest that there were some rocks in the mix too.

Whatever it was, it's now under them. The jolt was from the treads rolling over the rocks and stones before Sixsmith could bring Rosie to a halt.

'Any damage?' Carlisle asks the driver now.

Sixsmith consults the diagnostic board, shakes her head. 'Nothing in the red, sir. We're good. Should I get out and verify?'

'Not here,' Carlisle says. 'Move us on a mile or so. We'll take a look when we're well clear.'

Sixsmith rolls Rosie forward an inch at a time, alert for any suspect vibration, any hint of trouble. She waits until she can see the barricade in the rear-views before she hits the throttle.

In the event, they drive almost four miles before Carlisle

calls a halt. He waits until the forest on both sides thins out and they're in relatively open country. Even then, he makes Phillips do another 360 with the infra-red goggles.

In the crew quarters, he assembles the escort and assigns details. Sixsmith will stay at the wheel; Foss will man the turret guns. He himself will go outside with McQueen and Phillips to inspect the damage, if any. The colonel was expecting to have to field anxious questions from the science team, but they have migrated en masse into the lab.

While McQueen and Phillips kit up, the colonel goes astern to check on Dr Khan's status. She fell down when Rosie stopped. She is still on the ground, ashen pale, not speaking or trying to move. Her lab coat and shirt are thrown open and Akimwe holds a stethoscope to her bare abdomen. The remaining members of the science team stand around, extraneous and unhappy. Stephen Greaves is rigid with misery and fear. His head is bowed and both of his fists are pressed hard against his forehead. Almost imperceptibly, his upper body rocks backwards and forwards. John Sealey kneels beside Khan, both embracing her and holding her head up off the cold steel of the deck. His cover, the colonel assumes, is now blown even for the slowest of uptake. As if on cue, Dr Fournier enters from the engine room, blinking in the harsh light from the neon strips.

Akimwe assures the colonel that there are no bones broken. Carlisle's glance goes down to Khan's abdomen. 'The baby seems to be fine too,' Akimwe says. 'It has a very strong pulse.'

'Good,' Carlisle says gruffly. 'I'm glad of it. All of you, stay in here. Full lockdown. We'll assess the situation and then we'll tell you where we stand.'

He kneels and squeezes Khan's hand, just for a moment. 'I'm relieved you weren't hurt,' he says.

'Me too,' Khan mutters. She tries to smile but the effect is far from convincing.

The colonel leaves her there, after instructing Dr Akimwe to see her safely back to her seat and strap her in. 'Take care of Mr Greaves too,' he adds.

'Do you have any suggestions as to how I might do that?' Akimwe inquires politely.

Carlisle doesn't, so says nothing. He refreshes his e-blocker, noting with approval that McQueen and Phillips are doing the same. Then with the two men at his back he opens the mid-section door and steps out.

Into a raw, clear afternoon. Mist lies on the ground, but from knees on up there's good line of sight. Perhaps there are hidden attackers snaking through the long grass on their bellies. If so, their snaking skills are commendable and they have found a way to fit grass blades with silencers.

Notwithstanding this, Carlisle elects not to speak. He signals to McQueen to cover him and Phillips while they check the treads and the underside of the vehicle.

Once again they feel the absence of Private Lutes, who knew Rosie's skin like his own. They are able to verify that they haven't blown a tread and that there is no visible damage to the chassis. Confident now that they are alone, Carlisle brings Sixsmith out from the cockpit to join them. As the most competent engineer out of the five of them, she is best qualified to make a full visual inspection of the tread connects. The colonel also orders her to check the rear-mounted air vents. The vents are high enough off the road that it's unlikely they would have been touched, but he doesn't want to neglect something so crucial to their survival.

Everything is fine, or seems to be.

'Was that an ambush?' McQueen demands. From the crew quarters, he wasn't able to see a thing when they actually rolled over the obstacle, which is clearly a sore point.

'There was definitely a built barricade,' Carlisle says, sticking to what he knows. 'Branches. Stones. Some sharpened stakes.'

'Stakes?' McQueen is incredulous.

Carlisle sketches in the air. 'Lengths of wood about four to six feet long, split at one end and with glass shards wedged into the fork.'

'It was an ambush,' Sixsmith says flatly. 'You need to see this.'

On Rosie's rear right flank there are shallow scratch marks, scoring the olive-drab paint. Below them, a small soot-blackened ellipse shows where someone tried to set a fire. The four of them stare at these baffling signs as though they're trying to read them like runes.

'Last night?' McQueen demands at last.

'Has to be,' Sixsmith says. 'We were A-one at Lloyd's after we got out of Invercrae. I went over every inch.'

'Why didn't this show in the MAC checks?' the colonel demands.

Sixsmith shoots him a hunted look. He has impugned her and she feels it, especially after running right into the barricade. 'Sir, the MAC is about moving parts. We don't go over the armour.'

McQueen is still focused on the invisible enemy – the crucial point here. 'So someone got through the motion sensors and the traps and had a go at us?'

'Yeah, but with penknives,' Phillips says, with a nervous laugh. 'Penknives and a cook-up. Who tries to stab a tank?'

McQueen is not amused. He scans the empty horizon, scowling like a demon. 'Who tries to stab a tank?' he repeats.

213

'The same people who went up against us in Invercrae yesterday with slingshots. The same people who killed Lutes with fucking kitchenware. They've followed us.'

Carlisle shakes his head. He has considered this, but it seems entirely implausible to him. 'And got ahead of us? On this road? How, Mr McQueen? No, if this was an ambush, it was laid for someone else. Someone who's not riding inside four inches of steel and ceramic laminate.'

But there is another possibility, he allows in his own mind. It could be someone who saw them coming and preposterously underestimated them. If he and his team had stepped out to inspect the treads on the spot, would woad-painted savages have run out of the trees to attack them with spears and clubs?

No, of course not. It has only been ten years since civilisation fell apart. People don't devolve to the stone age in a single decade. In any case, Phillips did a thorough scan with the thermal goggles and saw nobody in the woods beside the road. Even if you were to accept the hypothesis that this could have been done by savages, there would still seem to be a logical contradiction in the idea of savages who set an ambush and then wander off to pick flowers.

Despite his orders, Dr Fournier emerges from Rosie, exiting via the cab rather than through the mid-section door. Unused to the high running board, he almost slips and falls. He is very flustered as he crosses to join them, indignation and belligerence clearly visible on his face. Something else is there too, disguised and half-effaced under these banner-headline emotions. Carlisle puts it down to fear. It is understandable for the doctor to be afraid, and to want to hide it. There is no reason as far as he knows to believe that Fournier has anything else to hide.

*

Fournier is trembling uncontrollably, and his stomach churns with nausea. He has just disabled the radio in Rosie's cab. The circuit board he pried out of it is sitting in his pocket now, along with the Allen key he used to detach the radio's fascia from the console and get access to its innards.

All the while he was working, he was in full view of the colonel and his soldiers. They could have turned at any point and seen him, and then come back to the cockpit to find out what he was doing there. It was, quite simply, the bravest thing he has ever done, and he is amazed at himself. He was amazed even as he was doing it, to find that he was capable of such reckless courage.

Now he is suffering the reaction, surplus adrenalin making his body rebel against his conscious will like an unbroken horse. There is no way that he can come across as his normal self, so he lets the soldiers see that he is out of control. They will mistake it for cowardice, but that's fine. For once, their lack of respect for him will work in his favour.

'Is it too much to ask that you brief me on what just happened?' he asks Carlisle. The pitch of his voice wavers. Good. Let it.

'We hit a roadblock, Doctor,' the colonel explains. 'We took no harm, and we can be on our way again.'

Which is very good news under the circumstances, but flushed with the success of his recent exploits Fournier senses an opportunity to make it even better. The brigadier's orders to him were to see that Rosie was delayed: this looks like a perfect justification for a delay, and if there is no actual danger then so much the better. He demands details, and more details on top of those. As civilian commander, he announces with calculated shrillness, he has a right to know.

The colonel visibly contains his impatience. He gives Fournier a full and circumstantial run-down of recent events and speculations. The rest of the escort stand in the tall, sodden grass swapping glances of contempt and disbelief.

As he listens, Fournier considers how best to play this situation – how long a standstill he can negotiate. 'We can't go on until we can be absolutely certain there's no danger,' he says when the colonel is done with his report. 'I refuse to submit my crew to any unnecessary risk.'

On Fournier's left-hand side but not out of his line of sight, one of the soldiers, Sixsmith, shakes her head in wonder.

'Doctor, the only sensible response is to keep going,' the colonel says levelly. 'If there is a threat, the best thing we can do is outrun it.'

'I absolutely disagree,' Fournier says. 'We have no idea what we might be running into. Rosie should stay right here while your men reconnoitre further up the road and ascertain whether there's anything else in our way.'

'And if there is?' Carlisle's voice is stiff with the effort of being polite. 'We'll still be making the same decision, which is either to plough through or to go around. It does no good to have these soldiers expose themselves on foot to hazards that Rosie is well equipped to deal with. You can see we took no damage.'

Fournier digs in. He really doesn't have any choice, and he can't afford to lose the argument. 'This trap could be the first of many. To sound us out. Test our resources. So they can hit us harder next time. We can't assume that because there was no damage done this time there's no threat. In fact they could be deliberately encouraging us to underestimate their capabilities.'

The colonel raises both hands to indicate the emptiness all around. 'Who,' he asks, 'are *they*?'

Fournier is aware of the risk he is taking, the very real dangers he is inviting. If whoever set the barricade did mean it for them, then moving on quickly minimises the window for further ambushes. Standing here and arguing widens it. But he has a job to do. The fate of Beacon is in his hands, and it outweighs the fates of these individuals. Even his own fate, although he shies away from that thought. He wants very much to believe that the real threat is small, even while he talks it up into a crisis.

The adrenalin that flooded his system after his act of espionage in the cockpit has at last begun to ebb. In a more measured voice, he draws his line in the sand. 'Driving on into more roadblocks and ambushes is not an option, Colonel. If you refuse to carry out proper reconnaissance, we'll have to take other counter-measures. We have a vehicle that was specifically designed to function off-road. I suggest we use that capability.'

'What the actual fuck?' Private Sixsmith says, making no effort to lower her voice.

The colonel puts a thin veneer over the same sentiment. 'We'll lose time, Doctor. A great deal of time. The going will be harder and we'll have to stop earlier when the light gets poor. And the slower we travel, of course, the easier it is for any potential saboteurs to follow us. Are you sure this is what you want to do?'

'Entirely,' Fournier says.

'Permission to speak, sir,' Private Sixsmith says. Carlisle nods. 'Going overland all the way means taking longer, and that's got knock-ons. We'll run out of water unless we restock. But what I'm wondering is what happens if we blow a tread?'

217

'You're qualified to deal with that, aren't you?' Fournier demands.

'I've done it as a drill, Dr Fournier. But I'm not Brendan Lutes. If we get into serious trouble, I'll take twice as long and I'll do half the job. It probably won't happen, but I thought you should know going in. These hills all around, these are the Cairngorms. Off-road means uphill, and it will get pretty steep pretty quick. If we land in trouble in there, we might not be able to pull ourselves out again.'

Carlisle nods. 'Thank you, Private. I appreciate your honesty.'

Fournier doesn't appreciate it all, but the word Cairngorms has triggered a memory and now he teases it out. An ace in the hole, or at least an argument that he can win. 'There's another reason why I was considering a detour at this point,' he says, trying to look like a man who has thought deeply about this and is not just flailing around at random. 'The cache we missed on the way up is very close to here, on Ben Macdhui. If we leave the road and go east, overland, we'll hit it within a day.'

The idea lands like a dead fish. Everyone is looking at him as if he has just suggested that they camp out in the open and watch the stars.

'Doctor, it was your decision to omit that cache in the first place,' Carlisle points out brusquely. 'You argued that it would be too difficult to reach. I don't really see how our situation is any more favourable now. If anything—'

'I always held open the possibility of retrieving it on the return journey,' Fournier breaks in. 'And now, with no findings of any consequence to report, it's our last chance to find significant data.'

'Why should this lot be more significant than the other ninety-nine?' McQueen demands. Sixsmith and Phillips exchange a glance of amused contempt which they make no effort to disguise. But the colonel says nothing. Clearly the mission statement still has some sway over him. Fournier has picked the right lever.

'The road is straight all the way from here to the Firth,' he presses. 'One highway, going south. If we stick to it, we give these people a very easy target. They can set their ambushes at any point they like and we'll roll right into them. Overland is slower but safer, and it gives us an opportunity to retrieve the cache.'

Carlisle nods at last, prompting angry mutters from the soldiers. 'Very well,' he says. 'We'll go overland. As far as Ben Macdhui, at least. Private Sixsmith, you'll keep the speed low and stick to level ground wherever possible.'

'Level ground? Ben Macdhui is a bloody mountain,' McQueen points out. 'Sir, I volunteer to scout the road ahead and see if it's safe.'

'Thank you for the offer, Private McQueen,' the colonel says. 'Your concerns are noted, but for now we'll do as the doctor suggests. We'll find the cache, and then we'll re-join the road at the Forth estuary. Hopefully we'll only lose a day.'

'Dismiss,' Dr Fournier says, which is pure wishful thinking brought on by having won his point. The soldiers wait, seemingly deaf. Even McQueen doesn't move until Carlisle gives the nod. He may hate the colonel, Fournier reflects sourly, but to take orders from a civilian? Clearly he hates that idea even more.

The new regime in Beacon will have its downside for a thinking man with no military background. Fortunately, his own status will be secure. He will have proved his allegiance beyond doubt.

29

Private Sixsmith turns Rosie through a tight arc and cuts her loose. With no buildings to worry about, she is quick and confident, almost showy. There is barely a jolt as they leave the asphalt for the wild green yonder.

Phillips is back up in the turret. The mid-section platform is empty now, since the bumps and shocks of their overland progress make standing up more of a challenge. Dr Fournier is in the engine room, the colonel and Sixsmith in the cockpit. Everybody else is sitting in the crew quarters.

Everybody except for Dr Khan, who has retired to her bunk. The excuse she gave was that she was still feeling woozy after her fall, but she flashed John Sealey a look as she retreated – if a sideways removal of less than two yards counts as a retreat. Now she's waiting for him to take the hint.

Waiting with the curtains closed, and with a caldera of tears boiling inside her. She feels a surge of undirected anger.

She never cries. The worst thing about all this is that she has lost control enough to feel she might cry.

Almost. Almost the worst thing.

Poor Stephen! He was so helpless when she fell. Earlier, when he saw her mixing up some emergency medication for herself, he was right there with a chemical solution to her chemical problem. But when he saw her hurt, he was paralysed.

No sign of John. All he has to do is say he's crashing early with a good book (one of the three on board). He must have seen her give the high sign. But he doesn't come. Does he know what she wants to say to him? Is he staying away in order to stop this box from being opened?

Not going to work, John. It's coming, ready or not.

'Anyone feel like a game?' McQueen's voice, faux-casual. He lives for his poker, and the worse his mood gets, the more he needs his fix. There are murmurs of assent from Foss, Akimwe and Penny. A flat no from Stephen. Then John's voice, the weariness just as studied as McQueen's nonchalance. 'Count me out. I think I'll read.'

She hears him cross to the bunks. The metallic rattle of his feet on the boost-step, then a creak as he settles. She's waiting for one more sound, but it doesn't come. He's taking his time. Playing it cool.

'Dealer's choice,' McQueen says. Akimwe declares that his choice is Oxford stud with a high-low split. As the bidding starts, there is (at last!) a muted swish of fabric. Sealey's curtain being drawn across.

'Goodnight, John-boy,' Foss calls.

'Goodnight, Calamity Jane,' Sealey replies, which causes Akimwe to giggle like a schoolboy.

John waits a good five minutes before rolling his mattress

221

back and removing the top slat. His face appears in the gap directly above Khan, peering down. He is instantly alarmed by the sight of her red-rimmed eyes. 'Hey,' he says, his voice a murmur designed to stay within the bunks. 'You okay?'

Khan shakes her head.

John finishes the excavation and leans down to join her, insofar as that's possible. To close the gap, at any rate. In a crazy way, the risk is less because they're doing this by day and on the move. The engine noise will help to cover any sounds they make, and nobody else is likely to head for the bunks any time soon.

Tentatively, with due regard to the narrow space, the crazy angle and her fragility, he puts his arms around her. He doesn't ask any questions, just waits for her to talk.

Which she does. She has held it in long enough, and to hell with stiff upper lips.

'When we were running for cover in Invercrae, I got a contraction,' she says. She talks into his chest to mute the sound. Also so he doesn't have to look at her flushed, out-of-control face. 'When it didn't come back, I thought it must just have been a stomach-ache, but this morning I got three in the space of an hour. I've been dosing myself up with home-made tocolytics. Magnesium sulphate at first, then Stephen told me there was nifedipine in the med kit. I'm fine now, but I'd lay ten to one odds I'm going to drop this payload before we get anywhere near Beacon.'

There's a long silence. His arms tighten around her just a little, transmitting reassurance. 'Okay,' he says at last. 'So you have the baby in Rosie. It's okay, Rina. We can make the lab sterile, and you're surrounded by biologists. We know how it works. Plus Lucien's got masses of first-aid training.

222

Penny too, I think. You'll be as safe here as anywhere else. Safer, even. You name me another maternity ward that's got its own flamethrower.'

She smiles at the incongruous image. In her current mood, she finds it has a certain insane appeal. But the thought of what's to come still weighs on her: the known unknowns of giving birth inside a tank in the middle of a war zone. She feels a sudden, dizzying sense of dislocation, a keen awareness of unfathomable distances: between here and Beacon; between the past and the present; between the world as it is and how she would wish it to be.

Paradoxically, though these thoughts give her pause, they don't cow her into despair. There is the baby now, a new and unknowable factor. The baby could be the bridge over all these abysses.

'Hey,' she says, trying for a bantering tone. 'Do you want to volunteer to pick up that last specimen cache?'

Stark horror makes John's eyes open wide as saucers. 'Rina, it's halfway up a mountain!' he protests.

She shakes her head. 'Near the top, I think. Eight hundred metres up.'

'Do you want to give birth on a rock ledge?' He hugs her close as if he could protect her from her own recklessness.

'I was kidding,' Khan whispers.

'Don't.'

30

The land east of the A82 is rugged and broken, with a topography that changes from mile to mile. Rosie makes indifferent speed even with full daylight. As the sun drops and the shadows lengthen, she slows to a crawl.

The poker session is equally desultory. Brendan Lutes' ghost hovers over it, making the usual raucous banter seem like a slap in his ectoplasmic face. Finally, the game dribbles to a halt.

McQueen strolls out to the mid-section to oil his gun. And to brood, something that he feels is best done alone. He is unused to giving way to his emotions, or at least – he corrects himself wryly – to being aware that he is doing it. It sits badly with him, like most things that have happened since Invercrae.

He admitted he was wrong to fire the flamethrower. The colonel had a chance to admit, in his turn, that – orders or no orders – McQueen pulled all their arses out of the fire. He didn't do that. They could have met in the middle but they didn't, so they have retired to their corners instead.

At some point, the bell is going to ring for round two.

In the meantime, they've got someone on their tail and McQueen knows in his gut that it's the exact same bastards who killed Lutes. Said bastards have cars or – his best guess – bikes, and they know enough to stay out of the range of the infra-red scopes. Wouldn't have been hard to slip down some back crack out here in the fucked-up wilderness and flank them. Find a good spot to dig in and wait for fireworks.

So leaving the road was pretty much the stupidest thing they could have done. It makes them a little bit harder to track, sure, but they're the only thing moving out here so how hard can it be? And the slower they go, the more chance the Invercrae posse have to get ahead of them again.

Tonight, tomorrow or the next day – soon, anyway – they are going to find themselves in the middle of another surprise party, probably a lot wilder than the last one. When that happens, they're going to need him. Need him on the big guns, up in the turret, laying down serious hurt. And he will do his duty, as per the oath he swore when he joined up. He'll do whatever has to be done to keep them all alive.

Even if that means putting a bullet in the colonel's head and assuming command himself.

While he is musing on these matters with the rifle completely disassembled, the Robot comes tripping through from the crew quarters, heading for the lab. McQueen snaps out a warning, but the kid steps nimbly between the components and the grease rags. Doesn't touch a spring or a bolt. McQueen finds this irritating without being able to say why.

'This is delicate equipment,' he says sternly. 'Each of these little bits and pieces has got a job to do, sunshine. Don't mess them up.'

Greaves turns around and faces him. Well, that's probably stretching it a little; the Robot keeps his eyes on the ground the way he always does. But he is looking at the ground in front of McQueen in a way that's maybe a little sassier than usual.

He points to the dismounted pieces of ordnance laid out neatly on the floor, and as he points he names them. 'Operating rod. Bolt. Firing mechanism and trigger guard. Magazine. Takedown pin. Pivot pin. Charging handle. Bolt carrier assembly. Buffer assembly. Spring.'

Considering how inflectionless his voice is, it's amazing how much defiance and sarcasm it carries. McQueen is nonplussed, and even a little impressed.

'Well, hooray for you,' he says. 'Ever use one?'

'Yes.'

Of course he has. Everyone in Beacon has to do their civil defence, even people who manifestly shouldn't be allowed to use sharp pencils.

'Ever hit anything?'

'No.'

'Right. So you stick to your test tubes and I'll look out for the guns, okay?'

'Okay,' Greaves agrees. He walks on into the lab, but he mumbles something as he goes.

'What was that?' McQueen calls. Because he's not taking any cheek from this reality-challenged little snot.

The Robot stops and half-turns around, so he is talking to his own shoulder now. 'You're going to get a hammer follow,' he says, and he slides the lab door across between them.

'The fucking hell you say,' McQueen says to the closed door. Indignant. Like anyone could tell that without even bending down to inspect the gun parts up close. But of course he has to check now.

And of course (because what's a joke without a punchline?) the Robot is right. There is wear on the hammer face and on the sear, so McQueen probably would have got a hammer follow and a bad misfire sometime in the next ten or twenty shots.

He changes out the sear spring and the disconnector. He is thinking dark thoughts when he starts, but by the time he's done he finds it hard to keep from grinning. He set out to school the Robot and got schooled himself. That is pretty funny, any way you look at it.

Everything is a lesson. This one is about not judging by appearances. Just because the kid has a face as empty as a bucket with a hole in it doesn't mean he's stupid. And just because he creeps around like a whipped puppy doesn't mean he's got no spirit.

Everyone is special, right?

31

In the end, it's McQueen and Phillips who climb Ben Macdhui and bring the specimen cache down. They're professional about it, but they let their irritation show. If going cross-country was a bad idea, parking up to run errands makes it catastrophic.

But Sixsmith makes it easy for them, taking Rosie up the shallow slopes of the Cairngorm plateau almost to the summit. It's such a bravura performance, they're barely aware they're climbing.

'Door to door,' she jokes, as she brings them to a halt at the mid-point of the Lairig Ghru, directly below the peak.

'Keep the engine running,' McQueen tells her. 'We're not sticking around.'

It's cold as hell on the slope and the ice makes the going precarious, but fifteen minutes' slog brings them out above the treeline. The world opens out, suddenly. They can see

Braeriach to the west, and lonely Ben Nevis beyond like a sleeping god who has turned his face from them, pulling the mantle of the snow up around his shoulders. Right at their feet, the valley dips and bends all the way down to the loch in switchback curves like a roller coaster.

Phillips stops to gawk. Stubbornly resisting the beauty of the vista, McQueen urges him on and up. He has seen the splash of orange on the ridge above them and wants very much to get this over with.

Phillips is looking thoughtful as they climb the last hundred feet to the cache. It's an unusual enough occurrence that McQueen feels it needs to be checked out.

'What?' he demands. He grudges the spent breath a little, and the gulp of frigid air he swallows to replenish it.

'I was just thinking,' Phillips admits. 'I wonder what we look like from space.'

McQueen looks around at the rust-brown scrub and general desolation. 'Like two ants on a turd,' he grunts.

'They reckon you used to be able to see the Wall of China from the moon,' Phillips pursues, refusing to be sidetracked. 'But by the time it all went to bits, there would have been lots of human stuff you could see, wouldn't there?'

They've reached the cache by this time. They lean against the rock to rest up for a few seconds before they get busy again. 'Cities and towns would have been big grey areas,' Phillips says. 'Going on for miles. Only now they're not, are they? The forests have gone in and taken over again. From a hundred miles up or so, it would all look the same. London would just be more jungle.'

'So?'

'So here we are up on a mountain. And I bet this bright

orange dot here is one of the last human things you could still see from all the way up there.'

McQueen gives a snort. The condensed breath hangs in front of his face, a visible index of his emotion. Most of the satellites fell out of the sky long ago so this is academic in any case, but he doesn't see what's so great about leaving your mark on things. You have a life and then it ends and you're dead. Living it is the point, not proving to other people that you were there. The whole thing is really just water pouring down a plughole, but that's absolutely fine. Standing water gets stagnant.

'Let's get this done,' he says.

He opens up the cache and takes out the first of the cylinders. The seal seems to be intact but there's nothing growing inside the glass jar: just a smear of brown jelly at the base of it. He's seen enough of them by now to know that that's wrong.

'Bloody waste of time,' he mutters.

'What? Why?'

McQueen shakes his head. It's not worth explaining. The cold is starting to bite into him and the way down is going to be harder because they'll have to be careful not to damage the specimen jars. 'Come on,' he says. 'Load up.'

There are twelve jars. They take six each, stowing them in their packs between layers of wadded towels. Phillips dawdles, distracted by the view and by unprofitable thoughts. When they're done, he's still eyeing up the cache itself. McQueen can tell he's thinking about history and the point where he butts up against it. He's about to snap his fingers under the private's nose, but then an idea occurs to him and very much to his own surprise he voices it.

'Leave your dogtags.'

Phillips gives him a sidelong glance, alarmed at having his mind read so easily.

'For future generations,' McQueen says. 'In case there are any. Why the fuck not?'

'The colonel will have my guts.'

'The colonel won't care. I doubt he'll even notice. Go on, if you want to. We haven't got time for you to write a personal message.'

Phillips nods slowly. He unfastens his dogtags and sets them down in the bottom of the cache. He fastens the lid back on carefully, testing it to make sure that it will hold against the insistent easterly wind.

'All right?' McQueen tries to keep all inflection out of his voice.

'Yeah.'

'Then for fuck's sake let's go.'

He gives the plastic crate a ringing kick. It stays where it is: steel brackets at each corner have been driven down into the rock, holding it firmly in place.

'You're all good, Phillips. That's what eternity sounds like.'

Normally Greaves finds the lab a calming and comforting place to be. It's a place full of certainties, and it's a place where new certainties can be hammered out.

But today he can't find comfort and can't make himself be calm. He keeps seeing Rina falling backwards, her face twisted in pain and shock; hearing the sharp huff of breath as she hits the floor. His perfect memory torments him with perfect reproduction.

She could have died. In many different ways, the fall was potentially fatal.

Her head could have hit one of the storage or base units, causing a haematoma, intraparenchymal haemorrhage or crush injury to the brain.

The shock of the impact could have brought on an early labour, with significant risk of death from post-partum bleeding, infection or hypertensive disorders.

Conversely, she could have suffered a miscarriage, necessitating surgical removal of the dead foetus in an environment in which medical support and expertise are limited.

Greaves runs through all the scenarios he can think of that would have ended with Rina lying dead at his feet. There are dozens. Though none of them happened, he feels them clustering around him, thickening the air in the lab until he starts to hyperventilate. His vision darkens.

If Rina were to die, what would he do?

But that's the wrong question. What can he do to make sure she *doesn't* die? They are surrounded by risks both quantifiable and otherwise. Granted, they are inside an impregnable tank, but outside its hull is a world where life expectancy has dropped back to levels not seen since the early middle ages. Even Beacon isn't safe, although it is safer than Rosie by several orders of magnitude.

He will have to be vigilant until they get back there, and he will have to make sure that if dangerous situations arise the risks are borne by others. The soldiers for example, who have the best weapons, the most relevant skill set and a specific brief to protect the science team. They should be ready to fight and die to protect Rina if the need arises.

He will be ready too. He is ready right here and now, and that won't change. He will keep her safe, no matter what.

With his mood a little restored, he turns his attention to the tissue samples.

But the calm does not last. The samples and the findings he is getting continue to confound him.

Should he classify the dead child as a hungry? Amazingly (and it hurts a little, burrows through his nerves and makes them twinge) he is still undecided.

For: the boy had the *Cordyceps* infection in an advanced form, and some of the salient behavioural symptoms. Specifically, he had the consuming urge to feed on fresh protein from a living source.

Against: in other ways his behavioural repertoire was more like that of a human being. He was still capable of thought, and of emotional attachment. If he was an animal, he was a social animal. And a tool-using one.

A hungry, then, but with provisos. A hungry of a type that Greaves has never observed or seen described. He notes, with a slight prickle of alarm, that by using the personal pronoun he has partially prejudged the question he is meant to be deciding. That isn't like him. He watches himself for subjective error all the time, alert for premonitory urgings of presumption or prejudice. His mind is an instrument, and you have to keep all your instruments in balance if you want them to be fit for purpose.

The brain. The explanation for this paradox has to lie in the child's (no, the specimen's) brain. *Cordyceps* is abundantly present there, as Greaves has already verified. But natural brain tissue is healthy and robust. And whereas in a regular hungry the tide of native neurotransmitters has ebbed once and for all, in this brain roughly half of all chemical messengers are present and correct.

So who is in charge here? The human or the fungus? And either way, what is the afferent mechanism that carries orders from the control room – wherever that is – to the nerves and muscles of the body?

Greaves draws off more samples. He adds more stains and reagents, searching all over again for the brain's missing messengers. Dopamine. Acetylcholine. Adenosine. Noradrenaline.

He doesn't find them. They're not there to be found.

But he finds something else.

Checks, finds it again.

And again.

And again.

The brain is swimming in mycoproteins, long-chain molecules manufactured by the fungus. Greaves has dissected and studied the brains of fifty or sixty hungries, and he has never seen any of these molecular structures before.

A suspicion strikes him. A hypothesis.

With a micro-pipetting frame and one of Rosie's carefully maintained population of Sprague Dawley rats, he is able to stimulate measurable brain activity with low concentrations of each of these fungal proteins. The results are consistent, predictable and repeatable.

The mycoproteins are neurotransmitters, running the brain's errands for it in the absence of the regular staff. *Cordyceps* is doing good deeds by stealth. Its mere presence messes up the chemical balance of the brain, which is why so many of those native neurotransmitters have dried up, but now it is repairing that imbalance with its own exquisite forgeries.

The mass of fungus in the brain has turned itself into a protein factory. It is manufacturing copies of the missing neurotransmitters in the form of long-chain mycoproteins built to order. The fake, fungal neurotransmitters seem perfectly capable of doing the job the real ones would have done, carrying nerve messages from the human brain tissue to the peripheral nervous system. To the rest of the body. This is the main trick in the *Cordyceps* repertoire, of course. But in every other hungry he has examined – every hungry ever documented – the result is a hostile takeover. The fungus hijacks the host.

In this boy, *Cordyceps* was filling in the gaps in brain function caused by its own presence. Building bridges instead of torching buildings. It was helping the brain to think, not tripping it up and hog-tying it.

Greaves feels as though his head is splitting open, not with pain but with the chain reaction of thought on thought on thought. This is a find that vindicates the entire expedition, but it's so much more than that. It's—

What?

The Holy Grail.

The philosopher's stone.

The *elixir vitae*.

The cure.

If he figures out how to fake it. How to make an uninfected brain do whatever this brain is doing and turn the fungal invader into a friend and fellow traveller. A symbiont.

When the pressure in his head gets to be too much, Greaves sits down quickly on the floor of the lab and hides his face in his hands.

He can do it. He knows he can.

He can make a vaccine.

One by one, he defines the procedural obstacles in his mind and considers how they might be addressed. This will have to be a live vaccine, not even attenuated. And it will be heterotypic, including not just cells from the pathogen but also cells from this child's spectacularly modified brain. Embed the symbiotic tissue like a seed crystal, to teach a normal human brain how to welcome the invader. How to collaborate instead of resisting.

But there are thousands of human brains in Beacon. The task will be huge. He calculates the volume of serum that would be required.

And how it might be obtained.

Five minutes later, he is still sitting in the same position. Still paralysed by the implications of what he is about to do.

32

They're moving again, back down across the plateau on a roughly south-westerly vector. Foss is up in the turret, and wishing very hard that she was somewhere else.

All through the day she has been seeing things. Flicks of movement in the furze, the long grass, behind the occasional rock ridge or up on the elbow of a messy tumble of scree. Nothing odd about that, of course. There are plenty of things out there that might be moving. But it doesn't feel quite random enough: it feels like every time she doesn't quite see something, it's the identical something she didn't quite see last time. There is some trick of tone or colour or velocity that makes her scalp prickle with *déjà vu*.

It's just paranoia. It has to be. Living in a tank will do that to you. Any kind of enclosed space, for that matter. The horizon is too close, and it never moves. Then when you get up in the turret and take a look outside, any movement you do see gets exaggerated. It takes a while to push past that, to get your eye in again.

But it shouldn't take all bloody day.

The afternoon is petering out into tardy, sullen evening. Rosie seems to empathise, slowing more or less to human walking speed. She will be stopping soon, since driving cross-country at night on unknown terrain is outside even Sixsmith's skill set.

The sky starts to put its sunset colours on, which is a fine thing to see and distracts Foss from her growing obsession for all of five minutes. But the rapidly cooling air gives her an opportunity to try something new. She takes out the UV glasses. Toggled to N-NORMAL, they are maximally receptive in the 22–33 degrees Celsius range and at distances of less than 100 metres. On that setting, they show Rosie as more or less alone in the endless night. There are a few yellow-green blurs at ground level where small nocturnal mammals are hunting and being hunted. The rest is cold, passive blue.

Foss is prepared to buy that, but there is one more thing she can do to see what the night has up its sleeve.

She resets the goggles to E-ENHANCED. In this mode, she can access the headset's processing software and tweak the resolution to focus on a specific temperature range.

She goes low. Then lower. Then right to the bottom of the gauge.

And Jesus Christ almighty, the little bastards are everywhere.

'What are we talking about?' Fournier asks for about the tenth time. 'What exactly are we talking about? Give me facts, Private, not conjecture.'

238

Well, I wasn't a private when I signed up for this job, Foss reflects, and I'm sure as hell not a private now, so clearly you can't have been talking to me. Accordingly she addresses herself to the colonel and to McQueen.

They're all jammed into the crew quarters, elbow to elbow, so there's no need for her to raise her voice. Everybody is right up in everybody else's face except for the Robot, who has flattened himself against the latrine door out of pure holy terror of someone accidentally touching him.

'These things are in the blue,' she says. 'Cold-passive. Shaped like people, but if they were people they'd be dead. They don't show up at all unless you dial the contrast all the way up, and even then they're so close to background you pretty much only see them when they move. I'd put their core temperature around 13 Celsius.'

She speaks slowly and clearly. Part of her wants to yell and wave and point, but this is her first official debriefing in her new role and rank and she wants to do it right. Plus, it's not as if they're going anywhere. They are dug in for the night now, having lost what was left of the light ten or twenty minutes ago. Bad timing, but it's not as though Foss could have done what she just did any earlier in the day.

'That temperature reading is spot-on for hungries,' Sealey says. Foss is grateful. Someone had to play the straight man here.

'Yeah, but the movement isn't,' she says. 'They were jogging along on either side of us, keeping pace with Rosie but not closing. And they were in formation. Like a kind of wedge on either side, with one pacemaker and then a bunch of them strung out along a widening line. Does any of that sound like hungries to you?'

Nobody answers. The colonel takes the goggles and goes to see for himself, leaving everyone in the crew quarters taking turns to open their mouth, find nothing to say and close it again.

McQueen catches up quickly though, and he ends up in the same place Foss did. 'If these are the guys who set up that barricade . . .'

'They can't be,' Akimwe interjects. 'We've covered forty miles on bad ground since we left the road. Even hungries would have hit the wall by now.'

Foss begs to differ, but she doesn't bother to say it. They stopped to go up the mountain, after all. And you hear stories about squads driving for days on end in a jeep or a hummer on good tarmac with a hungry chasing their tail the whole way. It's a moot point, though. She doesn't think these are hungries. She has no idea what they are. She didn't even mention the creepiest part, which is that they're pint-sized. Human body plan, just way too small.

Man-eating hobbits? Feral ten-year-olds?

The colonel comes back from the mid-section and hands the goggles back to her. He is very quiet.

Foss has to ask. 'Did you see them, sir?'

He shakes his head. 'Nothing in sight.'

'But they're out there,' Foss blurts. 'I didn't imagine this!'

'I don't for a moment believe you did, Foss,' Carlisle says. 'I'm assuming they're still close by, and that they went to ground when we stopped.'

'Wouldn't have had to stop if we'd stayed on the road,' Sixsmith says. Her voice has a raw edge to it. Everybody turns to stare at her and she shrugs, defensive but still angry. 'I'm sorry, but it's true. We could have outrun them on asphalt and we could have kept on going through the night if we had to. As it is, we're stuck here until morning. Assuming they tried to trap us with that barricade, we finessed ourselves into the trap when we ran away from them.'

Fournier gets to his feet, all on his dignity but also really rattled. To Foss, he looks like he's standing up to add to his physical size the way a scared cat does. 'May I remind you,' he says frigidly, 'that going off-road was a decision made by myself and Colonel Carlisle jointly, in response to a real threat.'

McQueen gives a mirthless chuckle. 'Nobody saw a threat apart from you,' he says. 'But I imagine that happens to you a lot.'

Carlisle moves in quickly to shut McQueen down. Ours not to reason why, evidently. 'That's enough, all of you. Foss, is there anything you can add to what you've already told us? Numbers? Appearance?'

'I saw eight of them,' Foss says. There's no doubt about that: she took the time to count. 'But there could easily be more, because like I said they were running in a pretty loose sort of formation. Maybe I was only seeing the ones who were closest to us. There could have been more of them hanging back, or flanking us. I wouldn't have got much of a reading through the trees.'

'Were they armed?'

'I can't be sure, sir.'

'Did you get a sense of what they look like?'

Foss could have done without that question but she answers it anyway, knowing that she's going to sound like an idiot. 'They were way below normal adult height. The tallest one I saw was only about four feet or so.' She hesitates for a moment, but there's no point in holding back details that

241

might be important. 'Visible light was poor, obviously. That's why I went to enhanced thermal. But it looked like some of them were holding things. Weapons, maybe.'

'Oh my God!' Dr Penny bleats. She turns to look at Khan. 'I told you, Rina. I saw children down by the loch right after the cull. You remember?'

'Children?' Dr Fournier's tone is one of bewilderment tinged with contempt. 'We're not being pursued by children.'

'I just said they were small,' Foss snaps, all out of patience. 'Did you hear me mention children?'

'Pygmies, then?' Fournier inquires snidely. 'It's a shame you weren't properly trained in observation.'

The colonel comes in again, saving Dr Fournier from a short sharp meal of rifle butt. 'Please. Let's deal with the situation on the ground. Since we don't know the first thing about what we're facing, we have to assume that their intentions are hostile and prepare accordingly. I want a three-man watch throughout the night. The cockpit, the turret and the mid-section platform. Sixsmith, let's have the intracom wide open at all points so we'll all know instantly if there's a sighting.'

As Sixsmith heads aft, Foss does the maths. 'Sir, a three-man watch—'

'I know. With a man down, one of us will have to double up. That might as well be me, since I've had the least to do today. You and Sixsmith will take second watch. Mr McQueen, Private Phillips, you're with me. Dr Fournier, you and your team had best get some sleep. We'll move on as soon as there's adequate light.'

'With respect, Colonel.' It's Khan speaking up this time, which shouldn't come as any surprise since she's got the

242

biggest mouth of anyone on the science team (Foss hasn't forgotten that *idiot* jibe). But she hardly ever makes a peep when the colonel is talking. For some reason he gets a free ride while Khan talks to the rest of the escort like they're shit on her shoe. Even now she is respectful, almost apologising for disagreeing with him. 'I don't think we should move on. Not right away. I think we need to find out what these things are.'

She looks around at Fournier, at the rest of the whitecoats. 'Don't we? I mean, look at the facts. If they're that cold they're not baseline human. The safe call would have to be hungries – especially if they've been keeping pace with us across all this distance. If you were human, trying to maintain that speed, your heart would burst. But hungries don't use tools, so this doesn't add up. We have to find out what it is we've got here.'

'I said I didn't see what they were holding,' Foss points out. Although maybe she did, she just isn't sure. Until she is, she is more than happy to be disagreeing with Khan.

Which is mutual, clearly. Khan rounds on her. 'The barricade back there was a tool,' she says coldly. 'It was meant to break our treads or trap us. That's why I think we should stop and check this out. If they're hungries, we need to know how they can make that kind of calculation. Or build structures, for that matter.'

'We're not sure that they did,' Sealey objects. 'Is there any evidence that these . . . entities we're seeing now had anything to do with the ambush back there?'

'What kind of evidence would you be looking for?' Akimwe says. 'Seriously, John, there's no point in kidding ourselves here. We were targeted long before we met the barricade. As far back as Invercrae. We were attacked there and we had to run. But we didn't run fast enough and we were followed, from Invercrae to that barricade and from the barricade all the way to here. Or are you saying we've somehow run across three separate groups of people who all have unfriendly agendas?'

'People,' McQueen says, with no particular inflection so you can't tell if it's a question or not.

'You know what I mean.'

McQueen blows out his cheeks. 'Well, I presume you mean what you say. But that's precisely what you don't actually know.' He looks from Akimwe to Sealey and then to Carlisle. There's a real intensity in that look, a challenge. This isn't just him saying black because the colonel said white. McQueen has got something between his teeth. Finally he nods his head towards Khan. 'She's right. You know bloody well she is. Foss's bogeys are around four feet tall. Dr Penny confirms she saw something that fits that profile back at the loch. And they show on the thermals as hungries, not people. I mean Jesus, isn't looking for oddballs part of the mission statement? I can't believe any of you are seriously considering walking away from this.'

The colonel seems about to speak, but he hesitates, weighing his words.

Dr Fournier jumps adroitly into the gap. 'Yes,' he says quickly. 'I can see an argument for stopping here and finding out who or what these things are. For as long as it takes. We should make camp and investigate. Stay here until we've got answers.'

It's difficult to keep up the calm, judicious tone – difficult to speak the words at all. Really he thinks running away makes

244

much, much more sense, but his brief from the brigadier is to introduce as much delay as he can. Going off-road was a start, but this is better. It could hold them up for days, especially if – as he hopes and prays – there's nothing out there to be found.

Two or three other people try to speak at once, but Sixsmith interrupts them all when she returns with the news that the intracom is dead. Her face is grim and angry.

'You mean the reception is poor?' the colonel asks her.

'No, sir, I mean it's dead. It's not working at all. Permission to speak to you privately about that.'

'We can worry about the intracom later,' Fournier says quickly. The less said about that the better, since it was probably him taking that component out of the cockpit radio that killed their internal comms. 'Colonel, Dr Khan has made an excellent point. What we're seeing here speaks directly to our core mission statement. I believe we have to stop and investigate further.'

The colonel doesn't answer at once. When he does, it's with a heavy emphasis. It almost looks to Fournier as though he's gritting his teeth. As though he knows how this is going to go, but he feels he has to say his piece anyway. 'Going by Foss's account,' he says, 'we don't know the numerical strength of the opposition we'll face or how they're armed. When you talk about investigating further, Doctor, do you envisage my people or yours doing the investigating?'

'Ask for volunteers,' Dr Khan suggests. 'Nobody has to go who doesn't want to. And we can keep the engine running.'

'Rina—' Carlisle begins.

'I'll lead a team,' McQueen breaks in. 'Happy to.'

'I'll go too,' Foss says. 'I mean, if that's the decision, Colonel. I volunteer.'

'That seems eminently reasonable,' Dr Fournier says happily. 'A team of volunteers.'

'To do what?' the colonel demands, with strained patience. 'To track our pursuers down and bring one back alive for interrogation? Or for medical testing? How does that scenario play out, Doctor?'

But Fournier can see that the colonel has lost the argument. Everyone else in the room is up for this. The scientists are excited at the prospect of finding something entirely new, and the soldiers are seeing some possible payback for Private Lutes.

The only one who seems to be less than happy about the situation – apart from Carlisle himself – is Greaves. The boy has a stricken look, and his mouth seems to be moving without any sound as though he's speaking under his breath.

Fournier ignores him. 'I would expect,' he says, 'that this would be like a regular sampling run in most respects. We choose our targets, then we clear and collect.'

'We?' Foss repeats. 'Will you be leading the science team then, Dr Fournier?'

Fournier pretends he hasn't heard. His presence isn't needed on sampling runs. Everybody knows that. There's no point in rehashing old arguments. He looks to the colonel, whose sombre face suggests that he hasn't yet reached a verdict.

'If the feeling is that we should do this,' Carlisle says at last, with visible reluctance, 'and if that feeling is unanimous apart from me, then I'll withdraw my objections. If there's a split vote, then we don't proceed.'

'All those in favour,' says McQueen before anyone else can. 'Let's see those hands.' His own is already raised.

One by one they join him. Khan and Fournier first.

Phillips. Sealey. Sixsmith. Penny. Akimwe. Finally, almost apologetically, Foss.

If the colonel is chagrined at the defeat, he doesn't let it show in his face. 'Very well,' he says. 'It's decided.'

But something is happening on the other side of the room, and it's happening to Stephen Greaves. He seems to be building up to a crisis of some kind, moving his weight from one foot to the other as though he's walking on the spot.

'Over to you, Lieutenant,' McQueen says to Foss. 'But count me in.'

'I'll draw up a roster,' Foss says. But everybody's eyes are shifting to the Robot now. He's going to say something, for sure. Well, either that or throw up.

In the event, what he does is to shake his head. He does this with some vigour, like a dog coming up out of a river.

'Stephen,' Dr Khan says. 'Are you all right?'

'No,' Greaves says loudly. And then, inexplicably, 'It's not.'

He has the floor. It's a rare enough event for him to speak up at all when they're all together like this, and it's unheard of for him to raise his voice. Most of the time he keeps his head down and speaks into the breast pocket of his lab coat, as though he keeps a hidden microphone in there.

'Not what?' Khan coaxes.

Greaves shakes his head again, even more emphatically than before. McQueen rolls his eyes. 'Kid, the grown-ups are—'

'It's not decided,' Greaves says in his goat-bleat voice. 'Colonel, you said you'd change your mind if everybody else voted the same way. But it's not everybody. I didn't vote.'

There is an avalanche of sidelong glances. Everyone looks at everyone else rather than meeting Greaves' eyes (although catching that skittering gaze is a difficult feat at the best of times). The plain fact of the matter is that Greaves does not merit a vote because he's just a child. He is only here at all because Dr Khan forced him onto the roster by delivering an ultimatum. All of this is self-evident. But apparently it's not self-evident to Greaves himself.

'Wow,' Phillips says, summing up the general sentiment. Nobody else says anything at all. They are all waiting for the colonel to find some diplomatic way of telling Greaves to sit down and be still.

'You're right, Stephen,' Carlisle says gravely. 'I did say that I would only yield to a unanimous verdict. And I appreciate your support. But the two of us together don't make a consensus. I think the majority has spoken.'

Greaves is not deterred, although it's clearly costing him a considerable effort to speak up in public like this. His face has gone red. His breath is uneven. 'I have a report,' he says. 'I want to make a report. It's relevant to your decision.'

Fournier is embarrassed for him. It seems as though everybody else is, too. They wait in silence for a few moments, then a few moments more. Greaves can't get the words out, though his throat works hard to make a sound. It's like he's trying to regurgitate something big and angular that's stuck in his gullet.

'Was it something you saw while you were off on your own in Invercrae?' Khan coaxes. And then before Greaves can scrape up an answer, 'Do you want to make your report to me, Stephen? Would that be easier?'

Greaves nods gratefully.

'Okay,' Khan says. 'Dr Fournier, can we use the engine room?'

Fournier is about to agree, but a half-formed presentiment

makes him hesitate. The argument is won. It's highly unlikely that anything Greaves can say will change that; but it's not impossible. 'I think enough has been said on this subject already,' he says instead.

'What harm does it do to hear him out?' Dr Sealey demands, with a quick look at Khan which she meets halfway. Fournier has very little insight into other people's sexual chemistry, being all but celibate himself, but he realises as he tracks the pathways of their mutual gaze that Sealey is Khan's lover and the father of her unborn child. That will go into his next report, he decides, as soon as everything gets back to normal.

'No harm at all,' he says, getting to his feet. 'Stephen, if you have any information that bears on the current situation, whether it's a sighting in Invercrae or an observation based on what we've seen tonight, you can of course report it to me as mission commander. I'll be happy to hear anything you have to say. Apart from that, I'm going to consider this conversation closed. We'll want to make an early start in the morning, so I suggest we use this opportunity to get some sleep.'

For once, his assumption of authority actually works. With very few words, most of them sideways on to the subject, they break up by ones and twos and find their bunks.

When Foss passes through the mid-section a few minutes later to retrieve her fatigue jacket, which she had left hanging on the rail of the turret stairs, she sees Stephen Greaves sitting in the airlock with his head buried in his folded arms. He has taken a blanket in there, too. It won't be the first time he's slept in the airlock. Not even the hundred and first. He likes his own space. Foss is surprised to find herself speculating on what it must have cost him to come out on this little road trip, to voluntarily lock himself up in a steel box for most of a year with other people's voices, presences, personalities.

Greaves comes across like a startled mouse most of the time, but maybe that's a trick of perspective. Like Dr Fournier measuring everyone else on board by his own weasel length. People only make sense from the inside, Foss has found. And that's if you're lucky.

33

At 0800 the next morning, the hunting party leaves Rosie. Foss chooses to lead it herself, which feels right, and she rounds out the escort with McQueen and Private Phillips. Drs Sealey and Akimwe are there to represent the science team.

Sixsmith remains in Rosie on the grounds that she is the best driver they've got by a country mile. And country miles are what they're dealing with here. They've come down half a thousand feet and south a couple of dozen miles from Ben Macdhui but they're still on the plateau, a landscape of mountains and moorland intersected by dozens of small rivers. It was wild even before the Breakdown and now it's a whole lot wilder. If they get into trouble, Rosie might have to ride to the rescue. Nobody besides Sixsmith would have a chance of finding a safe way through this sprawling mess.

There is going to be a problem with the short-range radios too, Sixsmith tells them. 'Well, unless you stay on the near side of those hills. There's nothing to boost the signal now the cockpit radio's fucked, and nothing to bounce it off. It's just got to go through every bloody thing it hits.'

'We'll definitely be going over the ridge,' McQueen says, forgetting in the heat of the moment his new place in the pecking order. 'You'll have to figure something out, that's all.'

Sixsmith chews it over. 'Two possible work-arounds,' she says. 'Either we find a high spot and park Rosie up there, or we put someone up in a tree with a radio to be a relay.'

The trouble is, they're running out of someones. It doesn't feel like a good idea to anyone to split the party up further, and making Rosie do another steep climb is such an obviously bad move that nobody mentions it again.

'We'll make do,' Foss decides. 'We'll go out of range when we have to, but we'll check in again as soon as we've got elevation.'

'Do we have to stay inside while you're gone?' Dr Penny asks, which probably means that most of this fraught conversation has gone over her head. 'Or can we search the immediate area?'

'Search it for what?' Foss interjects. 'Four-leaf clovers?'

Penny seems surprised at the sarcasm. 'Footprints. Artefacts.'

Foss doesn't have words. She shrugs and looks to the colonel.

'I think that would be unwise,' Carlisle says mildly. 'Given that we still have no idea what we're facing.'

Penny almost pouts. 'Then I'd like to join the hunting party. Or lead a second party to search the immediate area.'

The colonel vetoes that too, and the hunters leave (thank God) without any more conversation. Foss breaks the trail herself. She has a plan that involves getting up on some high

252

ground and then circling Rosie on a widening spiral until they catch a glimpse of something. McQueen is carrying the thermal goggles and his sniper rifle. Foss herself has taken one of the heavy assault rifles. She is not conceding that McQueen has better aim: she's just taking the grunt work and leaving the glamorous part to him because that's what leaders have to do. Their place is in the thick of things. She has learned that much from Colonel Carlisle, at least.

So if they come across one of last night's goblins, McQueen will take the shot while she and Phillips run whatever interference is needed. Then the scientists will slice and dice, and they will all be home in time for tea. That's the plan, if you can call it a plan.

But they don't get to implement it, because they don't find anything. It seems they are all alone out here with only the squirrels and the crows for company. For the first hour or so, that doesn't bother anyone. It's a crisp autumn day painted in crazy colours. The fresh air is a novelty and the freedom, the sense of space is intoxicating.

A couple of hours later, though, they're starting to get a little sick of it.

If Foss hadn't seen the goblins herself the night before, she would be thinking that they were an illusion. A glitch. A false sighting. But she did see them, and there is no way she could have been mistaken. So either the little bastards are deliberately avoiding them or else they've actually left the building.

And if it's option A, then they're pretty damn good at it. They're not just staying out of eyeshot, they're hanging far enough back not to show on the thermals.

It is possible, of course, that the goblins have an agenda

of their own. Suddenly uneasy, Foss climbs to the top of the nearest rise and radios back to Rosie for a status update. It's less than half an hour since she spoke to Sixsmith and obviously there is nothing new to report but she does it anyway, just for peace of mind.

'Nothing going on down here, either,' Sixsmith confirms. 'Quiet as the grave. Except that the Robot was having a little cry a while back.'

'He was?' Foss feels a little sad about that, after last night's show of (relative) strength. 'What about?'

'No idea,' Sixsmith says. 'He's stopped now. Khan gave him a cuddle, I suppose.'

But a cuddle wouldn't have done the trick, of course. It would just have made Greaves cry harder.

Khan bides her time until Dr Fournier has retreated once again into the engine room, which he was inevitably going to do. The colonel is up in the turret, Sixsmith is in the driving seat and Penny is sulking in her bunk.

Stephen hasn't stirred from the shower, where he went immediately after the hunting party evicted him from the airlock. There is no sound of running water and there are no clothes on the rack outside the shower door.

'Stephen?' she says quietly. 'Are you in there?'

'Yes.' Greaves' hoarse mutter is even lower than her own, and there's a crack in it.

'Will you come out and talk to me?'

He goes so far as to pull the curtain aside. He is sitting fully clothed on the floor of the shower, his knees drawn up to his chest. Clearly he is using it in the same way he uses the airlock, as a space in which he can reliably be alone.

Khan feels a little pang of remorse at disturbing him. He has the hollowed-out look of someone who hasn't slept.

'Are you okay?' she asks.

'No,' Greaves admits. 'I don't think so.'

Khan sits down facing him, putting a towel between herself and the cold metal before she carefully lowers her awkward bulk to the floor. 'Is it about what you were going to tell us last night? Is it still weighing on your mind?'

'Yes.'

'And you still think it's important?'

'Yes.'

'Did you tell Dr Fournier?'

Stephen grimaces, unaccustomed anger showing in his face. 'Dr Fournier doesn't want to know.'

Khan is surprised at the accuracy of that assessment. Maybe Stephen is getting better at reading other people's emotions.

'No,' she agrees. 'He doesn't. But I do. Was it something you saw before we started heading south again?'

Stephen makes a fending-off gesture with his hands, palms out. He is not agreeing or disagreeing; he's just asking for space. Khan waits patiently. It's a long time before he speaks. 'Something I did,' he says eventually.

'Tell me,' Khan suggests, and then when that elicits no response, 'or show me, if it's something you can show?'

Unexpectedly, Stephen starts to cry. Ragged, unwieldy sobs that sound like hiccups. 'Hey,' Khan whispers. 'Hey. Stephen. It's all right. You haven't done anything wrong. Just show me. Come on.' She rubs her fingertip gently against the back of his hand until at last he wipes his eyes and pulls himself together.

Stephen climbs slowly to his feet, his breathing still ragged.

255

'I wanted to show you before,' he says, sounding lost. 'There wasn't a time when I felt like I could do it.'

'Show me now,' Khan prompts him gently.

He nods, and walks past her through the mid-section into the lab. There is a faint thud of bass from Penny's bunk: it seems she has retrieved her CD player from the engine room. They won't be disturbed or overheard, which feels like a good thing. Stephen's state of agitation is worrying Khan, even though she is still more than half convinced it will turn out to be nothing.

Then he opens freezer cabinet ten, and it's not nothing. It is very definitely something. Khan stares at the diminutive corpse in amazement, then in blank dismay. There is no grey threading anywhere on the body, no sign of fungal outgrowth. For a moment, she's just looking at a dead child. It is – it has to be – a hungry, but that doesn't make this okay. It hasn't been logged. It has no reason to be here.

And in the light of last night's alarm, it's a question mark a mile high.

'Stephen,' she demands, 'what is this? What am I looking at?'

'I think it might be a second-generation hungry.'

'A . . . a what?' She stares at him blankly. The words make no sense. Hungries don't breed. They don't do anything except eat.

'I don't know, Rina, that's only a guess. But there were children in Invercrae, and they were different. They're infected but they've got normal brain function. Behavioural reper-toires like primitive humans. And Private Lutes found them. That was what started the fight. He shot one of them – this one – and then they killed him. I felt bad because I'd seen them first and I could have told everyone they were there. I

256

should have said. I should have told all of you, but I didn't and then it was too late.'

He points out the bullet wounds, his face crumpling with sorrow. For the dead hungry, or for the damage done to its brain? Khan isn't sure. 'I found this body right after Private Lutes shot it. I thought I should take it and bring it on board and study it, because the children were so different. I thought this might be the breakthrough we'd been looking for. I was going to tell you, but Lutes was dead and I felt like it was my fault so I wanted to wait until there was something to show you all. Something solid. Their brains are—' His voice catches and he swallows. 'I should have told you, Rina. I'm sorry.'

Khan doesn't answer. She feels bile rise in her mouth, and it's not because of the blood and exposed brain. 'Stephen,' she says, trying to keep her voice level and uninflected, 'was Lutes . . . ? What was Lutes doing while you were finding this sample and bagging it? Did you just leave him there?'

Greaves is horrified at this suggestion. 'I never even saw him! I heard some of his shots. He was using a suppressor so I must have been close, but when I got there, all I saw was . . .' His voice trails off and he just points. Khan looks up from the freezer cabinet to see his eyes tight shut, tears welling out from under the lids.

'It's all right,' she says automatically. She tries to find words that will talk him down from his crisis. Dr Fournier is going to ascend the walls and scream at him from the ceiling, but there's no point in worrying about that now. There are so many other things to worry about. 'This is an important find, and you did right to retrieve it.'

'I tried to tell you last night.'

257

'I know you did. We all saw Dr Fournier shut you down. But before that . . .'

No point. She needs to tell the hunting party they're on a fool's errand. They've already got an intact specimen.

She heads for the engine room, then changes her mind and climbs the turret steps instead. Her head pokes up between the colonel's feet. He looks down, surprised to see her there.

'Rina. What can I do for you?'

'You can call the team in from the field, Colonel. We've got the goods.' She doesn't elaborate; she just retreats. She needs time to think of an explanation that doesn't leave Stephen hanging off the wrong end of a court martial. But of course the colonel can't leave it at that. What she has just told him sounds like gibberish.

He comes down and follows her into the lab. Stephen has closed the freezer cabinet, but Khan opens it up again and shows Carlisle what's inside. 'Stephen found him in Invercrae. This is what's following us. There's no need to hunt them down.'

Carlisle nods but says nothing. He is probably wondering why Khan has waited until now to explode this bombshell. 'I didn't know,' she says inadequately. 'I'm sorry.'

The colonel heads aft. Sixsmith needs to deliver the news to the hunting party and get them back inside as quickly as possible. This is a big mess already but it could easily get much bigger.

Khan follows, and Stephen follows her. They watch, tense and silent, as Sixsmith tries three times to raise the field team on one of the hand-helds. It doesn't take.

'Foss said she'd check in every time they get a clear line,' she points out at last. 'We can tell her the next time she pings us.'

258

Carlisle shakes his head. 'I'll tell her myself. Now.'

He kits up. So does Khan. 'Standard procedure,' she reminds him when he questions her with a look. 'You going out there by yourself makes no sense at all, Isaac. Sorry.'

Penny walks in on them while they're checking their magazines. She volunteers too, and the colonel tells her to man the airlock. When they come back, it's possible they might be in a hurry. Having someone on hand to let them in could make a difference.

Dr Fournier is next. He ventures out of his engine-room lair to demand an explanation for why they are all going outside. They leave Sixsmith to give it.

It's only when they're through the airlock and a hundred yards from Rosie that Khan realises Stephen has followed them. It's too late by then to send him back.

They walk together up a steep incline that is parti-coloured and precarious with old leaf mulch and this season's fall. At the top, the colonel tries the radio.

Nothing.

He tries again.

34

McQueen is a tracker of considerable skill and experience. It pisses him off, therefore, to find that there is nothing to track.

Actually that's not quite true. There is the occasional footprint, wherever the trail is softest. Small and shallow, they confirm Foss's visual description of their quarry. They look like the prints of barefooted children.

But there is no consistent direction. If one print leads west, the next will almost certainly point them east, or south. If the trail leads upslope, they'll just find another print at the crest of a hill that's heading downward again. Either the goblins are dancing in a big fucking ring or they are deliberately smoking their tracks. McQueen is unwilling to accept either of these two hypotheses.

But he is starting to lean towards the second one. Foss saw a whole pack chasing Rosie, and these prints only ever come solo. If they're not following the herd then they're following a decoy.

A decoy would do just fine, of course, if they could catch him. Maybe that's what keeps McQueen from suggesting that they give up and turn back. Foss doesn't suggest it either, but then this is her first field op since Carlisle bumped her up to lieutenant. Obviously she's not going to want to come across as a coward or a screw-up. Phillips is a buck private. He'll do exactly as he's told.

And the whitecoats are actually enjoying themselves. Akimwe has been taking photos of the footprints. Sealey has been measuring them. Both men have gone down on their knees, for Christ's ineffable sake, and had a good sniff. They have been talking the whole time about stride lengths, interdigital gaps, whatever else. Foss has told them three times to shut up but they're like schoolkids on an outing. Only a smack in the mouth will do the job, and he is seriously tempted. There's no way they're catching this little barefoot bastard if they're clashing their cymbals and singing 'Hare Krishna' as they come.

Although McQueen is honest enough to admit that keeping quiet might not help much. It's possible that the goblins have their number in any case.

He is just about to broach the delicate subject of throwing in the towel when the radio on his belt vibrates. Foss must have got the call too and she beats him to the draw because the assault rifle is lighter and less unwieldy than his M407.

'This is Carlisle, field team,' the colonel's voice tells them, as if they didn't know. 'Time to come home. Wherever you are, return to Rosie by the nearest route.'

'Affirmative,' Foss confirms. She looks relieved. She must

261

have known as well as McQueen did that they were getting nowhere slowly. 'Anything we should know, sir?'

A few moments of crackle on the line make it seem like she has lost the signal, but then Carlisle's voice comes through clear again. 'We already have a sample specimen. Repeat, we have a specimen on ice that's fit for purpose.'

'What the fuck?' The words are forced out of Foss. It's not in mission-speak, but it has to be said. 'Sorry, sir. Did you say you already caught one of these things?'

'I said there's one on board, Lieutenant. In fact it was Mr Greaves who obtained it – back in Invercrae, apparently. I'll be debriefing him in due course, as I imagine will Dr Fournier. In the meantime, you should abandon your mission and come in. There's nothing to stop us going on our way.'

A number of emotions play across Foss's face. She looks at McQueen, who mimes shooting himself in the head. But it's really not his own brains he'd like to see spread around.

So he doesn't get to bag one of the things that killed Lutes, because the Robot got there first. The fucking Robot! It's like you had your eye on some hot, sweet lady and Stephen Hawking beat your time.

Except that Stephen Hawking, by all accounts, was pretty smart.

'We are going to have words about this,' McQueen prophesies grimly.

'On our way, sir,' Foss says. 'Out.'

Akimwe and Sealey are looking comically surprised. Probably feeling like Greaves cock-blocked them too. 'Any takers for one last sweep?' McQueen demands.

'I'm in,' Phillips says. Akimwe is a couple of seconds behind him, but he votes with his heart and that's three.

But Foss isn't counting hands. 'We've got our orders,' she says. 'Let's go.'

Good for you, McQueen thinks reluctantly. And because he doesn't want to foul her in her first match, he falls right in behind her.

But by the same token, the Robot is going to get it in the neck. And parts way, way south.

Carlisle lowers the walkie-talkie and nods. 'They're coming,' he tells Khan.

She sags with relief. She has been afraid all this time that there might be some kind of catastrophe and that it might be brought back, somehow, to Stephen. Even though he has problems that nobody has allowed for. Even though it's Fournier's fault as much as anyone's that he didn't get a chance to speak. But it's okay, after all. It's going to be fine.

They retrace their steps from the top of the ridge. It's harder going on the way down, and particularly hard for Khan because she can't jump, run or take a chance on a tumble. She has to lower herself a step at a time, with due regard for her precious cargo.

The colonel utters a sudden, intemperate oath. Khan is surprised until she sees what he has seen: Penny is walking towards them from Rosie, aiming to meet them halfway.

When she is close enough for him to speak to her without raising his voice, Carlisle chews her out. 'I told you to wait, Doctor,' he says. 'Not to leave the airlock open and unattended.'

'I closed it behind me!' Penny says indignantly. 'I just wanted to . . .' Her voice trails off, but the end of that sentence is easy to fill in. She didn't want to be the last member of the science team left on the sidelines, and for these purposes she doesn't count Dr Fournier as a scientist any more than the rest of them do.

The colonel doesn't waste time on remonstrances. He ushers them on with a brusque nod of the head, and Penny reluctantly turns to make the march of shame back to Rosie. She even takes the first step.

But in between the first step and the second, the children emerge from the forest on all sides of them. It's as quick and as seamless as ink soaking through a paper towel. One moment they're alone, the next they're surrounded.

They stop dead. There is no other option: the children's cordon bristles with points and edges. They are equipped with a terrifying array of found objects, as though a primary-school outing had armed themselves from their parents' kitchen cabinets and toolboxes before setting off. With a dizzying sense of unreality, almost as though she is looking at a puzzle picture (can you find seventeen sharp things in this woodland scene?), Khan's gaze is drawn to a carving fork, a drill bit, a Stanley knife, a ski pole, a chisel. The children hold these things in readiness but make no move to strike.

Khan experiences a weird fissioning of her vision. At first glance, she is seeing children. Scary human children, either playing war games or going full-on *Lord of the Flies*. On the double-take she sees that the whites of their eyes aren't white. They're grey. *Cordyceps* infection, when it reaches the brain, deposits mycelial matter in the visceral humour of the eye. These are hungries.

But regular hungries are like rays of light. Once they start moving, they can't stop until they hit a target. They don't *choose* to stop. And they don't watch anything the way the children are watching them now: intent, appraising, ready to move again from one moment to the next. Khan feels her legs weaken, almost falls but steels herself and stays upright.

One of the children steps forward. Their leader? It's hard to tell. Like the rest she is dressed in outlandish offcuts, faded and scuffed with wear. A hundred keychains hang at her waist, and her red hair is a still-frame from an explosion. But she has an air of authority, and the others track her movements with a hushed expectancy. She might be nine years old. The worm of an old scar winds across her pretty face. Her grey-on-grey eyes are open more than a little too wide, the pupils visible as perfect circles.

She goes to Stephen. She is aware of Khan, of the colonel, but she doesn't seem interested in them. She is as lithe as a cat: the keychains barely jangle when she moves.

She places her hand in the centre of Stephen's chest. To Khan's astonishment, Stephen accepts the touch with no sign of discomfort. If anyone in Rosie, even Khan herself, laid a hand on him like that he would flinch away so violently that he would ricochet off the far wall.

For several heartbeats, the girl's hand, with the fingers spread, rests against the thin fabric of Stephen's shirt. Then she removes it and presses it to her own breastbone. Holds it there.

And drops her arm, once again, to her side.

There is a long, strained silence. It's as though they're in a play and everyone has forgotten their lines. The colonel's hand drifts by almost imperceptible degrees towards the gun holstered on his belt.

Stephen is just a little faster.

He reaches into the pocket of his fatigues and brings something out. A lozenge of red plastic with a white ring dangling from it on a string. He tugs the string, pulls it out to its full length and then releases it.

'*At light speed,*' a voice says, '*we'll be there before you know it.*' It's an analogue voice, a gravelly rasp made almost incomprehensible by hiss and sputter. As the words are spoken, the string rewinds back into its casing until the ring bumps up once again against its side.

For a moment, Stephen stares at the thing in his hands, a frown of thought on his face. Khan hasn't seen the thing in his hands for eight years but she knows exactly what it is. Captain Power comes back to her in a sudden flood of recollection. The toy Stephen was clutching when they found him, and all the way back to Beacon. The one she found, broken, and gave back to him. The voice box must be all that's left of it now.

Stephen holds it out on the flattened palm of his hand.

The girl takes it and turns it in her hands. She makes a chirping, clicking sound, baring her teeth. This seems to signify approval. At any rate she tucks it into her belt by the ring, which she loops around three times. She studies the keychains that hang beside it with great thought, and finally selects one.

She unhooks the keychain and hands it to Stephen. Its shape isn't clear to Khan until Stephen takes it and holds it up. It's a plastic figurine from some long-forgotten toy franchise: a small, moustachioed man in red and blue overalls and a red hat that bears a capital letter M. His limpid blue eyes roll satirically, and his right hand is raised in a salute.

Stephen bobs his head in acknowledgement as he takes the little gewgaw from the girl. He snaps the business end open, hooks it on one of the loops of his own belt and shuts it again. He pats it approvingly, makes a convincing show of liking how it sits there.

Throughout all of this, Khan and the colonel and Dr Penny have stood frozen. Khan can see, and she assumes the others can, that this is a ritual of first contact. Their lives — at the very least — depend on its going well.

Apparently the gift-exchange phase is complete. The scarred girl repeats the gesture with which she started all this, putting her hand first on Stephen's chest and then on her own. *You,* she says. *And me.*

When she can see that they've all registered this gesture — her own people as well as the four adults — she brings the hand down so her whole forearm is extended horizontally. She holds it in that position for a few seconds. Then she extends both arms towards them, as though she wants to be picked up and cuddled or as though she's asking for applause.

Her eyes are on Stephen again now, hard and questioning. Her fingertips flicker and her lips move, but like him she makes no sound.

Khan feels a throb of wonder so intense it's almost a physical pain. These signs are stripped down to the barest basics, not because the girl's understanding is basic, but because she is making no assumptions about theirs. She is keeping it simple for their benefit.

Khan sees the colonel's stance, his wary readiness, and Penny's bloodless face a second or two away from a scream or a sob.

Hungries that can talk! Hungries that can reason!

Reasoning is very much Stephen's thing, but talking he does poorly. His hands are twitching. He is building up to an attempt, but Khan can't trust their chances of survival to him getting the signals right when he is so bad at talking to his own kind.

She brings up her own arms, left and then right, in a decisive motion.

Now hear this.

The girl's gaze flicks between her and Stephen. She doesn't seem to appreciate the interruption. 'Over here,' Khan says. Her voice breaks a little, but the words do the job. She's got the girl's attention.

She points to herself, to Stephen, to the colonel. Draws three vertical lines in the air. Then she lets her arm fall, as the girl did, until it lies horizontal at the level of her midriff. The horizontal line means the dead boy, she's pretty much certain. And the girl's pantomime plea meant *give him back*.

The children have come all this way for a corpse. For a burial. Running hour after hour, keeping formation, leaving their home and everything they knew behind them. Following an idea. Even more than their ability to communicate, this fact proves their humanity beyond a doubt.

'You took samples?' Khan asks Stephen, keeping her voice low and flat.

'Yes.'

'From the brain?'

'Brain. Spinal column. Heart. Kidney. Spleen. Muscle. Dermis. Epidermis.'

'Dr Khan,' Carlisle says in a conversational murmur, 'would you please explain to me what you're doing.'

'I'm negotiating,' Khan answers in the same tone. 'For our lives.'

With Stephen's samples safe and stowed, they can afford to give up the body. It might not save them, of course: when she sees how it has been dishonoured, the scarred girl may feel like there's still an issue to settle. And part of me wouldn't blame her, Khan thinks. She is seeing herself and all of them, suddenly, startlingly, from the children's perspective. It's not a pretty sight.

268

She points to Rosie. Puts her hands in front of her face to mime the airlock doors opening, closing, opening.

The girl bares her teeth, head tilted to one side. Impossible to know whether she gets it, but she is listening. Watching. Waiting for Khan to lay out the deal.

Khan walks the fingers of her right hand across the open palm of her left. Points to Stephen and the colonel and Penny and finally herself.

Him. Him. Her. Me. All of us. We walk.

And then . . .

The clinching argument. She makes the dead-boy sign again, arm held out flat from the elbow, and slides it very slowly across the space between them until it's almost touching the girl's shoulder.

We bring him out to you.

The girl looks her in the eye. Hard. The way anyone would when there's a deal on the table and they want to get a sense of how much weight your word will bear. Khan is wondering that too, but she means what she says. She'll do it, if the scarred girl lets them go. She'll keep the bargain, mend what was broken back in Invercrae, and take her chances on the consequences.

And it's looking good, Khan thinks. Nobody has been eaten, or stabbed, or shot. We can do this.

But they can't.

The tableau breaks up. Without warning and contrary to sense, one of the children is slammed backwards off his feet. It's the boy standing immediately to the scarred girl's right: he is there and then he's gone, so suddenly it's almost as though he's being reeled in on a line. Khan registers the sound of the gunshot, as soft as one hand clapping, a full heartbeat later.

After that, things do not go well.

269

35

McQueen has deployed every ounce of tracking craft he possesses and got nowhere. Then, as they retrace their steps down the near side of the ridge, chance hands him what he has been searching for.

In the clearing below them, barely fifty yards from Rosie, Colonel Carlisle (along with Dr Khan, Dr Penny and the Robot, but you can't expect any better of them) has allowed himself to be ambushed. They all see it. But unlike McQueen they are stopped dead by it. Paralysed. Maybe they see children, but McQueen is expecting things that *look* like children and he is not taken in.

He ships his rifle with the casual virtuosity of a drum majorette doing a baton twirl. It ends up in optimal balance, the sight to his eye and the rest against his shoulder. With his left arm he points to where the bullet will fall. With his right hand he pulls the trigger.

The first target goes down clean. Externally clean, at least. On the inside, that fragmenting hollow-point bullet has turned it into the kind of stuff that clogs up the drains in an abattoir. And an abattoir is what this is about to become.

But his first shot breaks the tableau into blurs of untrackable turbulence. The goblins are everywhere and then they're nowhere, faster than he would have imagined possible. In their wake, Penny and Khan are down. Penny is self-evidently dead before she falls, blood gouting from her open throat. Khan is clutching her arm, which is red from shoulder to elbow.

John Sealey gives a yell of formless horror and rage and he's off down the slope, cutting straight across McQueen's line of sight but that doesn't even matter. There is nothing to aim at. Literally nothing. Foss is running too, quartering back towards Rosie, and she's firing into the air which is a sound idea. Throw the little bastards a scare at least, and maybe hide the noise of her own booted feet as she sprints downhill.

The enemy is still right there, he knows, despite what his eyes are telling him. The only way they could disappear so fast is by dropping down into the long grass. With the wind coming out of the east the grass should be leaning to his left, so wherever it does anything else something is moving. And to his amazement the movement is in his direction. The goblins aren't running away, they're coming on strong.

He squeezes off three more shots in quick succession, aiming at those suspect movements in the grass, and each one does some good. But Phillips falls too, cut down right beside him by means not yet clear. A downhill charge won't help. It certainly hasn't helped Sealey, who has vanished from sight, plucked down into the hungry undergrowth.

The time for precision is past. McQueen lets it go with maybe the faintest twinge of regret. Now is the time for violent excess.

He drops to one knee, sets down the M407 and picks up Phillips' SCAR-H. He notes in passing that what killed Phillips was a thrown knife that ended its trajectory in his jugular. That was an impressive throw across a barely credible distance. He salutes a fellow professional.

He hefts the SCAR and stands, pressing down firmly on the trigger. The rifle speaks a spiked and rolling polysyllable as he turns it slowly, from left to right and back again. The long grass writhes and thrashes.

36

Khan is the still centre of a world of turbulence. The stillness is not through choice, she just can't react fast enough.

The boy goes down.

The other children scatter – but scatter is the wrong word. They rise up like a wave. They flow over and past and through anything and everything that's in their path.

One of them, in passing, smacks down Khan's arm which is still raised as part of her diplomatic pantomime. Another cuts Elaine Penny's throat. Then they drop into the long grass and vanish from her sight.

Penny flinches away from the attack, but only after it has already happened. Flailing, helpless, she puts up both hands to clasp the ragged wound, from which blood has started to spill in the gulp-gulp-pause rhythm of water being poured out of a jug. She opens her mouth, fights very briefly to speak, but it turns out that's all she has to say.

Gulp. Gulp. Pause.

She staggers. Khan reaches out to steady her, to hold her. The blood, she thinks. The first thing is to stop the blood. But one look tells her it's futile. That slashing cut left nothing intact to build on.

Penny crumples from the knees and falls.

Khan is left staring at her own right arm. Some of that blood isn't Penny's, it's hers. It wasn't a slap she felt, it was a stab. The gash is shockingly wide and deep. Blood is lying in it like a pool, overflowing like a waterfall.

She presses the arm to her body, wincing from the contact and from the throbbing pain that is only now making itself felt.

More shots ring out from up the slope. High-pitched shrieks indicate that they found their targets, or at least something that was alive. Khan is stupefied. She knows she needs to find cover but she can't turn that thought into action. Stephen is keening beside her, his clenched fists in front of his face like a boxer on the ropes.

She catches her first glimpse of the people who are shooting. McQueen striding slowly down the slope, Foss running away from them at a steep angle with her rifle pointed at the sky. Where is she going?

And John. John is sprinting downhill to join her, his face flushed red with effort. Then he trips and falls headlong, disappearing into the long grass.

Khan runs towards him. He's not alone down there, and he didn't just fall. Invisible in the undergrowth, the children are moving. Three of them swarm across John as he sprawls and flails. A small girl hugs his arm, bends it backwards with fierce concentration. A boy of the same age claws at his face,

274

blinds him. Another, older, punches him again and again in the stomach with a blade no longer than a pizza-cutter.

Khan grabs the older boy by the shoulders and drags him away. His face is a painted-on skull, the real teeth extended above and below his jaws into a terrifying, unreal rictus. The boy squirms in her arms, impossible to contain, and bites deep into her already wounded arm. When he raises his head again, there is a gobbet of her flesh between his teeth. She feels no pain, but the shock of it drops her to her hands and knees.

Which is just as well. Bullets scythe the grass at what would have been her chest height. They pluck the boy apart.

Khan tries to stand. Tries to think. Freezing fog is pouring into her brain, filling the orbits of her eyes. She's wounded, but that's nothing. She's infected. If these children are hungries, she's infected. She has to do something, but there isn't anything. If she had a knife. If she cut off her arm right now . . .

But she doesn't carry a knife, and in any case it's probably already too late. That's not a race anyone has ever won.

Hands are hauling at her waist, lifting her up. Someone is trying to carry her, and whoever it is they're finding her weight hard to manage. She struggles, thinking it must be the children come back to take her. To finish the job. The hands shift, clamp down hard around her middle and she's lifted into the air, dumped down heavily over someone's back.

She lets the fog swallow her. It's a relief not to have to be conscious while *Cordyceps* remakes her in its image.

Foss makes her call and sticks to it.

McQueen may or may not have the edge on her, very slightly, as a shooter. But the logistics of firing downhill into a crowd that includes her own people don't thrill her.

So she runs for Rosie, picks a spot halfway down the near side where the airlock housing gives her some cover and drops into a shooting stance. She would have preferred to have her M407 in her hands, but the SCAR on semi-auto will deal out the damage a lot faster and this feels like a situation where more is more.

'On me!' she shouts. 'Back this way! Now!'

The colonel gets it at once, but he's not going to be the first to come. He has his sidearm unholstered and he's firing up the slope, where the tall weeds are crawling with quick, darting shapes. Between the two of them they're making a corridor down which the science team can retreat.

Dr Akimwe takes the invitation, arms and legs pumping. Foss sights on him then ranges left because that's where the undergrowth is thickest. She sees the movement and gooses the trigger. One. Two. Three.

She thinks she hit what she was aiming for, and she sure as hell didn't hit Akimwe. Whatever takes him down takes him at foot level and trips him hard. He's winded but still conscious, still moving, so why the hell doesn't he get up?

Because there is something knotted around his ankles. They got him with a bolas of some kind.

But the colonel is on it. He backs towards her, towards Akimwe, firing as he goes. McQueen is out of sight, which Foss hopes means he's found a good hide somewhere up on the hillside. She can see Sealey and Penny but they're not moving.

Nothing is moving now. There isn't a sound and the grass is finally in some kind of consensus with the wind. Maybe it's over.

The stone that whips past her face comes from above, rings against Rosie's armoured flank like a dinner gong. That's what the lull meant. While she was watching the weeds the kids have taken the high ground. More stones slash and punctuate the air, punch the ground and the trees all around her.

Could this get any more fucked up?

Foss switches her aim to the leaves overhead and lets off a long, meandering volley. Sorry, squirrels. Anything off the ground is fair game.

And here's some good news at last. The turret rotates and the flamethrower kicks in, drenching the canopy overhead with yellow-white flames. When they get out of this she's going to have to kiss Sixsmith on the mouth, even if people will talk. The fire catches and the rain of stones drops off sharply, presumably as the kids find some vantage point where they won't be roasted.

Something big and shapeless comes blundering towards her down the slope and she almost cuts it down before she realises what it is. It's the Robot, weaving like a drunk, carrying Dr Khan over his shoulder. She looks like she's already dead but you do what you can.

The pelting rain of stones resumes as Greaves lurches past her towards the airlock. Foss locks the SCAR-H on full auto and gives him a 51 mm umbrella.

Greaves makes it to the airlock, but then he has to put Khan down so he can cycle the door. Further up the slope McQueen is on the move again, taking the same route she did. He's walking at a steady, deliberate pace, turning the rifle in a bendy figure-of-eight to take in the grass and the trees from his nine o'clock to his three.

Now Colonel Carlisle is coming in too, on Foss's right-hand side. He stops long enough to get Akimwe upright, although the scientist isn't walking properly.

Two dead, maybe three. The science team fucking decimated. The colonel was right about staying indoors and she should have backed his call. None of this had to happen.

Greaves has got the door open, thank God. He stoops to gather up his burden.

Foss fights the urge to run straight for the door. She still needs to give the others some cover as they come. She backs towards Rosie's mid-section one step at a time, while the colonel and Akimwe converge with McQueen to form a ragged but effective skirmish line. The kids may be wicked little wizards with their stones and their penknives but that

278

doesn't mean shit if they can't pop their heads up without getting them blown off.

She reaches the airlock, steps up onto the plate.

And the door slams shut in her face. She hears the scrape and smack of the latches sliding into their grooves, the hiss of the cycling air.

Greaves has locked them out.

38

Every second counts, so Greaves has been counting them. He is up to seventy. He has set a metronome ticking in his mind. He trusts its accuracy, has no need to check a watch. And no time. No time at all.

Seventy seconds from the moment when Rina was bitten, and two minutes is the average time – not the shortest, only the arithmetic mean – that the *Cordyceps* pathogen takes to cross the meningeal barrier and set up house in the brain.

Fifty seconds, then, before Rina is gone.

Set her down. Close and secure the airlock door. Forty-nine. He can't let anybody see this. Forty-eight. Nobody. Forty-seven. The lock is still set to respond to the day code if it is correctly keyed in from outside. Reset the day code. Forty-six. Forty-five. He has to choose a number he will remember, so he can let the rest of the team back in once he has done what needs to be done. He chooses pi to ten places. Too obvious? He cheats and rounds the final five down instead of up.

Forty-four. Forty-three. Forty-two. He kneels and picks Rina up again. She is convulsing, twisting in his grip. He staggers, almost loses his balance, but manages to right himself again.

Forty-one. Forty. Sixsmith is in the turret, directly above his head. Busy. Greaves walks on by without even looking up.

The lab can be secured from the mid-section by a sliding bulkhead of interlocking plates. But he has to put Rina down again, on the workbench this time, scattering racks and retorts and equipment trays, pushing everything else aside to make room for her. Thirty-nine. Thirty-eight. And then before he can deal with the bulkhead Dr Fournier comes striding out of the engine room, full of panic and righteous fury.

'What's all the noise? Greaves, what are the soldiers firing at? Why—?'

Thirty-seven.

Greaves charges him full on. Before Fournier knows what's happening Greaves' lowered head has slammed into his face and Greaves' forward momentum has pushed him back into the engine room where he falls and sprawls.

Thirty . . . six? Allow one for a skipped beat, lost in that painful impact. Thirty-four.

Fournier is looking up at him in dazed horror, his face smeared with his own blood. He is mouthing Greaves' name in a slurred and bewildered tone, interrogating the impossible thing that just happened.

The engine room isn't really a room, fortunately. It bolts and locks from the outside. Greaves steps back quickly into the lab, slams the door and slides the bolt. Thirty-three. Thirty-two.

Footsteps on the mid-section platform. He races across the lab and closes the bulkhead door across, just in time, as Sixsmith comes down the turret ladder, dropping the last few feet onto the platform.

Thirty-one. Thirty. Twenty-nine. The metal reverberates to her pounding. 'Greaves, are you fucking insane? What have you done to the door?'

No time. No time. He shuts out the noise, concentrates on the tick of the metronome.

Twenty-eight	draw Rina's blood
Twenty-seven	try to
Twenty-six	try to draw Rina's blood but she's
Twenty-five	struggling, fighting him doesn't
Twenty-four	recognise him so he has to
Twenty-three	lean his weight on her
Twenty-two	pin her down as her hands
Twenty-one	find his face. Push. Claw at his face.
Twenty	Draw Rina's blood. Twenty cc.
Nineteen	With one hand uncap the test tube
Eighteen	the wrong test tube, he needs
Seventeen	the latest batch, unlabelled, this one. Here.
Sixteen	Insert the hypo, still one-handed.
Fifteen	Drop the plunger. Rina's blood mixing
Fourteen	so slowly
Thirteen	with the dead boy's cerebrospinal fluid
Twelve	and the T-cells of unnamed patient 13631

Eleven	whose resistance to Cordyceps was promising
Ten	but who knows? Who knows, really?
Nine	Draw it back up again
Eight	all of it
Seven	Rina's hands force his head back
Six	so he's blind and in his panic the metronome breaks. The ticking stops. His fingers grope and slide and don't find a purchase. He needs a dispersal point in the muscle of her upper shoulder close – very close – to her neck. Intra-muscular injection will take advantage of the massive blood flow through that part of the body. Take-up should be instantaneous, and it will have to be.

Because he's out of time.

He stabs down, hits the plunger, drops the untested medicine into a part of Rina's body that he can't even see.

Then gives up the fight, loses his balance and falls.

Rina falling off the table along with him, landing right beside him, face up.

She's not moving.

Until she opens her eyes, opens her mouth, and screams.

Greaves holds her as she shakes. It's not easy for him to be so close to another human body, to feel its alien movement against his own skin, but in her convulsions she might injure herself or kill the baby she's carrying.

Eventually she quiets.

'Please,' he whispers into her ear, in case she can hear him. 'Please. Please. Please. Don't tell them, Rina.'

They can't know – nobody can, not anybody, not ever – what he has just done.

39

Sixsmith is nobody's idea of an engineer but she is far from stupid. With the mid-section door out of action, the cockpit will have to stand in. The main problem is that it opens like the door of a truck's cab, occulting about half the visual field as it swings out.

Weighing against that, there are doors on both sides.

She fires up the engine and brings Rosie around in a half-circle, driving a steel wedge between the beleaguered crew and the little fuckers who appear to be trying (with some success) to kill them all.

She throws the nearside door open and yells out something that more or less boils down to 'come and get it'. And one by one they come. Akimwe, limping and sobbing, as pale as a whitewashed wall. Then Foss and McQueen, still firing up into the blazing canopy even though there is no response from up there now. And finally the colonel, who doesn't even make a move until everyone else is inside.

They don't stay in the cab – it's barely big enough for a driver and a shotgun. One by one they clamber through the gloryhole into the crew quarters. Slamming the door shut, Sixsmith guns the engine and relocates at maximum warp. The fire is catching. The whole damn forest is burning down, and the flames will go where the wind carries them. The only sane place to be is way out in front of that.

She gets about two miles – not even that far, not two – when she blows a track.

40

By the time Foss makes her way through to the mid-section, Greaves has unlocked both the bulkhead door and the engine room. Dr Fournier is screaming into Greaves' face, his own forehead bearing a bright-dark smear of blood, while Dr Khan, on the floor, lies sobbing and wheezing for breath. Her long dark hair trails into the pool of vomit she has just deposited there. Her wounded arm has been newly but not neatly dressed.

They only just got out of that with their lives and maybe they should be counting their blessings, but Foss has a sense that things are still coming apart. McQueen strides past her, past the colonel, pushes Fournier out of the way one-handed and grabs Greaves' lapels to lift him off the ground and slam him hard against the wall.

Then he hauls him back and slams him again, even harder.

'Mr McQueen,' Carlisle says. 'That's enough.'

McQueen evidently doesn't agree because he goes for the hattrick. The Robot hits the wall so hard that Foss can feel the vibrations through the steel plates under her feet.

Which seems to be the straw that broke the camel's back. The colonel's handgun is suddenly up against McQueen's ear. McQueen lets go and Greaves slumps, sliding down the wall until he is sitting on the floor.

'Discipline is a habit of mind,' Carlisle says, with deadly calm. 'Acquire it. Right now.'

McQueen stares down at the Robot. His teeth are bared and his eyes show very wide. 'I want this bastard off the bus,' he says hoarsely. 'He almost killed us all!'

Carlisle doesn't look too impressed with this argument. His brow furrows a little and his face flushes red with the effort of self-control. 'Actually I believe that honour belongs to you,' he says. 'Dr Khan was talking to the children. Negotiating with them. They didn't attack until you shot at them.'

McQueen turns. He makes a big show of being under the gun, of only holding back because the gun is there, so Carlisle holsters it and holds him with a glare.

'There will be a full inquiry,' the colonel says, 'when we get back to Beacon. Until that time, we are all members of the same crew and we will behave as though that means something.'

'Try telling that to this little shit,' McQueen says, prodding Greaves with the toe of his boot.

'He trapped me in the engine room,' Fournier pipes up plaintively. 'He assaulted me and locked me inside. Now I can't get any sense out of him. I demand to know what happened out there and where the rest of my crew is.'

'They're dead,' Foss says shortly. She's had about enough of the civilian commander. They've just lost three people, for Christ's sake, and on top of that Greaves panicked and almost killed them all, and here's Fournier bleating on about his own little bit of lost dignity like that's the salient point.

Dr Khan is trying to climb to her feet. Foss offers her a hand but she shrugs it off even though she has to grab hold of a grip-rail to stay upright. 'Where's John?' she whispers. 'Did he make it?'

'Sealey's dead,' McQueen says. 'Penny and Phillips too. And the rest of us were this close.' He holds forefinger and thumb an inch apart, an inch from Greaves' face. 'That was when boy genius locked the door on us.'

'I demand to know—' Fournier says again.

'Oh, shut the fuck up,' Foss interrupts. 'If you want to know something, stick your head around the door once in a while and take a look.'

Fournier swells like a bullfrog but he doesn't answer, so that's a plus.

Khan is stricken. She falls back against the lab bench and almost slides down onto the floor again. Foss doesn't like her much, but she knows that look of blank despair. She has seen it often, both in Beacon and in the times right after the Breakdown before Beacon was a thing. Impulsively, not really knowing why, she puts a hand on Khan's shoulder. 'Hey,' she says. 'Be strong. For the baby.'

Khan looks round at her. She doesn't seem to have got the sense of the words, but the touch calms her a little. At any rate she stays upright, and her breathing slows a little from the two-stroke staccato she had going on there. She's doing her best to hold herself together, Foss thinks, and her best isn't bad. All the same, the doctor keeps blinking as though she is having a hard time bringing the world into focus.

There's more yapping. Fournier goes on about insubordination; McQueen goes on about locking the Robot up or throwing him out, swinging back and forth between the two options. They're both still reeling from what just happened, Foss sees, and maybe being angry keeps them from thinking about it too much. And all this while, Akimwe is crying as though he's never going to stop.

Rosie just rolled to a halt, Foss realises suddenly. She goes forward to see where Sixsmith has parked them. Right now, looking at the scenery feels like a much better idea than listening to all this bullshit and watching all this heartache.

41

Rosie has stalled. And the people inside her, likewise.

In the face of Khan's grief, which is silent, and Akimwe's hysteria, which is loud and inescapable, Dr Fournier retreats once more into the engine room. He knows how bad this habit of self-imposed purdah looks to the rest of the crew, especially now, but he needs to get in touch with the brigadier and tell her what has happened. That the team has suffered a catastrophe. That the hungry pathogen has metastasised in some unforeseen way to produce an entirely new pattern of symptoms, possibly becoming even more dangerous. And that Rosie is carrying the proof, in the form of a valuable and hitherto unseen specimen.

He wants the brigadier to give him permission to come home. What they have just found takes precedence over politics. Surely Fry has to see that!

His decision to go overland in the first place quite possibly led directly to this disaster, by slowing them down enough for the feral children to keep pace. Certainly it was a factor in Rosie blowing a track, which is why they're not moving although there is now so much they need to run away from. Fournier is keenly aware of all this. He feels the weight of the crew's unspoken verdicts. He is the commander, and every call he has made since they turned around and headed for home has been wrong. There is no way for them to know that he has been wrong for the best reasons, on direct orders from the Beacon Muster. This is necessary. All of it. He is on the right side of history.

With the blood of three people on his hands.

He feels himself surrounded, and it brings him close to panic. He is guilty and ashamed, but he wants to explain to the others the conditionality of his guilt, the unimpeachable rightness of his disastrous decisions.

He can't. He is not allowed to. His mission – his larger mission infolded in theirs – is ongoing. There may even be more deaths. How can he know? He has leaned out a long way past his centre of gravity, and gravity isn't a law you can exempt yourself from.

He places his work table against the door, wedging it closed, and calls the brigadier. Nobody answers. He hits the signal button again and again without hearing anything apart from the infuriating insect chirps of static. The radio has just the one frequency so he can't tune it. He can't do anything except keep on pressing.

Finally he breaks down and cries, utterly alone in his misery. Even Greaves has Samrina Khan, but he has nobody. No friend or confidant, nobody to justify him in the face of the world. Of course it's only in Rosie that he is despised, for now, but when they go back to Beacon it will be the whole world. Everyone will hear how he caused the deaths of a third of his crew. The Muster can protect his person but not his reputation, and the one is scant use without the other.

It's not his fault. He is not a free agent.

The free agents around him should have done better.

A heavy knock on the door makes Fournier start violently. He ducks down to floor level to stow the radio and slip the plate back in place over the hidden recess. It's getting a little crowded in the hidey-hole now, because the circuit board from the cockpit radio is in there, too.

What about his face? Is it obvious that he has been crying? With the heels of his hands he wipes his cheeks.

He straightens, smoothing down his shirt. 'Yes?'

'Dr Fournier.' It's Carlisle's voice, infuriatingly calm and even. 'May I come in?'

Fournier considers the various negative responses. He doubts that any of them will do. He pulls the desk away from the door and opens it. Carlisle steps inside and immediately pushes it closed again.

'Have we repaired the tread?' Fournier asks.

'Repairing the tread will take hours. And anyone who goes outside to do it will be hard put to protect themselves while they're working. It's broken ground out there, with plenty of cover.'

'Still, if we're to get moving again—'

'I'm very much aware of the urgency of the situation, Doctor. That's why I'm here.'

Fournier steels himself for some accusation or else for a question he can't answer.

'Decisions need to be made in the wake of what just

happened,' Carlisle says. 'The crew are badly shaken up – close to falling apart, in some cases – and they need us to show some leadership now. You can't stay in here.'

'No,' Fournier agrees. 'I won't. I just needed to— to compose myself . . .'

'But it's important that we agree on a course of action before we go out and speak to them, wouldn't you say? Given where disagreement has got us.'

'I . . . yes,' Fournier says. 'Of course, Colonel. That makes very good sense. Would you like to sit down?'

He indicates the only chair. He would very much like to claim it for himself because his legs feel weak, but from the perspective of non-verbal signals, body language, that has troubling implications. He doesn't want to look up at Carlisle, who already has the advantage of having been proved right.

The colonel shakes his head. 'There is a suggestion,' he tells Fournier, 'that we should go back and recover the bodies. It came from Dr Akimwe, but I suspect Khan and Sixsmith may feel the same way. I said I would consult you before deciding on anything.' He winces and shifts his weight.

'Your leg—' Fournier essays, pushing the chair forward a little.

Carlisle affects not to see it. 'My own thinking,' he says, 'is that we need to focus on our own survival. That means fixing the broken tread and then heading straight back to Beacon without any stops along the way. Do you agree?'

The straight question lands with a thudding impact. Of course Fournier agrees, with every nerve in his body. But his remit from Brigadier Fry runs in exactly the opposite direction.

'We mustn't act in haste, Colonel,' he says. 'This . . . this situation . . . Yes, we're in a very bad spot. I accept that. We've suffered losses, and . . . and we're still directly threatened. At risk. Very much at risk. But we've made a hugely important find. Surely it's incumbent on us to assemble as much data as we can before leaving the site.'

Carlisle's brows dip a little. 'We've already left the site,' he points out, his tone flat. 'And we have an intact specimen.'

'Yes,' Fournier admits. 'Yes, of course. But I mean in the wider sense. We need to see how far this new phenomenon has spread. Take . . . take measurements, and observations. That merits a short delay, I think. A day. Perhaps two. No more than that.'

Abruptly Carlisle changes his mind and sits, with a half-stifled sigh. He stares hard at Fournier.

Fournier opens his mouth to speak again, but the colonel makes an impatient gesture that silences him.

'This is why I decided to speak to you alone,' Carlisle says, still fixing him with that searching gaze. 'Doctor, the failure of the ship's intracom wasn't due to any accident or mechanical fault. Private Sixsmith informs me that a component is missing from the cockpit radio, which controls the intracom system as well as maintaining our only link to Beacon. Do you know anything about that?'

Fournier freefalls for a second before shaking his head vigorously. 'No. Nothing. But how could that happen? Missing in what sense?'

'In the sense of having been removed. It took Sixsmith a long time to discover what was wrong. She had to go back to the schematics. The missing part is an intermediate frequency transformer. Small enough that its absence is hard to spot, but as it turns out absolutely crucial.'

'Why would anyone disable the radio?' Fournier asks. It sounds like an appropriate question for an innocent man to offer.

'I have no idea,' the colonel admits. 'Possibly the aim was to make sure the radio wasn't used to talk to the outside world, and the failure of the intracom was an unlooked-for side effect, but that's just speculation. The reason I ask you, Doctor, is because of the timing of all this. The intracom failed shortly after we crashed that barricade back on the road. And I remember that when we were examining Rosie in the aftermath of that incident you came out to join us via the cockpit door. It's the only time I've ever known you to use it.'

'It was the quickest way!' Fournier exclaims indignantly. Indignation feels highly plausible. 'Good God! I'm under suspicion for choosing the wrong door?'

'My suspicion is spread fairly evenly at this point.'

'But surely after today Greaves has to be the most likely culprit? He clearly can't be trusted. Whether it's some mental aberration or a malicious act intended to . . . to . . .'

Fournier stops in mid-sentence. The only intention he can think of is the real one, the brigadier's, as actioned by him. *To prevent you from finding out that there has been a coup d'état in Beacon, in case you feel called on to interfere.*

Carlisle shrugs. 'I'm making no accusations. I asked you purely because I know you had the opportunity. As to the motive, well . . . I presume we can agree that it falls under the broad heading of sabotage?'

Reluctantly, Fournier nods. He doesn't like the colonel's choice of words. People get shot for sabotage. He thinks he has been discreet, but being a double agent in an enclosed space is an insanely demanding discipline. He can't be sure he has left no clues behind him.

'And if it was sabotage,' Carlisle continues, 'whoever carried it out wanted us to be unable to talk to Beacon. I can imagine some circumstances in which that would be an issue. All of them are extreme and unlikely, but then so is the prospect of a saboteur in this crew.' He is still examining Fournier's face as he says this, with minute and clinical interest. Fournier does his best to look concerned, affronted and honest.

'How does this bear on our current situation?' he asks at last.

Carlisle shifts his weight in the chair, wincing again. 'I should have thought that was obvious,' he says. 'If someone wants us to stay incommunicado, then we have to return to Beacon as quickly and directly as we can. Your suggestion that we explore further makes no sense to me, especially in our weakened condition. We're short-handed, some of the crew are traumatised and for all we know the feral children are still pursuing us. They seem to be outside the normal human range for both strength and speed, just as the hungries are. It seems very likely that they *are* hungries, of a new and unidentified kind. It's imperative that we stay ahead of them, and it's imperative that we return to Beacon in one piece to deliver what we've discovered. You understand me?'

'You make a strong case,' Fournier allows. 'But still, in the interests of—'

'Doctor,' Carlisle cuts in, 'the question was not "do you agree?" but "do you understand?" I'm not negotiating with you. I'm explaining to you what we are going to do. I expect you to go out there now and tell the crew that this is a decision we've reached together. If you feel unable to do so, I'm going to shoot you in the head and tell them myself.'

Fournier laughs at the absurdity of this image, but it stops being funny as he takes in the colonel's sombre tone and the solemn, unhappy set of his face. He means it.

'Are you mad?' Fournier gasps.

'Possibly,' the colonel says. 'But I don't believe so. At any rate, I'm fully cognisant of what I'm doing, and I'll take full responsibility for it. I intend to get this crew back to Beacon alive. If you propose any course of action that exposes them to further danger, you make yourself an active threat. In which case killing you becomes the least of several evils.'

'But . . .' Appalled, Fournier tries to cling to rationality. 'You can't just threaten me like that!'

'I don't do it lightly, Doctor. When we get back to Beacon, you can report that I coerced you and threatened you with violence. I won't contradict you. In the meantime, of course, it will have to be our secret. As I've already told you, I don't want to compromise morale when it's at such a low ebb.'

'We . . . we share this command. I have as much right as you to say what the mission is!'

'Up to now, yes. Not any more.'

The colonel draws his field pistol from its holster and lays it across his lap. He waits in silence, presumably for Fournier to decide between death and surrender.

There is a middle ground, though, whatever the colonel thinks. Fournier can say whatever he needs to say to get out of this room, and then go back on it. Carlisle won't dare to kill him in front of the crew.

Which means, of course, that he won't dare to do it here in the engine room either. The closed door hides nothing. If he shoots Fournier, everyone will hear the shot. Everyone will know it was murder.

'I'm sorry, Colonel,' the doctor says. 'I won't be threatened or dictated to. I have the right to express my own opinions, and the right to enforce them as civilian commander.'

'Very well then,' Carlisle says. He runs his left hand across the side of the handgun. There is a single click, soft and discreet but full of sinister import. He stands, without a word.

'Wait!' Fournier blurts.

Carlisle presses the barrel of the handgun against the side of the doctor's head. Fournier's eyes close involuntarily against the flash and ruin that's about to come. His knees give and he sinks to the floor. He raises his hands to wrest the gun from the colonel's hands, but then leaves them up in a gesture of abject submission.

'Don't,' he pleads.

'I don't want to,' the colonel says again. But the gun doesn't move from Fournier's temple. 'I want us to come out of this intact, with no further loss of life. Work with me, Doctor. Until we get home, at least. After that, you can do as you like.'

Fournier can taste bile in his mouth. He thinks he might be about to vomit, which would make his humiliation complete. 'I'll work with you,' he says, the words thick and oily in his mouth. 'I promise.'

The cold pressure at his forehead goes away. 'Thank you,' Carlisle says. 'You are sure, Dr Fournier, that you don't have that missing radio component? If you did, we could contact Beacon right now. Make a full report and get our orders direct. The report would of course include the conversation we've just had. I won't try to stop you from laying a formal complaint against me.'

Fournier climbs weakly to his feet. He feels strange and distant from himself, tingling and prickling with dread and nausea, but that makes it easier to lie. Nobody could read his body language now, when it's slack and sick and strange even to him.

'I don't know what happened to the radio,' he says.

'Very well. But we're agreed about the mission?'

'Yes, Colonel. We're agreed.' *And I'll make my report in my own way. In my own time.*

'Then that's all that matters for the present. Thank you. I'll give you some time to compose yourself, Doctor. Ten minutes. Then I'll convene the crew.'

42

There is a meeting in the crew quarters, to which everyone except Stephen Greaves is summoned. He is the spectre at the feast, Khan thinks, only a few feet away but invisible, sitting on his bunk with the curtains drawn. Present and absent at the same time. He has changed into his blue cotton pyjamas, as though this is his bedtime, and withdrawn into himself in the way he often does. The rest of the crew have pulled up their drawbridges too, in ways that are only marginally less obvious. Greaves might as well be in another country.

Foss has been patched in from the turret via the short-range walkie-talkies, since the ship's intracom is still shot. Khan is present too, for some value of that word. Mostly she is aware of the tides of her own blood and her own emotions, while the conversation rolls around and over her.

She is still human. The moment when she was bitten plays on a continuous loop in her brain, vivid and terrifying, but

301

it must be an illusion. A trauma artefact. She must have been stabbed or scratched or sliced, or else something scraped against her open wound and caused that sharp spike of pain. She has managed to evade the (literally) once-in-a-lifetime opportunity to study the hungry pathogen very briefly from the inside.

All the same, something is very wrong. Under the bandage her skin is alive, crawling, as though it wants to migrate to some other part of her. Her head is heavy and hot. Her stomach too, an oven baking her dry. When she cried for John, which she did long and hard, no tears came from her eyes.

Everybody, by this time, has made the pilgrimage to the lab's freezers and inspected the tiny corpse in cabinet ten. Everybody has accepted that it is what Greaves says it is: one of the hungry children they just encountered. The children who all but slaughtered them from a standing start despite the adults' massive superiority in weapons and training.

If they had only known, John might be alive. And Penny. And Phillips. Khan has always been able up to now to make allowances for how Stephen thinks. How he behaves. And she knows he tried his best to tell them his secret. But for now, and for the first time ever, she finds it hard to look at him or to think kindly of him.

Words wash around her. Meanings follow at their own pace, or some of them do. She is not always at home to take delivery.

Akimwe argues for going back. His lover, Private First Class Gary Phillips, is among the dead. He asserts, over and over again, that they can't just leave him there. Leave them all there, like rubbish dumped along the road.

John is there too, Khan thinks. *I should feel the same way*

Akimwe feels. But she doesn't. When she thinks of John Sealey, she thinks of their bodies pressed together between the upper and middle bunks – the narrow space that they defended against the world. That's important. The scientist in her insists on it. Her memories are John's mortal remains, and that roadside carrion is nothing.

But the living owe a duty to the dead. Even the feral children know that. That's why they ran and ran in Rosie's wake, all the way from Invercrae. They want their brother, their friend, their own to be returned to them. Which is exactly what Akimwe wants.

She sees it all in that moment. Everything that's happening, and has to happen. But it slips away again. Her mind won't make a fist to hold it in.

So it is left to Dr Fournier to explain how important the specimen in freezer ten is. How unique it is. McQueen scoffs at that word. How can it be unique, when they're surrounded by the evil little fuckers? And it's true that Fournier's words ring a little hollow right now. In fact, everything about him is hollow. He looks like a cardboard cut-out of himself stood up as a point-of-sale display in the days when smiling faces sold things. Not that he's smiling.

The children are – or seem to be – something completely new, he tells the silent room. They are infected but they can still think. Properly focused research might be able to pinpoint the mechanism involved and then duplicate it. To find a cure, or a vaccine. This is the single most important discovery anyone has made since the Breakdown began.

Fournier speculates, briefly, on what the children might be. The offspring of women who were already pregnant when they were infected, or else the children of atypical hungries who retained some human drives apart from feeding. Second generation, almost certainly. The *Cordyceps* pathogen has to have been mediated through something in order to explain these functional and structural changes, and the most likely candidate is a placenta.

Khan feels a vibration, as Fournier says that word, from the depths of her own abdomen. It feels for a moment as though Rosie is still moving, but it's just her: a freight train with a single carriage, a single passenger, destination still unknown.

Fournier seems to have realised at last how little anyone cares about his speculations. He pulls himself together and sums up quickly. They have to get the sample – the child from Invercrae – back to Beacon, along with their report. The scientific effort that is needed now will involve dozens or hundreds of researchers and years of time. And that work can't start until they get their specimen home. With the radio out, they can't even let the Main Table know what they've found. They have to bring the sample back, or everything they have done will be wasted.

It's quite a long speech. Dr Fournier makes it, for the most part, with his eyes down, staring at the steel-latticed floor. But when he has finished he looks at Colonel Carlisle, just once, as if he is searching for approval or agreement in the colonel's eyes.

Foss, over the walkie-talkie, says thank you. She says she likes to know what she's shooting, especially when it's cuter than kittens. She adds that if they are ever going to get started on those fucking treads they've got maybe an hour or so of daylight left.

McQueen says he doesn't think daylight is going to make much difference. They've got the spotlights, and all the kit.

The trouble is that as soon as they step outside the doors all hell is probably going to break loose again. They're stuck here for the duration, which might mean until they're all dead. Right now he is more concerned with the question of what they're going to do with Greaves – only he doesn't say Greaves, he says 'the Robot'. He offers some suggestions. The mildest is that they shove Greaves out of the airlock and leave him to die. Another, not the most extreme, involves a bayonet.

The colonel states, without inflection, that he has written up Stephen's actions and will refer them for adjudication and punishment as soon as they're back in Beacon.

McQueen says that's not good enough. Akimwe agrees, and the whole room tenses for a confrontation that seems to have been a very long time in coming. It's awful, all of this is awful, but Khan feels as though she is watching it through the wrong end of a telescope. At the same time, everything is too close, too confined. Rosie is full of the rank sourness of human bodies pressed and rolled against each other like cheese in a vat. Every time she inhales, the smell hits the back of her nose, tickles and scorches there.

John is dead and there is nothing left that isn't burning to the ground. Except her baby. Except that little sliver of life that caught in her and quickened.

'He saved me,' she whispers. She clears her throat and says it again, louder.

They're the first words she has spoken. Everybody looks at her and she holds up her bandaged arm. 'Stephen saved me, after I was hurt.'

'That's beside the point,' McQueen says.

'Not to me.'

'He almost killed the rest of us.'

'Well, you did that first,' Khan points out. 'You shot one of them without even looking at what was happening, and everything went to hell. We were fine up until then. And by the way, you should know that unless we leave that body here for them to find, they'll keep coming after us. That's what this is about. That's what it's been about all along.'

'And who brought the damn thing on board in the first place?' McQueen demands. 'Thanks. You've made my point. It's way past time we stopped talking about this and just fucking dealt with it.'

The ex-lieutenant seems to be all done with words. He stands up, slowly, making a big deal out of it.

'We need a little leadership here,' he says. 'That little tosser hung us out to dry, and he probably spiked the radio too. Now are you going to show him the door or do I have to do it myself?'

With a heavy sense of inevitability, Khan finds a fork – the only sharp implement on the table – and grabs a hold of it with her good left hand. She is so tired and so sick, she would much rather just sit here, but if McQueen is going to square off against the colonel to decide Stephen's fate then he's going to do it with three tines lodged in his kidney.

But Stephen breaks the tableau. He pulls the curtains of his bunk aside and peers out at them, as though all this time he has only been waiting for his cue. His face is pale and his eyes are wide, but his tone when he speaks is calm and precise.

He says, 'I'm happy to go outside. I was actually going to suggest it.' And then, although Khan thinks she must have misheard this part: 'I'll need to put my suit on.'

43

Private Sixsmith is not a good teacher, Greaves thinks. She locates and assembles the hydraulic track puller and drills him in its use, but she omits several pieces of information that he considers crucial.

One: she doesn't tell him that the Rosalind Franklin has 'live' rather than 'dead' track, held under tension by the rubber brushings in each track block so there is less risk of a throw as it passes over the return rollers. If he didn't know this already he would expect the treads on the upper span to be under lower tension than those on the ground span.

Two: she tells him to set the puller to deliver 1,800 mechanical horsepower, the maximum it will output. This is only appropriate if the break is in the middle of a span, and must be adjusted depending on the distance from the return rollers.

Three: she omits to mention that Greaves will need to replace the existing connectors on the intact blocks adjacent to the damaged ones. Even if they look sound, they may be stressed in the plane of the existing break. Fitting new blocks to mounts that have been stressed in this way will practically guarantee another track throw.

As it happens, none of these omissions causes Greaves any practical difficulties. He read the track puller's manual from cover to cover on the second week out from Beacon. He read the manuals for all the onboard equipment, even the ones that were already familiar to him from Rina's lab. Still, it's useful to see a live demonstration, and in this respect he has no complaints to make about Sixsmith's instructions. She shows him how to position the pump, and the safest angle from which to fire the tapping-bit. These are useful things to know and the manual did not explicitly address them.

'A few wars ago, this was a four-man job,' Sixsmith tells him. 'Tanker bar, cheater pipe, the whole frigging wardrobe. Even now, I don't envy you doing it alone. The puller makes it possible but it doesn't make it easy.'

'Thank you, Private Sixsmith,' Greaves says meekly. 'I'll do the best I can.'

'And you're sure you don't want to take a gun?'

'We are not,' McQueen says, 'giving this fucking retard a gun.'

Greaves doesn't answer, since McQueen's response has made his own unnecessary. He absolutely does not want a gun. He won't have either of his hands free to carry a weapon, and he wouldn't be able to use one in any case. He read all the manuals for the guns and rifles too, of course, but only in order to understand their functioning. Not because he ever seriously thought about firing one.

They all watch as he puts on the suit. Its existence seems

to make Dr Fournier very angry, though he says nothing. Perhaps he feels that he is the only one on board who should be allowed to keep secrets from the others. Perhaps secrets are meant to be a privilege of rank.

'That is grotesque,' McQueen says, shaking his head.

Greaves tries to explain that form follows function. 'The principle is heat diffusion via the placement of—'

'I don't want to know the principle, fuckwit. I just want you to get out there and do the job. Or get yourself eaten, so we know where we stand.'

Dr Khan is not present. She has pronounced herself unwell and taken to her bunk. Greaves had thought she might try to dissuade him from going outside, but she seems to be having difficulty at the moment focusing her mind on her surroundings. When he saw her last, as she withdrew, her face was flushed and she had a visible tremor in her hands.

Greaves frets. What are these things a symptom of? Just shock, or something worse? Has his cure – or rather his desperate, ad hoc work-around – been effective or has it failed? If the latter, the infection could become active again at any moment.

But he can't help her unless he goes outside and acquires what he needs. That's the whole point of volunteering to repair the broken tread.

Lie.

Liar.

Not the *whole* point. There's something else he needs to do. Will risk his life to do, although he has no idea why it matters so much. It ought not to matter at all.

He pulls on the facemask and hood with a sense of relief. If they can't see his face, they can't see his thoughts.

'Here you go, you little lunatic.' Sixsmith says this without heat, almost with respect. She hands him, one by one, the track puller, the slender cylinder of compressed air in its shoulder sling, and the toolbox.

'I'd like my sampling kit too,' Greaves mumbles. 'Please.'

McQueen rolls his eyes, but they humour him. They think he is sticking to a routine, just for the comfort it brings. They think, as always, that they understand him. Acting Lieutenant Foss brings the kit, and Greaves clips it to his belt, which he has deliberately worn on top of the heat-dispersal suit.

Then Foss opens up the inside door of the airlock for him, and he steps in. Greaves is used to missing the signals other people send with their faces and making up the lost information in other ways, but he sees the moment when Dr Akimwe looks away. Dr Akimwe blames him for the death of Private Phillips, whom he loved. He knows, of course, that Private Phillips died before Greaves sealed the mid-section door. But the logic that is operating here is not a simple, linear one. Guilt and innocence are tangled up in each other, elided.

Foss drops back as Carlisle steps up, taking her place at the airlock controls. 'Are you sure you want to do this, Stephen?' the colonel asks.

Stephen nods. He's very sure – and very grateful for the vagueness of the word 'this'. He is sure of what he wants to do, and has no wish at all to explain it.

'Be careful,' the colonel says. 'And come back inside at the first sign of movement.' He knows Greaves well enough not to try to touch him, but he gives him a nod of reassurance and perhaps acknowledgement. Then he closes the inner door.

Greaves is committed now.

Inside the mask he smiles, because of the certainty. Because being committed means a reduction of randomness, a paring down of possibilities. It will be hard, and he might die, but it's good to have a clear through-line and to depend on nothing but his own abilities.

The outer door opens. He steps through it.

It is very dark at first. The moon has filled out a little since his last night-walk but rags of cloud are racing across the sky so it comes and goes.

He is alone in the night, as far as he can tell. All the rest of the crew are inside the hull. They can't see him or interact with him. Sixsmith had tried to fit him with a radio microphone but had given up when she saw how tightly the mask and hood fitted him. A mike that broke one of the suit's seals would be worse than useless.

Because from another point of view, he is far from alone. The children are out here somewhere, possibly very close. Greaves has stepped out of his own world into theirs. At night, he knows, they can only see heat. Their sight in the visible spectrum is no better than his, so the suit will disguise him. But it won't muffle the noise he makes as he works, which will be considerable. His best hope, or perhaps his only hope, is that the fire started by Rosie's flamethrower has forced them to relocate.

He addresses himself to the repairs. This is the first time he has ever used any of these tools, but their operation is simple and the task has an algorithmic structure that appeals to him.

Locate the damaged tread blocks. There are only two, which is good.

Break the track by knocking out the end connectors on their inside and outside edges. The puller has a tapping-bit attachment like a blunt-ended road drill specifically for this. The bit is powered by the gas cylinder and delivers a colossal amount of power to an area perhaps two square inches in cross-section. It feels to Greaves as though he is swinging a sledgehammer without having to raise it. The recoil frightens him a little, but the connectors pop away with almost no resistance.

Replace the damaged blocks with whole ones. He has brought ten and uses four – swapping out both the damaged blocks and their nearest neighbour on either side.

Attach the puller's clamps to the two loose ends of the track, then set the main gauge to 1,500 horsepower, which he has judged by eye to be sufficient. The hydraulics go to work as he operates the pump, dragging the broken ends together under higher and higher tension until at last they are where they need to be. The puller is now holding the tread together like a fingertip on a knot.

Fit new end connectors, again using the tapping-bit.

And release the puller. This is far and away the most dangerous part: if he has miscalculated the tension, the tread will snap and he will be standing right in front of it – perfectly positioned to be slapped across the face with a gauntlet of modular steel plates moving at eighty to one hundred metres per second.

He has not misjudged. The puller slides free and the tread holds.

Greaves' inner clock tells him he has been out here for forty minutes. Lacking any visual confirmation of the extent of the damage, Sixsmith had estimated that repairs would most likely take around three hours. Greaves resets the notional timer with a half-painful prickling of tension. He has told nobody what he intends to do now. He has allowed them to believe that he will finish repairing the tread and then return immediately to the airlock.

But he hasn't actually told a lie. That Rubicon glistens in the dark in front of his eyes, still and deep and treacherous.

Greaves puts down the puller, the cylinder, the toolbox. He walks away from Rosie into the dark and the silence, following one of the two flattened paths left by the vehicle's treads. This is wilderness, uneven and unpredictable, but the going is relatively easy as long as he sticks to the path. He makes good progress.

After half an hour, he is back among the trees. He can feel the residual heat from that afternoon's fire but the smell doesn't reach him. He wonders whether it would include scorched flesh as well as charred wood and vegetable matter. He wonders whether he has come here on a fool's errand.

But the bodies are intact. The flamethrower was pointed at the canopy and the east wind spread the blaze away to the west, leaving them untouched. And the living children, as far as he can see, have not yet returned to claim their dead. Greaves sits and waits until the moon comes out from the scudding clouds, letting him see to work.

Seven of the children died in the afternoon's encounter. He draws off cerebrospinal fluid from each of them, inserting his sampling needle into the subarachnoid space between the third and fourth lumbar vertebrae.

He fills every vial in his kit. He will need as much CSF as he can get. He thinks that if he is going to die tonight it will be now, as he robs the dead. If any of the children are watching, they will be full of outrage and vengeful fury. But he can't let that stop him: there is too much at stake.

Rina. Rina is at stake.

Also there is the other thing, the smaller thing, but not so small now that he is looking down at the small, curled bodies. He checks to see that the scarred girl is not here. He wants her to be still alive.

He looks at each face in turn as he works.

Not her.

Not her.

Not her.

Not her.

Not her.

Not her.

Not her.

His chest, where she kicked him back at the water-testing plant, aches a little. It's as though they are still touching.

As soon as the last vial is full, he turns and walks away. He imagines the children watching him go: in the branches, sitting in long lines with the smallest way up high so the bigger ones further down can keep them safe if anything fierce climbs up from the forest floor. It's nice, for a second, to imagine that phantom company. But the fact that he is still alive proves that he's all by himself out here after all.

314

PART THREE

BIRTH

BIRTH

44

With the treads repaired and Greaves back on board (he did the job inside the three hours that Sixsmith predicted, with five minutes to spare) they continue south. Acting on the colonel's orders, Sixsmith is aiming to pick up the main road again at Pitlochry. Once she is on tarmac, she will floor the accelerator. In the meantime, she coaxes Rosie with fretful patience over the rugged ground, giving the new tracks plenty of time to bed in. Outdistancing their pursuers will have to go on the to-do list for tomorrow. That's the bad news.

The worse news is that the feral kids are still out there. Nobody sees them through the day, and everyone on board is starting to get their hopes up, but as soon as it starts to get dark Foss dons the night-vision goggles and dials the sensitivity up all the way. Abracadabra. The dusk is full of sprinting fairy lights. The children are behind Rosie and off to both sides of her, maintaining a wide, loose formation despite the rough terrain. Effortlessly keeping up.

The mood on board is volatile. That's a polite word for it anyway, Foss thinks. The Robot's little trick with the track puller has bought him a little bit of leeway from the haters. The prevailing sentiment now is that when he locked them out he was just panicking because Dr Khan had been injured. Everyone except for McQueen seems prepared to accept that in mitigation – and even McQueen is on record as saying that the kid scores higher on a ball-count than might have been expected. He hasn't forgotten the spiked radio, though, and he has told Foss privately that he is going to be the Robot's shadow for the rest of the journey. Eyes on the prize all the way, until they get back to Beacon, drive in through the front gates and actually park. 'There's something going on in there,' he says, when Foss tries to joke him out of this promise. 'You've only got to look at the kid's face.'

Which is true enough. But then there's something going on behind all of their faces.

In Akimwe's case, it's grief, simple and bottomless. Foss had always assumed that he and Phillips were just shagging out of convenience and proximity, which goes to show how little she knows. Akimwe is down fathoms deep and not coming up again soon.

Fournier is sunk about the same distance, but his medium is self-pity and – in Foss's opinion – terror. He stiffens at loud noises, his voice breaks unexpectedly when he's talking and his eyes seem perpetually wet with unshed tears. It's just as well he spends most of his time in the engine room because he's a one-man funeral.

McQueen is a ball of compacted rage.

Khan is sleepwalking and looking for a way to wake up.

The colonel is . . . what? Waiting, maybe. Like he sees where all the rest of them are heading and he means to step along and join them in his own good time.

Only Sixsmith seems to have her mind on her job, and given what her job is that's just as well. The tracks won't slip again while she is at that wheel.

At about 2100 hours, when they come down onto relatively level ground, Sixsmith puts the pedal down hard. This was a plan of the colonel's: take it slow and steady until dusk and then — conditions allowing — accelerate just as the kids are slowing down. It's too much to hope that Sixsmith will give them the slip altogether, but if she grabs some distance she can put it to good use.

About an hour later, the colonel flags up a good defensible spot on a scree slope outside of Dunkeld, where they stop and dig in. Properly. Motion sensors, razor-wire barricades, anti-personnel mines, the whole shop. They are maybe five miles from where Birnam Wood made its unexpected visit to Dunsinane castle in the play *Macbeth*, but there is no danger of that here. Carlisle has picked a spot with no ground cover for half a mile in any direction. Birnam Wood would need to put on a good turn of speed to get past Foss, who is up in the turret with the guns warmed up and ready. Of course, it's not trees she's looking to set light to.

The colonel takes the mid-section platform, despite having pulled double-duty the night before.

Tomorrow they'll find the road again. Tonight they'll sleep.

★

Or in Dr Fournier's case, catch up on some phone calls. He tries the brigadier's line again and again. It seems unlikely that she will pick up on the hundredth hail after ignoring the ninety-nine that came before, but he can't stop himself. He needs to explain to her that they're coming in. He has done all he can, and all that anyone could expect him to do, but they are coming in. Let the Muster deal with Colonel Carlisle. It's the Muster, after all, that has a problem with him.

The doctor falls asleep at last, with the radio clutched in his hand.

And wakes to find it whispering, vibrating in his grip.

'Yes!' he yelps, a little too loud. He winces at the sound of his own voice in the brittle silence. Pressing the radio to his lips he murmurs, 'It's me! Fournier!'

'You've been trying to reach me, Doctor.' The brigadier's voice is calm and cold.

'Yes! Since yesterday. There have been some developments. Things have happened that I have to report. We've lost Penny and Sealey and Private Phillips in an engagement with—'

'Be quiet.'

Fry stops him dead with those two words. Fournier's lips continue to move, but without any sound, without any breath.

'I'll take your report later, if there's time,' Fry says. 'The situation here has become . . .' There is an audible pause before she continues. '. . . unstable. The subversive elements in Beacon have managed to claim some territory and hold onto it. We're fighting on several fronts, when we ought to be consolidating. Your losses are highly regrettable but I don't have time right now to hear an itemised account.'

'I— I understand,' Fournier says. He thinks: unstable? What have they done to Beacon? What is happening back there?

Meanwhile, Fry goes on without a break. 'So my question for you is this, Dr Fournier. Can you deliver the Rosalind Franklin to a specific location in a specific time frame?'

Fournier is aghast. 'No!' he exclaims. 'Definitely not! Brigadier, the chain of command has broken down here. Colonel Carlisle has threatened me. Physically threatened me. He suspects I disabled the radio and he— he's watching me all the time. He won't entertain any suggestion from me, not for a moment.'

Silence at the other end of the line, shot through with cycling static.

'All right,' Fry says at last, with grim resignation. 'Explain.'

Fournier tries, but does poorly. The events of the previous day sprawl across his mind like debris from a landslide. He struggles to find a through-line, and clearly he doesn't succeed. Fry seems confused about the children and absolutely uninterested in Colonel Carlisle's threatening to murder him. She does take the point that they have encountered a new form of hungry and obtained an intact specimen. She congratulates him – perfunctorily – on that achievement, but she doesn't seem to appreciate what it might mean.

When he tries to explain, the brigadier returns to something he told her during their last conversation.

'You said there was some kind of personal friction between Carlisle and McQueen. Is that still true?'

Fournier is nonplussed. 'Well, yes,' he says. 'They came close to fighting yesterday. The colonel broke McQueen back down to the ranks, after all. McQueen hasn't forgiven that.'

'Then let me talk to McQueen.'

Fournier thinks he must have misheard, so he ignores the order and goes back to his main theme. 'The specimen is

321

a child. It may have been born to an infected mother, and its brain tissue—'

'Later,' Fry interrupts. 'Your salient point is that you have new and pertinent data to bring home. That's excellent news, and you'll be rewarded in due course. But it's for others to examine and interpret. Right now I need you to bring McQueen into the engine room and let me speak to him.'

So he did hear correctly. But after all these months of complete secrecy he finds this shift in operating parameters hard to process. 'But then . . . if McQueen finds out I've been reporting to you . . .'

'As ordered,' the brigadier reminds him. 'You've done nothing wrong. This is about Beacon's survival, and there is only one right side in that struggle. Bring him, Dr Fournier, please. I assume he's still awake?'

'I think they're all awake. I can hear them talking. They're in the crew quarters, most likely playing poker.'

'Then go and fetch him.'

It's not as easy as it sounds. For once, the colonel is in the mid-section rather than in the cockpit, keeping watch along with Foss, so Fournier has to walk past him on his way to the crew quarters – eyes on the ground, unable to meet his gaze – and will have to walk past him again on his way back.

He needs a plausible cover for a private conversation with the former lieutenant, and he can't think of anything that will not look suspicious. McQueen is not under his direct command. There just isn't any reason why he would need to talk to the man about anything that wouldn't normally route through Carlisle. And they're all so intent on their endless poker game that McQueen probably won't even listen to him.

Inspiration strikes in the moment when he walks in on

them. A diminished game, with just McQueen, Sixsmith and Akimwe at the table (and Akimwe there in body only, like a propped-up dummy). They don't look up.

Until Fournier gathers the cards up from the table and holds out his hand for the ones they're holding.

'What the fuck?' Sixsmith demands, bemused.

'I'm confiscating this deck of cards,' Fournier says. 'It's bad for morale.' And since they're still keeping tight hold of the cards in their hands he turns and walks away with the bulk of the deck as his prize.

'Goodnight, Colonel,' he mutters as he walks through the mid-section. 'I hope we see no activity out there.' He moves on quickly. If there's a reply, he doesn't hear it.

He shuts himself in the engine room again and waits there in an agony of anticipation. Has he misjudged? He thought he knew McQueen well enough to be sure he wouldn't sit still for such a high-handed intervention, but they are all so beaten down in the wake of the attack that for once it might pass without comment.

There is a knock on the door. A single, peremptory thud. Then it opens and McQueen is standing in the gap. 'I'm going to need those cards,' he says. His tone is grim, his face set in a warning scowl.

'Of course,' Fournier says quickly. 'But come in, and close the door.'

McQueen has come prepared to argue. He is not expecting instant surrender and he doesn't seem enthused by it. He beckons impatiently for the cards.

'Please,' Fournier says. 'This is a really important matter . . . Lieutenant.'

His deliberate pause loads the last word with emphasis.

And it does the job. McQueen steps inside, kicking the door shut with his heel. He tries for indifference, but with indifferent success.

'What?' he says truculently.

Fournier holds up the radio. 'Brigadier Fry,' he says, omitting what would have to be a lengthy and complicated explanation. 'She's calling from Beacon. She wants to talk to you.'

Surprise makes McQueen's normally forbidding face, for a moment or two, a perfect blank. He takes the radio, but stares at it as though he is not certain what to do with it. When he puts it to his ear, he does so warily, with visible mistrust.

'McQueen,' he says. 'Over.'

He listens in silence for a long time. Fournier listens too, but though he strains to hear he gets no hint of what Brigadier Fry is saying. He is physically trembling with frustration and impatience when McQueen finally turns to him, covering the tiny radio with his big hand as though it's the mouthpiece of a phone.

'She says to tell you this is private,' he says, shrugging with his eyebrows as if to convey a shared exasperation with the vagaries of high-ranking officers. 'Sorry. You'll have to step out.'

45

Stephen Greaves dreams about the scarred girl.

In the dream she can talk, and she tells him about the life she lives with the other children. *It's really nice*, she says. *We don't remember our mums and dads at all, ever, and we don't need them. We've got each other.*

This sounds good to Greaves, but he is disconcerted to be having the conversation in the kitchen of the old house, where he lived with his mother and father until the day the hungries came. It reminds him of what he has lost, when the girl is denying the reality of loss.

Conflicting symbolism, some part of his mind comments. You want to believe, but you're telling yourself not to. Greaves leaves the thought parked in a storage bay somewhere behind or below the level of the dream. He thinks: behind? And then: below. He needs to be clear about spatial relationships even in dreams, where space is purely abstract and notional.

The kitchen is very fully realised, not abstract at all. His school bag stands on the table with Captain Power guarding it. His mother's last ever THINGS TO DO list is pinned to the fridge with magnet Homer and magnet Marge. It says:

EVACUATION 12.00 NOON LIBRARY!!!

I think you're all second generation, Greaves tells the scarred girl. *Children of the infected. So your mother had the pathogen in her system before you were born. You would never have known her as a human being.*

A human being is a very hard thing to be, the girl says gravely. Greaves agrees.

But seriously, she tells him. *Come and live with us. Bring Dr Khan.*

I can't do that. Greaves is sad to have to say it, but he knows it's true. *I can't be like you, and neither can Rina. I'm absolutely sure you need to be exposed to the infection in utero in order to form the symbiotic attachment to the* Cordyceps *fungus that you and the other children have.*

You're very clever, Stephen, the scarred girl says admiringly. *Thank you.*

But then, what's going to happen to Dr Khan?

As she says it, she points. Behind him. Greaves is meant to turn, and see what she is pointing at. That's the way the dream is meant to work. When he resists it, when he refuses to move his head, something clamps down on his shoulder. A hand.

Rina's hand.

She is there, at his back. Already changed. Already gone from herself for ever, sequestrated or erased by the infection.

I don't want to see, he pleads.

The girl nods. She understands. She gives him dispensation. *You don't have to look if you don't want to. But you have to decide. You have to know what you're going to do.*

Rina's grip tightens on his shoulder. She can't think any more, but clearly she agrees just the same.

And then it comes to him that it's not Rina's hand that's gripping him; it's Rina's teeth. In an access of pure panic, he tries to pull away. If she infects him, if he becomes a hungry, there won't be anybody who can save her. Losing him, she will lose herself.

As his muscle tears between her tightening jaws, he wakes. His face is drenched with tears, and his body with rank sweat. He is noxious and appalling to himself. If he went outside now, hungries would flock to him like bees to a flower. Like crows to the newly dead.

He sits up. The crew quarters are absolutely silent. Without even opening his curtain, Greaves slides out and down. His bare feet touch the metal of the floor and he almost gasps at the shocking cold. He hates that he doesn't have any shoes on but he is not prepared to take the risk of opening his locker. The less noise he makes, the less chance there is that he will be challenged, and pressed with questions that he can't answer.

By the light that filters in from the mid-section platform, he retrieves the sampling kit from his bag. Then he moves on tiptoe to the door, clutching the plastic vials protectively against his chest.

The platform seems to be empty, but as he moves across it he sees the colonel sitting against the airlock door, his head bowed onto his chest. Greaves is about to say hello when someone hails him from above with an urgent, repeated click of the tongue. He looks up. It's Sixsmith, manning the turret. Foss's watch is over, evidently, and she has taken the next stint.

She points to the colonel. 'Let him sleep,' she whispers. 'He was on his feet for forty hours straight.'

Greaves nods to show that he understands.

'What's going on in there that couldn't wait until morning?' Sixsmith demands in the same *sotto voce*. 'Never mind, don't tell me. But keep your voices down, and close the bulkhead door. We're meant to be going dark.'

Stephen is parsing these words as he steps into the lab, and one word in particular. *Voices*, plural.

Rina is standing at the work station beside the freezer. Actually she is leaning forward with both elbows on the bench. Her face is close up against the eyepiece of the TCM400 inverted phase microscope but her eyes, Greaves can see, are closed. They come open slowly as he pulls the bulkhead door across, and she turns to face him. She seems to have expected him, or at least she shows no surprise at his arrival.

On Stephen's side, the surprise is absolute. He has come here to be alone. To do work that nobody else must see. And for a moment he mistakes the vials and jars on the bench in front of Rina for his own samples. But they're not. They're the last batch of legacy cultures from the Charles Darwin, the ones that Private McQueen and Private Phillips brought down from Ben Macdhui the day before. Back when Private Phillips was still alive, along with Dr Sealey and Dr Penny.

So long ago.

Rina comes away from the bench with a wince of pain or effort, and crosses to where Greaves is standing. In this constricted space, it takes only four steps. She stares into his eyes. Normally she would know not to do that, would remember how hard it is for him to bear the searchlight beams of other people's gaze. Her own eyes are open very wide, the full circumference of each pupil clearly visible, and her irises are bigger than he has ever seen. They don't constrict at all, although the fluorescent tubes are very bright. Shadows like bruises underline them with savage emphasis, visible even on Rina's olive skin.

'What did you do to me?' she asks him. The words come out low but forceful, with a growl of exhaled breath. She smells of sickness. Her breath is freighted with bile and medicine.

'Rina,' Stephen says. And for a moment that is all he can offer her. Her own name, like a badge, like an incantation to conjure her back into herself.

She clutches at the lapels of his pyjamas and drags him close with surprising strength. 'What did you do?' she repeats. Greaves is still struggling with the words, still not quite able to marshal them into a coherent sequence, but in any case Rina lets him go, as suddenly as she seized him. Her finger-tips scrawl wavering lines down his chest as she turns away. Abruptly she sits down, in the middle of the floor. Her head sinks onto her clenched fists.

'It wasn't you,' she mutters. 'I'm sorry. I shouldn't take it out on you. John is dead, and I feel . . . I don't feel *enough*. It's as though I'm a long way away from you all. From everything here. None of it is real.'

Greaves is filled with dismay. Rina is reporting altered affect, which probably means that the inoculation's effect is wearing off. He has to make up another batch of serum immediately, using the new tissue samples he took from the dead children after he repaired the treads.

Also he has to answer her questions. Holding back the truth – although he has done so recently, with terrible effect – is for him like stopping a truck from rolling down a steep slope just with his hands.

He dumps the sampling kit down on the workbench and starts to remove the individual containers from their receptacles.

'It was,' he says. Quickly. Running across a minefield made of words. 'It was me, Rina. One of the children bit you and I had to stop you from changing. I gave you medicine I made out of the dead boy's cerebrospinal fluid. I came in here now to make some more.' He holds up two of the sampling tubes, one in each hand, to show her; but Rina isn't looking at him. Her head is drooping at an odd angle on her neck, as though it is too heavy to hold up, and she is staring with wide-open eyes at her bandaged arm. The bandages dangle loosely: at some point she must have removed the dressing and looked inside. She must have seen the bitemarks on her forearm.

'Yes,' she mutters at last. 'I knew that, really. I just forgot.'

Memory lapses. Another warning sign. He has to do this now, and he has to do it right.

He tells Rina the whole story as he works, in great haste, to prepare another batch of the serum. He doesn't really believe she's listening. He is just throwing out the words in the hope of holding her there – her consciousness, her Rina-ness – for a few minutes longer. He throws out questions, too. Does she remember what happened after they got back inside Rosie? How he locked the door, and how he pushed

Dr Fournier back into the engine room? 'You should have seen his face, Rina,' he babbles. 'You would have laughed!' It's only a guess. Not even that: it's something people say, about strange and grotesque moments when people act out of character or something unexpected happens. You should have seen their faces!

He can't look at her face, as he mixes and filters the live vaccine. He draws off seven millilitres, which leaves about twenty-five in the retort. It's a slightly bigger dose than before, but with the ingredients in exactly the same ratio. What he did before worked: he can't afford the luxury of experimentation.

Remembering the traumatic wrestling match that happened last time Greaves stays away from Rina's neck and injects instead into the median cubital vein, inside her left elbow. Rina helps, tapping the vein to make it dilate and protrude. That reassures him, but only for a moment. Does it mean she understands what he's doing, or is it only a muscle memory stimulated by the sight of the hypo?

He kneels beside her and waits in a nightmare of anxiety for her to respond. To say or do something that will tell him whether she's still there with him or gone for good. His interior clock keeps time: he can't turn it off. For seventeen desolate, drawn-out seconds there is nothing.

Then she reaches out and touches the back of his hand. With the tip of her index finger.

He lets out a held breath, trembling all over with relief.

'Hey,' Rina whispers weakly. 'Stephen. When did you get here?'

'Hey,' Greaves answers. His voice thickens and he can get no further.

Dr Khan's head comes up, slowly. Their eyes meet. Only

for a moment this time. She knows to look away at the moment when he starts to tense. But her fingertip presses harder against his skin. 'I need a drink,' she croaks.

They can't go through to the crew quarters without passing under Sixsmith's gaze, and neither of them is ready to do that. Also, it would be impossible for them to talk in there. Rina has some instant coffee hidden away at the back of a shelf, a precious store that John found on one of the forays they made when they were heading north. She draws off water from one of the stowed drums into a beaker and heats it with a Bunsen burner. They sit side by side on the workbench, their legs dangling, and take alternate sips. It's too bitter and too hot: the only comfort it brings is from the fact of their sharing it.

They talk in low voices.

'So how did Alan react when you told him?' Rina asks.

'When I told him what?'

'Duh! What do you think? About what you've made here, Stephen. About the—'

'I haven't told him.' He steps in quickly. If she doesn't say it, doesn't use the word *cure*, he doesn't have to unsay it.

'Great. I want to be there when you do. You know, I can't quite believe it. I can't believe it was this easy. My God, if John— if he had just lived a day longer . . .' She runs out of words, completes the thought with the smallest flexing of her hand.

Greaves shakes his head. He's walking a tightrope over the abyss of an outright lie. 'It will take more than a day,' he mumbles.

'You know what I mean,' Rina says. She touches the back of his hand again for a moment, her emotions overflowing in a way that scares him. 'You succeeded where everyone else failed. I'm proud of you.'

It's more than Greaves can bear. 'No, Rina, no,' he says. It sounds as though he's pleading. Perhaps he is. He pushes his clenched fist against his mouth to slow the words coming out, but he can't stop them.

'What do you mean, no?'

He is helpless in the grip of his compulsion.

'I didn't cure you,' he whispers. 'And I won't. I can't.'

46

With the first hint of light, when the air is still chill enough to use the enhanced mode on the glasses, Sixsmith takes a reading and declares that they're alone. McQueen doesn't really believe that, but he keeps up the pretence as they pack away the sensors and the traps, expecting at every moment to be caught in a cloudburst of slingshot stones and baby-faced monsters.

The aim is to move out quick and quiet, to be on the road and up to speed before the feral kids know they're gone. That timetable hits a slight snag when Foss does a head count and discovers that Dr Akimwe is no longer on board. McQueen is not in the least surprised. If he has ever seen a dead man walking it was Akimwe, from the very moment he was told that Gary Phillips hadn't made it.

None of the doctor's possessions are missing, but he has opened up the gun locker (Phillips must have given him the code) and removed one of the handguns. 'The doss fucker hasn't taken any ammo though,' McQueen reports after a thorough check. 'The magazine ought to have been full, but after that he's on his own.'

Rosie's electronic log indicates that the passenger-side cockpit door opened and closed again at 2.17 a.m. Sixsmith was still on watch in the turret, and saw and heard nothing.

There is yet another yack-athon in the crew quarters, and they all get into a pointless shouting match over the odds of finding Akimwe if they turn around. They just won't, it's as simple as that. Not unless he sticks to the road, and if he intended to do that there wouldn't be much point in sneaking away like a ninja in the first place.

'He's gone to bury Phillips,' Sixsmith says. 'That's where we'll find him.'

'Yeah, but no,' McQueen observes. 'He's not going to get that far.'

'For fuck's sake!' Sixsmith is on her feet, glaring at him. 'Four KIAs aren't enough for you? If we go slowly, we can pick him up with the infra-reds. He can't have got far.'

But they would be driving back towards the children, and that's a bridge too far for all of them. When the colonel gives the order to keep on going south, nobody raises a squeak. Not even Sixsmith. McQueen guesses that she's just feeling bad because she let the doctor sneak out past her. Like it's on her somehow that Akimwe decided to kill himself. If they did manage to catch up with him, McQueen thinks, the first thing he personally would do is smack Akimwe in the head with a rifle butt for stealing the handgun. The handgun is actually useful.

They get moving at last. The atmosphere on board is

as tense as hell. It feels to McQueen as though they're all counting odds. All except for him, anyway. What he is doing is brooding over an imaginary Venn diagram entitled 'my enemy's enemy is my friend'. Brigadier Fry has promised to give him back his commission if he will help her with a little problem, the problem in question being Colonel Isaac Carlisle.

There is absolutely no downside to dropping the colonel in a bathtub full of broken glass. But conspiracies, cabals, other people's agendas, it all sticks in McQueen's throat a little and makes him want to balk. He'd rather just go round and round with the colonel on a little patch of grass somewhere. Hand him a split lip, a few broken ribs, maybe the odd tooth. Shepherd him to a few conclusions about human dignity.

But that's not going to happen. And if Beacon is going all to pieces, with the brigadier doing the carving, he will need to find a place to stand. Might as well pick the one that comes with the fringe benefit of the colonel getting his ticket punched. They're all as bad as each other, in his opinion, but the colonel is the only one McQueen ever had some respect for, and therefore the only one who has ever disappointed him. He has this coming.

He goes to Carlisle, in the cockpit, and asks for permission to speak in private – with a pointed sideways glance at Sixsmith in the driving seat. They go astern, all the way to the lab. Nobody is working there. The colonel closes the door and waits for McQueen to speak.

McQueen puts Fournier's little radio down on the workbench. Carlisle stares at it, a slow frown descending over his face. 'Whose?' he says. He knows what he's looking at, and probably he has guessed right away what it means.

'Fournier's. It's a one-to-one. Permanently welded to a single freq. In case you're wondering who's on the other end, it's Brigadier Fry.'

Carlisle nods, accepting the explanation without question. Because why not? It makes so much sense. 'And how did you come by it?' he asks McQueen.

'Heard him talking, walked in on him. He spilled it all without me even asking. Fry wanted someone to keep an eye on us out here. Playing the political game, some such fuckery. I suppose she picked Fournier because she knew he'd roll over when he was told to. He wasn't ever going to say no.'

Carlisle picks the radio up at last. 'It's still functional?'

McQueen nods. 'I didn't talk to Fry, but I could hear an adjutant repeating a call sign for a couple of minutes after I took it away from Fournier.' This is looking good. The old sod is buying the whole prospectus. It's not as though he has a lot of choice, at this point. The radio is a big deal no matter how you look at it. A lifeline. They were lost, and now they're found. Carlisle can't do anything but take it and use it.

McQueen waits. The colonel says nothing.

'Might have bruised the doctor a little bit in passing,' McQueen offers. 'I hope I'm not on a charge or anything. He really didn't want to let go.'

Carlisle looks at him hard. Really searches his face. McQueen endures the scrutiny, deadpan to a fault.

'Yeah, you're very welcome,' he says at last, to break the heavy silence.

Carlisle doesn't even say 'dismissed'. He just pockets the radio and walks back to the cockpit. Turns his back on McQueen like McQueen isn't even there.

Oh shit, does he have this coming.

On his way through the crew quarters, Carlisle has time to notice how quiet things are. Not a good quiet, an enervated one. Foss is lying in her bunk with an arm thrown across her eyes, too exhausted even to sleep. Stephen Greaves sits at the table with his arms in his lap, staring at nothing. Samrina Khan is in the galley area gripping the counter top on either side of the sink, head down as though she is about to throw up or else just has.

The colonel is perturbed about the radio, and even more so about McQueen. He has always been reasonably skilled in the assessment of character but there is something in McQueen that is opaque to him. Perhaps he has allowed some mistrust to take root in his mind for that reason alone, quite apart from his doubts about the man's fitness as a soldier. But finding the radio was a good thing, and handing it over was a better one.

The radio. It's a godsend, but Carlisle strongly dislikes what it implies. When he takes his seat next to Sixsmith, when he sets the small device down on the cockpit's console, he feels as though he has picked up a great weight rather than shedding an insignificant one.

Sixsmith is staring at the radio in wonder. 'Where the bloody hell did that come from?' she demands.

'A contribution from Dr Fournier,' the colonel observes, keeping his tone carefully neutral. There is no point in letting his anger show. No point in feeling it, although that ship has

338

already sailed. There has never been trust between himself and the brigadier. When he tried to resign his commission – the most passive of protests – she read it as open rebellion and argued him out of it. She has been afraid ever since that he will attack her again from a different direction. And he has felt close, recently, to doing it. That was why Fry sent him away. But clearly sending him away wasn't enough.

'Dr Fournier,' Sixsmith repeats, making the name sound like a swearword.

'Apparently this was issued to him when we left Beacon, as a fallback in case of emergency. I think our current circumstances qualify.' There's no more to be said on that topic; no more, at least, that Carlisle can trust himself to say. 'I'm going to call Beacon, Private,' he tells Sixsmith. 'If I get through, I may need your help in maintaining the contact. This is a very small and very directional device. If we start to lose signal strength, please slow the vehicle and be prepared to stop if I tell you to.'

Sixsmith shoots him a look freighted with unspoken questions. 'Yes, sir.'

Carlisle switches on the radio and waits. There is almost no static, just a low hum of electronics. After a while a male voice speaks. 'Brigadier Fry's field line.'

'This is Colonel Carlisle,' the colonel says. 'I'd like to speak with the brigadier if she's available.'

There is no pause at all, and no surprise in the man's tone. 'Yes, Colonel. One moment.' They were expecting me, Carlisle thinks. Most likely the doctor missed a scheduled call-in and they drew their own conclusions.

'Isaac.' Fry's voice this time, and although she sounds weary and stressed she makes more of a performance out of being caught unawares. 'How did you find this frequency? I don't recall giving it to you.'

'I'm calling you on Dr Fournier's radio, Brigadier.' He doesn't offer an explanation, but moves straight to the substance of his report. 'We're now heading south towards the northern end of the M1, and making good speed. But there have been developments of the utmost significance of which you and the whole of the Main Table need to be apprised.'

'Go ahead,' Fry says.

He doesn't waste words. First he details Greaves' find, because that's the nub of the matter. They are carrying a specimen that is absolutely unique and whose scientific importance cannot be overstated. A child who seems to have a partial immunity to the hungry pathogen! A child whose remains might hold the key to a cure.

Only after that does he fill in the details about the botched search party and the deaths. He states, formally and for the record, that he is taking full responsibility for these things. Finally he makes it clear that Rosie is running for home, non-negotiably, and that she might not be alone when she arrives.

When he has finished speaking, there is a long silence. To his right and at the periphery of his vision, Private Sixmith's hands grip the wheel more tightly than is strictly necessary.

'So after seven months of nothing to report,' Brigadier Fry says at last, 'you're now saying that you may have made a definitive breakthrough?' Her tone is clinical, with no trace of enthusiasm or curiosity.

'Yes. Exactly.'

'The timing is interesting, Isaac. I might almost be tempted to say suspicious.'

Carlisle is baffled, both by the words and by the coldly accusing way in which they're spoken. 'Suspicious?' he repeats. 'I don't understand, Brigadier. What is it that you suspect?'

Another silence. 'It's not important,' Fry says at last. 'I'll consider what needs to be done. Keep the radio open on this frequency.'

This last instruction is meaningless, since the little radio lacks a tuner. Lutes might have been able to tweak it onto another frequency using parts from the main cockpit radio, but nobody else on board would have a clue how to do that.

But the dead air from the radio makes it clear that Fry has signed off. Evidently Sixsmith feels free, now, to draw the moral. 'So Dr Fournier has been spying on us all ever since we hit the road.'

'Beacon was at liberty to set up multiple reporting systems,' Carlisle says carefully. Mechanically defending the status quo. Why does he do that? Why has he spent his whole life servicing and sanctioning bad decisions made by people he can only despise? He lets out a breath that turns out to be a sigh.

'Yes,' he admits. 'Dr Fournier has been filing secret reports to the Muster, although he's meant to be civilian commander. I'll make an official complaint on our return to Beacon.'

'How about an unofficial smack in the face?' Sixsmith's tone is tight, and the colonel doesn't believe she is joking.

'Private,' he says, 'it's not worth risking a reprimand or a dishonourable discharge over—'

Fry's voice cuts him off. The channel is open again, and might have been all along. 'I've arranged an escort for you,' the brigadier says without preamble. 'It's of the utmost importance

341

that your specimen is taken back to Beacon for further study, and the Rosalind Franklin alone is too vulnerable to attack.'

'Very well,' Carlisle says. 'What are your orders?'

'Rendezvous at base Hotel Echo, near Bedford, forty-eight hours from now. If you're going to have trouble making that rendezvous, let me know well in advance.'

'I'm not familiar with Hotel Echo,' Carlisle admits.

'There's no reason why you should be, Colonel. It doesn't exist yet. It's the former RAF Henlow. We're refitting it as a forward base for tech retrieval runs into Stevenage and Milton Keynes. Take down the coordinates.'

Carlisle does. The brigadier goes on to give him more detailed instructions for the rendezvous. She will arrange for a squad of twenty soldiers to be present, along with three armoured vehicles, all under the command of a Captain Manolis. If they are not present, Carlisle is simply to wait. On no account is he to use the radio, either to speak to the brigadier herself or to attempt to make contact with anyone else at Beacon. When Captain Manolis makes himself known, Carlisle will turn Rosie over to him and ride in a staff car to Beacon, ahead of the rest of the column, for immediate debriefing.

Carlisle believes he knows what debriefing will entail in this context. Despite their revolutionary discovery, the expedition has sustained unacceptable losses and by military logic someone has to be to blame. He will take that blame, while Fournier takes the credit for the new specimen. Possibly this or something like it has been the plan all along, from before they even left Beacon. Possibly the only purpose of the expedition in the brigadier's mind was to allow Carlisle a public opportunity to fail.

Fry is still talking him through the protocols for the rendezvous. Assuming the absence of hungries, she tells the colonel, he and his people are to exit Rosie first, bringing the specimen with them, and assemble on base Hotel Echo's main parade ground. Manolis and his squad will then make themselves known, retrieve the specimen and carry out a handover in good order.

Fry asks Carlisle to confirm and accept these orders. He does, but he feels compelled to add something despite Sixsmith's presence beside him. 'You should have trusted me, Geraldine. I've never given you any reason to question my loyalty to Beacon or to the Muster.'

'Well,' Fry says. The word hangs by itself for a moment. 'Loyalty is just the wheels on the bus, Isaac.'

'Meaning what?'

'Meaning that it keeps things moving but it's neutral when it comes to the direction they move in.'

The colonel contains a twinge of exasperation. 'I believe that's actually the point I was making. I've been neutral to a degree that could fairly be called pathological. Yet you decided you needed eyes on me all the same. Can I ask why that is?'

There is a pause, filled only with static.

'We've missed you, Isaac,' the brigadier says. 'I look forward to hearing all about your adventures north of the border.'

She cuts the channel.

He knows the answer to his question in any case. Fry is a political animal engaged perpetually in a zero-sum game: she plays it skilfully, in all circumstances, and she has an unerring sense of the cards that other people are holding. As she has consolidated her hold on power, Carlisle has been almost the only Muster officer with the combination of high profile and public approval to challenge her. She has never stopped waiting for him to play out the hand.

The colonel stares out of the forward windscreen. The road opens ahead of them, miraculously clear. They are making good progress for the first time since they rolled out of Invercrae.

But where are they going?

47

In the crew quarters, Dr Khan is falling.

Her hands are braced against the edge of the sink, her feet firmly planted on the steel plates of Rosie's floor, but all the same she is in freefall. She has been like this for hours – ever since she spoke to Stephen in the lab – and she still hasn't hit bottom. Perhaps there is no bottom.

Lieutenant Foss mutters in her sleep. Something about roast chicken. Something about time. Khan plummets through the diffuse froth of the lieutenant's voice without slowing.

They're going home, but that's not real. John is dead, which is just about as real as it gets, but even that is just a fact she has to remind herself of every few minutes, to keep her grieving fresh.

'The road is going to get bumpy,' Sixsmith calls from the cockpit. In the absence of the intracom, she has to rely on her own natural bellow. 'There's a heap of old cars ahead, but they're mostly just rust and moss. I think they'll pretty much break apart when we hit them, but you'll feel a jolt. Hold on tight.'

Khan holds on tight. It makes no difference.

'Rina,' Stephen says at her elbow. 'You'd better strap in. The baby . . .'

The baby. Yes. All right. She slows herself, opens her eyes on a present moment where she desperately wants not to be. A fierceness rises in her, ballasts her. She pulls herself together; brings herself, by the application of her will, to a dead halt – although Rosie rumbles on. The baby needs her to make rational decisions about her own safety, since her safety ensures its own.

She crosses to a chair, hands cradling her swollen belly, sits down, straps in. Stephen takes the seat beside her and checks the straps, making sure that they're not crossed or twisted and that the inertia reel is running free. Sixsmith's warning has woken Foss but she just turns over in the bunk and digs in out of sight.

'Lieutenant Foss,' Stephen calls out. 'We need to—'

'I'll take my chances,' Foss grunts.

Rosie shudders and rocks. The deck plates creak. They're flung from side to side by sudden shifts, lurches, stops and starts. Khan stares straight ahead, braced tight in her chair.

It's not a cure, Stephen had said. In the lab. When they spoke. When they spoke before. *I know what the cure will look like, but I didn't have the time to make it. All I could do was stabilise you, in a sort of brute force way. The feral children secrete their own neurotransmitters that talk back to the fungus, and now your brain has those chemicals, too.* Cordyceps *thinks you're a friend.* Cordyceps *thinks you're all part of one big fungal colony.*

'But that *is* a cure,' Khan whispered. In her desperation she had held onto his sleeve, almost touching him, almost invading him. 'That's the definition of a cure, Stephen — a way to keep the pathogen from changing us. It's what we've been looking for all along! It's enough. Isn't it enough?'

No.

Yes.

Maybe, if there was enough medicine. But there won't be. Even for her, he won't keep making it. He'll keep her stabilised until the birth, until the life inside her has undocked. That will use up all the serum he has on hand, and he won't go hunting for fresh ingredients. Not given where they would have to come from.

Which is to say the brains and spinal columns of the feral children.

He won't commit murder for her.

When he told her that, and when she realised that her life as a human being was measurable in days or perhaps in hours, she felt herself fall. She fell away from him and Rosie and her stolid, helpless self, from everything that demanded an answer out of her.

Such a luxury. Such a mountain of self-pity. She hates herself for having that traitor inside her, that coward. She is back now. In the driving seat, whatever that might mean. She will see this through for the baby's sake, given that as of now she has no sake of her own.

It helps to think of herself as a vessel. Like Rosie. Carrying a precious cargo over rough terrain, heading for a harbour where most likely — having served her purpose — she will be mothballed and dismantled. There is no shame in that. No stigma in being dead once you've done everything you needed to do. She has this payload to deliver. She needs to keep her armour up until the job is finished.

A sudden clenching of her stomach promises that the job will be finished soon.

What if she outed him? Shouted out Stephen's secret to the rest of the crew? McQueen would get the recipe out of him at the point of a bayonet, squeeze him like a sponge. The world would be saved.

But no. It wouldn't. The treatment seems to require regular top-ups, like the Td toxoid vaccine for tetanus. Khan glimpses a future in which the feral children are caught, brought to maturity, bred in pens the way pigs and sheep used to be before the Breakdown. Farmed for their nerve tissue.

How many lives is my life worth? she wonders, dazed and sickened. She can't do the maths. While the baby is still inside her, she won't even try.

But she'll keep her mouth shut, as they rush towards separation. What happens after that will depend on who she is when they get there.

48

Night falls and they keep on moving. Slowly, with circum-
spection, but always pushing forward. It's a calculated risk.
The road is wide and flat and they can see a long way out in
front of them. This far north the obstacles are few, and since
Sixsmith has charted them on their way up she is unlikely
to be surprised.

With the first hint of dawn, she accelerates again. Rosie
attains her ponderous top speed and eats up the miles.
Hungries see them and give chase – not the children, just
the regular kind – but mostly they don't get close. When they
do, Rosie ploughs them under with a barely perceptible bump.

They are still two days out of Beacon by anybody's reck-
oning, but they're not heading for Beacon now. If they keep
to this speed, they've got one more day, one more night.
They'll make it to the rendezvous sometime around sun-up
tomorrow. There has been talk of helicopter gunships. They

will ride home in style, leaving Rosie behind them like a steel rind, a shed skin.

That thought causes Lieutenant Foss a twinge of melancholy, but in every other respect the news is good. She has had more than enough of the field. She wants a hot bath, a sweaty fuck (these thoughts are not coming in any kind of logical sequence) and above all the feeling that if she lets her guard down nothing will take a bite out of her. This is what she's living for now, and it's close enough that the pleasant fantasies she is indulging feel like promises to herself that she can actually keep.

Looking around her, though, she's not seeing the same enthusiasm. Okay, the whitecoats are in mourning. She gets that, and she respects it. But the colonel isn't saying a word to anyone, Sixsmith is sullen and even McQueen has closed up tighter than a nun's hope chest.

She finds him in the mid-section, making ammunition. It's something she does herself, but she has never seen him take an interest. The RIH cartridges and vintage Lapua Magnums that Beacon uses as standard issue seem to suit him well enough, and he hasn't seemed impressed by her highly technical arguments about long-range stopping power versus short-range accuracy. Now he's sitting there on the floor with a non-electric press and a Lee Challenger reloader (she is pretty sure it's hers), cleaning out spent primers with the quiet intensity of a monk flicking through the best bits of his rosary.

'You pick your times,' Foss says, nudging his shoulder with her knee. 'What do you think you're going to be shooting?'

'You never know,' McQueen says. He doesn't look up from his work.

Foss leans back against the turret rail and watches the landscape roll on by. She feels a strong determination to squeeze a companionable moment out of this. 'Remember that time on the way up when we got stuck in the mud and had to hammer the front winch into the fucking asphalt because there was nothing else to tie it to?'

McQueen tamps another primer down, decants powder into the Challenger's narrow hopper. 'What about it?'

'Nothing. I'm just looking forward to never doing it again, that's all.'

No response.

'What are you looking forward to?' Foss prompts.

He looks up at her now, his eyes cold. 'Some peace and quiet,' he says.

Foss can take a hint. 'Fine,' she says. 'Enjoy.' She leaves him to his home-mades, which frankly are not up to the standard of hers. He is sloppy with the calipers and uneven with the powder.

The crew quarters feel uncomfortably empty, like a jawline with some fresh, raw gaps between the teeth. Khan is lying down, her pale face shiny with sweat. The Robot is soaking a towel at the sink, which he carries across to her. She is clutching her big belly and muttering to herself under her breath. Counting, it sounds like. Foss puts two and two together and gets a total of *holy shit!*

'You're kidding me,' she says. 'It's coming? It's coming *now*?'

'Soon,' Greaves says, giving Foss a quick, anguished glance. 'The contractions are fifteen minutes apart.' Khan says nothing. Her eyes are open and she's staring at the ceiling. She is deep inside herself somewhere, barely aware of her surroundings.

351

'Okay,' Foss says. But what the hell does that mean? Should she do something, or just let this run its course? What's the significance of fifteen minutes apart? How long does that give them?

The last question is the pertinent one. 'Khan,' she says, 'are you about to drop? Give me an ETA, for the love of Christ.'

'It could be a few hours yet,' the Robot tells her. 'When she's fully dilated, the contractions will come a lot faster. And probably her waters will break.' Still nothing from Khan, not even a look.

Foss turns her attention back to Greaves. 'Can you do the necessary?' she asks him. The Robot! She can't believe the words that are coming out of her mouth. But what's the alternative? Somehow she can't imagine either Fournier or McQueen telling Khan to bear down – and the colonel and Sixsmith have other fish to fry. It's going to be the two of them, God help them, and Foss has no idea which of them will turn out to be the better qualified. She's pretty sure Greaves has never touched a woman in his life, but he sounds like he's got the theory all down. They'll just have to do the best they can.

She sticks around in the crew quarters, out of a general sense that Zero Hour won't be long in coming. To pass the time she plays patience. McQueen has her loader, and in any case she's stacked up all the ammo she needs.

About an hour into this vigil Khan starts to thrash and snarl. It's not a symptom of imminent childbirth that Foss has ever heard of. The doctor sounds fucking alarming, no doubt about it. But Greaves runs to the lab and comes back a minute or so later with a hypo, which he empties into Khan's arm, and she quietens down again.

'What was that?' Foss asks. She expects a one-word answer

– painkiller, maybe, or sedative, or maybe some medical word she won't understand. But the Robot doesn't answer at all. He gives a low moan, as though he's in pain, and rocks on the spot, from one foot to the other.

'Shit!' Foss exclaims. 'Greaves . . .'

'Hold back the symptoms,' the Robot moans. His face flushes and his hands flutter in the air, describing some complicated, abstract shape. 'The progression. It's a suppressant. Palliative. Palliative care. Not . . . it's not a cure.'

'Okay,' Foss says, softly softly. A cure for pregnancy? She'd love to see what that might look like. 'I withdraw the question. Don't sweat it.'

'Thank you,' Greaves mutters, his shoulders sagging a little. He actually looks relieved, as though her saying that was a real concession.

Foss changes the subject, for his sake. 'Hey, should I boil some water? Is that a thing?'

'I've already sterilised the lab,' Greaves says, eyes intently down as though he's checking that the deck plates are still there. 'We don't need water.'

'Okay then,' Foss agrees. 'All good.'

And they're all good for about three hours or so after that. It's actually quite peaceful in the crew quarters. Foss playing endless games of patience, lost in the algorithmic flow like it's a Zen meditation, and Khan pumping air through her teeth in a rhythm that accelerates and then falls back again and again like the tide hitting the base of a cliff.

Then, just as Foss is teasing out her third ace, Doctor Khan's waters go like Niagara fucking Falls, dripping through her inch-thick mattress to rain down on the bottom bunk (which is Dr Fournier's, so no harm done).

'Looks like we're on, sugar lump,' Foss says lightly.

When you're a mile outside the limits of your competence, there is some comfort to be had in sounding like you know what you're doing.

49

I'm still me, Khan thinks.

Checking. Making sure it's true. It should be true by definition – she thinks therefore she is – but maybe the voice in your mind goes stumbling on after the lights go out, just doing its own thing because that's all it knows.

So she forces herself to remember. Making love with John, the viva exam she gave when she delivered her doctoral thesis, fragments of her childhood. She reviews them in her mind and she goes over their meanings. Because if they have meanings then she is still human.

But she has to do these things in the gaps between the contractions, and the gaps are getting shorter. Every ten minutes, then every five, then every three, her body closes like a vice and the horizon rushes right in. There is nothing beyond the pain.

At the edges of it, something. The cold metal of the

dissecting table under her back and her bum and the soles of her feet. The tang of disinfectant, her profession's holy incense, in the air. She's in the lab. They've brought her to the lab, because it's her time.

She is sailing the ship out of the bottle, pushing another human being out of her body. A tiny, imperfect replica of herself, or it might be of John, whipped up out of whatever pieces of them were available, milled and ground and mixed and left to rise in the oven of her abdomen. And at the last moment, the extra, top-secret ingredient: *Cordyceps*.

She moans aloud.

'You're doing fine, Doctor.' That's Foss. Foss is here. And Stephen too, his touch taboo forgotten. Or not. His eyes are wide as he squeezes her hand, giving her the time signature for her breathing in a Morse code of pressure and release.

'Oh shit!' Foss says. 'I can see the head. I can see the baby's head!'

'You have to hold back,' Stephen murmurs urgently, leaning low over her with his eyes averted. 'Use the breathing to get through it. Relax, Rina. Try to relax.'

When she was six, her father put her on her brand-new bike and rolled it down a hill. *That's how you learn*, he said. The bike went faster and faster and she just held on to the handlebars for grim death, too terrified to brake or steer, until the bike strayed into a garden wall and she fell right off it, going full tilt. Her arm was broken. Her mother called her father a brainless bastard and he said again, stubbornly, *That's how you learn*.

Quae nocent saepe docent. Pain is the great teacher.

'Okay, now push! Bear down, Doctor Khan!'

'Bear down, Rina!'

Pain has no agenda at all. It teaches us nothing, except what hurts. And if you can't avoid the things that hurt then what use is the lesson?

Pain clenches in her, moves through her in drenching waves, until finally it finds an outlet.

Her baby cries.

'Holy fuck,' Lieutenant Foss shouts jubilantly. And then again, 'Holy fuck, the eagle has landed!'

There is concerted movement in the space between Khan's tented legs. Something parts from her. A fullness becomes a yawning absence. Cold air strums her sweat-soaked thighs.

'It's a boy. And he looks healthy. Nice work, Doctor Khan.' Then, in a different tone, 'He's covered in this gunk. Is that normal?'

'Yes,' Greaves says. 'It's normal. Let her hold him.'

The baby is placed in her arms. He smells of blood and of her. Of sweetness and the slaughterhouse. He has fought his furious way into the world and now he lies exhausted on her breast. Red-brown smears mark where his tiny fist slides against her skin.

'John,' she whispers.

'No,' Greaves says. 'It's me. It's Stephen.'

'She's naming the baby, dickhead. After its dad.'

But she's not. Nor is she forgetting that John is dead. She just wants to invoke him now, to have him be here for this in some way. She aches to have him touch her and say her name. More than that, she aches to have him see what they have made between the two of them. The miraculous solidity and presence of it. This is the other side of the equation. Thesis: John died. Antithesis: the baby is alive.

He finds her nipple, but does nothing with it. Just breathes, lips parted around the swollen teat.

50

On the A1(M), a little way north of Leeds, they hit a roadblock that they can't get around or roll over. Sheets of corrugated tin shored up with stacks of tyres into which concrete has been poured. Someone's idea of a border control, maybe. Keep the hungries way down south with the city bankers and the landed gentry, or alternatively push them up north with the chavs and the oiks. The occasional scatter of wind-bleached bones suggests that the barricade may not have been fit for purpose, either way. Hungries are stateless, their allegiance only to the next square meal.

The soldiers have to get out and clear a path. The white-coats too, except for Dr Khan who has a baby to look after, which everyone has to admit is a pretty solid excuse. Fournier pitches in with the rest of them, Sixsmith observes with grim approval. She would have dragged the treacherous little bastard out of the engine room by the back of his neck if he had tried to hide in there.

'How did we miss this mess coming up?' McQueen complains. He is massively hungover after a late-night session with a bottle of single malt he found in Dr Akimwe's personal effects.

'We made a side-trip into Wakefield,' Sixsmith grunts, rolling a concrete-filled tyre off the road. 'We didn't come up this stretch at all.' Her arms and back are aching and she's got to get back into the driving seat after they're finished here. She's in a foul mood and it's not getting better.

Colonel Carlisle suggests tersely that they save the conversation for later. It's a cold, clear day and the sound will carry. Better for all of them if it doesn't carry too far.

But Foss doesn't seem to have got the memo. She is looking back up the road, first of all shading her eyes and then sighting through the scope of her gun. 'We've got incoming,' she shouts. 'Guys, you've got to see this.'

Everyone turns to look. The cluster of moving dots more than a mile back along the road could be anything. Sheep. Stray dogs. Or hungries, always the odds-on favourite. But they're moving in a kind of loose formation, strung out across the road, and their pace is a steady, indefatigable jog rather than a hungry's swallow-dive sprint.

'No bloody way,' Sixsmith says, lodging a protest with reality.

'Oh my God!' Dr Fournier whispers.

It's the feral kids, still on the trail. And still keeping pace with them after more than a hundred and fifty miles.

The colonel raps out orders, but it's only the blindingly obvious. Get the last few bits and pieces off the road, get back into Rosie – stat! – and get moving.

Everybody jumps to it. Except for McQueen, who stands out in the road with his M407 in his hands and a contemplative look on his face. A mile is a long trip even for a gun like that, but the word is going around that McQueen has decided to roll his own ammunition for once. He's got to be tempted to try out his bespoke rounds on these obligingly available targets. Slowly he raises the rifle to the ready position.

'Mr McQueen,' the colonel calls. 'We need you here.'

McQueen gooses the scope, reads off distance and wind speed. His finger touches the trigger, starts to pull back with soft, even pressure. But then he turns, the rifle still in position. He's pointing it right at the Old Man now, his hand rock-steady, the trigger still drawn halfway back.

'Sorry, sir,' he says. 'What was that again?'

The colonel looks at McQueen down the barrel of the rifle, absolutely impassive. 'We need another pair of hands,' he says. 'Now. You can display your virtuosity another time, when it will actually do some good.'

Sixsmith braces herself for the big bang. It feels to her as though it has to happen. Because how could McQueen make a threat like that and then back down from it? They've all seen this. That alone should force the issue.

But McQueen doesn't fire. He just glares at the colonel over the rifle's sights, from which he has finally taken his eye.

'You're not nearly as fucking clever as you think you are,' he says. There's a bleakness in his voice, as though he is announcing the time of the patient's death.

Carlisle seems to consider this. 'Are any of us?' he asks at last. 'Move those stones, and that sheet.' And he turns away, as though the menace of the sniper rifle isn't something he needs to worry about or even acknowledge.

361

It could still happen, Sixsmith thinks. She takes a step forward, not knowing what she means to do but wanting to be close enough that doing it might be an option.

But there is no need. McQueen lets out a heavy, dissatisfied breath. Then he slings the M407 and gets to work. They're done in a minute, back inside Rosie in ninety seconds, battened down with the mid-section sealed.

'Go,' the colonel tells Sixsmith.

She bolts for the cockpit, fires up and goes. The wild things eat their exhaust.

For the next fifty miles or so, she is marvelling at two things, alternating so they both get a fair share of her attention.

The kids are keeping up, somehow. This is personal for them, it must be. They don't just want a meal, they want that specimen back. Or more likely they want blood.

And McQueen, in that long drawn-out moment, didn't. What he wanted wasn't clear at all.

51

Dr Khan is back in her own bunk. Stephen has changed the sheets and the mattress. With the gaps in the roster, there were plenty of spares lying ready to hand. She believes she is lying now on what was John's mattress, and the thought pleases her.

The baby sleeps, wakes, rests upon her. After that first coming-into-the-world cry, he hasn't uttered a sound. He also hasn't fed. From time to time, he mumbles and kneads at Khan's breast as though he's picking a fight with it, but he doesn't make any attempt to drink, no matter how much she coaxes.

She expresses milk with her fingers, wets the baby's lips with it. He wrinkles up his face in something like frustration. His mouth opens and closes but he doesn't lick his lips, doesn't swallow.

Khan is aware when Rosie stops, and when she starts

again. The question why does not occur to her. Her mind is engaged with another question, which looms a whole lot bigger.

A short while after their motion resumes, a shadow falls across the bunk's closed curtains.

'Rina,' Stephen whispers.

She sits up. 'Now?'

'I think so. It's better not to cut it too close.'

He withdraws again. Khan wraps the towelling robe – Akimwe's, opulently thick and fleecy, scavenged by Stephen from the doctor's locker – around herself and climbs awkwardly and gingerly out of the bunk. The baby is asleep again and she considers leaving him behind, well tucked in and bracketed by pillows so he can't fall out of the bunk. But it's too soon for them to be away from each other, her and this little separated part of her. She lifts him up, cradling his head, and posts him through the collar of the robe, holding him in there against the well-stoked furnace of her body, out of the world's cold airs.

There is nobody in sight. Presumably Fournier is asleep in his bunk, or in the engine room, and the soldiers are at their stations. Stephen is already walking astern and she follows him, padding softly on bare feet. The floor vibrates and rocks under her with Rosie's forward movement. She uses one hand to anchor herself, the other to hug the baby to her. If she falls, she will do her best to roll and land on her back, protecting him with her body.

Someone is up in the turret but Khan only sees boots in the gun-platform stirrups. Whoever is up there doesn't hear them, or at least doesn't look down.

The lab is a dark cave. It stinks of preserving chemicals

364

and (a soft undercurrent) of the things they have failed to preserve. Stephen doesn't turn on the lights at first. He draws the door across very slowly, avoiding any noise that might be heard over the sounds of the engine, the road and the wind.

Khan waits in the dark until the fluorescents shudder on. Then she waits in the light. Stephen prepares a hypo, taking minute care. Measuring, filtering, measuring again. Finally he turns.

'Roll up your sleeve,' he mutters.

But she can't. That would mean using both hands; would mean letting go of the baby.

'How long do I have?' she asks instead.

Stephen stands rigidly still. The hypo points at the ceiling and both his hands are clasped around its base. He looks like a knight in a pre-Raphaelite painting, pledging his sword to the service of God or some other random cause.

'How long?' she says again.

'There are two more doses after this. About the same size or a little smaller. They might last six or seven hours each. Maybe even eight, but that would be pushing it. I don't think they're . . . I don't see them lasting that long.'

A day then, at the outside. She looks at her watch, finds that it's a little after three in the morning. She will still be human when the sun comes up. She should even see it go down again. After that, all bets are off.

'Someone has to look after the baby,' she says. That's the most urgent thing. The only urgent thing. Slipping away from herself will be the easiest proposition in the world. It's staying here that's hard. But how can she die and leave her newborn son unprotected? The world is a threshing machine and she would just be letting him fall into the blades.

'I wanted,' Stephen mutters, 'to run some tests. On . . . John. After I've injected you.'

Khan steps back, both hands enfolding the tiny form. He moves, and he makes a sound; a soft, half-vocalised breath. But he doesn't wake. 'No,' she says. 'His name isn't John, and no.'

'Just to see,' Stephen insists.

'To see what?'

He hesitates, chooses his words. But he chooses very badly. 'What he is. To make sure.'

'He's human,' Khan snaps. 'As human as I am.'

Stephen doesn't pick up the warning in her tone. 'I think being human means something different now.'

Which is basically what he said already.

I didn't cure you. And I won't. Because the main ingredient of the cure would be the children, and I can't do that to them.

Can you imagine, Rina? Half a million people in Beacon. Half a million doses of vaccine, just to start with. If I bring this home, if I tell them . . . We'll scour the whole country, from one end to the other. Probably we'll have to send some raiding parties across the Channel, too. And then when that isn't enough – not nearly enough – we'll start a breeding programme. Capture female hungries alive and impregnate them. Take the babies, and . . .

Mulch them down. Liquidise and synthesise and mass produce.

Build massive battery farms full of insentient brood mares. Fill them and empty them again and again.

Perhaps if it were just hungries they were talking about it would be bearable. But Khan remembers the potlatch in the forest. The scarred girl accepting the plastic voice box, then taking the keychain from her belt and handing it to Stephen. She looks down at his waist, sees that it's still there:

the little plastic man saluting her with his expression of arch amusement.

Marco? Mario? Something like that. A child's toy, manufactured by the billions in an age when everything – life, food, comfort, safety – came without effort.

The children are human in every way that counts. Growing up in the wild, with no adult role models except the hungries, figuring it out for themselves. It's a miracle they have come so far so fast. That they have formed a family instead of beating each other's skulls in and eating the best parts. Clubs and knives and slings and stones notwithstanding, Lutes and John and Phillips and Penny notwithstanding, they're nobody's monsters.

What would be monstrous would be pulping their brains and spines to make medicine. Khan understands why Stephen can't bring himself to do that, even for her.

'I never thought I'd be sorry you had too much empathy,' she says. She tries to smile, to take the sting out of her words. If the smile looks from the outside as bad as it feels on her face then it must be a pretty awful counterfeit. 'Pretend I didn't say that,' she says, 'I get it. You're not into genocide. I just . . . I wish . . .' She runs out of words and finishes the sentence with a shrug.

When her hand falls back onto the counter, Stephen rolls up her sleeve and injects her. For a moment she thinks about stopping him. If her life is over, why shouldn't it be over now? But this grubby miracle gives her a few more hours with her newborn son. A few hours to get to know him, and – if there's a way, if there's any way at all – to save him.

'I want to run some tests,' Stephen says again.

Khan bends her head to touch the baby's forehead with

367

her lips and nose. He gurgles breathily, stretches out his tiny hands to touch her cheeks. 'Forget it,' Khan mutters.

'Rina, we have to know.'

'Why?'

'Because it will make a difference.'

She almost hates him for that circumlocution. 'Not to me,' she says, between her teeth.

The baby kicks and wriggles, suddenly restless. His mouth gapes wide, and Khan finds herself staring at reddened gums, four tiny teeth already coming in on the lower jaw – to either side, a canine and its neighbour incisor. Tilting the baby's head she finds the same pattern on the upper jaw.

Her child is not a hungry, no matter what corruption is churning in his blood. He is already alert, already taking an interest in his surroundings. He is not a puppet with its strings cut or a shark scenting chum, and the hungries are only ever one of those two things.

'I'll need to do a lumbar puncture,' Stephen is saying. He wanders around the lab assembling the tools he needs.

No difference. No difference at all. It's not as if she can be made to love this little wind-blown speck of humanity any more, or any less.

Stephen carries out his tests. When the baby cries, Khan holds him close and sings softly. The same lullaby her mother sang to her.

'Positive,' Stephen whispers. 'I'm sorry, Rina. I'm so sorry.'

She goes right on singing.

Hush.

Hush little baby.

Don't say a word.

52

They keep on rolling south as the horizon pales from pitch-black to milk-shot blue.

There have been three sightings of the children in the course of the night. Always very close, always running at the same steady pace – the same colour on the scopes as regular hungries, but easily distinguishable because they stay in that arrowhead formation, strung out across the road. That's just the vanguard. There are other little groups sprinting through the weed-choked ground on either side of the carriageway. They seem to be keeping pace, which presumably means that the ones on the road are slowing down to let the others keep up.

But they don't make a move. Rosie rolls on unmolested through the day, which waxes and wanes around them as though they're in a time-lapse movie. They're eating up the miles that on their outward journey took so many arduous months. Some weird gravity has them in its grip.

Stephen Greaves and Dr Khan visit the lab in the middle of the morning and again in late afternoon. Each time they spend about ten minutes closeted together, unsupervised. The rest of the crew make the logical assumption, that Greaves is Khan's physician now. Given that the only other candidate is Dr Fournier this passes without comment.

They reach their junction at last and turn off onto what used to be an A road. A cute, cartoony sign depicting a shire horse with a smiling duck on its back welcomes them to Alconbury Weston. Twenty or thirty burned-out shells of buildings show where the town once stood. Sixsmith doesn't feel very welcome and she doesn't slow. She's conscious of the kids chugging right along behind.

They are thirty miles or so by the map from base Hotel Echo. Normally the thing to do now would be to throw out some chatter and see who else is around, but they've been told to stay off the radio – which in any case only talks on a single frequency. All they can do is send up a couple of flares: green for friendly, white for incoming. Five minutes later they do the same thing again so that anyone actually watching from the base can take a bearing and an estimate.

Put the kettle on, in other words.

It's the colonel who fires both sets of flares, and after the second time he orders a halt. He climbs down out of the cockpit and stands in the road for a while scoping around with a pair of field glasses. Not the infra-reds, just a regular pair. Without waiting to be invited, Sixsmith gets down behind him and unships her rifle. The mid-section door opens and Foss steps out, too. Looks like they both had the same idea: since trouble is definitely coming, they might as well meet it halfway.

Carlisle looks ahead, to where the base is meant to be. Maybe he's hoping for an answering flare, but if so he is disappointed. Then he turns and looks back the way they've just come.

Sixsmith joins Foss at the mid-section door. 'If Beacon's late at the meet, those kids are going to be all over us,' she mutters.

'Yeah, but round two will be different,' Foss says.

'Will it? Why?'

'Won't just be us. We'll have more people and more guns. And this time we'll see them coming.'

Sixsmith feels obliged to point out the obvious. 'Same goes for them though, doesn't it? They know what our guns can do now, and how far they can fire. I doubt they're going to stroll out into the open again.'

'They're just kids,' Foss says.

'Yeah,' Sixsmith says. 'They are. But they nearly slaughtered us back there when you had the drop on them and you were firing from the top of a gradient.'

Foss doesn't seem to like that version of events much. 'How about if you drive,' she suggests, 'and I shoot. You okay with that?'

Better off without it, frankly, Sixsmith thinks but doesn't say.

The colonel is done with his eyeballing. They all get back inside and the magical mystery tour continues.

The road gets rougher. They're driving through weeds that are high enough in places to obstruct the view ahead and to blur the distinction between the carriageway and what's around it. Sixsmith has to take it slow in order to avoid nasty surprises, sudden drops or hidden obstructions that might foul their treads. The Robot did a great repair

371

job last time, against all the sensible betting, but there's no point in tempting providence.

The colonel navigates and tells her when to turn, but he's going by the compass more than the map most of the time. This is ground that looks like it hasn't been walked on since the Breakdown. Mother Nature has had plenty of time to settle in and get comfortable, effacing the road signs and the white lines on the asphalt and most of the structures that used to serve as reference points. Church with a spire? Somewhere off that way, behind the three-metre-high brambles. Or more likely in the middle of them. The day goes by in these tomfooleries.

Then a long straight stretch reveals the children dead centred in the rear-view, surprisingly close, jogging tirelessly behind them. 'Sir . . .' Sixsmith says.

'I see them,' the colonel acknowledges. 'Can we go any faster?'

'Not safely, sir, no. The surface is a mess and the weeds are hiding most of it. The ditches are easily deep enough to fuck our axle.' She hesitates. 'I could go off the road.'

'I suspect that might slow us more than them,' the colonel says dryly.

So they're between a rock and a hard place. When Sixsmith isn't watching the road, she watches the colonel's face, on which a pantomime of inner conflict plays out. She knows what he's thinking. They can't arrive at the rendezvous point bringing actual hostiles with them. But they've been ordered to maintain radio silence, so they can't reschedule or relocate.

Finally he stands.

'Keep to this speed, Private,' he orders her. 'Or as close to it as you can.'

Without another word, he goes astern. Sixsmith concentrates on her driving, until movement in the mid-section catches her eye. She glances in the mirror and gapes in open-mouthed astonishment. After that lecture up in Scotland, after McQueen losing his commission, she doesn't expect to see what she's seeing now.

The flamethrower extends and elevates. The primer puffs a few fat balls of flame.

And the forest is alight. Behind them and then on both sides as the spray of fire and black smoke vomits out in thick, greasy saccades. The turret turns and the flamethrower weaves an oxbow river of fire. It spreads away from them, quickly becoming a sea.

Sixsmith's first thought is: he's gone mad. We are bloody well going to burn.

Her second: but so clever! The colonel's craziness belongs to the fox or some related species. The children can't run through the fire and it's going to be a long trip around the edge of it. When they find the road again, Rosie will be long gone. Not only that, but the cues that hungries usually rely on – smell and body heat – will be monumentally messed up by the stench and residual heat of the burning.

They don't catch fire. The colonel's hand on the flame-thrower is deft and precise. He keeps it pointing backwards, rotating the turret within sixty degrees of arc. They outrun the destruction, leaving the feral kids to deal with it.

When Carlisle comes back to the cockpit, Sixsmith shoots him a grin. 'Good thinking, sir.'

But the colonel is sombre. Of course he is. You don't forget something like the burn runs. Not if you flew in them, and still less if you ordered them.

There are no further sightings. They seem to have thrown the kids at last.

And they get to Hotel Echo in plenty of time. But things go downhill from there because Hotel Echo is just a fence around some more of the same terrain they've been traversing.

There is no trace of activity here at all. No clearance, even: weeds right the way up to the fence. They roll halfway around the perimeter until they find what used to be the main gate, and in all that time they see no sign of life inside.

The gate is almost lost in the weeds. It wears a thick padlock that has rendered down into a red rosette of bristling rust. 'Sir,' Sixsmith says, 'is there any chance the brigadier meant somewhere else? This doesn't look like a forward base to me.'

Carlisle just points. To the left of the gate, almost lost in the overgrowth, is a sign that reads RAF HENLOW. Smaller signs on the same post announce that this is the home of the RAF CENTRE OF AVIATION MEDICINE and the TACTICAL PROVOST SQUADRON. Yeah, well, that was then. Now it's about 200 acres of bugger all.

'The coordinates are right,' Carlisle says. 'This is definitely the rendezvous the brigadier had in mind. She only said that it had been selected as a possible forward base. She didn't indicate that it had been cleared or fortified.'

'But then where do we go?' Sixsmith demands, her exasperation getting the better of her. 'If it's like this all the way, we'll be playing hide and seek in a sodding jungle.'

'The rendezvous point is the main parade ground. That at least ought to be partially clear, even if no work has been done on it. Proceed as ordered, Private.'

Sixsmith proceeds as ordered. She goes out with the bolt cutters and takes the padlock off, the skin on the back of her neck prickling the whole time like a bad sunburn. There is no way of getting the gates open by hand. The mass of vegetable growth is too high and too deep. Back in the cockpit, she nudges Rosie through, the forward ram clearing the way for them.

Then she reverses into the gates to close them again. One excursion outside Rosie's hull feels like plenty just now.

They find a road, or something that used to be a road, and follow it around the inside of the perimeter. Some sort of major ordnance must have been stored here once, because the concrete bunkers they're driving past look like they were built to withstand the smackdowns of Biblical proportions. Brambles pour out of their blind windows like barbed-wire tears.

They find the remains of a runway and turn onto it. It takes them west, towards the setting sun, and finally they reach a parade ground. There is nobody waiting for them. There is nothing moving on the face of the whole ruined Earth apart from Rosie, and when the engine stops the silence swallows them whole.

'Orders, sir?' Sixsmith inquires glumly.

The colonel folds the map and sets it down on top of the console.

'We wait,' he says. 'Until they come.'

Sixsmith doesn't ask which *they* he means.

53

Dr Fournier is sensitive to moods, and the mood inside Rosie has soured to the point where he can no longer bear it. He is hiding from the crew, from the colonel and from his duties.

Of course, this isn't entirely a new thing. Hiding has been an important part of his repertoire ever since they left Beacon. That was why he colonised the engine room in the first place, and it has served him well. Now, though, he has added some layers to his concealment. He is hiding from new and unfamiliar things. From McQueen, for example, who has taken his radio and seems by doing so to have taken his place as Brigadier Fry's agent on board the Rosalind Franklin.

More significantly, he is hiding from the hateful revelation that he has placed himself on the wrong side of a crucial argument. The brigadier's coup in Beacon was reckless and badly thought out. It has led to civil war, which is something the rump of humanity can ill afford. Whether she wins or loses, Fry will have done terrible damage and dragged the whole population of the embattled enclave to the ragged and crumbling edge.

If she loses, that's the story that will be told. Fournier's name will be in it, among the misguided and the contemptible. Not prominent. Not up in the headlines. A grubby, derided footnote. Other people are coming back from this expedition with something of honour and something of success. He is coming back as an addendum.

He has tried to blunt the awareness of this in the time-honoured fashion, which is to say with strong spirits. But he has discovered again what he should have remembered, that whiskey even in moderate amounts doesn't agree with his constitution. Swigged from the bottle, it unmans and dismantles him.

Now he sits in the engine room with his shoulders against the engine cowling, his head tilted back so the crown of it rests directly on the cold metal. Rosie stopped moving some hours ago, but there is a yawing in his head and stomach that makes him terrified to stand up. He is at the stage of wanting very, very much not to vomit but finding that every movement brings it closer.

The door of the engine room sits ajar. On the other side of it, in the lab, Stephen Greaves is moving around. With the lights off, invisible in the dark, Fournier watches him through the gap between door and frame. Greaves is working diligently with the contents of several containers taken from his sample kit. When he was in there earlier, he was with Samrina Khan. Fournier almost spoke to them, but speaking is one of the things he thinks might cause him to throw up.

So he only sat and watched as Greaves mixed up some kind of home-made medicine and injected Khan with it.

They talked about the feral children, and about Dr Khan's baby. They talked about a cure. Most of it rolled over Dr Fournier unheeded, but now he finds that some of what they said has lodged in his mind after all.

They were talking about a cure as something that could actually happen. Or . . . *had* happened? Fournier wonders belatedly what that medicine was, and what Greaves is working on so assiduously now. The supposed savant (Fournier has seen no compelling evidence of that!) mutters to himself as he works – two different voices, two sides of a conversation. Fournier can't hear everything, but he gets the gist. Greaves is addressing someone as 'Captain' and then answering his own questions in a deeper, exaggeratedly masculine tone.

'But it's not going to be enough,' he says as himself. 'It's going to run out!'

'You work with what you've got, kid,' he answers in the other voice. 'Can't squeeze orange juice out of a stone.'

'I've got to save her!' Greaves' usual voice again, trembling and petulant. 'I've got to!'

'Fine. But you better count the cost before you get into paying it. There are lives at stake here. Not just hers, but the children's, too. How far are you prepared to go?'

'But I've still got some spinal fluid here. That might be enough to . . . to make something that works. Not a suppressant. Something that works properly!'

Fournier has raised the whiskey bottle to his lips for another sip, a long time before, and it has stayed there ever since. He sets it down again now, carefully and quietly.

'It isn't.' The deeper voice. 'It isn't enough.'

'It might be.'

'No.'

'You don't know!' Greaves' voice rises to a squeak of protest. 'You don't know, Captain.'

'Kid, I know the cells you're working with are dead, and I know you need live ones. I know prion contamination has reached 14 per cent. How many batches would you be looking to grow? That pipette is probably enough for ten at best, so you've got a maximum of ten configurations that you can test for. And since that would use up all the spinal fluid you've got left, you wouldn't be able to dose her up again – which means you've got to get positive results in the next three hours, before her current dose wears off. How is anything supposed to grow in three hours?'

Greaves has stopped dead in the course of this speech. His hands are frozen in the air, a pipette in one of them so he looks like a conductor about to give the orchestra their cue to start the symphony.

'You don't know,' he says again, his voice barely a whisper.

He seems to collapse in slow motion, going down on one knee and then on both. His head bows down into his lap.

'I'll have to tell,' he moans. 'I'll have to tell if they ask.'

That's good to hear, Dr Fournier thinks. Because he intends to ask.

54

The christening party is Foss's idea, and she surprises herself.

She finds powdered egg and sugar, flour and a thin scraping of lard, and bakes up a kind of a sponge, with coffee and gelatin and a lot more sugar for icing. And she drags everyone into the crew quarters, whether they like it or not, to wet the baby's head with the liquor of their choice. As long as that's water or single malt, or single malt cut with a little water.

'What the hell is this about?' McQueen demands truculently when she hauls him down out of the turret.

Since he blew her off the day before, she hasn't felt like she owes McQueen anything very much, and certainly not an explanation. But maybe she's really explaining to herself.

'This time tomorrow we're going to be back in Beacon,' she says. 'And we're going to go our separate ways. Some of us will bump into each other again, but we'll never be *this* again. This crew.'

'Thank Christ for that,' McQueen mutters.

'Yeah, but it matters. We were part of something, and I hate to see that just fade away without . . . you know.'

'No. I don't.'

'Without doing something. All of us together, one last time. And after that, fuck it. We let it pass. But it's wrong to let it pass without a proper goodbye. Call it superstition, if you want to. But where's the harm in it? Come and have one last drink. Meet the rug-rat. Make your peace with the colonel.'

That last was a mistake. McQueen was looking half-persuaded but now he bridles and fixes her with a glare. 'You don't know fuck all about me and the colonel,' he says.

'No,' Foss admits. 'And I don't need to. It's over, mate. That's all I'm saying. It's over and this is a good way to wave goodbye to it.'

He comes along at last. Everyone comes except for Dr Fournier, who in a slightly slurred voice claims to have work to do. Well, he's welcome to it, and out of all of them he's the only one whose absence in Foss's opinion will leave no hole.

So there are six of them, which is a bigger crowd than the crew quarters has hosted since Invercrae. Khan doesn't seem all that into it at first, but she laughs weakly when Foss brings out the sponge. And then cries, which puts a bit of a damper on the proceedings.

Foss pours out tots of whiskey. McQueen winces and pushes his aside, but then on second thoughts he takes it back. Everyone else takes a glass except the Robot. Colonel Carlisle solemnly proposes a toast to the newest member of the human race and to his eminent parent. After a moment's thought, he adds John Sealey's name to the toast.

They knock back the booze and Foss tops them up. Khan

is still in an odd mood that Foss can't read, but she supposes that giving birth takes the edge off your game in all sorts of ways. 'So you're going with John,' Foss says. 'John Khan.'

Khan shakes her head. 'No,' she mutters. 'I don't know. I haven't decided.'

'Well, if you want to give the little sausage a middle name, I think Foss has got a nice ring to it. Just saying. Jonathan Foss Khan. Someone with a name like that, they'd damn well get respect.'

It takes a little persuasion but Khan lets them all hold the baby. Or everyone who wants to, which (with hard passes from Sixsmith and McQueen) is Foss and then the colonel. And then Foss again. She is just full of surprises today. She hasn't ever given a moment's thought to having kids of her own, but this unnaturally quiet little bundle of joy puts her into an odd and not unpleasant reverie. It's sort of a reassurance, she thinks, and sort of a promise. Things don't end, after all. They only change, and you keep changing with them.

Impulsively she holds the baby out to McQueen. 'Go ahead,' she says. 'Meet the one member of the crew who's got a smaller vocabulary than you do.'

McQueen shakes his head. 'I'm good,' he says.

'Coward. It's just a baby.'

'Everyone's just a baby sometime, Foss. That's how it starts.'

Foss gives it up. 'Let's have another toast then,' she says. 'To the Rosalind Franklin, and all who sailed in her. Fuck the brass and fuck the Main Table. We're the ones who make it happen.'

There's an emphatic 'Yes!' from Sixsmith, a rueful snort of laughter from McQueen. He swirls his whiskey in its plastic cup for a long while before he drinks.

382

'Well, we did it, people,' Foss says. She's still not sure why she's going to so much effort, but for some reason she really wants to make them feel this. Feel something, at least, even if she has to hammer together an atmosphere out of wood and shingle. 'We came and we saw and we frigging well conquered. Lutes and Phillips and the others didn't die for nothing. They died to get us here. One more for the five of them, yeah? To the memory of—'

McQueen puts his empty cup down, shoving it away from him across the table. 'Stop it, for fuck's sake,' he says. 'We're no use to anyone if we're pissed.'

He walks back out to the mid-section.

'To Lutes, Penny, Sealey, Phillips and Akimwe,' the colonel says quietly. He takes the bottle, pours himself a glass and empties it. Foss follows suit, but the mood has gone all to hell. Khan is crying again.

No, not crying. It's a different sound, a sort of hacking exhalation as though she's trying to spit something up. The baby is back in her lap but she's not holding it. Her fists are tightly clenched, the knuckles white.

'Samrina,' the colonel says. 'Are you all right?'

Greaves is on his feet. 'It's complications,' he says too quickly, too urgently. 'From . . . complications from . . .' His hands make shapes in the air. 'She needs medicine. Come on, Rina.'

He tugs on her shoulder. That's a strange sight, Foss realises: the Robot touching someone, instead of backing away in all directions at once into his own rigid little space. And those are some pretty complicated complications. Dr Khan's mouth is gaping wide and she is blinking in rapid semaphore. It looks like she's about to have a fit.

'You've got medicine for this?' Foss asks Greaves. 'Okay, let's get her into the lab.'

She moves to help Khan get up. The Robot is in her way. 'I'll do it,' he bleats. 'I can do it. Leave her alone.'

'Shit, Greaves, I'm only trying to—'

She doesn't get to say what she's only trying to do. The movement sensors go off like a chorus of chirping crickets and drown her words right out.

They've got company.

55

Colonel Carlisle makes the worst-case assumption – that the children have caught up with them again – and scrambles them all to battle stations. Foss takes the turret guns (and the infra-red goggles), McQueen the mid-section platform, the colonel and Sixsmith the cockpit. Each grabs a walkie-talkie as they go. With no intracom, they'll have to squawk each other and hope for the best.

From the cockpit, nothing is visible. Night has dropped over them like a black-out curtain. If the children are out there they've got the advantage because they're hunting by scent. There is nothing to be done but stay inside and let them come, hoping they haven't got anything in their arsenal that can inconvenience a tank.

Carlisle is still debating whether or not to turn the head-lights on when someone else makes the decision for him. Twin beams light up the night. Then another two, and finally a bank of six ferocious halogen spots, all of them pointed at Rosie from source points about a hundred yards away. Human figures walk back and forth in front of the spotlights with a lack of discipline the colonel finds bizarre and a little shocking.

'Hold your fire,' he says into his walkie-talkie, 'but stand ready. I believe this is our escort, but let's take nothing for granted.'

The broken radio rules out a normal hail. He tells Sixsmith to use the headlights to send a two-word message in Morse code. *Rosalind Franklin.*

One of the two pairs of headlights facing them blinks in response, sending four words back. *Beacon. Manolis. Present selves.*

Carlisle stands and clips the walkie-talkie to his belt. Sixsmith gets to her feet too, but he shakes his head. 'I'll go out to them,' he tells her. 'Those were the brigadier's orders.'

'Sir—' Sixsmith begins. She doesn't look happy.

'At ease, Private. This is Beacon. It's appropriate that I meet the senior officer and formally hand over command to him. I can also see what provisions they've made for us and satisfy myself that you'll all be looked after. There's no problem here.'

Sixsmith stays on her feet. 'Well, there might be, sir, if those kids have sniffed us out again. I'm just saying. Shouldn't we fill the escort in on the situation before anyone goes outside? That's just good sense, right?'

And it is, Carlisle can't deny it. 'Very well, Private,' he says. 'Send another message.'

'Yes, sir. Thank you, sir.' Sixsmith is visibly relieved. She sits down again and gets busy with the headlights. But she is only a few dots and dashes in when the lights over the way start flickering too, interrupting her in mid-flow.

Present selves, they spell.

Sixsmith is disgusted. 'Fucking jokers,' she mutters. She starts her message string again.

And the same thing happens. The other vehicle's headlights flash across her, abrupt and intemperate. The same sequence as before: *present selves*.

Sixsmith shakes her head in disbelief. 'Maybe I should try signalling with the fucking turret gun,' she mutters. 'Sir, permission to give this one more—'

'Yes,' Carlisle says. 'Go ahead, Private. Try again.'

Sixsmith does. And this time, at least, her opposite number allows her to finish her message. *Fence compromised. Possible hostiles.*

After half a minute the answer comes, with a grim inevitability.

Present selves.

'We're dealing with a moron,' Sixsmith marvels.

The colonel picks up the walkie-talkie and squawks Foss. 'Sir?'

'What are you seeing on the scope, Lieutenant?'

'Couple of dozen ground troops, sir, with about as much fieldcraft as a fucking high-school picnic. And three vehicles. There's something a bit odd about the vehicles. One of them is a tank – probably a Challenger, judging from the turret config. The other two . . . well, they could be staff cars but one of them looks more like a bus. And the other is pulling a limber of some kind. High sides like a caravan. I'm not seeing a chopper.'

A presentiment runs through Carlisle. He shies away from it by main force.

'Any sign of the feral children?' he asks.

'No, sir. Nothing. But there's a lot of shrubbery out there. Lines of sight don't extend as far as I'd like.'

'Thank you, Lieutenant. I'm coming through to join you.'

He tells Sixsmith to keep the engine running and goes astern. The crew quarters are deserted. Presumably Greaves has taken Dr Khan into the lab to examine or treat her.

A doubt is nagging at him now, and he can't quieten it. *Present selves?* In the dark, in an insecure location with no attempt to set up a perimeter? Possibly Sixsmith is right and Captain Manolis is an imbecile. The alternative is more troubling.

McQueen is waiting on the mid-section platform. He looks angry. His left hand grips the turret ladder hard, the knuckles white. Lieutenant Foss comes down out of the turret to join them. There is a muffled clatter from the lab where some sort of commotion seems to be going on, but the colonel has no time to concern himself with that.

'Open the door,' he orders. 'But close it behind me. I'll go out to them alone.'

'Sir,' Foss says, 'with respect, there's something not quite right about those vehicles out there. You could do with someone riding shotgun. I'm happy to come along.'

'Or I will,' McQueen chips in.

'No,' the colonel says. 'I don't anticipate problems, but if any arise it's better if Rosie is secure.'

'She'll still be secure if you've got a tailgunner,' McQueen says. Tension makes his voice flat and harsh.

'Thank you for your concern, Mr McQueen.' Carlisle stares into the man's eyes. 'As I said, if anything complicates the handover I'd prefer to know that you're here. I trust you – both of you – to protect the science team and Rosie.'

He reaches out to tap the keypad and open the airlock door. McQueen's hand is faster, gripping Carlisle's wrist. His face is reddening. Something is working there now, a rage that seems to have no object.

'Mr McQueen—'

'Just how stupid are you?' McQueen spits the words out. 'Can't you tell a fucking ambush when you see one?'

The colonel wrests his hand free, but he doesn't touch the keypad. 'Go on,' he says quietly.

McQueen grimaces and shakes his head, but he gets it out with a sort of grim disgust, like a man spitting blood and disinfectant into a bucket after getting dental work done. 'They brought you here so they could kill you and take Rosie. That's the only reason they told Fournier to pass the radio on to you. So they could get you out here in the middle of nowhere and take you out of the equation.'

'What the hell are you talking about?' Foss demands. She laughs, and she looks to the colonel as though she expects him to laugh, too.

'Dr Fournier didn't give me the radio,' Carlisle reminds McQueen. 'You did.'

McQueen raises his hands in sardonic surrender. 'Shit! I'm not saying I'm not involved. Can we stick to the point? Fry wants you gone, and the whole idea of meeting up out here instead of back in Beacon is to make that happen. No fuss, no reporting. You just don't come home.'

Carlisle feels a dull certainty settling on him, but he fights against it. 'Why should it matter if I come home or not? I have no authority in Beacon. I'm no threat to the brigadier.'

'Yeah, well you might be now. While we were away, she decided to take over the Main Table, but they're fighting

389

back. She had bad losses, so she had to reach out and make a deal. With the junkers. Those are junker battle-trucks out there. Now she's worried you might pitch in on the opposite side. Plus she needs Rosie because of the guns and armour, and she doesn't think you're likely to just hand over the keys.'

Foss hasn't said another word all this time. She's just been looking at McQueen. Now she slings her rifle to free her hands, moving briskly but carefully, and punches him in the mouth. It's a solid punch. It rocks McQueen on his heels a little. He takes it in silence: just wipes the blood off his lip and probes the damage with the tip of his thumb.

'You stupid, stupid bastard!' Foss yells.

'Okay,' McQueen mutters. 'Fine.'

'Junkers? A deal with the junkers? What, with their— their recreational rape and their fucking cannibalism, and— shit! Shit!'

'Get it all off your chest,' McQueen says bleakly, rolling his eyes.

'What did you think was going to happen to the rest of us after they killed the colonel? You really expect them to fly us out of here in a gunship? Cocktails and fluffy pillows? He didn't walk into an ambush, *you* did. We're toast when we go out there! You utter fucking moron!'

She raises clenched fists. Another punch seems imminent. McQueen looks away from her overflowing anger, out into the opaque night.

'Lieutenant,' Carlisle says. His mild tone works. Foss gets a grip, though she is still trembling with suppressed fury. Carlisle has seen her copy McQueen's mannerisms in the field; the swagger in his walk, the way he uses the heel of his hand to take the safety off the SCAR-H when he's obliged to use one. Her disillusionment is a freefall plunge.

'Set aside your differences,' he says to both of them. 'Now, please. I'm inclined to agree with Foss's assessment. If killing me is the main agenda, it's hard to imagine that the killing will end there – especially if we're witnesses to an illegal alliance with Beacon's enemies. We need to keep Rosie from falling into unauthorised hands and we need to protect the science team. In addition, and this is more important than anything, we need to make sure that the news of what we've discovered gets back to Beacon. We can't do any of those things unless we're all fighting on the same side.'

It's not eloquent, but it's the best he can do. The measured words sound pusillanimous even to him, but the alternative is to stand here trading punches while Fry surrounds them.

'So what's it to be, numb-nuts?' Foss snarls the words into McQueen's face.

There is a long, strained pause. At last McQueen shrugs. 'I don't care whether you live or die,' he tells Carlisle. 'On the whole I'd prefer to watch you bleed. If Beacon falls apart, it's because you stood by and let it when you could have turned it into something better. But I'll admit I didn't think this through. I'm with you until we sort this and get out of here.'

Foss draws her sidearm and shoves it up against McQueen's cheek. For all her fury her hand doesn't shake. 'Just so you know,' she says. 'If anyone bleeds, it's going to be you. Sir, what are your orders?'

First things first, Carlisle decides. 'Man the turret guns, Lieutenant. If we're attacked, we'll need to be in a position to return fire.' He turns to go back into the cockpit. Sixsmith is right behind him, holding up Fournier's radio.

'Colonel,' she says. 'We're being hailed.'

'By Captain Manolis?'

'No, sir. By Brigadier Fry. She's somewhere out there. And she wants to talk to you.'

56

It's not like the other times. It's a lot worse.

Dr Khan's eyes are rolling back into her head, showing pure white for seconds at a time. Her movements are violent and uncoordinated. Several times on the short journey from the crew quarters to the lab she almost falls.

As Greaves tries to mix the serum, she is scrabbling at his arm, clutching blindly at his head. She has made no attempt to bite him, but there is an urgency to her movements, almost a desperation. The sense of need is waking up inside her, moving her. It can only be a matter of minutes, Greaves thinks, maybe seconds, before the *Cordyceps* in her blood and brain is able to make her do what it wants.

Babbling apologies in an endless stream, he attempts to strap Dr Khan to the workbench. When the bench was installed, the vivisection of hungries without anaesthetic was unflinchingly taken into account and catered for. It's easy to loop and tighten the first strap, around Rina's left wrist. After that she fights harder, kicking and clawing at him. Her jaws are starting to work, opening and closing with a grating click of cartilage. In the end he has to leave her with just the one arm restrained.

'It will be okay,' he promises her. 'I'll just . . . I'll make up the dose. Don't worry. Don't worry.'

Tears blind him as he works. This is the last batch of serum. This is goodbye. Each dose has worked for a shorter period than the one before it, and this one is the dregs of the batch, smaller than the preceding doses and of course not so fresh. It might not work at all, he might have left it too late, and if it does work it will be for a few scant hours. After that Rina will go away, for ever, and all that will be left will be an animal that wears her face. What will he do without her? What will he do with what remains of her?

And what will happen to her baby?

When he approaches Rina with the needle she snaps and snarls at him. Drool flecks her lips, which have receded a long way from her bared teeth. There is no recognition in her wide eyes.

Greaves grabs her free arm and rolls up her sleeve, using his shoulder and the weight of his body to force her head back against the bench. He can feel Rina's jaws opening and closing against his upper arm, but there are several thicknesses of fabric there and he doesn't think she will have time to chew her way through.

She is struggling furiously. He stabs the needle into her arm but misses the cubital vein by a fraction of an inch. The second time he's not even close. The third time, with Rina's teeth grinding against his shoulder, he gets a bullseye and sinks the plunger in.

Cloth tears as he pulls himself free from her. A tiny shred of fabric stays between her clenched teeth, like the seat of the burglar's trousers in the dog's jaws in an ancient comic book he saw once at the orphanage. She spits it out and strains to get to him, to try for another bite. He is forced to retreat around the bench, out of her reach.

He waits to see if she will recognise him. He's crying again, wrenching sobs that shake and hurt him as they're expelled. Every few seconds, he says her name aloud in the hope that she will answer.

She doesn't, but her breathing calms and gradually she closes her mouth. She sinks down onto her knees, her legs bending under her, and sags a little although her bound wrist keeps her more or less upright. The blank look goes out of her eyes. Now she just looks exhausted and confused, her brows furrowed with thought as she stares around the lab. She blinks slowly, screwing her eyes closed for several seconds before opening them again and taking a second look – as though she hopes a second throw of the dice might have a better outcome.

'Rina?' Stephen says again.

Again, she doesn't speak. But when he holds out his hand to her she touches his palm with the tip of one finger. He gives a tearful laugh, returning the one-finger hug. Rina turns her head, her eyelids flickering a little as she stares at the strap around her wrist. She tugs against it to see if it will give. Fumbles at it with the fingers of her free hand.

'I'm sorry, I'm sorry,' Stephen says thickly. 'I had to. I'm sorry.' He steps forward quickly to untie her.

But he doesn't get there. Dr Fournier steps out of the dark of the engine room, whose door has been open all this time, and blocks his way. It's so sudden that Stephen jumps backwards and slams his elbow painfully on the corner of the freezer cabinet. He yelps and folds his arms around the pain.

'Don't touch her,' Dr Fournier snaps. And then, 'What did you do, Greaves? Tell me what you did. My God, she's infected. She's infected, and you found a way to control it. You found a cure.'

'No!' Stephen says. It's completely involuntary. Presented with the false statement, he has no choice but to correct it.

'I know what I saw. Tell me. Tell me how you did this.'

'I can't,' Stephen yelps. 'Please!'

In the intensity of his feeling, Dr Fournier grabs Stephen's shoulders and pushes him back against the freezer cabinet. 'Tell me!' he roars.

The shock of physical contact freezes Stephen on the spot. He doesn't even struggle. Words well up behind his teeth, start to spill out. 'C . . . cerebrospinal fluid of the captured hungry. You take a b . . . base mass of between twenty and fifty cc and fix with—'

There is a sound like the dull ringing of a gong. Dr Fournier grunts, stiffens and falls headlong, unconscious before he hits the deck plates.

Rina lets the steel clamp stand slide from between her fingers. It hits the doctor again when it falls, leaving a triangular gash on his cheek.

Rina's eyes roll, wide and wild. She blinks and shakes her head, makes a *brrrrrrr* sound. 'That's better,' she growls through clenched teeth. 'Hear myself think.'

57

'This is Carlisle to Brigadier Fry,' the colonel says. 'Carlisle to Fry, or to the Beacon Muster, over.' He has turned the radio's gain up as far as it will go, and most of the remaining members of Rosie's military escort are crowded into the cockpit with him, Only Foss is missing, manning the turret again to warn him if the other vehicles out on the tarmac make a move.

The response is a long time in coming, and the brigadier sounds very relaxed when she finally answers the colonel's hail. 'Isaac. Welcome to base Hotel Echo. Did you have any trouble finding us?'

Carlisle isn't tempted by the invitation to small talk. 'Brigadier,' he says, 'we identify hostiles in the immediate area. I request leave to pursue our original course and rendezvous at Beacon. This place isn't safe.'

'Request denied,' Fry says, in the same calm tone. 'Those aren't hostiles, they're allies. Now, bearing in mind my explicit instructions to you yesterday, please open your doors and assemble on the tarmac. My troops will take Rosie from here, along with the specimen you mentioned – assuming it actually exists – and you'll be transferred to Beacon.'

And here they are, at the point where polite pretence has to break down.

'Transferred how?' Carlisle says. 'We see junker battle-trucks and junker cadres on the ground. I'm not convinced you can guarantee our safety.'

'I can guarantee your safety if you come out immediately. Not if you continue to waste my time.' The brigadier sounds just a little testy now, as though she's trying hard to avoid unpleasantness but is reluctantly acknowledging that it may become necessary after all. 'We'll drive back together, right now. Your orders stand, Isaac. Please come out.'

At the brink of direct insubordination, Carlisle feels the familiar reluctance to press forward. Instead, he marches in place. 'Geraldine, you're making common cause with murderers and rapists who oppose everything we believe in. I refuse to endorse that decision. Let me take Rosie back to Beacon and we'll perform the handover there in due course.'

'That's not possible,' Fry says bluntly. 'Isaac, let me explain the situation to you. There is no room here for argument, or negotiation. The alliances I've made are absolutely necessary to ensure Beacon's survival. I'm not offering you any kind of an explanation, or any apology. I'm your senior officer and you will obey me. I am requisitioning your vehicle for the Beacon Muster. Right here. Right now. If you fail to surrender it, you – along with all your crew – will be guilty of mutiny and treason and you will be treated accordingly. As enemies of the Muster and the polity.'

'She's bluffing,' McQueen says from behind him. 'She wants Rosie intact, not in pieces.'

'Is that Lieutenant McQueen?' Fry asks. 'If so, please tell him to be quiet and observe the chain of command. And if you share his optimism, Isaac, bear in mind that having Rosie in pieces is preferable to having her – and you – take the field against us.'

'Geraldine,' Carlisle says, making one last appeal to reason. 'I haven't lied to you. We have encountered a new type of hungry and we have obtained a specimen. It's vitally important that we deliver it to Beacon intact.'

'So you told me,' Fry snaps. 'I have to say that it seems unlikely after seven months of zero findings. I'm inclined to think that you saw this moment coming and finessed accordingly. But if you're telling the truth, that's all the more reason for you to give up without a fight and let Beacon have the benefit of your success.'

Carlisle grimaces. For a second he presses the radio against his chest while he formulates a response. 'Yes,' he admits at last. 'I can follow the logic of that argument. I'm prepared to hand over the specimen if we can agree a way to do it. But I can't surrender Rosie. I need to think about the safety of my crew. And in that regard, you should know that we also have a baby in here. Samrina Khan gave birth two days ago.'

There is the smallest perceptible pause. 'Really?' Fry says. 'That's wonderful. Against mission regs, of course, but these things happen. I look forward to wetting the baby's head. No more arguments, Isaac. You, your people, Rosie, the specimen. You will entrust them all to me, and you will do it right now. You have five minutes. Use them wisely. I'll be training

399

a scope on your mid-section door. The timer doesn't stop until the door opens and I see you step out.'

'Brigadier—' But she has broken contact.

'Sir.' Foss, on the walkie-talkie, her voice quick and urgent. 'The odds just got worse. Two more vehicles are rolling in behind us with their lights out. Definitely junker ordnance – barbed-wire trim, welded-on bits of shit all over them. There are some more ground troops too, moving in on our three o'clock and our nine.'

So they can't retreat, and they can't advance. If there is an unexcluded middle he's not seeing it. They're out of options and almost out of time.

'Foss,' he says, 'stay where you are and prime the field pounder. But don't rotate the turret. That may prompt them to start firing.' He turns to Sixsmith. 'Bring the remaining members of the science team to the crew quarters, Private,' he tells her.

Sixsmith rips off a salute and goes astern to the lab. Carlisle goes to the crew quarters himself to await their arrival. He glances towards the bunks, with a poignant ache of nostalgia. He is wearied to death, and it seems unlikely he will sleep again on this side of the grave.

Sixsmith brings Dr Khan and Stephen Greaves. McQueen follows them in. Khan is very much the worse for wear, leaning against Sixsmith until she is able to sink down into a chair.

'What about Dr Fournier?' Carlisle demands.

'Sir, he was unconscious.'

'He was . . . ?'

'I smacked him in the head with a clamp stand,' Dr Khan explains. 'He was assaulting Stephen and I acted without thinking. Sorry.'

'Don't beat yourself up about it,' Sixsmith says. 'Seriously.'

Carlisle has no time to tease out the story, and very little interest. He sums up what's happening in as few words as he can manage, and explains his own decision.

'Brigadier Fry has offered to take all of you back to Beacon,' he tells them, 'as long as I hand Rosie over to her within the next few minutes. If I believed that offer was sincere, I would already have surrendered. But I don't. I think she intends to kill all of us. Given that her troops seem to consist mainly of junkers, I can't even guarantee that death will be a quick one.'

'Fucking traitor,' Sixsmith says. 'Filthy fucking traitor.' Nobody else says anything at all.

'That being the case,' Carlisle goes on, 'the choice seems to me to be a clear one. I don't want to hand Rosie over to be used as the closing argument in a *coup d'état*. But the only alternative I can see is to make a run for it. The junker battle-trucks are civilian vehicles, much lighter than Rosie. It would be possible to ram one of them out of the way and push on past. But we're heavily outnumbered, even just on the basis of the vehicles we can actually see. There could easily be more positioned behind the bunkers, and it's almost certain that the footsoldiers who have moved in on our flanks are carrying RPGs.'

'Affirmative, sir,' Foss says, via the squawk-box. 'I've seen two already. Bazookas or grenade-launchers, heavy duty.'

'So each of you has to decide,' Carlisle concludes, 'whether you want to stay on board and make that attempt, or get out of here. I'm sorry I have no better options to offer you. If any of you want to leave, I'll mount the airlock and open the mid-section door. My belief is that you'll be giving

401

yourself up to torturers and murderers that the brigadier will be unable to rein in even if she wishes to, but it's possible that I'm wrong.'

The slightly stunned silence persists. The soldiers know all this already, of course. It's only Dr Khan and Greaves who are hearing it for the first time.

'I told them about your baby, Samrina,' he adds. 'That may work in your favour, if you should decide—'

'I'm not going out there,' Khan says. She wipes her eyes – which are red and swollen – with the heel of her hand. 'I'll take my chances with you.'

'Me too,' Sixsmith agrees. And Foss, over the walkie-talkie, says the same.

Finally McQueen shrugs and nods. 'I don't see what the hell else we can do,' he says. 'Stand or run, they're going to blow us to shit. We might as well take a few of the bastards with us.'

'Some of them are Beacon soldiers,' Carlisle reminds him. 'Like you. Part of their function is to obey even when they don't entirely understand.'

'That shouldn't be part of anybody's function.'

Reluctantly, Carlisle nods. 'Perhaps not,' he concedes. He feels as though he is throwing half his life onto the fire with those two words.

Only Stephen Greaves has failed to give an answer. Carlisle knows now what the consequences were of not allowing him a voice the last time they spoke like this. He nods to the boy, then deliberately lowers his gaze to make it easier for Stephen to find the words.

'I think going out might be a good idea,' Greaves says.

'You heard what I said, Stephen? The likelihood is—'

'No, I know, I know.' Greaves gestures with his hands in an

402

accelerating rhythm, not illustrating anything but building up the momentum to speak. 'A lot of people will die, but if we're careful it won't be us. Because we'll know they're coming.'

'Know *who* is coming?' Sixsmith asks blankly.

Stephen acknowledges the question by darting her a glance that lasts about a tenth of a second.

'The children,' he says. 'We can bring them.'

58

Lieutenant Foss extends and mounts the airlock, and they assemble on the mid-section platform.

Five of them, not the full roster.

One of the missing is Dr Fournier, who is still unconscious. When Khan went back into the lab to check on his status, she took the precaution of propping him up against the workbench and fastening his wrists, both together, to one of the straps. He is breathing shallowly but evenly and she suspects it might be some time before he wakes, but when he does she wants to make sure he stays exactly where he is.

Because the other two crew members who are staying on board are Stephen, who will close the airlock behind them, and her baby.

'This could go horribly wrong,' she tells Stephen, just before they leave. 'Even if it works. Even if they come, we could all end up dead. I'm leaving him with you because I trust you to . . . to make sure he's okay.' She flails for a second on the frictionless slope of that concept. 'Don't let them take him, Stephen. Whatever happens, don't let them take him.'

'I won't,' he promises her. 'I'll do what we said. Whatever happens.'

She touches the back of his hand with her fingertip, presses hard. 'Keep yourself safe too,' she says, her voice shaking. 'I love you, Stephen.'

All he can offer her in answer is a tremulous nod. 'I— I—' he tries, and then 'Rina.' He closes his eyes, folds himself in on the emotion to lock it down. Even ordinary social embarrassments are torture for him, so Khan can't imagine what he's feeling now. She wishes his condition would allow her to take him in her arms and stroke his head. She feels as though she's leaving both her children behind. Her whole family. But they can't embrace, they can only say goodbye, and drawing it out will hurt him more.

So she leaves, without any more words and without breaching the *cordon sanitaire* around his frail body. She is full to the brim with pain. And the fact that she will soon be empty is the most painful thing of all.

The soldiers are all in the airlock when they get there. Foss is talking to McQueen about bullets. 'You might get to try out those home-mades after all. Just wait until I'm somewhere else, okay?'

'Top notch, these are,' McQueen says. 'You'll be begging me for the recipe.'

'Oh, I know the recipe. That's what bloody worries me.'

For all their talk of weaponry, their rifles remain strapped across their backs. Their hands are empty.

'A word, Colonel,' Khan says. She beckons him close.

405

'Of course.' Carlisle leans down towards her and she whispers in his ear – a few terse sentences. The only gift she can give him, but it's not a small one. When she steps back and he straightens, he stares at her in solemn perplexity. 'Are you sure?' he asks her.

'Yes.' She's sure.

'But that changes—' He doesn't finish the sentence, so Khan doesn't have to disagree. Here, now, it changes nothing. It's just the punchline to a joke she won't be alive to tell.

Carlisle looks as though he wants to say more, but at that moment Stephen steps out of the crew quarters into the mid-section. He has brought the baby to see her off, and the baby's presence somehow eclipses everything else.

Stephen holds the tightly wrapped bundle out gingerly, uncertainly, his eyes flicking from side to side as he tries to avoid so many closely clustered gazes. Khan wraps the baby's tiny hand in both of hers and leans down to kiss him on the crown of his head, which is covered in unbelievably fine downy hair. 'Godspeed, buster,' she whispers.

'Takes after his dad,' Foss says. 'Poor little bastard.'

There seems nothing else to say. The moment is suddenly on them. The colonel taps the keypad. The deck plates shake as the airlock's hydraulics wake up.

The doors slide back and the soldiers step out onto the broken concrete. Khan climbs down right behind them, wincing as her feet touch down on the parade ground. Her muscles feel wasted, recoilless. But she lines up with the rest as they stand, spotlit by the multiple rows of headlights, showing their empty hands.

Showing their number, too. Brigadier Fry knows that Rosie's full complement stands at seven. She has to be aware, as the airlock doors slide closed again at their backs, that two crew members have remained inside. This is an invitation to negotiate, not a full surrender.

So the decision rests with her.

A man steps into the focus of the headlight beams, where he turns at once into a two-dimensional silhouette. He's not a soldier. He wears an ancient T-shirt with an indecipherable slogan, torn and mud-spattered jeans and orange snow boots. He waves to them to advance.

Khan takes one last glance back at Rosie. Her home through the long months of the mission, and the last one she will ever know. No, almost the last. Her body is a house too, for something subtle and ineffable that answers to its name. She carries her last home with her, walks it forward across weeds and concrete into a light that is alive with drifting dust motes.

Everything, she thinks. Everything is alive. I wish I'd noticed that before.

They walk a hundred yards. Another hundred.

'Far enough,' says a voice. A woman's voice. Brigadier Fry's.

Khan has only met the brigadier once, on the day of their departure, when she told them in front of a crowd of seventy or eighty thousand that the future of Beacon rode with them. The doctor barely recognises the short, trim figure who steps forward now, in urban camo designed for a bigger frame, in black boots on which hardly any black shows through the accreted dust and mud. The brigadier looks tired. There is a droop to her mouth that reminds Khan of a line from the play *Macbeth*. *I have supped full with horrors.*

But who hasn't, these days?

Fry gestures. Men and women deploy behind them, cutting them off from Rosie. More move in to either side of the brigadier, rifles raised and aimed. Around three dozen, Khan guesses, possibly more. A third of them are in military fatigues and hefting Beacon-issue rifles. The remainder wear anything, carry anything. She can see machetes and handmade bows in among the automatic weapons.

Like oil and water, the soldiers and the junkers aren't mixing much. The soldiers seem to be holding specific patches of ground between the strutting junker warriors, standing stock still and watching their new allies warily out of the corners of their eyes.

The junkers whoop and catcall, nudge and lean on each other as they hold their rough positions or shift for a better look at what's going down. One of them throws a stone in Rosie's direction, along with a few obscene words. The soldiers stand rigid and silent. Nobody is even pretending that this is business as usual.

Fry's gaze scans the little party, and the corners of her mouth tug down. 'There are only five of you,' she says. 'Where are the others?'

'Still on board,' Carlisle says. 'With the door locked. They're waiting on my orders, brigadier – whether to surrender Rosie or to scupper her, along with the uniquely valuable specimen we talked about earlier.'

Fry is only a few yards from Carlisle now. The men on either side of her are tense and watchful. The colonel will die if he moves his hand towards his sidearm – probably if he moves at all. Fry seems to find his answer mildly puzzling. 'To scupper Rosie?' she repeats. 'How would you do that?'

'If we reach an amicable agreement here, you'll never have to find out.'

Fry smiles. It's a little bleak, a little washed out, but it's there. This is another reason why they're still alive, Khan realises. The brigadier has built this moment up in her mind, has promised herself the luxury of a conversation. She wants her moment and she wants Colonel Carlisle to share it.

'I've already given you all the assurances I can, Isaac,' she says. 'And really you have no bargaining power here. You mentioned a baby. Yet now I'm expected to believe that you – and the mother – have come up with a plan in which the baby remains behind in Rosie to be blown up or burned to death if we fail to see eye to eye. I know you better than that.'

The colonel lets his gaze sweep across the ragged line of junker warriors. 'I imagine we've both moved on from the opinions we expressed the last time we talked,' he says.

And on and on, Khan thinks. Go ahead. Keep it up. While their invisible signal flare goes out into the night. They washed off their e-blocker before they stepped out of Rosie, every one of them. Even normal hungries can follow very tiny chemical gradients for miles: the feral children have shown themselves more tenacious again, and much more resourceful.

Come on, kids. We're right here, so let's party!

But the kids don't come and Khan's mind feels like a febrile flame, drawing up the light and heat from the searing headlights and turning them into something lighter and hotter still. She's going. She knows she is. Her consciousness will sublime away into the air. The dull-eyed animal that's left behind will make some purposeless movement that startles the soldiers and kicks off the slaughter.

That's not how this ends. It can't be. If they die, Fry will take Rosie. Stephen will spill everything he knows about the cure – he won't be able to stop himself – and her baby

409

will be picked apart on an autopsy slab while he's still alive. He will be the first of a great multitude.

'What?' Fry says to the colonel. 'You've finally realised that there's a downside to democracy? I find that hard to believe.' She turns to the officer at her side. 'Captain Manolis, lead a detail across to the Rosalind Franklin. Six men, including two engineers. Dismantle her treads so she is unable to move.'

The officer salutes and vanishes into the dark.

'I strongly advise you not to do that,' the colonel says. 'My men on board will interpret it as a hostile act.'

Fry all but smirks. 'Your men on board? I believe you're talking about the autistic boy, Stephen Greaves. And Dr Fournier, who answers to me and in any case is too much of a coward to contemplate killing himself.' The brigadier shakes her head. She has seen through all of Colonel Carlisle's subterfuges and she is expansive in her victory – but not too expansive. 'We can still do this without any unnecessary loss of life,' she says. 'Tell them to come out. Do it now. Otherwise I'll have to order the captain to block the air vents. Once they're all dead we can burn our way in through the airlock doing no damage to the hull at all.'

Carlisle takes a deep breath, and holds it. He tenses, and the soldiers all around them gather themselves visibly, interpreting his involuntary movement as a sign that he is about to attack the brigadier. But he doesn't. He only looks back across the distance that separates them from Rosie (it seems immense to Khan, an unbridgeable gulf) before settling his gaze on Fry again. 'May I remind you of the baby?' he says in a tone that is still very close to calm.

'Certainly, Isaac. May I remind you that I'm giving you the choice?'

There is a moment's silence. Fry raises her radio, watching Carlisle for a decision. Khan feels another wave of weakness, of fuzzed focus, of *absence* rush through her. She finds a thought and keeps it in the forefront of her mind. If Fry starts to speak into the radio, she will stop her. Whatever it costs her, that order isn't going to be spoken.

'Geraldine,' Carlisle says. 'You've made a terrible mistake.'

'Have I?' Fry inquires, with icy politeness. 'I don't think so.'

'But yes,' Carlisle insists, blatantly playing for time (and not very much of it, seconds at most). 'All of this, this entire situation, has been of your making. You were so sure that what humankind needed most was you that you were prepared to kill them all to prove your point. Which, by the way, you haven't. Even if you were right in the first place about Beacon needing a strong and centralised command structure, you've achieved precisely the opposite of what you intended. You've introduced chaos and randomness into a system that was barely surviving as it was. The junkers! You know what they've done, how they live. If Beacon survives, it will be in spite of you. I imagine that will be the kindest epitaph you'll get.'

'I beg to differ,' the brigadier says.

It's the conciseness of that reply, after the colonel's intentionally drawn-out *j'accuse*, that tells Khan the conversation is at an end. The children have failed them. They're out of time.

And so is she. There is nothing left to cling to. She's going out with the tide of her own breath. She will die and her friends will die and Stephen and then her baby last of all. She looks from face to face, trying to find an anchor that will hold her fragmenting mind in this place for a few seconds longer. But every face is turned away from her.

A soggy spark of realisation flickers, fades, almost dies. *Every* face is turned. The Beacon soldiers and the junkers have their guns trained on Carlisle. On Foss. On McQueen. On Sixsmith. The men and women in uniform, with rifles on their backs and pistols on their belts. The clear and present dangers. They have discounted the petite Asian woman in her soiled white lab coat. She is so clearly not a concern, not a factor in any of this.

She takes a half-step forward. 'Private,' she says. Her voice is a pitiful thing, hoarse and fractured, without breath to drive it.

She doesn't say it to anyone in particular and the man who glances in her direction isn't a soldier at all. He's a junker, an alpha male with corded muscle in his arms, braids in his shoulder-length hair and a moustache that reminds Khan of circus strongmen. The ultimate satirical statement of masculinity. His rifle still pointed at the colonel, he reaches out a hand to push her back.

Khan takes the hand in both of hers. Turns it so the fleshy part at the base of the thumb is clearly exposed. She might be trying to read his future. But he doesn't have one, any more than she does.

She lowers her head and bites down hard.

59

'If Beacon survives,' the colonel tells Geraldine Fry, 'it will be in spite of you. I imagine that will be the kindest epitaph you'll get.'

Fry gives him a glare of frank contempt. 'I beg to differ,' she says. Something in her bearing changes. It's not easy to define, but it's unmistakeable. She draws back a little way. The next time she speaks, Colonel Carlisle knows beyond a doubt, it will be to tell her men to open fire.

To her left and out of her direct line of sight, Samrina Khan reaches out and takes the hand of one of the junkers guarding them. Then she bends down – as far as he can tell – to kiss it. It's such a grotesque and unexpected sight that it makes Carlisle falter, stumbling over the temporising words he's trying to get out.

So he says nothing. He just laughs. Long and loud, dredging up the sound from the bottom of his chest. Drawing it out. Shaking his head and wiping imaginary tears from the corner of his eye.

Just to buy a few extra seconds, as Fry watches the panto-mime, stony-faced instead of giving the order.

'Would you care to share the joke, Isaac?' she demands as he subsides.

Carlisle waves a hand, as though he's still too helpless to speak.

'Ready rifles,' the brigadier raps out.

She gets no further than that. The man Dr Khan just kissed has flung himself violently upon the man beside him. Khan herself has progressed to the uniformed soldier on her other side, taking advantage of his momentary inattention to sink her teeth into his wrist. The man wrenches his hand away and raises his rifle to club her down. But before he completes the motion he freezes on the spot. The rifle slips from his grip and his feet shuffle as though he is trying to walk but forgetting the intricate rules. Abruptly he swivels and charges the private behind him, engulfing her in a clumsy, tight embrace. They topple together. Meanwhile both the junker Khan bit and the soldier he attacked have each found new partners and borne them down.

'Ready rifles!' Fry bellows again. But now the disturbance is spreading. That whole part of the line is involved in a complex wrestling match, the men Khan blessed with her laying on of hands – and teeth – passing the bad news along to their nearest comrades, who in their turn . . .

Every man and woman here has enough experience with this to know what they're seeing. This daisy chain is what they dread more than anything else in the world. It's what happens when people are exposed to the hungry pathogen.

Somehow, impossibly, Khan has infected them. She is the vector of this micro-epidemic, that is spreading now in waves outwards from her. There are shouts of panic. Men and women rising up from the ruck on the floor are summarily shot by those who haven't been affected yet. They haven't figured out that Khan is ground zero because she isn't flinging herself at them in the way the men she touched are. She just stands and watches the chaos she has caused through heavy-lidded eyes, as though she is suddenly exhausted.

Brigadier Fry is still yelling orders. They're good orders, too. Step back. Don't engage. Aim low. Isolate and incapacitate. The newly transformed hungries drop one by one.

But so do the men who are firing on them. Something whines by the colonel's ear, invisible, to smack into the skull of a junker ten yards away. A black stone, angular and highly polished. Volcanic glass, perhaps: northern Scotland, the colonel vaguely remembers, is rich in Mesolithic pitchstone. Whatever it is, it hits with enough force to remain embedded in the man's forehead as he falls.

The feral children have arrived at last.

Geraldine Fry looks from side to side, bewildered. She doesn't understand, in those first few moments, what this new threat is and where it is located. By the time she realises, her troops are falling like wheat.

She tries to rally them. Yells to them to fall back to the vehicles in good order. If they were used to serving in the same command, if they knew what good order was, they might be in with a chance. The junkers break in all directions. The Beacon soldiers can't even begin to hold the line that's left.

An adjutant over by the Challenger turns to relay the brigadier's orders. He dies with his mouth wide open and a spear through his neck cutting off the words he was about to say.

By this time, McQueen and Foss and Sixsmith have shrugged their rifles off their shoulders. Have brought them around and up to the ready. They're taking aim, as far as they need to. At this distance, the SCAR-H is not a discriminating weapon.

Firing at will, they move forward, away from Rosie and from the attacking children, through the ragged line of Beacon troops and the milling junkers who are in no formation at all. Nothing stands in their way, or at least not for long: they lay down a corridor in the chaos and walk on through it. Carlisle follows them, slower in his gait because of his limp and more deliberate in choosing targets. He shoots junkers, wherever he can, avoids the few uniforms he can see. His sympathies here are for the men and women – surely there must have been some – who thought they were fighting for something real.

Breaking through the line is much easier than he had feared. The junkers have scattered, which is a quick and easy suicide. The Beacon soldiers are doing what their training tells them to do, kneeling or throwing themselves prone to make a smaller target, using the towering weeds for cover. The enemy out in the night, seeing them by their body heat, kills them just the same.

The remnants of Rosie's military escort break out on the far side of the cordon and leave them to it. Predators and prey can sort it out among themselves. The little group sprints into the denser undergrowth at the edge of the concrete field, Carlisle still bringing up the rear. McQueen staggers, emitting a grunt of pain and surprise. He has taken a hit to the upper body, though it's impossible in the dark to say exactly where. His rifle clatters from his grip. He draws his pistol clumsily with his left hand and keeps on moving.

Finally they put the two staff cars and the Challenger between themselves and the worst of the gunfire.

The plan now is to carry on in as straight a line as they can manage until they reach the perimeter fence, and then follow it widdershins to the base's south gate, where Rosie will meet them. It's a terrible plan, built on the optimistic premise that their two enemies will obligingly break against each other and leave nobody standing to pursue them. It also assumes that they will not lose each other in the dark.

Unfortunately they already have. The colonel slows, realising suddenly that Dr Khan is no longer with them. He turns and looks back the way they've just come, but the headlights of the parked vehicles are the only illumination and they are all pointing at Rosie on the far side of the parade ground. Small, fleet figures race in and out of the beams. Like bats, they're almost too quick to see at all. When a burst of machine-gun fire rips apart the brambles a few feet away from Carlisle, he is forced to move forward again.

For another fifty yards. This time it's Sixsmith who stumbles to a halt. She points wordlessly off to the left.

'No way!' Foss exclaims incredulously. 'No fucking way!'

The brigadier would surely have left at least a token guard on the copter, but there is no sign of them now. Perhaps they went to join the fight. Perhaps, seeing the way things were going, they scattered and took cover. Whichever decision they went with, it will probably make no difference to their eventual fate.

The copter is a crude, functional thing: a bulbous egg at

417

the end of a fuselage that's no more than a single steel strut. 'What is this piece of shit?' McQueen grunts in disgust. He is bent over like an old man, his right arm folded against his chest. Wherever he was hit, Carlisle does not believe it's a flesh wound.

'MH-6,' Sixsmith mutters tersely, running past him and vaulting into the pilot seat. 'Little Bird. I can fly this. I can fly it all the way to Beacon.'

'Yeah, but we can't ride it,' Foss protests. 'There's no room.'

'It will take four.'

'There are fucking eight of us!'

'Four on the gun platform, I mean. Plus pilot and co-pilot. Khan can hold her baby and the civilian commander can fucking walk home.'

'Works for me,' McQueen says. He moves forward, but he doesn't seem able to raise his foot high enough to climb into the copter's rear. Foss has to lift and manhandle him in, which is a struggle. Then she clambers in after him.

Carlisle hesitates, looking back once more towards the parade ground where bursts of gunfire and screams of despair can still be heard, but at lengthening intervals.

He leaves it too long. And he lets his guard down, like a fool, thinking that the danger has stayed where it was put. Something cold touches his temple.

'You bastard,' Fry hisses into his ear. 'This was about our future. You've stolen our future!' Her fingers feel down his arm, find his pistol and tug it from his hand. He hears the heavy thud as it falls into the weeds. McQueen and Foss are inside the copter's passenger space and haven't realised what's happening. Sixsmith sees, but she has set her rifle down in the co-pilot seat to get to grips with the copter's controls. She glances across at it now, but there is no way she can get anywhere near it before Fry fires.

'You did that, Geraldine,' Carlisle says. 'When you started this. Nobody forced your hand.'

'I want Beacon to survive. That's what forced my hand. Tell your people to get out of my copter.'

'No.'

'Tell them, Isaac. Now.'

'No.'

'Fine.' Subconsciously he expects to hear the click of the safety, but why would the safety be on in the middle of a massacre? What he hears is the ringing, echoing roar of the brigadier's pistol discharging right beside his ear. The shot goes wide, though the range was point blank.

Fry's legs buckle under her and she folds backwards, her arms windmilling. Samrina Khan's jaws are locked in her throat. They hit the ground together.

Carlisle kneels quickly and gropes in the long grass for his pistol. Khan is on her knees too, her upper body leaning over the brigadier's and mostly hiding it from sight. The sounds, though, signal clearly that what is being hidden is extreme and cannibalistic in nature.

Carlisle finds the gun in the same moment that Samrina raises her head. The blood is black in the dim light, smeared across the lower half of the doctor's face like a highwayman's mask. Even her teeth are black, so her gaping mouth is just a tunnel.

Sixsmith has grabbed her rifle now: she hugs it to her chest like a comforter. But Foss jumps down from the rear platform with her weapon raised and ready.

Then she sees who it is that's crouching on her haunches in the grass. 'Oh shit!' she whispers.

Carlisle goes down on one knee, his stiff leg protesting at the harsh usage. 'Samrina,' he says. 'You have to get into the copter. Do you understand me?'

'Sir—' Foss protests.

'Now, Samrina. Quickly.'

'Sir, you can bloody well see she's turned!'

'Isaac,' Khan croaks. The word is barely audible.

'Yes, Samrina. Into the copter. Now.'

Khan raises her hand. The movement is jerky and effortful, stitched together out of a dozen separate acts of new will-power. She touches her extended fingertip to the centre of her forehead. 'Don't look back,' she says. Distinctly. Her eyes lose focus, as though she's peering with difficulty through the disordered drifts of memory into another time and place.

Her lips are still moving, but she has run out of words. It doesn't matter. There is no mistaking her meaning.

'Colonel, please! Get out of my way and give me a clear shot!'

Khan exhales – a long, breathy sibilance.

She gathers herself, her upper body ducking a little as she compacts the muscles of her legs and arms. Hands splayed wide. Jaws gaping.

In the instant before she leaps, Carlisle places his pistol against her forehead, exactly in the spot she indicated, and pulls the trigger.

Takes what was left of Samrina Khan and paints the grass and concrete with it.

The aborted attack carries her into his arms. He drops the pistol again to catch her, her insubstantial weight not even making him stagger. He lowers her to the ground with excessive care.

He is not crying. He makes no sound. The grief is wedged so deep within him that he can't turn it into breath.

Sixsmith is examining the brigadier's body. After a moment of wary circling she lowers her rifle. Most of Fry's throat and upper chest are gone, so there is nothing to be afraid of there. She turns her attention to Dr Khan, who is even more indubitably dead.

'What a waste,' she mutters. She struggles for words, comes up with nothing better. 'What a fucking . . . *waste*!'

'She saved us all from dying back there,' Carlisle snaps. 'And everyone on Rosie too. That's not waste. Don't ever call that waste.'

Lieutenant Foss leans down to help him to his feet but he stands unaided, though the pain forces a gasp out of him.

'Sir, we've got to get out of here,' Foss says.

The words make sense and he is about to follow her, but he makes the mistake of looking over his shoulder. He stays where he is, unmoving.

'Sir—'

'Rosie,' the colonel exclaims. It's the best he can manage.

'We'll rendezvous with Rosie at the south gate, as per plan,' Foss says. But then she follows his gaze and sees what he has seen.

Rosie isn't moving. And she is surrounded. Not by Captain Manolis and his detail, or by the junker warriors: the diminutive figures clustered around her front and her sides can only be the feral children. And the fact that they have come out of hiding presumably means that Fry's people are all dead or in the wind.

With an obscene oath, Foss takes aim.

The colonel grabs hold of the SCAR-H's barrel and forces it down.

The mid-section door has just slid open. Stephen Greaves emerges from the airlock and steps down into the midst of the children. He is holding Samrina Khan's baby in his arms.

'Listen to me, Lieutenant,' Carlisle snaps. He tells Foss what Khan told him in Rosie's airlock. He doesn't have to explain to her what it means. He tells her to get the survivors back to Beacon, and to spread the word to anyone they trust.

Then he heads back across the parade ground, picking his way around the dead.

60

With baby Khan tucked up in Rina's bunk, surrounded by her smell and her residual presence, Greaves watches the battle from up in the turret. He hates it, but he has to watch because he has made a promise to Rina that he means to keep. His window of opportunity, if it comes at all, will be narrow. He can't afford to miss it.

More distressingly, he has made a promise to Colonel Carlisle that he will ultimately break. He didn't lie – of course he didn't – but he knows that the colonel took a different meaning from his answer than the one that was in his own mind when he spoke.

'If this works, Stephen,' the colonel said, 'if the children come, I want you to meet us at the south gate as soon as it's safe to move. You can drive Rosie, I assume?'

And yes, Greaves said, he could. He had read the manual, and memorised it. He was confident that he could drive

Rosie at need. While he was saying these easy, obvious things, he prepared his answer to the bigger question.

'If you make it, Colonel . . . and if I make it . . . then I'll meet you at the south gate.'

He said it fiercely, forcing the words out of his mouth against the rebellion of his breath.

The colonel mistook his intensity for alarm. 'You should be fine,' he reassured Greaves. 'They won't fire on Rosie unless they absolutely have to, and our coming out will mean they don't have to. Or so they'll assume. We'll keep them talking until the children arrive, and after that they should have too much on their plates to worry about us.'

'Yes,' Greaves agreed. 'They'll have too much on their plates.'

'Here.' The colonel gave him the tiny hand-held radio that used to be Dr Fournier's. 'This is on the brigadier's frequency, so you can't use it to call us. Not yet. But once you get to the fence, if you don't find us, just keep this on and I'll talk you in.'

Then the colonel left.

And now he sits in the turret waiting and watching, knowing that he will never see the south gate. He has lied by omission. It sits in his stomach like a stone.

A voice from inside the lab, high but hoarse, scatters his thoughts. 'Colonel! McQueen! Anyone!' Dr Fournier has woken up and he seems very angry. Perhaps that's not surprising, given that he was rendered unconscious by means of blunt-instrument trauma and now finds himself tied to the workbench. Greaves tries not to listen, even when Dr Fournier demands shrilly and repeatedly to be let free. Even when his shouting wakes the baby, who starts to cry.

Dr Fournier is the other reason why Greaves is up in the

424

turret. He is afraid of the doctor, and seriously needs to keep a safe distance in case the doctor goes from complaining and demanding to asking questions again. Last time that happened, the only thing that kept Greaves from giving up everything he knew was Rina knocking the doctor out with the heavy steel clamp stand. Rina isn't here now so he has to be very careful.

The fight outside has reached a crescendo. Greaves switches to the infra-red goggles, which turn the bloodletting into an abstract play of shapes and colours. He bites his lower lip hard and tries not to think about punctured and perforated flesh. Teeth and stones and bullets. Blood running out onto the cracked asphalt. He hopes fervently that Rina and the others were able to get clear before the fighting started. That they're not out there in the middle of this killing field.

The movement outside goes on for a long time. The screams and yells, the pleading and cursing likewise, a very long time.

When the last of Fry's troops have been dispatched, the children move forward out of the brambles and the trees into the relative openness of the parade ground. They inspect the bodies, finishing off those who are still moving. Only then do they kneel down and feed. Perhaps it's Greaves' imagination but he believes he can see the moment when the scarred girl (he has recognised her from her silhouette and from the way she moves) nods her permission. He wonders if she is looking for him among the dead as he looked for her after the fire. He wonders what the captain's voice box told her that morning, assuming that she pulled the string and listened to the words. She wouldn't have understood them in any case. She doesn't speak the captain's language.

These are pointless thoughts. It's time, he decides. He needs to go down. He assumes the children will come in any case, to complete the errand that has brought them all this far, but just in case he will meet them more than halfway. He descends from the turret.

'Greaves!' Dr Fournier bellows. Stephen flinches. 'I can see you there. Untie me. Untie me right now, or you'll face a court martial. We're under military law! I can order you shot!'

Steeling himself, Greaves enters the lab. He is shaking with terror, but he has a contingency plan. If Dr Fournier asks him about the cure or starts any sentence with a question word, then Greaves will sing the theme tune from *Captain Power* loudly enough to drown out the words.

Dr Fournier sags with relief as he sees Greaves. 'Thank you!' he snarls with heavy sarcasm. Then he gasps out loud as Stephen walks right on past him. 'Greaves! Stop what you're doing and loosen these straps! I'm warning you—'

He's the hero of the spaceways, the galactic engineer, Greaves tells himself. He doesn't say it aloud but he's ready to. At a moment's notice. If a single dangerous word comes out of Dr Fournier's mouth. He keeps his face averted as he fills a canteen with water and loops its strap over his shoulder. As he opens freezer compartment ten and removes the dead boy. Then as he sets the cold corpse down on the work table a few inches from Fournier's head. Fournier pulls back from it with a yelp of protest.

'*I'm warning you* is tautologous,' Greaves says. He almost shouts it, his strained voice rising in pitch. This is the most dangerous moment, with the feral child actually in Dr Fournier's line of sight – a visual cue for the forbidden topic.

'What?' Dr Fournier splutters.

426

'To say you're warning somebody is to perform a self-enacting speech act. The warning is contained in the words used to announce that a warning is being given.' He's babbling, pushing the conversation like a boulder away from the place where it mustn't go.

'Greaves, are you mad?' The doctor's face has darkened to a deep red, almost purple.

Perhaps he is. There would be no way of knowing, which of course is always the problem – not just for him but for everyone. Sanity is a suspended state, moored in nothing but itself. You test the ground an inch in front of you, move forward as though it's solid. But the whole world is in freefall and you're in freefall with it.

'I don't know,' Greaves admits. 'I just don't know.'

He is staring at the small cadaver, guilty and desolate. The life that was here is long gone, but the dead boy's kindred have come a very long way to reclaim the part of him that they can still see. Greaves has disrespected that part. There are incisions and excavations where he took his tissue samples, raw wounds that have never bled because the blood had already congealed before the flesh was broken.

'Greaves.' Dr Fournier's tone has changed. He is staring at Stephen with a new urgency. 'Put that specimen back. You hear me? It belongs to the expedition. And your findings, your discovery – all of it! The colonel will be very angry with you if you do anything to jeopardise our mission. Our— our joint mission. He'll be angry and disappointed. Why would you put at risk everything we've—?'

Stephen slams the freezer cabinet shut and flees, taking the corpse with him. 'He's the hero of the spaceways!' he yells. 'The galactic engineer!'

'What? Greaves! Come back!'

The baby. The baby is next. Too many things, too many factors to keep straight in his head. He sets the dead boy down in the mid-section just inside the airlock door. His hands are shaking. There is no sequence here. None of the things he is doing are in the long, long list of things he has done before.

For a moment, he is completely lost. In a panic he almost hits the airlock's controls. No no no. Not yet. Not yet.

Dr Fournier's cries follow him into the crew quarters. They echo around him as he goes to collect the baby from Rina's bunk, but the shrilling of the crying child is louder and the pounding of his own blood seems louder still. It's easy now to shut out any meaning in the stream of sound coming from the lab.

The baby is lying on his back, screaming, his mouth an O of hysterical misery. He has kicked his blanket away. Greaves picks him up and swaddles him again with ginger care. Miraculously and very suddenly the baby stops crying at this point, as though human contact was all it wanted. As though all its sorrows came down to being alone. Perhaps that's true of everyone.

'Soon,' Stephen whispers, staring into the baby's solemn, inscrutable eyes.

The blanket is green, like all the blankets in Rosie. Army issue. Greaves takes another, from his own bunk, tugging it free one-handed with the baby cradled in his other arm. Dr Fournier continues to yell through all of this, but baby Khan stays quiet. Nonetheless he gapes his tiny mouth and tastes the air, which is no doubt rich with scents of possible food. Greaves notices that all the baby's teeth are now fully grown in.

He goes back out into the mid-section, carrying the baby in one hand and the spare blanket draped across his arm. Will it be enough? It's all he can do. He sets the baby down on the deck plates, making a nest out of the folded blanket to protect him a little against the cold metal. 'I won't be long,' he whispers.

On the other side of the airlock doors, the night is impenetrably black. But through the infra-reds, once he slips them on again, he sees a forest of bright blue lozenges converging on Rosie from all sides. Blue indicates a temperature between 10 and 14 degrees Celsius, barely higher than background ambient. The children are coming to meet him.

'Greaves, I demand that you untie me! This is your last warning!'

Stephen hesitates for a long time. Finally he goes back into the lab, opens one of the instrument drawers and finds a scalpel. He turns to face Dr Fournier.

The doctor tenses. He shrinks away as Stephen approaches, emitting a sound that's halfway between a whimper and a sigh.

Stephen slips the scalpel carefully between Dr Fournier's clenched fists. The doctor opens his hands and lets the scalpel drop. But then on the second try, when he realises that Stephen is not trying to murder him, he accepts it. 'You can cut yourself free,' Stephen tells him. 'Probably. But you'd better not follow me, Dr Fournier. It's not safe for you where I'm going.'

Fournier's eyes implore him. 'Greaves, wait. Tell me—'

'He's the hero of the spaceways, the galactic engineer! He brings the Terran Code to all the planets far and near!'

'For God's sake! *Greaves!*'

But he's gone, still singing. Captain Power's ship was called

429

Copernicus. He was a scientist as well as a hero, and knowledge was his greatest weapon. He would have hated Dr Fournier, who tries to turn knowledge into things he wants.

On the mid-section platform, Stephen kneels and makes ready. He finds the scarred girl's totem, her gift to him, and slips his little finger through the ring. The smiling man in the red hat and blue overalls dangles between his fingers.

He presses the airlock control. As the door slides open he steps out.

Into a mob. The children are everywhere, crowding dozens deep. So many! Have they brought reinforcements this time or were they always an army rather than a family?

But they *are* a family. The youngest press against the oldest or hide behind them, peeping out from cover. They grip onto the elbows of the bigger kids or swing from them, kicking their heels, as human children have always done. They are loved and protected, their place absolutely acknowledged.

They make no move towards Greaves. Perhaps having the door just slide open in front of them when they were gearing up for a siege throws them a little off their stride.

He holds up the key ring for them to see, and waits. He has no idea whether the little man with the M on his hat will make a difference, but once again it's all he's got. A ripple of interest goes through the children like a breeze through grass. They know whose sigil this is.

Then something else goes through them. The scarred girl herself, striding confidently along a corridor that opens ahead of her and closes again in her wake. The children step out of her path quickly enough that she is able to maintain a steady pace, never having to slow or stop.

She walks right to him.

430

She extends her hand and touches the key ring with the tip of one finger, as though she is acknowledging a kinship or a debt. They exchanged gifts. She remembers. Stephen looks down at her waist, expecting to see Captain Power's voice box among the baubles hanging there, but it's not. When he looks up again it's in her hand.

He releases a held breath. He still has far to go, but he feels as though he is on the right road.

Without shifting his ground, he half-turns and points – raising his hand slowly and carefully – behind him, towards the airlock. Actually towards the mid-section platform. He has left the lights on there, so they can see. More gifts . . .

Baby Khan lies on his back, quiet and good, kicking his legs just a little. Beside him, swathed in an identical green blanket, is the dead boy. It's not an equation. Greaves is not saying anything about their relative importance. He's just saying: they're both yours. One living, one dead, but they're yours. See that.

Two or three of the nearest children step forward, but the scarred girl stops them again with a single syllable. She is still looking at Stephen. She makes the exact same gesture he just made, points her finger at the living and the dead, then lets it fall.

It's probably a status thing. He has to come to her. He has to bring his offerings and lay them down before her.

He moves as slowly as he can, partly to avoid triggering any violent responses and partly to maintain the sense that this is a ritual. He steps onto the platform and picks up the dead boy.

The radio crackles in his pocket, speaks thin and broken words.

Reluctantly he sets the dead body down again, takes the radio out and puts it to his ear. 'Yes?'

'Greaves. It's Colonel Carlisle.'

Greaves considers many possible answers, settles on one that he hopes will fend off profitless questions. 'I can't talk right now, Colonel. I'm busy.'

'I know. I can see. I'm out on the parade ground, fifty yards away. If you close the airlock I think I can disperse the children without harming them.'

Greaves is appalled. 'No!' he yelps. 'Don't. Please, Colonel! Don't do that. Don't fire on them.'

'Then what support can I give you?'

Greaves looks out into the dark. He shakes his head, in case the colonel is actually close enough to see him. 'None,' he says.

'Lad, you're going to get yourself—'

'It's fine. I'll be fine. This is the only way, Colonel. The only way. Don't do anything.' He hesitates. There's so much he can't explain, but maybe one thing that he has to, to keep the colonel from running in with his rifle and ruining everything. But he's bad at explanations that aren't technical, and he is almost certain that the technical explanation won't work here. 'You know . . .' he tries, 'with kittens . . . if they smell wrong, or look wrong, sometimes the mother will eat them.'

'What are you talking about?' the colonel asks.

'Rina's baby. He has to go to his people, Colonel.'

'His people? But . . .'

For a few seconds there is nothing but static on the line.

Then the colonel's voice says, 'All right. I understand. Go on, Greaves.'

'That's all,' Greaves says. 'I want them to accept him. I

432

promised Rina. And if I do everything right, it might be okay. But if you fire . . . Please don't, Colonel. Please don't do anything, whatever you see.'

He switches the radio off and sets it down on the floor. Then he picks up the little corpse again and brings it out.

The whole tribe is waiting in silence, taking their cue from the scarred girl. But a shiver of movement goes through them all when they see – or perhaps smell – what Greaves is carrying. One of the children speaks, a murmur of liquid syllables. Another makes a sound like a soft moan.

The girl inclines her head and makes a brusque movement with her hand. She clicks her tongue. Four living children take the dead one from Stephen's hands and bear him to her. The scarred girl touches the boy's forehead, and then her own. They lay him at her feet, as softly as if they were trying not to wake him.

Stephen goes back inside, bends and scoops up baby Khan. The baby makes a small noise in his throat. *Geh*. His clenched fists paddle as though he is squaring up for a fight.

Stephen raises him high as he descends from the platform again. He walks to where the scarred girl stands, in the midst of her people. He turns slowly, letting all of them see baby Khan and smell him.

Moving as slowly and smoothly as he can he goes down on one knee, then on both. He holds out the fragile bundle for the scarred girl to take. She examines baby Khan critically for the space of two, three, four heartbeats.

She tucks Captain Power's voice box back into her belt.

She takes the baby from him. With one hand, she unwraps the blanket and casts it aside – almost with distaste. Her nostrils flare. The tableau holds, for one heartbeat and then another.

433

Finally she speaks: a melodious stream of sounds with no consonants in it, no hidden rocks to break the flow. One of the other children, a boy older and taller than her, shrugs off a woollen shawl he is wearing as a sash and offers it up. The scarred girl takes it and swaddles the baby in it. She licks the tip of her thumb and anoints his forehead very gently with her spit. A baptism.

And since it's a baptism, Stephen takes the risk of speaking. 'Sam,' he says. He points to the baby. Nods. Smiles. 'Sam.'

The boy who gave up his shawl goes to take up the fallen blanket — waste not, want not — but the scarred girl shakes her head and he backs away. Clearly there are boundaries here that matter.

'Thank you,' Stephen says.

The girl answers him, but he doesn't understand her any more than she understood him.

And now comes the hard part.

He rolls up his sleeve, all the way to the elbow. Taking the canteen of water from his shoulder, he unscrews the cap and pours the water over his exposed forearm. He rubs the whole area with the palm of his other hand, wiping away the e-blocker gel that disguised his scent. He holds up his wrist, which now (he hopes) smells of all things that are good to eat.

'Go ahead,' he says.

The scarred girl stares at him in perplexity. Her severe stare seems to ask a question: *is this how we treat our friends?*

'You have to,' Stephen explains, knowing the words are futile. He is relying on her instincts, not her understanding. 'Otherwise, when they ask me, I'll tell them. That there's a cure. How to make it. Men with weapons will come after you – many, many more than are here now. They'll take you and turn you into medicine. Kill you all, just so they can have a few more years of life themselves. They won't even feel sorry about it.'

The scarred girl seems to listen. Her mouth is bent into a trembling gull-wing scowl but she doesn't move. Greaves wonders how much control that takes, how much strength. And how much authority to make the others hold back, though they tilt their heads to catch the smell of him on the still air. The baby stirs and utters a thin wail of complaint, made suddenly aware of its hunger.

Helpless, Stephen plunges on. 'I can't kill myself. There are ways to do it without hurting, but . . . it's not one of the things I can do. So we have to do this instead.' He offers his arm again. The words are just a spur for his own faltering resolve: his dilemma would be almost impossible to explain even if they spoke the same language. He needs her to wipe the hard drive of his mind, so he can't give her and her people up to the dubious mercy of their predecessors, humanity 1.0.

Part of this is the promise he made to Rina. *Keep him safe. It doesn't matter what happens to me so long as you keep him safe.* And that means keeping the whole tribe safe. Which in turn means not letting out into the world the knowledge that will destroy them.

But it goes beyond even that strict imperative. Greaves has been thinking it through ever since he first met the scarred girl and her people. On one of the lowest levels of his mind, in a sub-routine set up for this alone, he has been working out the terms of the problem all this time. The solution is here. Now. It takes the form of a Venn diagram, two circles intersecting. The world of Beacon, dying slowly every year

435

even before it decided to dismember and eat itself; and the world of these children, which whatever it might be now has at least the potential to be something else. It's a seed. A dead tree can stand for years or decades as it hollows out. A seed has places to be and things to do.

Stephen has made up his mind. He's with the seeds, the scarred girl's tribe. He can't be one of them, but he has chosen his allegiance. The children are all that matters. And right now, though he's on their side he is the plague, the pathogen that could destroy them. The knowledge in his mind has to be safely disposed of.

'Please,' he begs.

The scarred girl makes a gesture. Her hand raised towards him, closed and then open. She knows what he wants her to do, but she won't do it.

It's a complex problem with a simple, inelegant solution. Stephen extends his hand to touch baby Khan's forehead.

'Sam,' he reminds them all. 'His name is Sam.'

He puts the tip of his thumb against the baby's lips. The baby's jaws work back and forth, sawing at Greaves' flesh. It's very hard for the tiny teeth to get a purchase, but once they do they punch through his skin cleanly and quickly. They're very sharp.

The baby takes its first meal.

Stephen lets go of his humanity with much more relief than fear. It was an awkward burden to carry at the best of times.

61

The colonel returns to Rosie across a field strewn with the bodies of the dead. All of the corpses he sees are adults and half-devoured. Brigadier Fry's troops seem to have given a poor account of themselves. Of course the children won the field and therefore have had the opportunity to take their dead away with them.

Certainly there is no sign of them now. Rosie's airlock still stands open, but the area around it is deserted. Carlisle is not surprised. He saw the moment when Stephen Greaves handed over Dr Khan's baby, and the moment shortly after when – in a different sense – he surrendered himself.

If Greaves were still present, Carlisle would shoot him just as he shot Samrina. Whatever the children are, or may become, an adult human on exposure to *Cordyceps* dies in that moment, or else becomes an unwilling passenger in a hijacked body. In the second case, the bullet is a mercy;

in the first, it's probably an irrelevance but it feels to the colonel like a mark of respect akin to covering the faces of the dead.

But there is no sign of Greaves. Perhaps when the children melted away into the dark he trailed along in their wake, moved by some half-remembered impulse. More likely he is out on the parade ground somewhere, feeding.

The *whup whup whup* of a helicopter's blades makes Carlisle look to the sky momentarily. Sixsmith is hovering the Little Bird about twenty feet up, right above his head. She gestures. A thumbs-up. She has her work to do, and he has his. He waves back, wishing her and the others well.

He hopes they will make it home. He hopes there will be a home for them to go back to. There is reason to hope. Brigadier Fry wouldn't have been out here in the wilderness making deals with the devil if her *coup d'état* had been thriving.

The Little Bird peels away. The last the colonel sees of it is the red light at the tail end of its fuselage lifting into the sky like a stray spark from an extinguished bonfire.

Carlisle is a practical man, and a soldier first and foremost. He enters Rosie via the cab, not the airlock, so that he can conduct a proper sweep from aft to stern. He finds no soldiers, no junkers and no children: nobody at all, in fact, except for Dr Fournier, who is cowering in the lab with his hands still tied to the workbench. When the colonel enters, Fournier starts to babble out a stream of complaints, demands, pleas, questions and explanations, the words falling over each other in his haste to get them out.

Carlisle checks the straps. They have been partially cut through, probably with the scalpel that is lying on the floor a little way away, but the doctor had not made much progress before he dropped the scalpel and it bounced or rolled out of his reach. The straps will hold.

When he sees that the colonel means to leave him there, Dr Fournier switches tack and starts to threaten. He has friends in Beacon. Friends with power and influence. He has been acting as Brigadier Fry's personal agent and representative. If he is harmed, if he is treated badly, the brigadier will not be happy.

Fry is dead, Carlisle tells him. If the doctor has any living friends he would be curious to know their names.

He puts the scalpel back in the instrument drawer where it will do no harm. In its place, he presses a full canteen of water into the doctor's hands. Whatever he eventually decides to do with Fournier, torturing him is not part of the plan.

He goes aft to the cockpit. Along the way, he closes the airlock door.

Driving Rosie isn't easy for a man with only one functional leg. There are a great many false starts before the colonel manages to get the vehicle turned around and moving away from the carnage. Then he wastes a great deal more time looking for the gate. Eventually he gives up the search and rams straight through the fence, which offers no resistance at all.

He is back on the M1 when dawn comes up, and by noon he is on the outskirts of London. When hungries chase him he does his best to outdistance them. Only as a last resort does he plough them under Rosie's wheels.

He is looking for a place to stop, but not any particular place. He will not be returning to Beacon, and he has no wish for Rosie to go back there either. He liked her best as an instrument of truth rather than a weapon of war. He will leave her somewhere where she is unlikely to be found by anyone in need of such a weapon. Somewhere in the capital's endless labyrinth of streets.

When the intransigent spike of the Senate House Library appears in the centre of the forward window, he knows he has reached his destination. He slows to a halt halfway along Malet Street, on the exact spot to which the shadow of the library's spire points.

He sits a while as the sun sinks down. The shadow swerves away from him, too slowly for him to see the movement: the hour hand of a clock, telling him his time is past.

But clocks are not infallible.

He goes and fetches Dr Fournier, freeing him from the workbench but keeping him at the point of a gun. When they are both seated side by side in the cockpit, he explains what he is about to do. He does this as a courtesy. To see death coming and be able to look it in the face is part of what human beings gained when they took the path that led them away from the rest of the living kingdoms. Part of what they lost, too, no doubt.

Distressed and terrified, Fournier pleads for his life. But he is indignant too. He demands to know what he has done to deserve a sentence of death.

'You conspired with Brigadier Fry to lead us into an ambush,' Carlisle says. It seems best to him to keep this brief, and simple. 'We were meant to die there. You would have died too, but you didn't know that. You were willing to sacrifice the whole of Rosie's crew to your own purposes.'

Fournier's face flushes red, with anger rather than shame. 'I was co-opted!' he says. 'Coerced. Nothing I did was by my own choice. Colonel, the brigadier gave me a direct order.

And she outranks you. You of all people have to understand—'
He falters, lacking the technical vocabulary.

'The chain of command,' Carlisle supplies. 'I do, Doctor. Very much so. I've always had what might be considered an exaggerated respect for it. But you're not a soldier and you weren't bound to obey. You had the luxury of choosing for yourself where your duty lay.'

'No, I didn't!' Fournier is shrill. 'She told me the only way I would be appointed to the mission was if I agreed to do as she said.'

'That,' the colonel points out gently, 'is what a choice looks like.' He nods his head out of the window at the Senate House. 'I was a student here,' he says. 'My degree was in history. I never imagined I'd live to see the end of it.'

Dr Fournier starts to plead again. He says that with Beacon split down the middle he couldn't be said to have committed treason, only to have chosen the wrong side. Carlisle listens for a long while, then holds up a hand to stop the logorrhoeic flow. 'Doctor, please. I was trying to explain, since you seem to feel you're being treated harshly. The point of history, the very essence of it as a field of study, is to find correspondences. You look at the past so that you can understand it, and through it you come to a better understanding of your own time. If you're lucky, sometimes you can even extrapolate to possible futures.'

'I'm not a historian,' Fournier points out.

'No,' Carlisle agrees. 'But biology is about correspondences too, surely? You study living things to understand yourself.'

Fournier is looking at him now with wary calculation. 'I suppose that's true,' he says, with no conviction at all.

'There's no need to humour me, Doctor. You're welcome to disagree. But it seems to me – am I wrong? – that all living

441

things form a sort of fractal pattern. The same features, the same structures, repeating themselves on different scales and in different configurations. You can't look at those things for long, surely, without finding yourself reflected in them.'

'I do,' Fournier agrees fulsomely. 'I find myself all the time.'

The colonel sighs. The man isn't listening to him at all. 'Well then,' he says wearily.

'Well then what?'

'Well, then you know what you betrayed. Not Beacon. Life. There were two sides and you didn't choose life. Did you even look at that last set of samples? The ones we brought down from Ben Macdhui?'

Fournier's face is blank. 'No, of course not. When would I have had time?'

'Dr Khan found the time. I'm not sure whether it was before she gave birth, or just after. She was surprised at what she found. None of the *Cordyceps* cultures from Ben Macdhui had germinated. Not one, out of twelve.'

Fournier blinks rapidly, several times. 'A mistake, presumably. Inert samples.' He is thinking it through even as he speaks. 'No, they would have been cultured separately. Grown in different media. But then . . . that would mean . . .'

'Exactly.' Carlisle nods. 'An environmental inhibitor, for the hungry plague. Something unique about the Cairngorm plateau, at least at its higher end. Altitude? Air pressure? Electro-magnetic fields? You'd be able to come up with a better guess than me, Doctor, I'm sure.

'Or perhaps it's nothing. Perhaps, as you suggested, the cultures were dead before they were put into the jars. Contaminated in some way. We've decided, though, to take the chance. To assume that it's not a mistake.'

'We?' Fournier echoes, with just a hint of a sneer. 'Your crew is gone, Colonel.'

'I know,' Carlisle says. 'But they haven't gone far. They probably arrived at Beacon before we reached London. They'll spread the word, as discreetly as they can, that there's an alternative now. Another choice. Beacon is becoming a terrible place, poisoned by its own isolation. Anyone who wants to leave, and try again, is welcome to come with us.'

'To Scotland?' Fournier is incredulous. 'To the Cairngorms?'

'Yes.'

'You won't last the first winter! Assuming you even get there in the first place!'

'Possibly not. But I believe it's worthwhile making the attempt. It gives me hope, and hope is important.'

Carlisle points out of the window again. When Fournier turns to look, he puts the gun against the side of the doctor's head and pulls the trigger. He is almost certain that Fournier didn't see it coming. As much mercy as he could manage, in the circumstances. Certainly a better death than the doctor would find for himself if he were left to walk home.

There is nowhere nearby to bury the body, and Carlisle has no tools that would serve. In any case, it seems to him, Rosie does very well as a coffin and London does tolerably well as a mausoleum.

He inflicts as much damage on the engine as he can bear to. He doesn't want Rosie ever to move again, ever to fight and kill again, but vandalism doesn't come easy to him.

He has a very long way to travel. He packs a rucksack with rations for a week or two, e-blocker for a month. If it takes longer than that then he probably won't make it at all.

But he will. He will make it. And Foss and Sixsmith and

McQueen will join him there, presently, with anyone from Beacon who has heard their message. That the Fireman is waiting for them high up in the snows and the frigid air. That he will build a new city, with their help. Or die trying.

He exits through the airlock, setting it to seal itself behind him.

He sets off walking. It's a beautiful evening. A beautiful place. He pretends as he walks that the old world never fell. That when he turns the corner he will see traffic roaring by. Foreign tourists waving selfie sticks like bishops' crosiers, office workers walking briskly from their hectic work to their hectic leisure.

And street upon street, the city. And city upon city, the world. Uncountable millions of people, as it was before.

He imagines that history stretches before him as well as behind, a river so broad and deep it makes the Thames look like nothing more than a teardrop rolling down the world's rugged cheek.

EPILOGUE

TWENTY YEARS LATER

The snow is eight inches deep, but you wouldn't want to trust to that too much. This is glacial moraine, sewn through and through with rifts and fissures into which snow has drifted until they filled to the brim. If you don't test every step before you take it, you can sink into a hollow that's deeper than your height, with rocks as sharp as teeth at the bottom of it.

Nonetheless, the little group of figures down on the eastern slope is making steady progress. They tack left and right, all together, and they keep on coming. There are places on the slope that are still in shadow, the blood-tinged dawn light poking patchily through the peaks above, but the six men and women don't slow down to probe the blank expanses ahead of them, and they don't put a foot wrong.

Foss is struck as she watches them come by, how young they look, the oldest barely thirty. That's not the most striking

447

thing about them, though. What she noticed first, and can't keep from thinking about, is how lightly they're dressed. Short jackets, open to the biting wind. No hats. If they were human — normal, baseline human, one-point-zero human — they'd be dead.

So they're what the colonel said they had to be when they were first sighted at the edge of the plateau. They're hungries.

And there are more of them down at the bottom of the slope, half a mile back. This is just the vanguard.

Foss turns and walks back the way she came, up to the top of the slope and then north along the razor-edge of what used to be called the Lairig Ghru pass. There are three sentries stationed in the rocks above the pass: they can see Foss as she comes and they can see each other. She raises her rifle horizontally and holds it in the air for several seconds, in her left hand. It's a pre-arranged signal that means *hold your positions and do nothing unless directly attacked*. The sentries, who have been straining every nerve since she went downslope, relax a little and return to their vigil. They have enough discipline not to shout questions at her as she walks on by.

Around the shoulder of the mountain, above the swollen exclamation point that is Loch Etchachan, is a settlement made of ninety tents and thirty-seven wooden huts. Sprawling, ragged and dirty, surrounded by mounds of its own rubbish that will stay on the mountain until the spring thaw makes it safe to take them down to the sink hole below the pass that is the settlement's official waste disposal.

On an ordinary day, even this early in the morning, there would be people walking or running across the open ground between the tents. Children on their way to school, men and women coming back from a hunt or from the barns along the line of the pass with sacks of turnips or onions on their backs.

But this isn't an ordinary day. A few more of Foss's people stand on guard at their posts on the upslope and at the ends of the tent-avenues. Everyone else is three miles down the pass, hidden in a defile whose mouth has been painstakingly camouflaged, ready to retreat up or down the mountain depending on which signal flare they see.

Foss goes to the council hut, where the colonel sits alone, and makes her report.

Carlisle gets to his feet. It's not a quick or easy process these days: the years have not been kind to his old injury or more generally to his hips and lower back. Foss has to resist the urge to give the frail old man a hand up, knowing that the reminder of his weakness shames him.

'We'll go down to them,' he says.

'Okay,' Foss agrees. 'But I'll lead, Isaac. You don't have to come.'

'Yes,' he tells her. 'I do.'

So it takes a good long time for them to get out onto the moraine, and after that they slow down more than somewhat. Foss could wish that the colonel had left this in her hands, though she knows why he hasn't. The people who left Beacon to found this precarious community put their trust in his name and reputation. He carries that responsibility like a physical weight.

All the same, she would have preferred for them to make their stand further down the plateau – if only because it will give the rest of the good citizens of Rosie's Town more of a head start if the balloon goes up.

A hundred yards down from the north-eastern edge of the

moraine, there is a rock shaped a little bit like a squatting rabbit. A small burn cuts in front of its base. McQueen is waiting for them there, and he gives them a nod of greeting as they come up.

'They're almost here,' he says, with a sidelong flick of his gaze. 'I've wired the rock with C4 in a couple of places, so we can throw them a decent party if we have to. This is a good enough place to wait.'

Foss agrees. The sentries above will be able to see them clearly, so she doesn't have to worry about getting the signal out.

They space themselves out to either side of the colonel, rifles at parade rest, while their visitors climb the last few hundred yards up the slope. When McQueen judges that they're close enough, he waves them to a halt. They understand his gesture and they obey it, which has to count as a good start. Nobody's ripping anybody's throat out, or at least not yet.

So young, Foss thinks again: and, weirdly, so beautiful. The whites of their eyes are *Cordyceps*-grey, but their skin is perfect – not dried out and broken with frost, scaly from vitamin B deficiency or ridged with keloid scars. They even look a little tanned, which suggests they may have started their journey a long way further south.

That's not true of their leader, though. She's white-blonde and albino-pale, her skin utterly without pigment. Her age is difficult to guess but she's certainly not the oldest here. She carries herself with an unselfconscious grace, without arrogance, almost without emphasis. Her short-sleeved shirt (it must be twenty below!) is a plain lemon yellow and her trousers – muddy, threadbare – are tucked into battered, well-worn boots. She wears no badge of office. But when she stands forward, the others drop back, deferential, attentive, completely silent.

'I'm Melanie,' she says. 'Good morning to you all.'

In polished English, beautifully enunciated. Foss's scalp prickles. What she has expected, up to now, is a sort of pantomime of grimaces and gesticulations. It never occurred to her that the second-gen hungries would have learned a language, or that if they did it would be this one.

'Isaac Carlisle,' the colonel says.

'*Colonel* Isaac Carlisle,' Foss corrects.

'And that is Kat Foss, while to my right is Daniel McQueen.'

The woman looks at each of them in turn, takes time to assess them. It's a close enough examination that Foss tenses a little and starts to measure distances and angles. If Snow White here wants to start something, they'll meet her halfway.

'We've been looking for you for a long time, Colonel Carlisle,' the woman says.

Carlisle says nothing, but McQueen rises to the bait and Foss is not surprised. 'Really?' he says. 'And why's that?'

The woman – Melanie – holds her arms out from her sides, palms open. 'We didn't think there were any of you left,' she says. 'It seemed too much to hope for. But we didn't want to give up the search while there was still a chance.'

Is it Foss's imagination, or did one of the guys further back just lick his lips? 'There are plenty of us left,' she says. 'Up here, and in lots of other places besides.'

'No.' The word is flat, unemphatic. Melanie shakes her head. 'The world is poison to you now. Apart from this one place, apparently. Beacon and the junker tribes died out at the same time, and then there was just us. Or so we thought.'

'That's a cute little euphemism,' McQueen observes. 'Died out. You mean they were eaten, right?'

'No.' Melanie looks cast down for a moment. Guilty, almost. 'The *Cordyceps* pathogen became airborne. All humans everywhere became hungries, all at once. Except for you.'

Foss is stunned by the words. Not because they come as a surprise. Nobody who has left the mountain has ever come back, in more than a decade, or else they came back changed, rabid, whether they had bite marks on them or not. It's been plain for a long time that the plateau is an island in an invisible but toxic ocean. But still, to hear it said fills her, in a few moments, with a decade's worth of fear and grieving. It's one thing to be an exile and another thing to know it. She hadn't even realised she was lying to herself until she feels the tears freezing on her cheeks.

'Then how did you know to look for us?' Carlisle demands. Mild, not confrontational, not acknowledging the hopelessness of their position.

Melanie's face creases with earnestness. 'We didn't,' she says. 'I told you. It was just that we wanted to do everything we could before we finally, officially gave up the search. Some friends of mine looked at old records from before the Breakdown, and drew up a list of places where extreme weather patterns or unusual microclimates might offer some . . .' she chooses the word with care '. . . protection for you. I've had teams searching those areas for years now, whenever they could be spared from other work. And finally, last year, they found you. Everyone was really excited when they brought the news back.'

'Yeah,' McQueen says, deadpan. 'I bet. Nothing like varying the menu.'

Melanie's five companions bridle at this. They try to keep up their expressions of disciplined impassivity, but anger shows itself momentarily, here and there, in the twitch of a mouth or the narrowing of an eye — like small sparks struck off grey stone. One of the five clenches his fists, then slowly relaxes them again as Melanie goes on in the same even tone.

'We didn't announce ourselves at once, because we wanted to be sure we understood your situation. We've been watching from a distance, as discreetly as we could. Building up a picture.'

'And do you?' Carlisle asks. 'Understand our situation?'

'I think so,' Melanie says. 'Yes.' Once again she looks at all three of them in turn, as though she's aware these words might hurt and is solicitous of their feelings. 'You're weak. Barely surviving. This is hard land to live in and even harder land to farm. Your harvest a few weeks ago was the worst since you arrived here. You don't have enough food left to see more than half of you through to next spring. Plus I'd imagine you're starting to see cases of scurvy and rickets because there isn't enough fruit or calcium in your diet. So even if you survive the winter, you're going to be in an even worse position going forward. Probably your colony has two or maybe three years left. Maybe not so long.'

She stops speaking, and dead silence follows. Foss exchanges a glance with McQueen, and she's happy to read in his face that they're on the same page. They'll let the colonel take the lead on this one, and they know exactly what he's going to say. He draws in a long breath and lets it out again, steadying himself, finding words that are equal to the moment.

'You won't take us easily,' he says, 'or without great cost to yourselves.' Melanie tries to break in but he goes on, speaking over her. 'I won't bother to deny what you've seen with your own eyes. Yes, we're weak. Our bodies are. But trust me when I tell you that the people who came here were the strongest Beacon had to offer. They walked four hundred miles for the bare chance of a new life. They'll do more for the chance to keep it.'

Melanie seems flustered, dismayed. 'But . . .' she says. 'Colonel—'

'So come when you're ready,' Carlisle invites her. 'You'll find us ready, too.'

'Colonel, we came here to help you.'

Carlisle is already turning away as she speaks. He's caught there, on the cusp of the movement. Melanie laughs – in pure embarrassment, as if she can't believe they were coming at this conversation from such different angles. That things she took as given still needed to be said.

Someone has to play straight man. Foss finds it's her. 'What are you talking about?' she inquires.

Melanie points off down the slope. The rest of her under-dressed entourage have advanced a little, and now they're setting down boxes and crates in a rough and ready cairn. 'Food,' she says, 'and medicines. The plastic coolers are full of rabbits, freshly caught as we came up. The wooden crates are apples and greengages. You can eat those, yes?'

'Greengages?' McQueen says. It's hard to read his tone, but Foss's mouth has filled with saliva just on hearing the word.

'We thought fresh fruit and protein would be your most pressing needs,' Melanie says. 'The rest is negotiable. We don't cultivate grain for ourselves, obviously, but we can grow it for you. You'll tell us what you need. What we don't have, we'll find or make.'

They're speechless for a moment or two. Then the colonel, who is still standing half-turned away from the girl, asks her the question that's uppermost in all their minds.

'Why?'

Melanie doesn't seem to understand, so he asks again. 'Why would you do this?'

'Because we can,' she says. She seems genuinely puzzled by the question. 'Because we thought you were all gone and we're so happy that we were wrong. That your people and my people can meet, and talk, and learn from each other. You'd just have been legends to us, otherwise.' She smiles, as though that thought strikes her as funny. 'I know how legends work. In a few generations, there'd be a thousand wild stories about you, and the truth . . . well, the truth would just be a story a little less interesting than the rest. Now that we've found you, we'll keep looking. Not just up here in Scotland, but elsewhere in the world. We've already started to equip an expedition to France and Switzerland. I mean, to the places that used to be France and Switzerland. You might not be the only ones after all.'

The crates and boxes are still piling up at the bottom of the slope. It's starting to look as though there might even be enough to make a difference.

'Thank you,' the colonel says, with awkward formality. 'We appreciate your offer of assistance.'

'You're very welcome, Colonel Carlisle. But we need to ask a favour in return.'

Here it comes, Foss thinks. The catch. There was bound to be one. Your old? Your sick? Your criminally insane? Who do they think we'll be prepared to throw into the lunchbasket?

'We're bringing you something else,' Melanie says, and

455

this time her smile is wider. There's definitely a joke they're not getting. 'Some*one* else, I should say. And we want you to make her at home. We want that very much. She's been on her own for a long time.'

The sound of an engine reaches them on the thin, clear air. It's coming from the road below the ridge, still hidden from sight by a frozen tide of drifted snow, and it's been twenty years but Foss would know that basso roar anywhere.

'Oh my sweet Jesus!' she exclaims. 'Oh no fucking way!'

Rosie crests the ridge like a ship cresting the horizon, with a stranger at the wheel. A dark-skinned woman in torn and faded fatigues, grimacing with effort as she urges the vehicle's unwieldy mass slantwise up the sliding scree.

It seems to Foss in the lightness and strangeness of that moment as though the past has swung open in front of her like a door. She never stopped being a part of that crew. Rosie is coming to collect her for another tour of duty, one last mission in-country. And something like relief floods through her at the sight of it. Something like joy.

She thinks: all journeys are the same journey, whether you know it or not, whether you're moving or not. And the things that look like endings are all just stations on the way.

Acknowledgements

When you live with a story for long enough, it saturates your life and you lose your objectivity and go a little bit crazy. You stop seeing the edges of the thing, so you've got nothing to judge it against. At that point, you need other people who either (a) love or understand the story or (b) are tolerably fond of you and will put up with you through endless repetitions of 'So what if I do this . . . ?' I had lots of these people, and I can only repay them with inadequate thanks and the odd pint or glass of red wine. My wife, Lin, and our wonderful kids, Louise, Ben and Davey. Colm McCarthy and Camille Gatin, who were with me on the amazing journey that was *The Girl With All the Gifts*, and who changed my life beyond recognition. My brilliant editors Anne Clarke and Anna Jackson and Jenni Hill, along with copy-editors Joanna Kramer and Sophie Hutton-Squire. My agent, Meg Davis. Publicists and people-who-magically-make-things-happen

Gemma Conley-Smith and Nazia Khatun. Foreign rights wonder-worker, Andy Hine. My brother, Dave, and his awesome wife, Jacque. My best friend from my teens to the present day, Chris Poppe. Once you start a list like this, of course, you realise very quickly that it has the capacity to go on for ever. If it takes a village to raise a child, it takes an army to keep an author more or less sane and more or less standing. If you're in that army, you know you're there. I don't deserve you, but I'm so happy to have you.

Look out for M. R. Carey's unmissable and highly original thriller, out now . . .

Fellside is a maximum security prison on the edge of the Yorkshire moors. It's not the kind of place you'd want to end up. But it's where Jess Moulson could be spending the rest of her life.

It's a place where even the walls whisper.

And one voice belongs to a little boy with a message for Jess.

Will she listen?

extras

about the author

M. R. Carey has been making up stories for most of his life. His novel *The Girl With All the Gifts* was a word-of-mouth bestseller and is now a major motion picture based on his own screenplay. Under the name Mike Carey he has written for both DC and Marvel, including critically acclaimed runs on *Lucifer*, *Hellblazer* and *X-Men*. His creator-owned series *The Unwritten* appeared regularly in the *New York Times* graphic fiction bestseller list. He also has several previous novels, games, radio plays and TV and movie screenplays to his credit.

Find out more about M. R. Carey and other Orbit authors by registering online for the free monthly newsletter at www.orbitbooks.net.

if you enjoyed
THE BOY ON THE BRIDGE

look out for

THE END OF
THE DAY

by

Claire North

Charlie meets everyone – but only once.

You might meet him in a hospital, in a warzone or at the scene of a traffic accident.

Then again, you might meet him at the North Pole – he gets everywhere, our Charlie.

Would you shake him by the hand, take the gift he offers, or would you pay no attention to the words he says?

Sometimes he is sent as a courtesy, sometimes as a warning. He never knows which.

Chapter 1

At the end, he sat in the hotel room and counted out the pills.

He did not do this with words, nor mathematics, nor did his hands move, nor could he especially blame anyone else.

It didn't occur to him that Death would come; not in the conscious way of things. Death was, Death is, Death shall be, Death is not, and all this was the truth, and he understood it perfectly, and for all those reasons, this ending was fine.

Tick tick tick.

The world turned and the clock ticked

tick tick tick

and as it ticked, he heard the countdown to Armageddon, and that was okay too. No point fighting it. The fight was what made everything worse.

He was fine.

He picked up the first pill, and felt a lot better about his career choices.

Chapter 2

At the beginning ...

The Harbinger of Death poured another shot of whiskey into the glass, lifted the old lady's head from the dark blue wall of pillows on which she lay, put the drink to her lips and said, "Best I ever heard was in Colorado."

The woman drank, the sky rushed overhead, dragged towards another storm, another thrashing of the sea on basalt rock, another ripping-up of tree and bending of corrugated rooftop, the third of this month, unseasonal it was; unseasonal, but weren't all things these days?

She blinked when she had drunk enough, and the Harbinger returned the glass to the bedside table. "Colorado?" she wheezed at last. "I didn't think there was anything in Colorado."

"Very big. Very empty. Very beautiful."

"But they have music?"

"She was travelling."

"Get an audience?"

"No. But I stopped to listen. This was student days, there was this girl who ... People won't be booking her for a high school prom any time soon, but I thought ... it was something very special."

"All the old songs are dying out."

"Not all of them."

The woman smiled, the expression turning into a grimace of pain, words unspoken: just you look at me, sonny, just you think about what you said. "A girl who?"

"What? Oh, yes, I was, um ... well, I hoped there'd be a relationship, and you know how these things sort of blur, and she thought it was one thing and I never really did say and then she was going out with someone else, but by then we'd booked the plane tickets and ... look, I don't know if I should ... I'm not sure I should talk about me."

"Why not?"

"Well, this is ... " An awkward shrug, taking in the room.

"You think that because I'm dying, I should talk and you should listen?"

"If you want."

"You talk. I'm tired."

The Harbinger of Death hesitated, then tapped the edge of

the whiskey glass, held it to her lips again, let her drink, put it down. "Sorry," he murmured, when she'd swallowed, licked her lips dry. "I'm new to this."

"You're doing fine."

"Thank you. I was worried that it would be ... What would you like to hear about? I'm interested in music. I thought maybe that when I travelled, I mean, for the work, I'd try and collect music, but not just CDs, I mean, all the music of all the places. I was told that was okay, that I was allowed to preserve ... not preserve, that's not ... Are you sure you wouldn't rather talk? When ... when my boss comes ..." Again his voice trailed off. He fumbled with the whiskey bottle, was surprised at how much had already been drunk.

"I know songs," she mused, as he struggled with the top. "But I don't think they're for you to sing. A woman once tried to preserve these things, said it would be a disaster if they died. I thought she was right. I thought that it mattered. Now ... it's only a song. Only that."

He looked away, not exactly rebuked, but nonplussed by the moment, and her resolve. To cover the silence, he refilled her glass. The tumbler was thick, clean crystal, with a clouded band at the bottom where the base was ridged like a deadly flower – one of a set. He'd carried all four up the ancient flagstone road from Cusco, even though only two would ever be used, not knowing what he'd do with the remainder but feeling it was somehow wrong to part one from the other. He'd also carried the whiskey, stowed in the side of his pack, and the mule driver who'd showed him the way across the treeless road where sometimes still the pilgrims came dressed in Inca robes and carrying a blackened cross had said, "In these parts, we just make our own," and looked hungrily at the bottle.

The Harbinger of Death had answered, "It's for an old woman who is dying," and the mule driver had replied, ah, Old Mother Sakinai, yes yes, it was another thirty miles though, and you had to be careful not to miss the turning; it didn't look like a split in the path, but it was, no help if you get lost. The mule driver did not look at the bottle again.

They had camped in a stone hut shaped like a beehive, no mortar between the slabs of slate, a hole in the roof for the smoke from the fire to escape, and in the morning the Harbinger of Death had watched the sun burn away the mist from the valley and seen, very faintly in the dry stone-splotched grass, the tracings of shapes and forms where once patterns miles wide had been carved to honour the sun, the moon, the river and the sky. Sometimes, the man with the three surprisingly docile mules said, helicopters came up here, for medical emergencies or filming or something like that, but no cars, not in these parts. And why was the foreigner visiting Mama Sakinai, so far from the tarmacked road?

"I'm the Harbinger of Death," he replied. "I'm sort of like the one who goes before."

At this the mule driver frowned and sucked on his bottom lip and at last replied, "Surely you should be travelling on a feathered serpent, or at the very least in a four-by-four?"

"Apparently my employer likes to travel the way the living do. He says it's good manners to understand what comes before the end." Having said these words, he played them back in his mind and found they sounded a bit ridiculous. Unable to stop himself, he added, "To be honest, I've been doing the job for a week. But ... that's what I was told. That's what the last Harbinger said."

The mule driver found he had very little to give in reply to this, and so on they walked, until the path divided – or rather, until a little spur of dark brown soil peeled away from the stones laid so many centuries ago by the dead peoples of the mountains, and the Harbinger of Death followed it, not quite certain if this was indeed a path used by people or merely the track of a wide and possibly hungry animal, down and down again into a valley where a tiny stream ran between white stones, and where a single house had been built the colour of the dry river bed, timber roof and straw on the porch, a black-eyed dog barking at him as he approached.

The Harbinger of Death stopped some ten feet from the

dog, crouched on his haunches, let it bark and dart around him, demanding who, what, why, another human, here, where no people came except once every two weeks Mama Sakinai's nephew, and once every three months the travelling district nurse with her heavy bags not heavy enough to cure its mistress.

"You'll want to learn how to deal with dogs," the last Harbinger had said as he shadowed her on her final trips. "Ask any postman."

Charlie had nodded earnestly, but in all honesty he wasn't bothered by dogs anyway. He liked most animals, and found that if he didn't make a fuss, most animals didn't seem to mind him. So finally, having grown bored of barking, the dog settled down, its chin on its paws, and the Harbinger waited a little while longer, and when all was settled save the whispering of the wind over the treeless ground and the trickling of the stream, he went to Mama Sakinai's door, knocked thrice and said, "Mama Sakinai? My name is Charlie, I'm the Harbinger of Death. I've brought some whiskey."